PRAISE *for* BARBARA WOOD

"The plot and pacing are masterful, and there is enough sex, betrayal,
murder, and intrigue to keep the most skeptical readers breathlessly
turning pages. Wood skillfully envisions a society set in biblical times,
with people-trading, marrying, and scheming in a thriving coastal
town at the center of ancient trade routes, rendered in soft focus but
with marvelous clarity and complexity."
—*Publishers Weekly,* for *The Serpent and the Staff*

"Barbara succeeds in illuminating a time in which Christianity hasn't
yet taken root and populates it with dynamic characters."
—The Historical Novel Society, for *The Divining*

"Wood shows herself a wizard at juggling action and romance,
maintaining the momentum and sparkle of both."
—*Kirkus Reviews*

"Barbara Wood is an entertainer."
—*Washington Post Book World*

"Absolutely splendid."
—Cynthia Freeman, *New York Times* bestselling author of
A World Full of Strangers and *Come Pour the Wine,* for *The Dreaming*

"Wood creates genuine, engaging characters whose
stories are fascinating."
—*Library Journal*

RAINBOWS ON THE MOON

RAINBOWS
ON THE
MOON

Barbara Wood

TURNER

Turner Publishing Company

424 Church Street · Suite 2240
Nashville, Tennessee 37219

445 Park Avenue · 9th Floor
New York, New York 10022

www.turnerpublishing.com

Rainbows on the Moon (A Novel)

Rainbows on the Moon is a work of historical fiction. Although
some events and people in this book are based on historical
fact, others are the products of the author's imagination.

Cover by Susan Olinsky
Interior design by Kym Whitley
Cover image: iStock/© Donyanedomam

Library of Congress Cataloging-in-Publication Data

Wood, Barbara, 1947-
Rainbows on the Moon / Barbara Wood.
    pages cm
ISBN 978-1-63026-088-0
1. Self-realization in women--Fiction. 2. Missionaries-
-Fiction. 3. Hawaii--History--19th century--Fiction. I.
Title.
PS3573.O5877R35 2014
813'.54--dc23
                          2014019215

ISBN: 978-1-63026-088-0 (Paperback), 978-1-63026-085-9 (Hardcover)

Printed in the United States of America
14 15 16 17 18 19 20—0 9 8 7 6 5 4 3 2 1

To my husband, Walt, with love

OTHER BOOKS *by* BARBARA WOOD

The Serpent and the Staff
The Divining
Virgins of Paradise
The Dreaming
Green City in the Sun
This Golden Land
Soul Flame
Vital Signs
Domina
The Watch Gods
Childsong
Night Trains
Yesterday's Child
Curse This House
Hounds and Jackals
The Prophetess
Perfect Harmony

BOOKS *by* KATHRYN HARVEY
Butterfly
Stars
Private Entrance

PART ONE

HILO ON THE ISLAND OF HAWAIʻI
1820

CHAPTER ONE

The first thing Emily saw, as the clipper ship *Triton* drew near land, was a strange object floating in the clear blue sky. It looked like a white veil, long and diaphanous, suspended horizontally in the air a mile above the island.

"It's an optical illusion," said Mr. Hampstead, who stood with Emily on the bow of the ship. "You're looking at Mauna Loa, an active volcano. The mountain is almost the same color as the sky. What looks like something floating in the sky is the snow-covered peak."

Emily was mesmerized. For seven long months she had fantasized about this moment, and now here she was, arriving at a land of palm trees and snow.

Closer in from the distant mountain, she saw emerald green cliffs, a flat lush plain dotted with houses made of grass, a sandy beach lined with coconut palms bending in the breeze. As the ship's crew dropped anchor and climbed the rigging to furl the sails, as the captain shouted orders and the passengers stood anxious and excited on the deck, Emily watched as the natives swarmed down to the beach, throwing off their clothing and dashing into the surf.

The sunlight amazed her in its sharpness and clarity—she couldn't recall ever seeing such unique luminosity in New England. The colors before her eyes were vivid and bright. The sea twinkled with broken bits of diamond sunlight. Ocean breakers rose and arched in lime-green splendor to crash in magnificent white froth. The trade wind was steady and brisk and tried to snatch her bonnet away. She watched the natives swim through the waves. She could hear their laughter. She had been warned of this. "The women and girls swim naked to the ships to welcome the sailors. It's a custom we're trying to break, but we haven't had much success. We're hoping the civilizing influence of Christian missionaries will put an end to it." So had said Mister Alcott, chairman of the Missionary Board to the Sandwich Islands, on the eve of Emily's departure from New Haven seven months prior.

As the women climbed aboard the *Triton* by ropes and ladders lowered by an eager crew, as they jumped onto the deck, naked and glistening and laughing, as members of the crew grinned and eagerly embraced the ladies, who then went around draping flower garlands over the passengers' heads—Emily turned toward the shore and saw outrigger canoes racing across the water. They were powered by thirty rowers each, strong brown men with garlands of green leaves around their necks, circlets of green leaves around their heads. When they neared the *Triton,* calling out and waving with big smiles, Emily hesitated to look down. But she saw with relief that the men, at least, wore clothing—loincloths that only just covered their privates.

Beyond, green mountains with deep chasms rose to misty clouds. Emily had never beheld such a beautiful sight. Waterfalls traced frothy white trails down cliffs covered in rain forest. Rainbows arched majestically against the mist. She knew that a few white people lived here—retired sailors and men who had come to explore and had stayed. But no white women. Emily Stone, twenty years old and a newlywed, was to be the first.

"We are ready to take you ashore, Mrs. Stone," Captain O'Brien said. He was a broad, gruff sea captain with a beard and the ruddy complexion of a man who takes one too many glasses of brandy at dinner.

She searched the crowded deck. Eight missionaries had made the nearly disastrous voyage from New Haven, as well as passengers continuing on to Honolulu on the island of O'ahu. They looked dressed for an afternoon garden party, as she herself did—ladies in day dresses of the fashionable high-necked, long-sleeved Empire style, with capes, bonnets and gloves, small handbags and parasols. The men were handsomely attired in snug breeches, linen shirts with perfectly tied cravats, black cutaway coats with tails, top hats, and boots.

One would not guess from this "Sabbath-best" crowd, she thought, that every single one of these cheerful men and women had only weeks prior been belowdecks, moaning in their bunks, retching into buckets, and calling out to the Almighty to end their misery. But these were New Englanders. Miseries were forgotten; they intended to arrive at the Sandwich Islands in style.

And there he was among them, the Reverend Isaac Stone, her husband.

Husband in name only, she reminded herself. There had been no time after their hasty wedding to consummate the union. Preparations for the long voyage, making the rounds of family and friends to say final farewells as it was unlikely Emily and Isaac would ever see New Haven again. Sleeping in separate rooms, Emily thinking that the wedding night would take place on board the *Triton,* which had sounded romantic at the time. But then the discovery of cramped quarters shared with strangers, everyone hearing everyone else's business, not a moment of privacy. And then the sea sickness and the high, rolling waves, and the desperate fight to pass around Cape Horn with the loss of two sailors who got washed overboard. A desperate, wretched journey that Emily swore she would never again experience.

But even afterward, sailing on the relatively calm Pacific with the help of the trade winds—even then, lack of privacy prevented Isaac from embracing his wife. And now here they were, about to set foot on land for the first time in a hundred and twenty days. "The natives will have a house ready for you," Mr. Alcott had assured them before they set sail with all their worldly goods, plus prayer books and Bibles. "They are eager to hear the Word of God."

So it will be tonight, Emily thought as she watched her lanky husband talk solemnly with two other men of the cloth—dour men, Emily thought, so intent on bringing the Gospel to the heathen that there seemed little room in their personalities for anything else.

Reverend Isaac Stone, twenty-six years old, graduate of Andover Theological Seminary, was a man of slight build, with soft, slender hands and a rather delicate face. Tall, but with a stoop, as if apologizing for his height. He needed spectacles for reading, which he did a lot, and he cleared his throat frequently, the habit of a man who was always calling for people's attention. Despite his looks, he was not a soft-spoken man. Isaac shouted. He yelled, bellowed, and boomed. "Must you be so loud?" his mother always said, and he would reply, "The Good Lord gave us the gift of speech and He expects us to put it to good use!"

Emily suspected it was because, no matter where he was, Isaac was always in the pulpit, and no matter the topic of conversation, he was always sermonizing.

Emily and Isaac were distant cousins. Emily's mother's brother had married a second cousin and Isaac was the result, and so Emily had encountered him over the years. They were attending the same Sabbath meeting when a Hawai'ian addressed the congregation. He was well-dressed and well-spoken, having learned English and civilized ways from merchant captains who anchored off the islands for fresh water and supplies. The dark-skinned young man had told them of godless ways and unspeakable ancient practices in his islands, and when Mr. Alcott had called from his pulpit for bold men and women to go forth among the heathen and spread the message of salvation, Emily had eagerly answered. The problem was, only married missionaries were allowed to go. As it turned out, Isaac had also eagerly answered the call, and so their families had gotten together and the marriage was arranged.

Two weeks later, they had set sail on the *Triton* for an unknown future filled with bright promise.

Emily knew that pride was a sin, but she couldn't help being proud of herself, proud that she was not like her mother and sisters and friends back home who had no taste for adventure. Here was proof! Riding the high seas in a frail ship, heading for an unknown destiny. How many women in New Haven could make such a boast? Most women needed convention, they lived by rules and etiquette and propriety. Living the way generations of women before them had lived.

But not I! Emily cried silently to a sky vaster than any seen over New England. *I was born for adventure. I flout convention. I am a New Woman on a holy purpose.*

The farewell tea before the missionaries had set sail: "You're so brave, Emily. You always were the strongest of us."

"God gives me the courage," Emily had replied in humility, but in her mind she had thought: Yes, I am terribly brave, aren't I?

The Hawai'ians sounded colorful and friendly, with their warlike past far behind them. It made her think of a trip she had taken with her family when she was little, to visit relatives in Uncasville in eastern Connecticut. Alongside the road they had come upon a small group of Mohegan Indians selling wood-splint baskets. They, too, were colorful, with their bronze skin and beaded headbands with a feather or two and moccasins, the women in knee-length skirts, the men in buckskin leggings. They had been shy and docile and polite and utterly tamed. Emily thought they were quaint. The Hawai'ians were going to be like that, she just knew.

I will be tolerant of their ways. Indeed, I shall express interest in all that they do, and perhaps even engage in some of their activities to show my friendship. I am tolerant of all humankind, as the Almighty instructs. I embrace every man as my brother, regardless of race.

As she trembled with excitement, watching the natives race toward the ship in their outriggers, she thought: They will be basket weavers, just like the Mohegan, and I shall sit with them as they create their quaint little baskets, I will learn that skill as I speak to them of God and Jesus. It will be perfect and wonderful.

Emily and the others were helped into special chairs attached to ropes and lowered down to the longboats. They were then rowed ashore to the accompaniment of swimmers in the water, waving and laughing, and outrigger canoes racing alongside. The longboats were met by cheering Hawai'ians who dashed into the surf to pull the boats ashore, and the Westerners were scooped up and carried to dry sand by sturdy sailors. There, Emily and her fellow travelers were met by a great crowd who surrounded them with greetings of "Aloha," and the gifts of beautiful floral garlands which the natives draped over the visitors' heads.

Emily thought she might faint from the press of the crowd, all of whom were in a state of near-undress, until the throng suddenly parted and a self-important man strode through. He was stout and wearing a plum-colored cutaway coat with tails, a striped waistcoat, and a cravat that was so full and elaborately tied that it almost tilted his head back. His top hat made of beaver skin looked as if it had seen better days. "Greetings!" he called, striding forward to shake everyone's hand. "William Clarkson, dock agent, at your service. Welcome to the Sandwich Islands."

As he drew near, Emily saw the unshaven chin, the bloodshot eyes. She was not surprised to detect the smell of rum about him. The new arrivals introduced themselves and then Clarkson said, "Come along, the chief is eager to meet you. The natives have been excited about this for days!"

But Isaac Stone, tall and lanky and bare-headed, clasped his prayer book and cried, "First we give thanks!" He dropped to his knees on the sand and held his hand up to help Emily down to his side. The missionaries knelt at once, while the rest of the passengers, hungry and weary, were slow to join them. When all were kneeling, Isaac shouted to the perfect blue sky, "Dear Lord, we thank you for bringing us to our destination in safety and in health, that we might commence the work of bringing light to these dark shores, to gather souls to reflect Your glory, to bring the word of Jesus Christ to those who have heard only evil. Into your compassionate and watchful care we humbly deliver ourselves. Amen."

As they traipsed across the beach, where fishing nets were spread out, and canoes lay like dead fish in the sun, and then up the grassy dunes, Emily saw ahead a large collection of huts, almost like a town, she thought, structures of different sizes and shapes, but all made of grass. To Emily they resembled great shaggy beasts, like sleeping woolly elephants that might any moment stir from slumber, rise up on tree-trunk legs, and wander away.

As they walked through the village, the natives crowded around the newcomers and pulled at their clothing.

"They're like children," Mr. Clarkson said. "They're in dire need of the white man to come and run things for them."

Isaac gave him a sharp look. "We have not come here to be their masters, Mr. Clarkson, but to lift them up from their dark, depraved state as our equals, and educate them so that they may read the Word of God for themselves, as is every man's right."

Clarkson mopped his face with a stained handkerchief. The day, despite the trade wind, was hot and humid. "They call us *haole*, which means without breath. We're so pale, I think they don't believe we're real people. I have to warn you, Mr. Stone, these people don't understand about souls. And they sure don't have any idea of heaven and hell."

"Then it is our duty to enlighten them so that they may find salvation through God's divine grace."

"Mr. Clarkson," Emily said, walking at the dock agent's side, "if they do not believe in heaven and hell, where do they believe they go when they die?"

"Their spirits go into animals and trees. They worship sharks because they think their ancestors turned into sharks. Everything on these islands has a spirit."

As the girls and women swarmed around Emily, tugging at her clothes, giggling, Clarkson said, "They've never seen white women before. And your clothing is a novelty."

"As is their lack of it," Emily said.

"Are you taking us to the king?" asked one of the other passengers, a merchant from Rhode Island hoping to establish a dry goods store in Honolulu.

"Kamehameha the Second is currently touring the islands with his wife, who also happens to be his sister. These islands haven't been united for long and they were centuries fighting among themselves, so the new king has to show the colors, as it were. And as he is only twenty-three, it is vital that he is ensured the same loyalty as was given to his father, old Kamehameha the First."

"How long have you lived here, Mr. Clarkson?"

"I came out ten years ago as a ship's chandler aboard an explorer vessel. Fell in love with the place and decided to stay. Old Kamehameha had already conquered all the islands with his one thousand war canoes and ten thousand warriors, so even a blind man could see that these islands, now that they are peaceful, are going to be a ripe plum for Westerners to come along and pluck. An enterprising white man can make a good living for himself here. I myself collect customs tax for the king from ships that drop anchor here and of course keep a fee for myself. A lot of white men with an eye to the future are starting to notice the value of this kingdom lying halfway between America and China. My own brother set himself up in the village of Honolulu, selling food and fresh water to whalers and other trading ships."

At the edge of the native village, facing the sea so that the scene was backdropped by the magnificent lush green crags and peaks and valleys of the mountains, stood a large pavilion consisting of posts anchored in the sand and a thatch roof. Beneath this woody canopy a group of impressively arrayed people sat, clearly the aristocracy of the islands, because as the visitors drew near, the great crowd of common people stayed back so that a broad space lay between them and the nobility in the pavilion.

These elite sat on a raised platform, sitting cross-legged on woven mats and great colorful sheets of cloth. The men were adorned with crowns of green spiky leaves, necklaces made of nuts, garlands of green leaves on their bare chests. Some had symbols painted on their skin, geometric patterns that Emily supposed must denote rank. There were women as well, wearing the wraparound garment that covered their legs but left their breasts bare, and adorned with flowers in their hair, around their necks and ankles and wrists.

They were the *ali'i*, Clarkson explained, the highest caste in the Hawai'ian social system, "the equivalent of European royalty and aristocracy," he said, and they all stared at the visitors with intense curiosity and eagerness, especially Emily and the other three ladies from New England.

Clarkson explained that the trio in the center were Chief Holokai and his son, a warrior named Kekoa, and the chief's daughter, Pua.

Holokai was a man of great stature and girth, a handsome nobleman with his close-cropped white hair decorated with green leaves. Around his thick neck, a choker made of green leaves, and matching circlets around his wrists and ankles. Upon his bare chest lay a necklace of shark's teeth. He wore a sarong of brown cloth, and carried a tall staff topped with a flower. A rope of yellow feathers encircled his waist—symbol of his high authority, Clarkson explained. Holokai's complexion was dark and glowed like bronze in the sunlight. His brow was thick and his eyes fierce.

Clarkson explained that the son, Kekoa, who appeared to be in his thirties with a strong resemblance to his father, was a *kahuna kilo 'ouli*—a character reader, trained from early boyhood to "read" people. The daughter, Pua, was a medicine woman.

Introductions and "alohas" were spoken, and then the chief

addressed Isaac. Clarkson translated. "He wants to know, if he believes in Jesus, will he get big ships, too?"

Before Isaac could reply, Clarkson said, "When the natives first saw Cook's ship and his firepower, forty years ago, they thought the white men's gods were more powerful than their own. They think that if they become Christians they will have all the trappings of Western culture."

"Jesus Christ," Isaac said in his booming voice, "brings you the promise of redemption and salvation and eternal life. It is God's love and mercy you must seek, sir, not material goods."

When Clarkson translated, and the chief grinned and nodded, Isaac suspected his words got lost in the translation. But he would remedy that soon enough.

The woman seated next to Holokai spoke and gestured to Emily. Clarkson said, "Pua is of the highest rank among the *ali'i*. She is High Chiefess and a *kahuna lapa'au*—mistress of healing. Pua's bloodline goes back many generations. She traces her ancestry to the First Ones, and therefore she is of the noblest line. Make friends with her and you've gone a long way toward winning the hearts of these savages."

Emily haltingly stepped up to the dais. Pua was beautiful. Dusky-skinned, voluptuous, and strong, with long flowing black hair and a garland of scarlet blossoms lying upon heavy, naked breasts, Emily judged she was around thirty. Pua's eyes were round and dark, with the slight fullness to the lower lid that seemed a mark of the Polynesian race. Her smile was like a sunrise, and when she reached up and brushed Emily's face, it was a gentle touch. "Aloha," she said, drawing out the second syllable, making the word almost sound like a song. She stroked Emily's cheeks and nose and forehead, and touched the deep brim of her bonnet, then she tapped Emily's shoulders, speaking in her native tongue. Clarkson translated: "Pua says you are very beautiful. You're like a flower. She says she wants you to be her friend. She says she wants to learn everything you know."

"Tell her I am honored."

Emily returned to Isaac's side and more dialogue continued, with Holokai questioning each of the visitors, asking many questions until Emily had to hold onto her husband's arm to keep from sagging.

Finally, Holokai rose from the platform, towering over the crowd with great stature, and made a loud announcement, his voice rolling out to the breakers on the beach. Clarkson translated: "Now the welcoming feast begins."

The guests were given places of honor near the platform, with clean, woven mats to sit on, while lesser nobles sat farther away from Chief Holokai, and the commoners, at the edge of the elite circle, sat wherever they felt like.

The sun was dipping toward the ocean as food was served. Emily was mortified to see the natives dig up a pit and remove a huge cooked boar. A priest chanted as the men ceremoniously carved the roast meat, and Clarkson explained that every move a Hawai'ian made was always accompanied by a blessing. In the instance of a memorable feast such as this, the priests were going to chant prayers all the way through.

Along with the boar, chickens and dogs had been roasted in the dug-out oven, which was called an *imu*, along with sweet potatoes, taro, and breadfruit. Mullet, shrimp, and crab were roasted on an enormous bed of hot coals. There was coconut milk to drink. Emily found it awkward to eat sitting on the ground, but told herself it was a picnic in the country. Still, there were no plates, no knives and forks. Slices of meat were delivered on large green leaves and had to be eaten with one's fingers. She wished she could unpack napkins from one of the many trunks they had brought from home. And she longed for a cup of tea.

But it was all part of the grand adventure and she gladly embraced the foreignness of it all.

Clarkson said, "By the way, Reverend, this is a show for you and your friends."

"How so?"

"Until just six months ago, there was a very rigid system of laws here, called *kapu,* which means forbidden. Laws that they've lived under for centuries but which were done away with when a powerful queen said she'd had enough. One of the kapu rules was that men and women were not allowed to eat together, and men got the better food. But that law has been banished and Chief Holokai wants to demonstrate how enlightened his people are, just like Westerners."

Entertainment followed, consisting of drums and chants, and a synchronized dance that shocked the Americans in its lewdness. The young ladies from New Haven tried not to watch, while their husbands frowned with displeasure. Mr. Clarkson, who could not take his eyes off the bare-breasted young women who were gyrating their hips in short skirts made of grass, explained that it was called hula, and that there were many forms, some for entertainment, some for sacred ritual, and some for "other matters."

Men danced as well, muscular specimens in skirts made of long green, spiky leaves, but their performance seemed to Emily more of a warriors' exercise as they stomped their feet in unison, and pounded their chests and shouted together in one voice. Perhaps designed to instill fear in an enemy, she thought, for they certainly were fearsome in their power and might.

Emily kept a handkerchief in the long sleeve of her dress, and she drew it out frequently to dab her cheeks and forehead, the day was so hot and humid. She thought she could not bear another moment sitting on the ground, drums pounding in her ears, every inch of her body fatigued from the voyage and from the anticipation of her new life, when Chief Holokai rose to make another announcement.

"They're taking you to your new house now," Clarkson said, groaning as he rose to his feet.

"Oh thank goodness," Emily said as he helped her up. "I do most look forward to some time alone. The ship was crowded."

"They built you and your husband a splendid house," Clarkson said as they fell into step behind the noble personages, with the commoners trailing behind so that they formed a solemn procession along a path at the edge of what looked to Emily like some sort of crop fields. Beyond, a waterfall tumbled from mountain heights into a sparkling river that emptied into the sea. There were no more native huts here, although she could see shacks down on the beach which she presumed were where the expatriate sailors lived.

They came to the edge of a beautiful lagoon beside which giant leafy trees spread shade over a flat expanse of grass. And in the middle of this acre stood . . .

Another grass hut.

It stood on a stone platform and was made of a framework of poles lashed together, clearly seen, with thick bundles of dried weeds tied to the poles. The roof was very steep and thatched. There was a door, in the front, with the familiar patterned cloth the Hawai'ians wore for clothing, hanging from a wooden rod. A square had been cut out of each wall to form a window. Emily and Isaac stepped inside. The ceiling consisted of rafters made of poles, above which could be seen the inside of the high, pitched grass roof. There were no rooms, no partitions. Isaac strode the length and breadth of it, counting out forty feet long and twenty feet wide. He deemed it a palace.

Emily was appalled.

But she quickly reminded herself that this was a good thing. That she was open to trying new ways. That whatever the natives endured, a New England woman certainly could. In fact, she couldn't wait to write her first letter home: "Dearest Mother, would you believe it? Mr. Stone and I have set up house in a hut made entirely of grass! We live exactly as the natives do and it is a welcome challenge."

Clarkson said, "The letter your Mission Board sent with a whaler out of Boston arrived two weeks ago, informing King Kamehameha of your decision to come. So he called for a special priest to roam the area and find the most auspicious place for your residence. The man prayed and called upon the gods and used all sorts of mumbo-jumbo to find the right spot. Then Chief Holokai put his men to work, whether they wanted to or not. There is no volunteerism here. What the chief says is rule. You disobey, you are seriously punished, sometimes executed. The construction was accompanied by prayers, chanting, rattling sacred objects, sprinkling sacred water over each bundle of weeds. I daresay an umbilical chord is buried in the foundation, for good luck. What I'm saying is, they'll expect you to appreciate their effort."

One of the chief's attendants, a wiry old man wearing a cloth cape and carrying bundles of green leaves, stepped forward and chanted over Emily and Isaac, and then shook the leaves at the house. When he was done, Holokai grinned and spoke, pointing to the interior, and Clarkson said, "The chief is reminding you to be sure to urinate along the walls of your house to keep evil spirits out. And he hopes that tonight will result in the birth of your first child."

The sun had slipped into the Pacific when the Stones said farewell to their fellow travelers, wishing them luck in their new homes here on Hawai'i Island and on O'ahu. The chief and his entourage,

Clarkson and the crowd all departed, and Reverend and Mrs. Stone were alone at last.

Emily was bone-weary and ready to drop. She longed for a bath and a big feather bed. But the bath, it turned out, was a bucket of water someone had thoughtfully placed in the hut, and the bed, at the far end of the hut, was a pile of woven mats.

Sailors from the *Triton* had already placed their trunks inside. While Emily got ready for bed in the dark, doing what she could with what little she had, Isaac said he wished to inspect the property while it was still dusk.

Emily found an oil lamp carefully packed in one of the trunks, and the flint needed to light it. By the lamplight she found her and her husband's nightclothes, which they had not been able to wear on the *Triton* because of the lack of privacy. Her heart raced as she undressed, washed herself, combed out her long hair, and slipped the nightgown over her head. Tonight was her bridal night.

Not knowing what else to do, she tried to get comfortable on the bed of woven mats and waited patiently in the dark. A breeze came through the windows, bringing the fragrance of exotic flowers. The air was sultry and heavy with promise. Emily wished she could remove her nightgown and feel the night air on her skin. She closed her eyes and thanked God that her bed no longer rolled and heaved with a ship. She prayed that she would never again have to set foot on a sailing vessel. She was drifting off to sleep when Isaac approached the bed.

He was in his long nightshirt with a nightcap on his head. "Mrs. Stone," he said solemnly, "there is an unpleasant duty I must perform. Forgive me, but it is long overdue. I shall be as quick about it as possible in deference to your chaste state."

He extinguished the oil lamp, knelt on the bed, lifted her nightgown in the darkness, fumbled about, then lifted his nightshirt and lay on top of her. Her mother had warned her there would be pain, and there was. Isaac buried his face in her neck and she put her arms around him as he thrust in and out. She tried to get comfortable beneath him but he seemed oblivious. She started to speak, to ask him to lift up, when he suddenly cried out, "Praise the Lord!" and collapsed on top of her.

He lay for a moment, panting, then he rolled off and said, "I shall not bother you again for another seven days. Good night."

Soon she heard his snores as she lay blinking up at the dark rafters.

As Emily drew water from the stream that fed the lagoon, she heard laughter on the wind and, turning toward the bay, saw native girls cavorting naked in the waves. The Hawai'ians, Emily had learned, spent half their lives in the water.

In the past seven days she had learned a few other things as well, foremost of which was why the Mission Board had insisted that only married couples could be missionaries here. The handful of white men who lived in the area had taken up with native women without benefit of clergy—Mr. Clarkson himself boasted having three wives! As much as Isaac tried to tell them that they were living in sin and dooming their souls to perdition, they didn't care. Emily could see the allure of these islands and the beautiful women who lived here—especially as the women seemed to possess no modesty or shame but rather gave willingly of themselves. Even the staunchest Christian male would be sorely tempted under such circumstances. Hence, married couples only.

She paused to watch Isaac assist in the construction of the meeting house. Tomorrow they would hold their first divine service there. Since seven days had passed, tonight he would perform his husbandly duty in the dark again.

Isaac was a hard worker, teaching the natives the value of honest labor through his own example. The natives were drawn to his power and his presence. He reminded her of her father, a strict, God-fearing man. When the natives had asked Emily what God looked like, she had replied, "The Almighty has no form, He is spirit." But even as she spoke the words, the image of her own father came into her mind—a cold man who believed a father should not show affection to his children as it would cause them to lose respect for him.

Emily was beginning to realize that Isaac was cut from the same cloth. Even on the night he did his husbandly duty, there had been no kissing, no caressing, and when he was done, he had rolled off and gone to sleep. Her mother had assured her that "love will come," and yet Emily had never seen any evidence of love between her parents.

Outside of the marriage bed, Isaac rarely touched her, so that when Emily observed the intense affection Hawai'ians showed for one another—touching, embracing, stroking—she felt a sharp pang. She had grown up in a home where all love was reserved for the Almighty, and now she lived in a place where the greeting, "Aloha," was also the word for love—a kingdom where families slept together in little shelters and gave each other gifts of flowers and food as tokens of love.

She went back inside, where she was working on making the hut a home, starting with curtains made of the native cloth that turned out to be made from the bark of the mulberry bush. A shadow fell across the open doorway. Emily was used to this, as the natives could not stay away, being curious about the white woman and her peculiar ways. Emily often found herself spied upon and took it in stride. "Aloha," she said without turning around.

"Aloha yourself," came a deep-voiced reply.

She spun around to see a stranger standing in the doorway.

He wore snug white breeches tucked into high black boots. His dark blue jacket with rows of brass buttons was fashionably narrow at the waist, but came to his thighs and was without tails. A white waistcoat was buttoned over a white muslin shirt, and his white cravat was elegantly tied, with the two ends trailing symmetrically on his broad chest. He removed his hat, exposing short, wavy brown hair. The hat identified him as a mariner. It was a flat-crowned dark-blue peaked cap with a visor, and the gold braid around the crown most likely identified him as the master of a vessel—twenty years ago, she thought, it would have been a white powdered wig and a fancy tricorn hat. He had the ruddy complexion indicative of a life spent at sea, Emily noticed.

She also thought he was extremely handsome, and the smile made her throat tighten inexplicably.

And then his smile froze when he got a good look at her. "God bless me," he said in shock. "When old Clarkie said there was a white woman on the island, the wife of a preacher, I pictured something else entirely. Older, farm-worn, matronly, with maybe a gaggle of kids. Not a pretty creature who belongs in a ballroom!"

"The dockmaster should have said there are *four* of us," she corrected him, suddenly aware of her own disheveled appearance, trying to remember if she was wearing one of her better gowns. "There is one lady in Waimea and two in Kona."

"But you're the prettiest I would wager."

"And married," she said pointedly.

Amazingly, the grin broadened. "So Clarkie said. And to a preacher no less."

He thrust out his hand. "MacKenzie Farrow, at your service."

She noticed he didn't step across the threshold. At least he knew his manners. Still, something didn't seem proper. "Shall we step outside, Mr. Farrow?"

He moved aside and Emily felt immediately relieved to be out in the open rather than in the intimate space of the dark hut. "Emily Stone," she said, shaking his hand and noticing the grip, the callouses. She also noticed he couldn't stop staring at her. "I would offer you a cup of tea, Mr. Farrow. But when they told me the natives would have a house for us, I was expecting something a little more habitable. There's no furniture. No cooking hearth."

"Hawai'ians don't live in their homes, except for sleeping. They spend all their time outdoors."

"There is my husband over there." She pointed across the lawn. "He is building our meetinghouse. Next will be a schoolhouse."

Farrow squinted at the work in progress—twelve tall, sturdy poles had been driven into the ground and natives were on the thatched roof, affixing thick bundles of weeds to it. The meetinghouse would be an open pavilion, Isaac had decided, to show the natives that all were welcome and that no walls or doors stood between them and God. Tomorrow, he and Emily hoped to see every inch of the mat-covered floor filled with those eager to hear the Gospel.

At that moment, Isaac looked up from his carpentry and, seeing a stranger at their door, broke out into a smile. Walking up, he boomed, "Welcome, stranger! Isaac Stone, at your service, and I see you have met my wife!"

They shook hands and Farrow explained that he had just anchored his clipper ship, the *Kestrel,* in the bay and that he still had to go and oversee the off-loading of cargo. But he had been in a hurry to see for himself the new Americans in Hilo.

"Then you must come back tonight!" Isaac shouted. "And join us for dinner!"

Glancing at Emily, pausing for a moment to search her face, Captain Farrow set his mariner's hat on his head, promised to return at sunset, and left.

You just missed meeting the great king that united these islands," Captain Farrow told his hosts. "When Kamehameha died last year, his body was hidden by his trusted friends, in the ancient custom called *hunakele,* which means to hide in secret. The *mana,* or power of a person, is considered to be sacred so, following ancient custom, his body was buried in a hidden place so no one could steal his mana. Kamehameha's final resting place will forever remain unknown."

They dined indoors by the light from three oil lamps and candles Emily had brought from New Haven. Nearby, in the night, they could hear the natives in their village as they cooked and ate, and told stories and laughed and engaged in leisurely activities outdoors by the light of *tiki* torches, as they had no form of lamps or indoor illumination. Emily made the best of what they had, turning their three trunks into makeshift chairs upon which they rather uncomfortably sat, while their "table" was a leather hatbox draped in a tablecloth in the center of the little circle.

Emily had tried her best to make cushions of her and Isaac's winter clothing, but even so the two men shifted on their buttocks and crossed and uncrossed their legs. They didn't complain, knowing the lengths to which she had gone to make the three of them feel at home.

Emily had also had Isaac suspend sheets of native cloth from a rafter to separate their sleeping area from the rest of the hut. It didn't seem right that this stranger, the first guest in their new home, should see their marriage bed.

Chief Holokai had sent two slave women to help Emily, but as she and Isaac were staunch abolitionists and were supporting the anti-slavery movement back home, she insisted on paying the two women a wage. It was small, but it wasn't slavery. They happily cooked outside and brought the meal in on china plates from New Haven, which they had stared at and examined a long time before laying the fried fish and roasted yams on them. Captain Farrow and his hosts ate with their dinners perched on their knees, but Emily had seen to it that each had a clean napkin spread over his lap. They ate with knives and forks, and drank fresh water from the nearby stream out of pewter cups.

It was an awkward arrangement, but all three, including the veteran sea captain, agreed that it was better than eating on board a rocking ship.

"Where do you hail from, Captain?" Isaac asked. He was formally dressed for this special occasion, in the black cutaway coat and tails he normally reserved for the Sabbath.

"I'm from Savannah, Georgia, Reverend Stone," Farrow said, filling the small hut with his deep voice. While Isaac tended to shout to drive home a point, Emily could not help thinking that the captain possessed a naturally commanding tone. "My father owns a cotton plantation, but I had a hankering to see the world. I was the youngest of seven, and had no desire to stay landlocked. My father and I had the usual arguments, and I ended up running away to sea. I started out as a cabin boy and then a deckhand. A merchant captain noticed that I was a natural. He took me under his wing and taught me everything I needed to know until I got my own master's ticket. But I didn't want to sail the Atlantic. I yearned for even farther horizons. A Canadian fur trapper told me about new trade routes opening up where a man could make a fortune, if he had the vision and the fortitude. So I came west, signed on with a small company that was willing to give me a share in profits if I was willing to take risks. The silk and fur trade between America and China is a lucrative one, and before long I was able to purchase my own ship, the *Kestrel,* and now I am my own master."

"You must miss your home, Captain," Emily said.

The look in his eyes took her aback as he said, "I've given scant thought to home . . . until now. Mrs. Stone, you have reminded me—" He caught himself and made a show of spooning salt out of a little bowl on the "table" and sprinkling it on his sweet potatoes. "I take it you are here to Christianize the natives, Reverend Stone?"

"Our first duty, Captain, is to teach the natives to read and write. They are being defrauded by sea captains who come into port for fresh water and provisions. Chief Holokai showed me a supposed contract he signed with the master of a whaler. The chief signed over a guaranteed measure of crops, pigs, and chickens, plus strong men to fill out the whaler's crew. As you know, crewmen on whalers are notorious for jumping ship. In return, Chief Holokai receives part ownership in the whaling vessel and is guaranteed a portion of the profits, which he will receive in coin with which he can purchase Western goods. He showed me the contract. It was written in gibberish. The chief is giving away valuable supplies and man power for nothing, and by the time he realizes he has been cheated and will never see a penny from the whaling captain, he will have no legal recourse should he take his case to the king."

Farrow nodded. "Unfortunately, there are scoundrels taking advantage of the illiterate chiefs of these islands."

"I and my brethren intend to remedy that outrage. Hawai'ians are to be treated with respect and as equals."

Farrow gave him a look. "You're the first Westerner I've heard express such a sentiment."

"John Calvin preached that all souls are equal before God, no matter the color of their earthly flesh. To this end, I and my brethren will see to it that all men understand this basic truth—natives and white men alike." Isaac sipped his tea, looking at his guest over the rim of his cup. "I trust, Captain Farrow, that you are not one of those scalawags?"

"Like yourself, Reverend Stone, I am a Christian and do not believe in defrauding my fellow man. It is a noble goal, educating the natives."

While they spoke and Emily watched the two very different men, it struck her that, by his manner and tone, Isaac seemed the older of the two, and yet she judged Farrow to be eight or nine years her husband's senior.

"After they have mastered reading and writing in English, they will learn to read and write in their own language, which necessitates our creating an alphabet as the Hawai'ians themselves have no system of written communication."

"Good luck with that," Farrow said. "The Hawai'ian language has all of twelve letters and a lot of vocal sounds that can't be assigned a letter."

"Then we will use other symbols."

"Captain Farrow, I am puzzled about something," Emily said. "What could Chief Holokai want so badly that he would pay so high a price for it?"

"Gloves!" Isaac blurted before Farrow could reply. "And boots! Breeches! Spyglasses! Pewter candle sticks! Top hats and canes! Pocket watches! For forty years they have gone aboard European and American vessels and seen goods that they'd never seen before and now they want them."

"But what use have the chiefs of such items?" she asked.

"Mrs. Stone," Farrow said. "What do you know of the history of these people?"

"Nothing, really."

When Isaac cleared his throat to speak, the captain said, "Reverend Stone, if I may? No one is certain exactly when people came to these islands, but the Hawai'ians' own oral tradition goes back many generations, perhaps over a thousand years. And in the past four decades, men of science and curiosity have come here to learn the mystery of these islands, and have discovered many things. Putting the science together with the oral tradition it is now known that nothing you see around you is native to these islands, which are in fact merely the tops of deep oceanic volcanoes."

While he spoke, Emily didn't touch her food. The atmosphere within the hut was close and intimate, with lamplight casting a soft glow on the captain's handsome features, the flickering candles glancing off his wavy hair in chestnut highlights. Although he commanded a merchant ship that carried Alaskan furs and Hawai'ian sandalwood to China, and brought back silk, spices, and jade, there was an air of high adventure about him. Well groomed and well spoken, Captain Farrow seemed the pinnacle of the civilized seafarer, yet in his presence Emily could not help think of dangerous pirates and privateers, men who lived on the edge of life, and who laughed at death.

She wondered if he was married.

"Some time around a thousand years ago or longer," he said, "a brown-skinned island race set forth from their homes in the South Pacific in double-hulled outrigger canoes to brave a hostile and unknown ocean in search of a new home.

"According to legend, guided only by stars and seagoing birds, they crossed the thousands of miles alone beneath the sky, unaware of other continents and races, bringing with them their wives and children, their pigs, dogs, and chickens, the idols of their gods, and cuttings and seeds of plants from home. How many months they paddled and sailed is unknown, how many perished along the way we do not know. Who they were, their names, and most of all their reasons for leaving their island homes is lost to memory.

"But on a date that was never recorded, the travelers finally spotted a string of islands on the horizon—the most isolated islands in the world, it turns out—and here, they brought their journey-scarred canoes onto virgin beaches, they planted the sacred standards of their gods and they called their new home Havaiki."

Emily was mesmerized by the narrative, while Isaac munched and chewed and ran bread around his plate.

"The legends tell us that the islands were inhospitable," Farrow said, his brown eyes on Emily, holding her in thrall. "There was no fruit, no edible plants. There were fish and a few species of birds, but these had to be skillfully trapped. There were no palm trees, no bamboo for making shelters. There were no bright flowers, no orchids or hibiscus to please the eye. Still, the newcomers made it their home. By luck, they had brought with them the essentials for survival: they planted coconut palms and bamboo, mulberry bushes for making cloth; they planted sweet potatoes, bananas, mangoes, and pineapple. They planted flowers from home until they turned the unfriendly volcanic peaks into paradise."

Farrow paused as the evening breeze found its way inside the grass house, stirring the cloth hangings. His eyes moved from Emily's face to her neck, where Emily felt curls that had strayed from underneath her white lace cap move against her neck. As it was evening, her collar wasn't high but square cut, revealing her collarbones and the hollow at her throat. She felt Captain Farrow's eyes roam every inch of face, neck, and hair, but no lower, staying respectful, while she felt her skin grow hot and heard her husband noisily refilling his teacup.

Presently, Farrow said, "The newcomers established a system of royalty and nobility, called the ali'i, who ruled over the commoners. They created a system of laws, called *kapu,* that if broken were punishable by death. They feared their gods and practiced human sacrifice. But they lived in a land that blessed them with sunshine, plentiful rain and food, and gentle trade winds, so that when not farming taro root or fishing in lagoons, the people entertained themselves with feasting and dancing and riding the waves on long wooden boards.

"Because there were no poisonous snakes in this paradise, no mosquitoes, no fevers or plagues or catastrophic illnesses, no predators or raptors (the newcomers found only two mammals here, the monk seal and a species of bat), the Pacific Islanders flourished and multiplied in their kingdom which was cut off from the rest of the world. They kept their culture unchanged for a thousand or more years, keeping strict observance of the kapu laws, and worshipping Pele, the goddess of volcanoes, because the islands shook and spewed forth lava on a regular basis. Once they had found Havaiki, the islanders never left again. They never went exploring, never sought an even newer home. They were content."

Farrow smiled and Emily released a breath.

"That was an interesting bit of history," Isaac said louder than was necessary. "Thank you for the lesson."

"That wasn't the interesting part," Captain Farrow said as he set his plate on the mat-covered floor and pressed the napkin to his lips. "The interesting part is that the islanders were unaware of other races, ones that were flourishing and multiplying, cultures that were evolving from the old ways to the new—other races that were born to explore and expand—Spaniards, Frenchmen, Englishmen, Germans, and Americans. Finally the day came when these white men set out in giant ships propelled by billowing sails and stumbled upon these isolated, 'undiscovered' islands, dropped anchor, and rowed ashore in longboats.

"It was just forty-two years ago when an Englishman named Captain James Cook claimed to have found a savage and naked race living in an earthly paradise."

Captain Farrow addressed Emily. "Now, Mrs. Stone, we come to your earlier question as to why Chief Holokai would pay such a high price for goods he didn't really need. Picture if you will, a people who knew neither the wheel nor the bow and arrow, who had no metals of any kind, nor precious gems, nor animals of prey, nor beasts of burden, whose only cloth was made from bark, whose only adornment came from flowers, feathers, and shells—a people who knew nothing of ceramics or glass, nor cotton or wool, who had never tasted wine or cheese or beef, who had no alphabet or books or writing of any kind, who knew nothing of clocks and teacups and fountain pens, or starched collars and violins. And then suddenly, upon this primitive and wanting stage, new actors emerged—men with white skin and brass buttons, carrying swords and guns and speaking of a world so vast and populous and full of wonders that surely those men were gods!

"The islanders, and you can't blame them, wanted to be like those men."

He fell silent and sounds drifted in through the windows and open doorway—the two serving girls outside, talking and laughing. The faint roar of the nearby waterfall. Voices and laughter from Chief Holokai's village. Dogs barking, children squealing.

Meanwhile, inside the hut, Reverend Stone sat deep in thought, his lips pursed over a problem he seemed unable to catch, and his wife found herself trapped in the hypnotic gaze of an exciting stranger.

Isaac spoke again, having caught his elusive thought. "Captain Farrow, I am discovering that the natives seem eager to learn about Jesus. We were told that we were going to have a difficult time bringing these people to the Lord, that first we needed to demonstrate that their gods are false and do not exist, and then tell them about the Almighty. But I have seen no resistance so far."

Farrow straightened his spine and squared his shoulders—he was clearly growing uncomfortable sitting on the trunk—and said, "That's because a very strange thing happened during your voyage, Reverend. Something unforeseen and rather shocking. Once Captain Cook reported back about these islands, it opened the way for other white men to come. For the past forty years, the natives have been exposed to Western influence and although they tried to hold onto their ancient ways, the influence of the West proved too great. Six months ago, while you and your party were on the high seas bound for these islands, Queen Ka'ahumanu, the new king's stepmother and co-ruler, decided she had had enough of the ancient kapu system and shocked everyone by sitting down at a feast and eating with the men. Her stepson, Prince Liholiho, who changed his name to Kamehameha the Second, gave in to her pressure and declared the kapu system to be obsolete."

Emily said, "It was that easy to dismiss a code of laws that had been in existence for centuries?"

He smiled. "The reason is simple. Under kapu, the people were told that if they broke any of the rules, the gods would punish them. And they believed it. But then they saw the white man breaking kapu all over the place and no divine punishment came. Queen Ka'ahumanu saw this as proof that the old gods were powerless. She ordered her people to destroy their idols. So you see, Reverend, your work here might not be as challenging as you had thought. The natives are empty vessels waiting to be filled with a new faith."

While his hosts pondered this unexpected revelation, Captain Farrow drew a fob watch from the pocket of his waistcoat, looked at it, and said, "I believe it's time to return to my ship."

He rose and collected his hat. "Mrs. Stone, I can't express enough my appreciation for your delightful hospitality."

"You must come again," she said.

"The *Kestrel* sails in the morning, I'm afraid. Off to China for several months."

They escorted him outside, where they found the breezes balmy and sweet. An ivory moon hung against the stars. On the other side of the Stone property, rented by the Mission Board from the Hawai'ian Crown, the village began and sprawled for a great distance, lighted with tiki torches and filled with the sounds of life and the aromas of food.

"Thank you again for your hospitality," Captain Farrow said and seated his mariner's cap on his head.

As he said good-bye to Emily, he stretched out his hand and she offered hers. But instead of a handshake, Captain Farrow *held* her hand and placed his left hand over hers, cradling her fingers in shocking intimacy. The warmth, the gentle squeeze sent a jolt through her. It was as if the captain had taken her entire body into his arms.

So small a gesture, yet so heavy with significance.

And Isaac, she noticed with relief, had been completely oblivious. "Godspeed," he boomed. "May the Almighty fill your sails with His divine breath and keep you safe on the seas!"

And they watched him disappear through the trees.

A jagged promontory overlooked Hilo Bay, created long ago by an ancient lava flow, the fiery molten rock running like a red river from a long since dormant volcanic vent, to run hot and then grow cool, to run hot again and cool again, over and over, layer by layer, until this cliff of black boulders stood high enough for a New Haven bride to look out at the ships riding at anchor, to watch the anchor of one of those ships, the *Kestrel,* rise up from the sea, to watch sails unfurl and to watch the sturdy clipper turn into the wind and slowly glide over the sunlit water, carrying Captain MacKenzie Farrow toward exotic climes.

Emily did not understand the feelings that swam in her heart. She knew only that when the ship grew smaller and smaller until it disappeared over the horizon, a part of herself disappeared with it, and that that part of herself would not return until Captain Farrow did.

CHAPTER TWO

Must you go, Isaac? We've barely been here four months."

"Many more souls await salvation, Emily," he said as he methodically packed his leather satchel. "I cannot stay in one place. The Lord sent his disciples out into the world to cast a wide net."

Emily wrung her hands. She hadn't known she was going to be left alone here. When he had informed her only the day before of his intention to visit the villages northward along the coast, she had been so shocked she had been unable to eat or sleep. And now she was a bundle of nerves.

Where had her adventurous spirit vanished to? Emily had discovered that she was terrified of being left alone with the natives, although she couldn't express why. It was their . . . *foreignness*. The Hawai'ians were kind and generous and seemed always to be smiling. But when Mr. Alcott had addressed the congregation of Emily's church, to speak of an island kingdom filled with souls doomed to perdition, he had failed to mention that there were more obstacles than the issue of religion. The children ran free, with no discipline whatsoever. But how could they know discipline when the adults had none? Their social life was based on impulse and whim. If the surf was high, everyone abandoned his or her labors to grab their long boards and take to the waves. And so it was with the school. In the first days, in the new thatched pavilion Isaac had built, Emily taught the alphabet to a crowd, children and adults alike, all showing up early and eager to be handed slates and chalk. Emily had been pleased. But then, some days, no one would show up and she had to go through the village, rounding up the unruly children.

And she couldn't put certain notions from her mind, once the odious Mr. Clarkson had planted them: telling her and Isaac, when he dropped by for tea and cakes, how just forty years ago these people were practicing human sacrifice. Even though Chief Holokai had assured Isaac that they no longer engaged in the abhorrent ritual, the urge must surely still be in their blood. And what if it was Isaac's presence that kept them in line, but once he was away from Hilo . . .

"I have heard of rampant fornication on this island," Isaac said as he tied his bag shut. "They have no concept of the union of marriage. They move from one partner to another as the whim strikes. And those who are married engage in sexual intercourse in front of their children. The whole family sleeps together. It is a tradition to which I am determined to put an end."

They went outside, where Isaac turned and laid his hands on her shoulders. "Remember that God is with us, Emily. There is nothing to fear. And it is time I took the light of the Lord to the other lost souls on this island. I leave you here to carry on my ministry, to correct our people when they stray, and to encourage them to believe in the Almighty and his Infinite Love for them."

Emily's faith didn't blaze across the heavens as her husband's did. Hers was a quiet, comfortable relationship with the Almighty. But she believed in the Devil and that there was evil in the world, and that the only salvation was through knowledge of the Most High. And so she had come, and had found a land so bright in its light, and deep in its beauty, that she wondered how darkness could prevail here. But then, hadn't Eden been beautiful? Hadn't it been a paradise where a man and a woman dwelled in blissful ignorance of evil? Ignorant even of their own nakedness, as these people were? Until a serpent had led them away from God's loving grace.

Shading her eyes, she scanned the surroundings—the lehua and ohia trees, the climbing vines and abundant flowers, the rushing waterfall and sparkling creek and deep, green lagoon, and thought: Yes, the Serpent is here, watching, waiting. . . .

"You must be strong in your faith, Emily," he said in his sermon voice. "God abhors weakness."

But Isaac didn't understand her feelings of isolation and loneliness. They did occasionally enjoy the company of white men, as ships anchored in the bay and all manner of gentlemen came ashore. Mostly sea captains, navigators, and explorers—civilized, educated men, with the common sailors being restricted to their vessels in order to keep the peace. Writers came as well, and artists, scientists, and naturalists who came to these exotic isles to see for themselves a world unspoiled. When they came ashore, they were always told that they could find a good meal and English conversation at the home of Reverend Isaac and his wife.

But never a white woman among them. And Emily craved the company of one of her own kind.

As Isaac mounted his horse, Emily touched his leg and said, "I have been thinking, Isaac. Perhaps we should have a proper house. We have the meetinghouse and the schoolhouse now. We need to build our permanent home. A grass hut is no fit place to entertain guests."

Emily had been struggling with the idea for days. She had arrived at this shore believing that she was open to trying new ways. That whatever the natives endured, a New England woman certainly could. But she had come to hate the grass hut.

And more. . . .

From the first day, when they landed, and naked women had climbed on board the ship, Emily had tried to convince herself it was simply their custom and, anyway, she and Isaac were there to change all that. But as tolerant as she tried to be, she was continually appalled by everything she saw. The natives were not at all how she had imagined they would be. The way they dressed, the way they ate, and the way they touched one another and exhibited lack of control or modesty. . . .

Emily had come from a world where overt displays of emotion were considered ill-bred. The Hawai'ians were highly emotional people and never held anything back. Whether anger or grief, or even extreme joy, they bellowed out their feelings, they wept waterfalls of tears, they shrieked with laughter until their bellies ached. How could she convey to them that well-bred persons controlled their feelings, their physical bodies, and their speech?

And it was not just the Hawai'ians. There was the intolerable Mr. Clarkson. Emily had never considered herself a snob. She had come prepared to befriend all who lived here, including the retired sailors and other expatriates who had settled in the tropics. But try as she might, Emily could not look upon the dock agent as a friend or an equal. She had been taught that icy politeness was a well-bred woman's best weapon in putting "vulgar mushrooms" in their place.

"Perhaps," she said now to Isaac, "we should not live like the natives after all. How else are we to civilize these people if not by example?"

But even as she spoke these very reasonable and logical words, Emily could not help but feel a small disappointment in herself.

"Indeed!" Isaac shouted with an enthusiastic smile, surprising her. "You are quite right, wife, and upon my return we shall commence the construction of a proper home! God be with you, Emily!"

As she watched him ride off and disappear into the forest, Emily turned to see a man coming up from the harbor. He was a surly, unkempt old sailor who lived in a shack on the beach and occasionally worked for Mr. Clarkson. "Letter for you, Missus," he called out, wiping his sweating face.

"A letter?" Her heart leapt. From home, yes! A letter from her parents! What a providential coincidence. And to have arrived so quickly.

But it turned out not to have been dispatched from New Haven but rather, strangely, from the middle of the ocean. Sea captains, the old salt explained, when they encountered friendly vessels going in the other direction, often asked for correspondence and other important news to be carried back, and so there was a packet of letters addressed to Reverend Isaac and Mrs. Stone from Captain MacKenzie Farrow.

Emily, in her sudden delight, pressed them to her bosom as she went back inside her grass house.

E mily hummed as she tied her bonnet ribbons under her chin and checked her appearance in the small looking glass brought from home.

She hadn't felt this cheerful in days.

Captain Farrow had written five letters, each a continuation of the last, covering a variety of topics, not the least of which was his expressed pleasure in knowing that the company of educated Christians now awaited him on his return to Hilo, and in looking forward to hearing about the progress of Reverend Stone's mission. Farrow talked about himself in greater detail, his family back in Georgia, and his travels to the Pacific Northwest where he enjoyed encounters with the various native peoples who lived a vastly different lifestyle from those who occupied the Sandwich Islands.

It was a long and interesting narrative but Emily wondered why he had written such personal letters to total strangers. She thought that, like herself, MacKenzie Farrow might be lonely out on the high seas, encountering foreign races and cultures, and that the opportunity to fill lonely hours by conducting a dialogue of sorts with newly made American friends was a welcome relief.

But then she came to the end of his final letter, in which he wrote:

"Mrs. Stone,

You made an impression on me. You reminded me of home, of the Southern ladies who had been in my family's circle. I have been away so long at sea, that I had forgotten fond memories which the sight of yourself suddenly brought back. Because of a falling out with my father, I had been content to let memories of my happy boyhood slip into oblivion. But you brought them back, Mrs. Stone, and for this you have my eternal gratitude.

"These memories, which seem like a gift from your kind self, have prompted me to write to my father, to reconcile our relationship. The Hawai'ians perform an ancient ritual called *ho'oponopono*. It involves confession, penitence, and forgiveness and it is usually conducted within a family to cure illness and bad luck. This letter to my father, which I pray you will pass on to a ship bound for the Atlantic, is my attempt at *ho'oponopono* in the hopes that he and I can heal the wounds between us."

Emily saw that the last in the packet of letters was addressed to a Colonel Beauregard Farrow, Savannah, Georgia, United States of America.

Emily pressed the letters to her breast and silently vowed that she would go down to the dock every day and make sure the precious letter was placed in the care of a conscientious captain. And as she made this vow, she wondered if more letters might be forthcoming from Captain Farrow, and now she had something to look forward to until her husband's return.

Isaac had been gone for three days now. Today was the first Sabbath on which he would not be delivering a sermon in their meetinghouse. But Emily was prepared. With her prayer book clasped in her gloved hands, she left the stifling grass hut. She brought along her umbrella because the weather in Hilo, she had discovered, was very unpredictable—one could be out in blazing sunshine and ten minutes later be drenched in a sudden soaking rain.

She crossed the green lawn—a natural landscape dotted with flowering shrubs and enormous leafy shade trees—to the "church" that had no walls. As usual, it was crowded. From Isaac's very first divine service, four months prior, attendance had been high. Every inch of the mat-covered floor was taken up with seated congregants, while others stood along the sides and at the back. Isaac's translator was a taro farmer named Kumu, who had been a boy when the first white men came to Hilo. Intelligent and a quick learner, Kumu had learned to speak English and now was eager to learn how to read it. In Emily's daily school, Kumu was one of the adults who sat with a primer and a slate, painstakingly writing the alphabet.

Emily smiled and said, *"Aloha,"* to the congregation. They were a colorful group, from infants to the elderly, the women wearing brightly patterned sarongs and floral leis, while some of the men wore trousers from the donations Emily had brought from New Haven. Unfortunately, many still wore the *malo,* a scant loincloth made from a narrow strip of bark cloth that only barely provided cover. Emily had been told that the sarong and *malo* were not worn for modesty, but to keep evil spirits from sneaking into the genitalia.

Isaac had preached many times on the necessity of covering oneself. He had also spoken out against the common practice of defecating and urinating in public, which the Hawai'ians seemed not to understand as unacceptable behavior. Emily decided that the focus of her sermon today would be the modesty of the women, and the need for them to cover up.

Isaac's sermons were always divided into two parts: the first concerned with how people should behave, while the second was about how to find the path to salvation. Strangely, it was the second half that the natives were most interested in hearing. Isaac had discovered, to his joy, that contrary to what Mr. Clarkson had averred, not all Hawai'ians wanted material goods and power. After it was demonstrated by Queen Ka'ahumanu that the old gods were powerless, many Hawai'ians were left without something higher to believe in. They warmed to the concept of an invisible, all powerful, and loving God watching over them. And as Captain Farrow had explained in his letter, the concept of forgiveness and redemption was nothing new to Hawai'ians.

Thus far, there were no official converts, Isaac had yet to baptize anyone into the faith, even though many enthusiastically declared their love for God. "Until they understand the concept of the soul," Isaac said, "and the difference between damnation and deliverance, I cannot call them Christians."

Emily stood before the congregation, opened her Bible, cleared her throat, and said, "Today I am going to read to you from Second Thessalonians, in which the apostle Paul wrote, 'Now we command you, brethren, in the name of our Lord Jesus Christ, that ye withdraw yourselves from every brother that walketh disorderly, and not after the tradition which he received of us—'"

"Where Mika Kalono?" a voice called from the back of the gathered company.

Emily looked up. "I beg your pardon?"

Another person spoke up: "You not Mika Kalono."

As the Hawai'ians could not pronounce the letters S and T, they substituted and so "Mister Stone" came out quite differently.

"The Reverend is away on a visit up the coast. He is taking the word of God to others of your people. I will be—"

Kumu the taro farmer, standing at her side, translated for those who could not speak English and the crowd was suddenly agitated.

"No Mika Kalono?" another cried out.

"Well, no, I'm sorry, but—" To her astonishment, one by one the congregants rose to their feet and shambled out, leaving her, moments later, standing alone beneath a deserted pavilion. Kumu grinned toothlessly and said, "I go now?"

A week later, as she dressed in her usual day gown with the long tight sleeves and high collar, wondering if the cloudy sky was going to deliver another day of rain, Emily decided she would try a different approach at the sermon. Instead of reading from a book, she would walk among the congregants and engage them directly and individually. Although most of them spoke no English, many knew a few words and phrases, and all were eager to learn. I shall make a pleasant game of it, she thought as she tied the ribbons on her bonnet. I will make it a sport, perhaps offer prizes of some sort.

She left the grass hut with hopes high and pleased with her ingenuity, but halfway across the lawn she stopped. The meetinghouse was deserted. Not even Kumu was waiting for her.

But she had gone through the village the day before, reminding them that tomorrow was the Sabbath and she hoped to see them here, and everyone had nodded and smiled and promised to come.

But now she knew the truth. Isaac was the force behind the Mission here. Emily had never felt so weak and useless.

I s there any mail for us, Mr. Clarkson?" Emily disliked the daily trek she took down to the dock where the agent had his customs office and a well-stocked trading post. But she was impatient for more letters—from home, from the Mission Board, but mostly from Captain Farrow. There were new ships in the bay, which meant the possibility of a mail delivery.

He grinned as he picked his yellow teeth. "Sorry, madam, nothing today."

She loathed the way he looked her up and down—an offense he had never dared commit when Isaac was home. However, her husband had been away for three weeks now and Emily was feeling increasingly vulnerable and defenseless.

But at least she had been able to hand Captain Farrow's letter to the captain of a clipper ship bound for the Atlantic who assured her he would see to it that the letter would be safely carried to the port of Savannah.

As she trudged up the dock, where natives were busily loading logs of sandalwood, harvested from higher elevation forests, into long-boats, Emily looked at the lush green mountains that towered over the little settlement of Hilo. Clouds had a mysterious way of suddenly materializing out of the blue, to darken the sky and let go a light drizzle, to break into mist against those craggy summits and give birth to magnificent rainbows. Hilo was a damp and humid place, but it was also beautiful beyond description.

She followed the path beside the lagoon and went past her own house, continuing on to the native village.

She was on a mission.

It had come to her last night during prayer. Alone in her grass hut, kneeling in the light of the oil lamp, trying not to let fear and loneliness weaken her faith in the Almighty's plans for her, she had talked out loud to her heavenly Father. His reply had come in the form of a thought: Focus on Pua. Convert the High Chiefess and the rest will follow.

While Pua, the beautiful thirty-year-old daughter of Chief Holokai, was an eager and quick pupil, she was an undependable one. In her capacity as *kahuna lapa'au,* she was called all over the island to diagnose illnesses, administer curative herbs, treat wounds and rashes, preside over childbirth, and generally be responsible for her people's overall health and fertility. Additionally, in her capacity as High Chiefess and as an ali'i, her presence was required at all rituals, ceremonies, and feast days. And as she was not yet Christianized, and even though the kapu system had been abolished and the gods declared nonexistent, Pua continued, along with thousands of other Hawai'ians, to participate in religious rites that sometimes took days. And so the remaining time that was allowed for learning to read and write was limited.

And Emily never knew Pua's schedule. The woman would simply disappear without a word, returning days later with no warning and expecting a lesson.

But Pua's brother, Kekoa, was seen in the village quite often.

A very influential man among his people, he had fought at old Kamehameha's side, and so the natives did whatever he said. *I shall ask Isaac to focus his proselytizing on Kekoa.*

Emily was well acquainted with the native village, knew where she could walk or could not, and which shelter belonged to which family.

Laid out in a haphazard pattern, some thirty huts, large and small, were home to Chief Holokai's people. Many called aloha to Emily, waving and smiling from their labors. Women sat in front of huts stringing flowers into garlands, or tending small vegetable patches, or nursing infants at their breasts. Dogs ran wild, as did children, and chickens scratched in the dirt.

The huts she passed were role-specific: there was the house where all family members slept together, then the men's meeting-house, forbidden to women, and the cooking house, also forbidden to women. There was the pavilion where bark cloth was made, an area forbidden to men, and the compound where canoes were hollowed out and fitted with outriggers, an area forbidden to women. On the fringe of the village were the simple shacks of outcasts and slaves, while the huts of the fishermen and canoe builders were closer to the beachfronts. At the far end of the village, which Emily now approached, stood the palatial thatched homes of the ali'i set on raised basalt foundations. Lastly, something called the sacred *heiau*— precinct of the old gods, surrounded by a high fence with fierce-looking idols guarding the gates.

A distance beyond this, and set apart from the main settlement, was the menstrual hut to which women retired once a month. So openly did they speak of this matter—men and women alike—that when the menses came, a woman wore a special flag upon her person to alert others to her condition. It was kapu for her blood, which they called Lehua's Tears, to touch another person or object. What was correctly and properly hidden in New England, was broadcast about in this savage culture, and Emily suspected that this was one custom she might not convince them to abandon.

But there were other ingrained customs that she and the other missionaries in the islands were determined to eradicate, with sexual promiscuity and incest at the top of the list.

As she walked past women harvesting flowers, stringing leis, making floral crowns and bracelets, and then past the cloth-making pavilion, it occurred to her that their adornments, except for seashells, were perishable. The cloth they made from mulberry bark did not last long and had to be constantly replaced. Even their homes eventually rotted or blew away in storms. Everything had to be continually renewed or replaced. To a New England native who was used to the permanency of brick and iron and glass, the Hawai'ian way of life seemed ephemeral, temporary. Nothing man-made among these people lasted. And yet . . . they were closer to nature. They worked with what they had, they did not manufacture what did not already exist in the world around them. And the constant renewal of their possessions made her think of the seasons and the earth's own constant rebirth.

The heiau was the Hawai'ian form of a temple, where priests made offerings to the gods. Constructed of piled lava rock, Chief Holokai's heiau was a square of about a hundred feet across, with walls eight feet high and four feet thick. A gateway opened in the middle of the north wall, through which Emily saw large stone platforms with various grass structures built upon them. She had been told that here was where the priests lived, and also where sacred items were stored. In the center of the compound stood an altar surrounded by idols of the gods.

She recognized High Chiefess Pua at the altar, laying down an offering of fruit and flowers as she chanted to a large stone that dominated the center of the altar.

"*Aloha,*" said a girl who stood at the gate.

"*Aloha,* my dear," Emily said, having met Pua's daughter on many occasions.

Mahina was thirteen years old, slender and pretty, with long wavy black hair and a colorful sarong around her hips. She was a shy, giggling girl who spoke some English. It occurred to Emily that Mahina was nearing the age when she would join the other girls who swam out to the ships to enjoy the company of sailors who had been months at sea.

Emily was helpless to stop the others from swimming out, but she vowed that she was going to see to it that Mahina never joined them.

"My mother give offering to Lono," Mahina said in her imperfect English.

"What is the significance of that stone on the altar?"

"That Lono's *piko ma'i*."

"I do not understand."

Mahina giggled and, through gestures, made her meaning clear. Emily stared at her for a moment, then looked back at the altar. Now that she saw the stone in another context, she realized there was no mistaking its symbolism: about four feet tall, carved smooth from black lava, the "idol" was cylindrical with what looked like a knob on the top.

Merciful heaven, she thought in shock. They worship the *male member*?

Momentarily speechless, she recalled what a physician, Dr. Franks, who was touring the islands, had said when he stopped by her house for tea. "Perhaps their faith and ours hold some things in common," Emily had said to him on the subject of the Hawai'ian religion. "For instance, we have been told that they practice circumcision. Through this common ground we can begin discourse on God's covenant with Moses."

"Yes, that's true," the doctor had said over biscuits and oolong, "circumcision is indeed practiced among these people. But it is not the circumcision of Abraham and Moses. It is in fact, not technically circumcision but something called 'subincision.' It does not remove the foreskin as a sign of God's covenant, but rather deforms the foreskin so that the man's pleasure during the procreative act is heightened."

Dr. Franks had spoken so matter-of-factly that Emily had nearly choked on her tea.

Physical intimacy seemed to be a topic of special interest among white men in these islands. Mr. Clarkson had enlightened Emily on another practice she had rather not heard about. But as the dock agent also happened to own the only trading post in Hilo, offering such needful merchandise as sewing needles and cloth, Emily had no choice but to be in the vicinity of his unpleasant banter. "It was their custom to have older women take boys to the beach at night, to teach them the ways of making love. And men teaching girls, indoctrinating them in lascivious ways, telling these innocent children that the ways of men and women behind closed doors is sacred. These sex practices, Mrs. Stone, have been outlawed, forbidden by the Hawai'ian monarchy itself. But everyone knows that away from the towns, out in the country, in villages, in darkness, the evil practices continue."

Finally, Pua ended her chant and left the heiau. *"Aloha!"* she said with delight at seeing Emily. She spoke rapidly and Mahina said, "My mother pray to Lono for you and Mika Kalona."

"Praying for us? Why?"

Mahina spoke to her mother, who said with a smile, "You and Mika Kalona twelve month?"

Emily frowned. "Oh, yes. We have been married a year, that is true."

"And no baby?"

"Well, no." Emily cleared her throat. She wasn't about to explain the circumstances of their marriage, that it had really only gotten its start just over four months ago. But ever since then, Isaac had been diligent and regular, every seven days.

And then the true significance of what Mahina had said sank in. Pua was praying to a stone effigy in the shape of a penis—for her and Isaac!

Emily suddenly felt soiled. As if something putrid had been poured over her. She instinctively fell back a step and looked at Pua in horror. "You must not do that, Pua!" she said. Emily couldn't put it into words—praying to idols was an abomination, yes, but not something that had filled her with revulsion. And yet in this instance it did, for now it was personal. Against her will, she and Isaac had been dragged into a heathenish practice of the most depraved kind.

She felt sick.

What was wrong with these people? Couldn't they see what an affront to God their ways were? Pua had asked, on several occasions, for Isaac to "make her a Christian," and he had explained that until she denounced her pagan ways she could never be baptized. How were they ever to get through to these people that they must give up the old ways before they could see God's divine light?

Emily was suddenly recalling the day King Kamehameha the Second had come through Hilo to visit his subjects and to receive reports from Chief Holokai. He had arrived with a retinue of foreign advisors, one of whom was the chairman of the Mission Board in Honolulu, a New Hampshire man named Jameson, who had introduced Reverend Stone and his wife to the monarch.

It was strange to Emily to see so dark-skinned a young man, with such distinct Polynesian features, dressed in a military tunic with brass buttons, medals, and a sash, with a plumed helmet on his head. And his eighteen-year-old wife, Queen Kamamalu, who wore a fashionable Empire-style gown with her hair swept up in a knot with ringlets over her ears, European style. Except for her dusky skin, Kamamalu would fit in at any court in Europe.

Emily had thought them a delightful young couple until Isaac had pointed out that the king's wife was also his sister.

And now she understood a truth. That, contrary to what Captain Farrow had said about bringing these people to Christianity being an easy task, it was in fact going to be an uphill battle. As long as their own royalty practiced incest and most likely other unspeakable practices, the likes of Pua and others were never going to know the Lord's love.

As she left the village, Emily still felt sick over her discovery of the obscene idol at the heiau. She had planned to spend the afternoon with sewing and mending, but her heart was filled with a heavy darkness. *I don't belong here! I was foolish and naïve to think I could make a difference in this savage place!*

She kept walking, blindly, past her hut, past the lagoon, down the worn path that led to the white-sand shore fringed with tall, swaying coconut palms.

She stumbled along the beach, clutching her shawl about her shoulders, and looked out over the ocean—looking for what, she did not know. All she knew was that this was a terrible place, that she did not belong here, and that at no time since coming here had she felt so acutely her loneliness and isolation.

As she gazed at the distant horizon, she thought of the thousands of miles that separated her from loved ones and all that was familiar. I am lonely and homesick! she silently cried, praying that the wind and the ocean waves would carry her plea back to her home in New Haven.

Mother, Father, dear sisters! she cried. Though I am surrounded by hundreds of friendly natives, I am an outsider. My yearning for home is like a sickness that overwhelms me and reduces me to tears. Dear family, help me!

She resumed walking—it was a stumbling gait, erratic, as she tripped on kelp and driftwood and sent sandpipers scattering in her path—trying not to think of the obscenity she had seen on the heathen altar. She clutched her stomach and prayed she would not be sick. Natives called out to her—young men with their surfing boards, older men mending fishing nets, women combing the grass at the base of palm trees, scavenging for fallen coconuts. All waved and smiled and Emily smiled back but it was a forced smile, her face felt wooden. It didn't matter how friendly they were—these people were brown-skinned and nearly naked and painted their bodies and adorned themselves with bones and shells and flowers.

A more alien world could not exist.

The wind tugged at her long dress. Sand found its way into her shoes. She wanted to go home. Not to the grass hut, but home. . . .

Sunday strolls on the Green after attending church on Temple Street. Picnicking in the woods on the Quinnipiac River. Sleigh riding in the winter. The changing colors of the leaves in autumn—oh, the golds and reds and oranges!

Emily's heart did a tumble and she released a bitter sob.

She pictured the house where she was born—a New England salt-box that had been built over a hundred years ago and was as sturdy and reliable as ever. Not like the grass huts of these islands, which got blown down in storms or rotted from dampness and mold and had to be rebuilt every year!

Emily stopped to stare at the surf rolling onto the beach and then retreating, leaving bits of foam and seaweed behind. Small shorebirds scurried about, dipping their beaks into the freshly wet sand. The tide came in again, causing old, decaying kelp to lift and swirl and settle back down when the water receded. It was hypnotic to watch.

Emily was reminded of family outings when she was a child, to New Haven Harbor where people had gathered to watch the construction of a lighthouse at the tip of Little Necke peninsula. There, too, she had been mesmerized by the ebb and flow of the sea, how it sometimes deposited items on the sand, or carried objects away from the beach in an eternal give-and-take.

She remembered finding a small seashell once. She couldn't remember what had become of it.

She sighed raggedly. Musings of home were not easing her melancholy. In fact, they were making her more homesick. She decided to head back to the grass shack that she feared she would never call home and, with her thoughts on needles and thread, resumed her trek across the beach.

Halfway to the dunes, her right toe struck something hard. She looked and saw a piece of wood buried in the sand. She bent and pulled it out, brushing it off to see what it was. It was a flat board, painted shiny and yellow, possibly from a shipwrecked vessel, that had washed up on shore.

She tossed it down, and as it fell, the board flipped over, exposing the other side. Emily froze. There, at her feet, was the word ROSE painted in black.

"Merciful heaven," she whispered, pressing her hand to her bosom.

Rose was clearly the name of a vessel lost at sea. It also happened to be her mother's name.

"Merciful heaven," she said again, louder, feeling the sun on her head and shoulders, the wind against her face, the sounds of native laughter and the crashing surf and, farther out, the shouts of sailors on ships riding at anchor.

Retrieving the plank, she pressed it to her heart and closed her eyes. She trembled. She held her breath. *No, this fragment of wood did not come from a shipwreck. It came from a shipyard in New Haven where the vessel was undergoing repairs. The name was damaged or perhaps changed. The workers tore it off and tossed it to the tides.*

Ocean currents and winds and gales carried this precious fragment down the Atlantic coast, all the way down to Cape Horn where, upon stormy seas, this little message from home was tossed upon icy waves until it found a current streaming into the Pacific and was carried here, all the way to this distant-most spot on earth, to be lifted onto the sand by the gentle Hawai'ian waters and deposited here, like a letter in a postal box, for me to find.

To tell me that God has seen the homesickness in my heart and has sent me a reassurance that no one has forgotten me, that the vast oceans are not a barrier between me and my loved ones, but a link that joins me to them.

With tears of joy, Emily hurried back up the path to the lagoon. Inside her grass hut, she placed the plank bearing her mother's name on a shelf Isaac had built for dishes and cups. And as she placed it here, Emily said out loud, "This board was sent to me by God from New Haven to let me know that despite distance and time, New England is still my home."

And she felt the pain of loneliness, of homesickness, start to fade.

As she turned away from her newfound treasure from home, Emily felt a strengthening of spirit and she thought of the shock she had received at the heiau. But now she knew she must not be repulsed. She must find courage. Suddenly, her determination to abolish sin in the Sandwich Islands intensified in that moment, as she vowed to make it her personal life's goal to bring High Chiefess Pua out of the darkness and into the light.

I n the glow of the full moon, Pua moved on silent feet.
Circling the dark hut where Emily Stone slept unaware, the High Chiefess wordlessly cast spells and magic into the night. She shook ti-leaves drenched with sacred water so that the drops sparkled on the sides of the grass house. She whispered chants and made sacred signs with her hands. And when she was finished, she smiled in satisfaction.

She had used a particularly potent spell.

When she returned to her sleeping hut, she found her handsome warrior waiting for her. Pua had no husband. Mahina's father had been one of Kamehameha's High Priests and Pua had spent four months of pleasure with him. Mahina's brother was the result of a union with a man of fine blood in Waimea, when Pua had attended a festival up there. Many other lovers had known Pua's artful lovemaking, and they had delighted her in return with their own.

These days, her heart belonged to one man, and it was to his mat she came tonight, where he welcomed her with open arms. She removed her sarong and laid her body alongside his, pressing her nose on either side of his, taking care not to let their lips touch, for that was kapu.

While they caressed and murmured words of love, she stroked his *piko ma'i* until it stood up as straight and hard as Lono's, and he fondled her *'amo hulu* until it was as moist as the deep rain forests on the slopes of Kilauea. She climbed on top of him, to straddle his hips and lower herself onto his shaft. Like all the girls of her race, Pua had been taught at an early age to manipulate her vaginal muscles to give her lover optimal pleasure.

As she delighted herself with his member, slowly and deliciously, she told him about the spell she had cast on the wife of the *haole* preacher. "She needs babies. She has nothing to do, nothing to love.

43

Her husband is cold, he has no breath, he is haole. But the wife has fire in her belly. I will pray every day, and I will chant magic spells, and I will place *ti*-leaves around her house. I will call upon the gods to give her a baby, and when she has one to love, she will stop trying to change us, telling us how to live."

Pua slowed her lovemaking to give him the most pleasure, this man she loved with all her heart—Kekoa, her brother.

CHAPTER THREE

The letter had come a week ago.

It had traveled thousands of miles from Savannah, Georgia, passed along from ship's captain to ship's captain, and it was addressed to Captain Farrow "in the care of Rev. and Mrs. Stone, Hilo, Hawai'i."

Emily could not stop staring at the writing. *In the care of . . .* Captain Farrow had placed himself and his father, and their unfortunate rift, in *her* care. . . .

She thought of what Captain Farrow had written in one of his letters, about the Hawai'ian ritual called *ho'oponopono* involving the Christian concepts of confession, penitence, forgiveness, and reconciliation. He had written a letter to his father as a form of *ho'oponopono* in the hopes that they could heal the wounds between them.

And now Emily held his father's response in her hands.

For the past seven days, she had gone out onto the promontory to watch for ships. Mr. Clarkson, who was familiar with Captain Farrow's route and schedule, estimated that he should be due back from China soon, bringing his cargo of jade and tea and silk and spices, to be sold in Honolulu to merchant captains who would then take the precious commodities to the Atlantic side of America and across the ocean to Europe where demand for the exotic Asian luxuries was high.

It had been nearly a year since her one encounter with the handsome captain, but his first letters and kind words had made a deep impression on her. And then more letters had come from China, handed to the captains of faster ships who would be stopping at Hilo for supplies, letters that regaled Emily with stories of the exotic Orient, hearing the captain's deep voice as she read them over and over, so that they had formed a bridge over the days and weeks, making it seem as if MacKenzie Farrow had dined with them only last night.

She still felt the warmth of his skin as he had cradled her hand in his.

The wind blew in off the Pacific, bringing rolling white clouds and churning the surf below, where boys rode the waves on their long boards. Emily recognized them. They were supposed to be in school. Yesterday, she had taught the alphabet and simple reading to thirty-one eager scholars. This morning, no one had showed up for a lesson. But then, she wanted to be out here as well, although for a different reason.

She shifted her attention between the distant horizon and, closer in, the tall coconut palms on the beach where youths had climbed high up among the fronds to engage in one of their favorite sports—to see who could spot new sails first.

When they started shouting and waving their arms, Emily saw, below on the dock, Mr. Clarkson come waddling out of his shack and lift a spyglass out to sea.

She held her breath.

She sometimes thought he purposely dragged this out, as he knew how anxious she was for letters, and for the return of Captain MacKenzie. But soon enough he lowered the glass, turned to look up at Emily on the promontory, cupped his hands around his mouth, and shouted, "Ahoy, Mrs. Stone! It's the *Kestrel* coming into port!"

She had not realized, until that moment, how desperately she wanted to see MacKenzie Farrow again, because now she almost fainted with joy. It took every bit of her willpower to keep from running down to the dock. With all the strength she could summon, she turned her back on the sparkling sea and the tiny sails on the horizon, and walked back to her grass house, where she would wait the eternity she must wait until Captain Farrow came to visit.

He arrived at sunset.

For the occasion, Emily had chosen one of her Sabbath dresses—a day gown of delicate muslin with a pattern of tiny blue flowers. The scoop neckline was low and would have exposed cleavage were it not for the addition of a fichu tucked in for modesty. She had decided to forgo her indoor lace mobcap so that her hair, clean and shiny and swept up into a Grecian knot, was exposed.

She told herself it was proper for her to wear her best clothes when a guest of honor was coming to visit. But in the back of her mind she hoped her appearance was pleasing to the captain.

And apparently it was because when she heard footsteps outside the hut, and she looked up, an expression of utter delight met her eyes. She had just finished setting the table that Isaac had constructed out of local wood. There were four chairs as well, but it was still a grass hut, and Emily was never more acutely aware of the rustic-ness of her home than in that moment.

"Good evening, Mrs. Stone," he said, removing his mariner's cap with the gold braid.

"Hello, Captain Farrow," she said. He was strikingly handsome in his blue mariner's coat, narrow at the waist with two rows of brass buttons. His tight breeches were white, his tall boots a shiny black.

"I trust I am not intruding?" His eyes went to the table set with a cloth and tableware.

"Not at all. I am pleased to see you."

He looked around. "Where is Reverend Stone?"

"On one of his many rounds about this island. He never rests in his drive to save every soul in Hawai'i."

His attention returned to the table, set for two. "Then I am intruding."

"Mr. Clarkson was kind enough to inform me of your imminent arrival. I was hoping you would dine with me."

"I can think of nothing I would like more."

His eyes held hers for a long moment, until Emily felt suddenly uncomfortable. "Shall we sit outside? It is terribly warm in the house."

As he turned to leave, Captain Farrow paused and looked at the shelf holding curiosities that could only have come from the beach: coral, sea glass, even the fragment of a wooden plank painted with a ship's name, *Rose*.

"When homesickness comes over me," Emily said, "I visit the beach and I always find something to comfort me. Last month, I found this large, smooth, curving chunk of amber sea glass. I held it up to the sun and saw warm colors swimming in the glass. And I knew at once that it came from a bottle that had contained ale. It looked just like the bottles Uncle Caleb drank from. I said to myself: This glass is not from a shipwreck but was thrown overboard in a moment of merry jubilance on the high seas. And it was carried here to remind me that those at home still think of me and that I can always go home someday."

She turned to MacKenzie. "Does that sound terribly silly of me?"

He met her gaze. "Not if it brings you comfort."

Isaac had built chairs for outdoors, as the Stones had adopted the Hawai'ian custom of spending very little time inside their hut. The two native girls who helped Emily were cooking over an open fire, turning a chicken on a spit and checking on vegetables in the coals. They glanced at the visitor and giggled.

"Tea, Captain Farrow?" Emily said, picking up the teapot.

"Yes, please, I could do with a cup."

As he watched her pour, Captain Farrow said, "Does your husband leave you here alone much?"

"He comes back long enough to refresh his growing flock here in Hilo," she said with a smile, but added silently: and to do his husbandly duty.

"The loneliness," MacKenzie said. "Does your husband know of this?"

"Isaac knows that he asks a lot of me, leaving me alone the way he does. I understand that and appreciate that he does the best he can in his own way. He has his hardships. It would not be fair of me to bring up my own troubles. I put up a good front for Isaac. He needs a strong woman. But I confess, Captain, that my spirit is weak. And I am disappointed in myself."

"Why on earth do you say that?"

She offered him the sugar bowl. "I had thought I was made of stronger stuff, but I am not the brave adventurer I fancied myself to be. I am sometimes so afraid of this place that I resort to familiar convention. In this way, I suppose, I remain in control, telling myself that I am doing all the right things. Every day, at four o'clock, I have tea in the white china cups. I make sure we have table linens and dress for dinner. If we had white neighbors, I would make morning calls and leave my card. I had thought I would leave all that behind."

"Please do not underestimate yourself, Mrs. Stone. I am impressed with how well you have adjusted and how well you cope with this strange life. It cannot be easy for you. A lesser woman would have packed up and sailed back to New Haven."

There was more, but Emily didn't know how to put it in words. It had to do with the Hawai'ians themselves. She was filled with a strange disquiet when she was around them. Her failings seemed larger when she was with the natives, as if the kanaka themselves were pointing them out to her, revealing her for what she really was: a New England woman just like the rest, in need of convention and familiar culture. It was as if they stood a looking glass before her and she was disappointed in what she saw, disillusioned with how she had turned out.

Disillusioned with the fact that, while she was committed to Isaac through marriage vows, she was in danger of falling in love with an adventurer who was forbidden to her.

"Perhaps you are right, Captain," she said. "Perhaps we need these comforts and, yes, we must keep to civilized ways. After all, do we not teach by example?"

But with each lump of sugar that went into her cup, Emily watched it dissolve and, with it, her previously high esteem of herself.

They sipped their tea, Chinese oolong, while tiki lights were lit in the village and drums sounded in the night and the air grew warm and sultry. Farrow was acutely aware of an ill-ease between himself and Emily Stone, so he cleared his throat and said, "Your husband must be making great inroads on this island, Mrs. Stone." And then he realized he had spoken the words, not to clear the air, but to remind himself that this winsome creature was *married*.

"The missions in Kona and Waimea, Captain Farrow, demand Isaac's assistance, which he gives willingly and at great sacrifice to his own comfort. Isaac is working, with two other ministers, to create a Hawai'ian alphabet using the English language, so that they can print Bibles in their native tongue. I am proud of my husband, Captain Farrow. There are fifteen thousand natives in the district, and Isaac must travel a hundred miles to reach them all. Some areas can only be reached with peril to limbs and even life. When horseback is not feasible, he traverses on foot, sometimes sliding down the sides of ravines, or climbing, or being let down by ropes from tree to tree. In times of heavy rain, he swims across swollen rivers, with a rope to prevent him from being carried away. He frequently preaches in wind and rain with his clothes saturated. It is a wonder he has not come down with pneumonia."

Farrow noticed how the flickering tiki light cast a fetching glow on her hair. Emily Stone was exactly the way he had remembered her these past lonely months. For the first time since he could remember, he had been eager to have a voyage come to an end. But only a brief end, he reminded himself now, because in a few days he must depart for northern waters to collect ivory and furs from Eskimos and Canadian trappers.

"I have brought gifts for you and your husband," MacKenzie said as he reached for a small sea chest he had set down next to his chair. Handing it to her, he added, "I hope Reverend Stone won't mind my forwardness."

Emily lifted the lid and found treasures from the Orient: a red silk scarf, a tea set made of white porcelain and painted with delicate flowers, packets of tea, and a small figurine that looked like a plump rabbit, carved from pink jade. Although she saw nothing in here for her husband specifically—except possibly the tea—she said, "Mr. Stone will be very pleased with his gifts." She closed the chest and reached into her skirt pocket.

"And I have a gift for *you*," she said, handing him the letter that had come from Savannah, Georgia. "Although," she added, "I really shouldn't take credit for it. This is a gift that comes from your father."

He stared at the envelope for a long time, then lifted damp eyes that glowed in the torchlight. "You are wrong, Mrs. Stone," he said softly. "It is a gift from *you*. A letter has little chance of making its destination from so far off and risky a route as China to the Atlantic seaboard. It needed a responsible caretaker at the halfway point to see to it that the letter was set into secure hands. And then to hold onto the return reply, for I doubt this little shred of paper could have made the final leg to China as we have been having typhoons and we have lost ships at sea."

He looked at the letter again and Emily felt his emotions stir in the evening air, as if they had escaped his body, like spirits, yearning to be free. "Aren't you going to read it?" she asked.

He smiled and slipped it into his coat pocket. "On the ship, when I am alone. I would not presume to waste a single moment of your valuable time, Mrs. Stone, by filling it with boring family news."

They engaged in pleasant conversation, with the captain entertaining her with tales of the Far East, and Emily being frank about the challenges of this mission and getting the natives to listen to her husband's message, and then the two girls served dinner and the New England wife and Southern sea captain dined as if they were in any house in America. But outside, they heard the drums and the chanting, they heard distant squeals and laughter coming from deep within the rain forest, and they felt the humidity of the sultry night, reminding them that they were both far from home.

As MacKenzie spun his tales of the mysterious Orient, Emily listened in rapt attention and thought: Speak to me of all the exotic places I cannot visit. Let your words be the ship that carries me to far-off adventures.

And she knew she had fallen in love.

Neither wanted the evening to end, but the captain had to return to his ship and Emily knew she must keep up appearances for the natives' sake. They shook hands and said good-night, but Farrow promised to come again the next day and Emily said she looked forward to it.

Neither slept that night.

MacKenzie Farrow watched from the back of the school pavilion as the children recited rhymes under the direction of Emily Stone. He doubted they knew who Mother Hubbard was or what a "cupboard" or a "coffin" were, but they chanted the English words in unison and with excellent pronunciation.

When they were done, Emily clapped her hands and the children scampered merrily away, clutching hornbooks, primers, and slates. He joined her as she straightened the woven mats and picked up pieces of chalk and bits of food. "It is nothing short of a miracle, Mrs. Stone. Your power of persuasion astounds me."

She straightened and gave him a long look. He wore his hat, although he now stood beneath the thatched roof, but no mariner's coat. Captain Farrow had arrived in waistcoat and shirt and he carried a mysterious package. She didn't know how to respond, being unused to praise. She had never heard it from her parents, and certainly not from Isaac. When she reported excellent school attendance to him, he said, "Praise God," giving all credit to the Lord. She had supposed he was correct, until now.

"It has not always been a success. In the beginning, I placed woven mats on the floor, spaced out evenly, with individual chalkboards and primers set out just so. A child at each mat, paying attention to me as I stood at the head of the class. The first few days were a success, but on the fifth day, no children arrived. I went down to the beach and there they were, riding the waves on their long boards!"

He laughed. "What do you expect, they're Hawai'ians!"

"I told myself that they were uncomfortable when they write. They need proper desks, I thought. That's what is lacking. I bided my time as I watched them ride the waves. The truants finally came out of the surf, tired and giddy and hungry. Sticking their boards in the sand, they ran off to their individual huts for a lunch of fish and poi. I had brought two brawny natives with me, and told them what to do.

"The next day the children showed up at the classroom because someone had stolen their surfboards and they had nothing else to do and so they thought another day of stories with Mika Emili would be a nice diversion. They stopped and stared when they saw their new desks—surfboards propped up on sturdy rocks."

Farrow smiled. "I would say that two lessons were learned that day."

"The children are like sponges, and the adults are eager to learn— when they feel like attending school. But the two whom I am most determined to save are High Chiefess Pua and her brother Kekoa. They worship . . . *disturbing* idols."

"What about Chief Holokai?"

"He refuses to give up the practice of polygamy and until he does, Isaac will not baptize him."

"Mrs. Stone, I was wondering—"

"Please call me Emily."

They strolled over the grass toward Emily's hut, where a flower garden bloomed in a riot of colors. Ahead, Hilo Bay stretched before them, with ships at anchor. To their left, the blue lagoon sparkled in the sunshine, and to their right, Chief Holokai's village was alive with daily life. Behind them, a lush and dense rain forest rose slowly on the gradual slope of Mount Kilauea, which Emily had been told was active and could at times show Pele's wrath. Thus far in the months since Emily had first arrived, the mountain had slept.

"Captain Farrow," she said, "did your father's letter contain good news?"

He smiled. "It did indeed. He could not express his relief enough when my own letter reached the plantation. The whole family rejoiced to hear my news and to learn that I wished a reconciliation." He stopped beneath the shade of a spreading banyan tree and looked down at her. "I came to thank you for your help in what would surely have been an impossible feat. Because of you, I am connected to my family again and I wish to show my appreciation in a small way."

She glanced at the mysterious box he was holding.

"Emily," he said, "if you have some free time this afternoon, I would like to show you an entertainment that I have brought back from China."

She hesitated. She should be working, doing washing and mending, or looking for Pua, who was overdue for a lesson, or weeding their garden patch, or engaging in any one of a multitude of tasks that demanded her attention. And wasn't her own husband at that moment toiling in some remote village to bring the light of the Lord to them? "I should love an entertainment, Captain Farrow," she said.

And he said, "Call me MacKenzie."

The mysterious bundle he carried turned out to be parts of a silk Chinese kite. Saying that the beach would be the best place for it, he and Emily were joined by a group of Hawai'ians and retired sailors and other idle white men, who clustered around to watch the American assemble the pieces. Emily had seen kites before, had helped her brother fly them, but those had been plain white cloth over diamond-shaped frames. Captain Farrow had brought a spectacle to Hilo!

The growing crowd made comments and sighs of admiration as a mythical creature evolved before their eyes. Upon a bamboo frame, Farrow stretched scarlet silk that had been painted in bright yellows and blacks. Gradually, they saw a giant bird, with great outstretched wings and a fearsome face that showed fangs.

"Fangs on a bird!" laughed one of the old sailors in the tattered uniform of the navy from which he had deserted.

When the eye-opening contraption was assembled and Captain Farrow stood with his arms outstretched to hold onto the giant wings, volunteers started shouting to be the one to get the kite into the air. But he grinned at Emily. "Perhaps the Reverend's wife would like the honor?"

She saw the challenge, and she felt something else, too, indefinable, in her breast, a skipped beat of her heart, a tightening of her lungs, the sudden desire to *do* something—anything—with this man. "I accept your challenge, sir," she called over roar of the surf and the wind and everyone talking at once.

Farrow placed the ball of twine in her hands, reminding her to keep the wind at her back, then he walked backwards, facing Emily, holding the unwieldy kite. The crowd parted behind him to let him through and to watch in awe. When he had gone thirty yards along the beach, leaving a bit of slack in the string, he stopped and called out, "Let me know when to release the kite."

Emily hadn't done this in a few years, but it came back to her. When she felt a good gust behind her, she tightened the string for tension and called out, "Release it!"

Farrow let go and the great mythical red and yellow and black bird with fangs and enormous wings soared into the air. The crowd cheered and clapped. Soon Emily had it going higher and higher. While she laughed and kept her eyes on the great unearthly raptor, and everyone on the beach looked up, MacKenzie Farrow kept his eyes on Emily.

Oh, it was a wonderful sight! Emily laughed as freely as Hawai'ians did, forgetting all proper ladylike comportment. She ran with the kite, lifting it higher. She looked up at the magnificent creature against the blue firmament and she thought: That is me up there! My soul is climbing to unimaginable heights and seeing the whole world, but it is tethered to the earth by a string. If I were to let go of this string, where would it take me? . . .

The wind picked up and Farrow saw that she might lose control. He sprinted back to her and just as she was saying, "It's too much!"

he stepped behind her, put an arm on either side of her and reached for the twine so that now the two controlled the flying creature from a land few white men had seen. Together, Emily and MacKenzie made the phoenix dance and soar and perform loops and tricks, much to the delight of the crowd while, on the nearby dock, Mr. Clarkson watched with a keen eye.

He was in his mariner's coat again, the gold-braided cap on his head, a solemn look on his face. Once more, he took Emily's hands in his and said, "I cannot recall when I have last enjoyed myself this much in port. And for the first time, I find myself reluctant to leave. But Alaska calls and I have a long voyage ahead of me."

She could barely speak. The past five days with MacKenzie had been a dream. They had gone for walks, visited lagoons and waterfalls, he had invited her aboard his ship, he had told her more enchanting tales while she had spoken of her girlhood in New Haven. Their behavior had been of the utmost propriety, with MacKenzie frequently expressing his dismay that he had missed the Reverend.

"I will write to you and your husband," he said, "and dispatch the letters with accommodating sea captains along the way."

"Isaac and I will look forward to reading them." Although, in truth, Isaac had not been interested in Captain Farrow's first letters, which had arrived six months ago. She doubted he was going to be interested in more.

But Emily herself . . . she was going to treasure them.

Once again she stood on the promontory to watch the *Kestrel* vanish over the horizon. But this time, she didn't feel just a part of herself going with it, but her *entire* self, and she knew she would not be whole until he returned.

We have arrived not a moment too soon, Emily, for these people are totally depraved, necessitating the sovereign grace of God for salvation. We try to make them see that such fallen people as themselves are morally and spiritually incapable of following God or redeeming themselves, that they need us to show them the way. Many are eager to become Christians. They flock to the meetinghouse and cry out that they want to be saved. We have to make them see that a person must believe the Gospel and then repent to be saved, and to take part in the sacraments of baptism and the Lord's Supper, which are signs and seals of the covenant of grace."

Emily tasted the soup that simmered in a pot over the outdoor fire. She added salt and continued stirring. Isaac had returned that afternoon and was so full of energy and bombast that she wondered if he would eat his dinner standing up.

"And this business of the marriage act!" he expounded, pacing in and out of the glow of tiki torches. "The islanders consider it an entertainment! They practice the procreative act in many positions. When I explain that the act is not for pleasure, but solely for the getting of more children for God, they do not understand. I tried forbidding one position or another but when I forbid one position, the islanders think this means the others are acceptable! So I told them that the face-to-face position is the only one permissible in the eyes of God. They complained that it was the least favorable for the woman's pleasure, but I said that the Almighty was less interested in a woman's pleasure than in her fecundity. The islanders told me they call this the 'missionary position,' which I think is very appropriate."

She paused in stirring the soup to look across the grass, through the trees, to the bay beyond. The beach ran at the base of the cliff, unseen from Reverend Stone's grass hut, but Emily saw it all the same. She felt the wind in her hair, the sunlight on the sea, the feel of a man's strong arms around her as together they controlled a bright red and yellow and black mythical bird in the air. It had been the most exhilarating moment of her life, and she yearned for it again.

The kite, disassembled and tucked away among her personal things, was Emily's secret. She would never show it to Isaac, who would call it a waste of materials and time, and never mind that such frivolous distractions tempted a man's mind away from God.

Isaac had returned from his island tour stirred up with evangelical zeal, his slender form, slightly stooped, whipped with enthusiasm. Emily could not help compare him to MacKenzie, who was also full of life and passion. But Isaac, it seemed, was only passionate when it came to other people's sins.

She quietly dished up his soup and asked him to take a seat. Placing the bowl in his hands, she then set slices of bread on the stool that served as their outdoor table.

She knew she shouldn't keep secrets from her husband, but she felt compelled to for reasons she could not name. The pink jade rabbit, which she brought out of its hiding place to hold and caress when Isaac wasn't there, was also hidden away with the red kite. She almost felt as if she were living a second life, and in a way she was. Isaac spent so much time away from home that at times she felt like a widow. And even then, when he did come home, his talk was all about the natives, so that Emily hardly felt like a wife at all.

Even when he came into bed every seventh night with an apology, even at that intimate time, when she was supposed to feel most like a man's wife, she hardly felt it at all.

"And then there is the custom of *haina,*" he said, shouting as usual even though it was just the two of them. "Giving children to other families to raise! They claim it's another way to keep the population in balance—those with many children share with those who have none. But I am putting a stop to it, Emily. I tell the natives that God wants children to be raised by their natural parents and are not to be given away like chickens!"

She watched him eat, spilling soup down the front of his white shirt, which she was going to have to boil later to get the stains out. He barely swallowed before he began another diatribe.

"Isaac," she said quietly as she watched clouds roll across the night sky and obliterate the stars. Was it going to rain tonight? *Again?* "Isaac, the roof leaks."

He stopped in mid-sentence and frowned at her. "What?"

"The roof leaks. I have to set pots and buckets out."

He waved a dismissive hand. "I'll have the natives throw some extra thatch on." And he resumed his sermon.

"Isaac, I want a proper house."

He laid his spoon in the bowl and said, "I understand, Emily. I truly do. And I promise that when I come back from Kau District we will get on it at once. You deserve a proper house, I do not deny that."

"When are you leaving for Kau?"

"Tomorrow! Reverend Michaels said that there are many souls there—"

"So soon?" she cried. "Isaac, you have been promising me a proper house for a year." Her heart raced in panic. The house was important—it was more than a sturdy shelter, it was a symbol, it was an anchor that kept her civilized. MacKenzie Farrow had stirred her soul and made her restless once again for adventure. But adventure meant becoming more like the natives, and that terrified her. No, the house was necessary for the saving of her sanity.

He gave her an admonishing look. "Our job here is to bring souls to the Lord, not to create a life of comfort and luxury for ourselves!"

That night, she lay in the darkness and when Isaac approached the pile of woven mats that served as their bed, Emily said, "I will not give you permission until I have a proper house. For every night that I am in this hut, we will not engage in the act."

"Woman!" he shouted in outrage. "It is a wife's duty to fulfill her husband's needs and to give him children!"

"And it is a husband's duty to fulfill his wife's needs and to give her a proper house. I will not change my mind."

Construction commenced the next day.

The new house, which took six months to build, was one story, constructed of coral blocks harvested from a nearby reef. It had four rooms and a wooden floor, with a small fireplace and windows. The roof, sealed with marine pitch and tar, did not leak. The furniture was basic and rudimentary, hand-crafted by Isaac: plain wooden tables and chairs, a bookcase and a bed raised off the floor. But the new home was a far cry from the grass hut and Emily was happy with it.

When the *Kestrel* was sighted out at sea, she got busy scrubbing the floors until they shone, straightening the curtains, polishing the few brass and silver items they had brought from home, placing flowers around the house, and lastly, choosing her favorite day dress and adding a cameo at her throat.

She greeted Captain Farrow at the front door and was pleased to see the look on his face. "Good day to you, Emily," he called. "I see your husband finally built you a proper house."

She could barely speak. It had been six months since she last saw him. Six months since he had stood behind her, his arms around her, his hands over hers as they guided the Chinese kite.

"All it took was a little patience and persuasion," she replied.

She saw, trudging behind him, a sailor puffing with a large wooden crate which he dropped unceremoniously at Emily's feet. With a salute and a nod, he turned and left.

"I took the liberty," Farrow said, "of bringing you a few supplies that I thought you might need. The trading posts in the Northwest are remarkably well stocked. Plus, I traded with other ship's captains."

Emily watched the sailor shamble down the path to the dock, where she saw Mr. Clarkson waylay the man and appear to engage him in dialogue. Then she brought her attention back to the crate, which Captain Farrow was in the process of opening.

"I thought of bringing you gifts of furs and walrus ivory," he said as he pulled the wooden slats away, "but what use would such things be in these islands?"

Emily's eyes widened as he produced bolts of cotton and muslin, tinned butter, sewing pins and needles. "Oh," she said. "The candles are a godsend. I don't know how I can thank you, Captain Farrow."

He studied her. "Is there something wrong, Emily?"

She glanced down at the dock. "I fear there is. After your last visit, Mr. Clarkson the dock agent started making unsavory comments in my presence."

His eyebrows rose. "Clarkson is an odious little toady, an unavoidable feature of life in islands so far removed from laws and authority. What sort of comments?"

"I cannot bring myself to repeat them, but he seems to be under the impression that you and I . . ." Her voice trailed off.

He stared at her. "He wouldn't dare," he said in disbelief. "Not even so scurrilous a fellow as Clarkson would stoop so low. To sully the good name of a preacher's wife—" He stopped himself and regained composure. "I will have a word with him. Don't worry, Emily."

The next day the dock agent was seen to have a black eye and he refused to talk about it.

This time they had only four days together, just long enough for Chief Holokai's workers to chop down sandalwood trees and haul them to the harbor, where they were loaded into longboats and rowed out to the *Kestrel*. Emily and MacKenzie filled their brief hours together with long walks, exploring the nearby forests and waterfalls and lagoons, always maintaining propriety but feeling a mutual yearning that was becoming unbearable.

At Mo'o Falls, where they stood high on a cliff to watch a waterfall tumble into a lagoon far below—an enchanted place where legend said that a dragon spirit lived, a place where natives left gifts for the gods— Farrow said, "I imagine the local people don't know what to make of your house." He said it to fill the silence between them, as more and more they walked quietly at each other's side, wondering if they were sharing the same forbidden thoughts, and such silences made him uncomfortable. Emily was a married woman. He needed words to stand as a barrier between her and his dangerous feelings.

She said, "During construction, as men brought coral blocks up from the beach, and Isaac showed them how to place them and line them up and join them with mortar, the people crowded around and watched. High Chiefess Pua was there more frequently than I would have expected. She seemed particularly interested in our new house. Once, when she asked me where I was going to sleep, and I pointed to the area where the bedroom would be, she stood over that spot and chanted for nearly an afternoon. I had no idea what that was about."

MacKenzie concealed his smile. He knew very well what the mistress of healing and fertility was up to.

"Pua has a remarkable store of remedies and cures," Emily said as the breeze shifted, sending a delightful mist their way, creating a rainbow at the same time. "I saw her treat the wounds of the workmen with remarkable skill. There were no infections, no fevers."

"The Hawai'ians have centuries of plant knowledge behind them. I would imagine a long process of trial and error has resulted in a pharmacopeia that European doctors would love to study. I doubt Pua would share her knowledge."

"I would like to know some of it myself, but the problem is, her medicine is intertwined with heathenish magic and witchcraft. I complained of a headache and she gave me an herb. I would have made a tea of it except that she told me I must pray to Lono when I drink it or the herb wouldn't work."

Emily fell silent and so did MacKenzie, as they stood close together in a concealed Eden where no one would see them. But MacKenzie was a man of honor and Emily knew that God was watching.

Two days before he was due to leave, Captain Farrow took Emily to see the lava. Word had reached Hilo that a new vent had opened up and Pele's "blood" was pouring out. "From my ship," he said, "you can see the smoke plume. It isn't a very big eruption. There haven't been any earthquakes. It will be safe to ride up there and take a look if you would like."

They went by horseback. Deep into the rain forest, they had to dismount and tether the horses to a tree. Emily could smell the sulfur and volcanic gas. The air in the forest was smoky with an acrid stench. The hike took a little more than an hour, a rugged trek until they were out of the forest and trudging over rocky, black lava that MacKenzie said was hundreds of years old.

They came to the edge of what looked like a narrow red river. To their right, a stark desert stretched away and up the gradual slope to distant Kilauea. To their left, miles away, clouds of steam rose up as lava cascaded into the ocean. The air was hot and sooty. Emily was mesmerized by the hot red flow from under the hard gray rock. Like fiery blood spewing from an artery. An angry, violent flow. *The island is alive. Pele is stirring from a long sleep.*

MacKenzie said, "You can see how a people who have no knowledge of Jehovah, who have never heard of Moses or Abraham, would see their god in this lava. Look around, Emily, the earth is still being created."

At Emily's feet, red viscous stuff was being belched from a wide black mouth, spreading out, darkening as it cooled, creating mesmerizing patterns. She felt the power of Pele, the power of Hawai'i.

And standing next to her, the power of MacKenzie Farrow.

She cried the night before his departure, and he awkwardly took her into his arms—one never knew who was close by, watching, or when Reverend Isaac might ride suddenly and unexpectedly into the village—and tried to console her.

"My loneliness is the worse pain," she sobbed. "Even when Isaac is here, he is deep in his work to translate the Gospel into Hawai'ian. There are no white women here except for those who pass through to go to other missions. In Kona, there are three mission families and a total of seven white women. I envy them. I have asked the Board to assign another family to Hilo, but as yet my request has gone unheard."

But she did not confess the real reason she wept, yet MacKenzie already knew. He wanted to cry for the same reason.

They are too sick, Mika Kalono," Kumu the taro farmer explained. Because Isaac was venturing into an area where few natives had had encounters with white men, he had brought Kumu along to translate.

They were sixty miles from Hilo, in the southernmost region of the islands—the place where, according to legend, the first people had arrived from an island called Kahiki many generations ago. It was a sacred forest and Kumu had to keep warning Mister Stone to watch where he stepped. "Many gods here, Mika Kalono. Many spirits. They get angry, haole walk here."

"Nonsense, my good man," Isaac would say. "All the world is God's land. And no man, brown or white, is restricted from entering into God's land."

They had spent the past few days at a village with no name, where the natives had given generously of their food and shelters and wives; the last of which Isaac had declined. While Isaac had been explaining his divine purpose in the islands, the chief had mentioned that the people in the next village might benefit more from praying to an all-powerful god whose sole job, it seemed, was to save people. The villagers in the next valley were very sick.

Isaac could not sit idle while heathens were dying without a chance to go to heaven.

But Kumu was afraid of this part of the island where Pele, a goddess known for fickleness and wrath, slumbered beneath the earth. All around them, as they cut through vines and ferns and dense forest, ancient volcanic vents stood in cold, dark testament to prior fire-storms and lava flows sent by Pele.

Yet Isaac would not be dissuaded. He had been put upon this earth to save souls from perdition, and if it meant hardship for himself, then so be it.

As they hacked and slashed through the dense growth, Isaac thought about Emily. He missed her. He wished sometimes God wasn't sending him out on so many errands of salvation, and at such distances. He appreciated Emily's quiet presence, her gentle manner of speech. And she had been so right about the house! What a proper home it was now, one could almost think oneself back in New England within those walls. Strangely, when he was in his new house, Isaac felt closer to God. He missed churches made of wood and stone with towers for bells. He missed a writing desk with quills and inkwells.

But mostly he missed Emily, of whom he was becoming quite fond. He prayed that children would start coming soon. She seemed a little restless of late, a little absentminded. A child would ground her and bring her closer to God.

"There is the village," Kumu said, pointing between the thick trunks of lehua and ohia trees.

But it appeared to be deserted, and then they heard wailing not far away. There had been sickness here. Were they already burying the dead, Isaac wondered. *Have I come too late?*

The natives were waving their arms and wailing at the edge of a clearing in the forest. Several yards ahead, Isaac saw a gaping hole in the ground. Kumu asked one of the men what had happened. He translated the response for Isaac, "A child wandered from the village and came here, and the ground gave way beneath him. This whole place, Mika Kalono, many lava tubes. Old lava beds, hollow caves underneath."

Isaac walked slowly and carefully toward the hole, feeling his way as he went, and when he reached the lip of the crater, looked in and saw, at the bottom, a little boy lying on his side, whimpering.

"Why the devil are these people just standing around? Why aren't they trying to rescue him?"

"They can't. Sacred ground. They afraid of gods."

"Then I will go after the child." Isaac shrugged off his rucksack and removed his jacket and hat.

"No, Mika Kalono. Too dangerous. The cave collapse. You die."

"I will not let that boy perish in a hole. While he has a breath in his body, I am going to find a way to save him. His immortal soul is at stake."

Isaac searched the terrain and found a thick creeper vine. "Kumu, come and help me!"

"No no, Mika Kalono. Sacred ground. Kapu."

"Kumu, you have been after me to baptize you. Now is the time to prove your faith in the Good Lord. Demonstrate to me that you turn your back on the old ways, deny the ancient gods and you will be rewarded with everlasting life!"

Kumu shifted nervously, and then slowly stepped forward, while the villagers backed away and cried, *"Auwe!"*

"Take hold of the vine," Isaac said as he tied it firmly around his waist. "I've secured it to that tree, but you will be a second anchor should it break. I will climb down into the cave as you feed me the vine."

The natives fell silent as the stranger got down on the ground and lowered himself into the hole. Isaac found handholds on the rocky walls of the cave-in. He wished belatedly he had gloves, as the ancient lava was rough and scraped his skin. Everyone watched in wonder as his light-brown hair vanished and Kumu struggled to control the vine. They heard bits of rock break away and cascade down the deep hole. They heard Isaac's heavy breathing, and then they couldn't hear him. Kumu inched closer and closer to the gaping maw, cold sweat breaking out over his body as he expected the ancient gods to strike him dead for setting foot on forbidden ground.

But he did not die, and presently he heard a voice call from deep in the cave, "Pull us up, Kumu!"

It was hard going and Kumu struggled. Three natives, making sure they stayed away from the kapu ground, took up the vine nearer the tree and pulled on it. It made Kumu's job easier, so that gradually the burden at the end of the vine reached the top. While the natives held the vine, Kumu ran forward to lift the boy from Isaac's shoulders and carry him to the anxious onlookers, who cheered and laughed and passed the child around.

The three men were so overjoyed to see the boy unharmed that, unthinkingly, they let go of the vine to join in the celebration. Isaac gave a cry and they heard a great thump.

Kumu shouted at them to take up the vine. And then the four of them frantically brought Isaac back up. Kumu helped him out of the hole, asking him if he was all right. Isaac said, "It's but a small break, it will mend," but Kumu saw in horror that the shinbone of Mister Stone's right leg protruded through the bloody skin.

A runner had been sent ahead to warn Mister Stone's wife, so that she was ready to receive Isaac as he emerged through the trees in the company of six natives. The grateful family of the rescued child had taken Isaac into their hut while the bonesetter, who lived in a coastal settlement, was sent for. Isaac had allowed the *kahuna* to set his leg between two stiff sticks and bind it in green leaves, but he had refused to drink the man's herbal concoctions, and absolutely forbade the local priest to chant over him. And then he had asked to be taken home.

So great was their joy over getting their boy back—without punishment from the gods for having falling into a hole in sacred ground—that the family had constructed a litter made of two long poles, vines, and woven pandanus leaves, and the six escorts had taken turns, over the long miles and difficult terrain, carrying the haole.

Emily ran to meet them, as did half the village. To her dismay, Isaac burned with fever and, when she lifted the bandage of leaves, she found a suppurating wound. "Bring him inside, please, and place him on the bed."

Kumu translated and Isaac was delivered to his final destination. The villagers crowded at the front door, curious and worried about Mika Kalono, while Emily wrung her hands over the infected wound.

She boiled water and tore one of her petticoats into strips. As she cleaned the wound, Isaac breathlessly recounted the story of his trek, leaving his accident for last and making light of it. "In a village near Kalapana, I sermonized for five days, at the end of which I had the natives throwing their idols onto a bonfire, and I left them with the first pages of the new Hawai'ian Bible Reverend Michaels and I are writing. When they learn to read, those people will be enlightened with Genesis, the first chapters."

"You saved a boy's life, Kumu told me."

"It was God who saved the boy. I was merely His instrument."

"Isaac, this wound looks bad. There is dirt in it. Let me send for Pua. She has special powders and leaves that cure infection."

"I will have nothing heathenish applied to my person. We will pray, Emily. The Good Lord did not bring me to this land to perish. He has many plans yet for me, but we need to ask His divine help."

The next day, Isaac continued to burn with fever. "The Almighty will repair my leg so that I can return to His service. Kneel and pray with me, Emily."

Emily slept on mats in the living room and awoke frequently to check on Isaac. On the fourth day, she knew by the smell that something terrible lay under the bandages. The wound had become gangrenous. "Please let me send for Pua." Again, he said no.

Isaac's condition worsened. The natives held vigil outside the house. Chief Holokai came to visit, which Isaac welcomed, but when the chief began to chant, Isaac sent him away. Then High Chiefess Pua came, speaking soothingly, laying a garland of flowers on his chest. She bent over him in a maternal way, even though she was only four years older. She stroked him and said gentle words. But when she produced a bundle of *ti*-leaves and started to shake it around the room, he dismissed her.

Again Emily begged him to let Pua apply a cure to his gangrenous wound, and again he said the Good Lord would not let him die.

The end came before dawn on the tenth day, when Emily awoke to find her husband cold and without life.

A storm was battering the eastern coast of the Big Island, causing palm trees to bend at an almost horizontal angle, with thatched roofs coming apart and flying off grass huts. Emily ran out of the house, leaving her dead husband in their bed, and plunged into the driving rain. She didn't know why she did this, or what she was doing. She hated this island, she hated the natives, she hated Isaac for dying.

Her hair came loose as she ran along the muddy path toward the bay, where clipper ships and schooners were tossed about like toy boats on a pond. The rain blinded her. She ran toward the dock. She needed to tell someone that Isaac was dead. She needed to tell a white man, even the odious Mr. Clarkson. She banged on his door, screaming his name, tears and rain mingling on her cheeks.

And then she felt strong hands on her arms, turning her around, and she looked up into warm, familiar eyes beneath the visor of a gold-braided cap. "He's dead!" she cried. MacKenzie pulled her into his arms and kicked down the door of the dock agent's office.

"We were heading out of Honolulu eastward toward China," he said when they got inside, "when I just knew something was wrong. I knew you needed me. I turned the *Kestrel* around and came back."

"Don't leave me, MacKenzie," she sobbed against his damp coat.

He stroked her wet hair. "My first mate, Mr. Riordon, recently achieved his Master's ticket. He is a capable man and wanting to skipper his own ship. I will have him take the *Kestrel* to China and I will stay with you, dearest Emily, for as long as you need me."

CHAPTER FOUR

The letter from the Mission Board in Honolulu was short and to the point.

"We are sorry for your loss, Mrs. Stone, but we must remind you that an unmarried woman may not serve in our mission. During your period of mourning, you may stay in the house that was built upon land we rent from the Crown, after which we strongly recommend that you return to New Haven and take a husband from among our congregation. Thus, with God's help, you may return to your divine work here in the Islands."

Emily's heart sank. She had written to them inquiring about her status, hoping that widowhood was sufficient to continue working here. But the Board made it clear that if she wished to continue with this mission, she must marry a member of their church. But how could she do that when she had given her heart to Captain MacKenzie Farrow?

True to his word, MacKenzie had stayed in Hilo and left the *Kestrel* in the capable hands of his first mate. While Emily and MacKenzie had spent much time in each other's company, and an unspoken yearning was palpable between them, they had not so much as shaken hands since the night of Isaac's death, six months prior. On that stormy night, when a strange intuition had made him turn his ship around and return to Hilo, MacKenzie had comforted her. But they had not kissed. It would not have been right. And then he had helped her bury her husband in a dry plot of land further inland, erecting a protective fence around the grave with a slab of coral crudely carved with his name and a cross.

In the days since, Emily had felt adrift. Isaac had been the backbone of this mission. He was the architect of salvation among the natives, their strong and guiding spirit. Without him, Emily felt untethered, like a red Chinese kite that might at any minute fly off the planet and disappear.

When MacKenzie was with her, she felt anchored. But they were careful to keep their time together at a minimum because gossip spread like wildfire and it would not take much for the Board to get wind of their friendship and send Emily packing at once, mourning or not.

She knew she could appeal her case to the Mission directors in New Haven, but it would take months for her letter to reach them, and more months for their reply to reach her. Possibly two years before she had her response, during which time she would be forced to vacate the house to make room for new missionaries.

When she saw MacKenzie coming up the path from the docks below, Emily tucked the letter into her pocket. She must think about it before she told him.

She knew he had feelings for her. She saw it in his eyes, and sensed it in the long silences when words failed and they just looked at each other. But they had not stepped over any lines. Emily knew she must act the proper widow and follow convention. But now the Mission Board was forcing her into a desperate decision. She had come to these islands to bring salvation to its people. But she could only do so by remarrying another missionary.

"Hello there!" MacKenzie called out.

"Good day to you, Captain."

Because he was temporarily without a ship, Farrow had built a sturdy grass hut for himself near the lagoon—not too far from Emily's little house, but far enough to satisfy propriety. Despite having delivered a painful message to Clarkson the nosy dock agent, MacKenzie knew that people were still watching them.

Emily wanted to run to him, but remained at the front of her little house, where she had been cooking and doing mending in the morning sunshine. Her two maids were hanging up washing.

They were the only natives Emily had been able to Christianize. Unfortunately they had no influence over the villagers because they were slaves. Emily wasn't certain what their crimes had been, but in the Hawai'ian social hierarchy they were only one step above outcasts, people who had broken serious kapus and could no longer have contact with the general population. These two sisters had been given to Emily and Isaac, but Emily treated them with respect. During Reverend Michaels' last visit, to preach and distribute Christian literature printed in the Hawai'ian language, he had baptized the sisters and now they were Mary and Hannah, names which they were able to pronounce.

Emily was also civilizing them. They did not wear dresses but had learned to wrap their sarongs under their arms and over their breasts. They ate with knives and forks and plates. Emily had taught them such skills as sewing and ironing, but their greatest gift was cooking, at which they excelled. Emily had taught them to bake bread, to roll dough for tarts and pies, to boil a perfect brisket and make a decent turnip sauce. With limited resources, Emily put out a surprisingly good New England meal—or so said the visitors who enjoyed her occasional hospitality. Emily missed cooking with apples and cheese, she missed mutton and lamb and often craved ice cream and maple syrup. But she had learned to savor pineapple and mango and the abundant seafood that fed these islands.

She had known Captain Farrow would be paying her a visit once his business at the docks was finished and so she had spent the morning personally seeing to a batch of jelly cakes which were now out of the oven and sliced into squares and ready to eat. She had used the last of her butter and milk to bake them, and who knew when more might be found? Beef was available whenever Chief Holokai sent men to capture and slaughter some of the wild cattle roaming the island, but domesticated cows were sparse, being mainly up in Kona, and so dairy products were scarce and costly. But the jelly cake was for MacKenzie, and she would use any of her precious, dwindling supplies to please him.

Emily's heart swelled at the sight of him striding toward her in the tropical sunshine, tall and handsome and commanding. She dreaded the day he would ship out on the *Kestrel*, as they both knew he must. But in the meantime, he was not idle. He spent his days in the company of ships' captains who came into port for fresh supplies. MacKenzie had entered into a trade business of sorts, purchasing cargo from passing ships, to stow it in a warehouse he had built near the docks, selling the goods to captains desiring his merchandise. It was a profitable arrangement, and with his earnings MacKenzie was going to buy a second ship.

A sailor plodded behind him, carrying a wooden crate. He was a stranger to Emily. But then, more and more sailors were jumping ship to stay on the island and take up with a native "wife." A scattered and disjointed little colony of white men was slowly growing along the beachfront, as men of various occupations—naturalists, geologists, artists, and explorers—came to stay for months on end to chronicle their discoveries here.

"I've brought you something," Farrow said as he drew near, grinning at the sight of Emily in her long pale-pink gown with the ubiquitous lace cap covering her shiny hair. She had worn mourning for three months following her husband's death, but the black bombazine had proved too much for the heat and humidity. After much coaxing from himself, and even from visiting missionaries, Emily had returned to her regular clothes.

"More gifts?" she said, laughing. Her little house was becoming filled to the bare rafters with MacKenzie Farrow's generosity.

"This one is more practical." He gestured to the sailor who dropped the chest to the grass and threw open the lid. The chest was filled with bolts of fabric.

"From the cotton fields of Georgia," Farrow said waving his arm proudly over the treasure, "to the mills of New England, and now to Hawai'i before continuing their journey up to California and the west coast. I traded these for Chinese jade."

Emily's eyes widened at the colorful chintzes, the pale muslins and white cotton. "Oh thank you, Captain! Please, come and have a seat. I just happen to have baked some jelly cakes and the mango juice is fresh and cold."

But he stayed where he was and seemed to go deep into thought. Gesturing to the sailor that he could leave, MacKenzie grew serious and, when they were alone, he said, "Emily, it's been six months since your husband died. It's a long time for a woman to be on her own."

"I'm not alone," she said with forced cheerfulness. "I have Mary and Hannah. I have many visitors. Pua and Mahina come by. And," she said in a lower voice, "I have you, Captain."

"That's just it, Emily," he said, stepping closer and respectfully removing his hat. "You do not truly have me. And I wish to make our arrangement a more permanent one."

"Oh!" she said. "Captain, you have caught me by surprise." She placed her hand on her bosom and felt her racing heart. A sudden surge of joy swept through her and the word, "Yes," stood on her lips. And then she remembered the letter in her pocket.

Showing it to him, and giving him a moment to read it, she said, "If I am to continue my work here, I must abide by their rules."

To her shock, MacKenzie took her by the shoulders and said with passion, "Marry me, Emily. You can still carry on your work here, no matter what the Mission Board says."

"MacKenzie," she said in a plaintiff tone, "the Board will move me out of this house! I won't be able to preach in the meetinghouse. They will send another teacher to replace me in the school."

"I will build you a house, Emily, and a schoolroom pavilion. You can carry on as you have been."

"It's not that simple. I won't have any standing here. The natives will be confused. They will think I am being punished. They will think my own people have cast me out, and in a way it will be true. If I am an outcast, then the natives will have nothing to do with me."

"I want you to be my wife, Emily!"

"And I want you to be my husband. But I also wish to serve God and continue the work Isaac started here and gave his life for! Oh, MacKenzie," she cried, "I only married Isaac so that I could be a missionary. If this work is taken from me, then what good am I? Why did I come all these thousands of miles?"

"To be with me," he said. His hands dropped away from her shoulders. "But I suppose that isn't enough. I don't blame you, Emily. I understand. But we can find a way. I'm sure of it."

She bent her head and twisted her fingers. "The Board has offered me another option," she said quietly.

His look turned hard and full of suspicion. "And what would that be?"

She lifted her head and met his gaze. "They say I can stay in this house and continue my work with the natives, with full status as a missionary . . . if I let them arrange for a husband to be sent to me."

He stared at her, then he whipped away. "By God, no!" he shouted. He faced her with a thunderous expression. "A proxy marriage? They would deliver you into the arms of a complete stranger? I will not have it Emily! Where are these self-righteous fools who think they can dictate your life? Are they in Honolulu? Then I will go to them and tell them to go to the Devil!"

"MacKenzie," she cried, grabbing his arm. "Wait. We have to be reasonable. We have to be level-headed. If you shout at them, they will send me home to New Haven in disgrace. Please. There has to be a compromise that will satisfy everyone. Give me time to think."

Reluctantly, he left her, marching down the path to the docks, stopping once to look back in indecision.

After he was gone, Emily lifted her shawl from its hook and struck off down the path to the beach.

The sunlight seemed particularly sharp, the island's colors more vibrant than usual. The mountains that rose behind the village of Hilo, sheer and sharp and overwhelming in their majesty, seemed to shimmer as if carved from emeralds. The tumbling white waterfalls, cascading from immense heights, spewed sparkling mists and colorful rainbows. The tips of sunlit palm fronds glittered like diamonds.

But Emily was oblivious to the tropical paradise surrounding her. Her thoughts were dark and troubled. Her heart was heavy with sadness and confusion—and a deep love for a man she should not love.

He understands me, she told herself as she walked along the damp sand where shorebirds scurried into the tide and kelp lay bleaching in the sun. Farther along, natives were working on canoes and surf-boards. *MacKenzie understands my need to help these people, he sees my worth, he gives me credit for my endeavors. But the Mission Board dismisses everything about me because I am not married to a preacher of my own congregation! Why must I have a missionary husband to validate my work, to give me worth in their eyes? We call one another "brother" and "sister," we preach equality to the natives, yet I am not recognized as a contributing missionary in my own right.*

She paused and looked out to sea where three ships, spread far apart, appeared on the horizon. Were they coming into Hilo or passing by to drop anchor at Honolulu? On any other day she would have been excited and joined everyone down at the docks to see who was coming, what cargo they were delivering (Emily desperately needed sewing needles and white flour), were they bringing letters and newspapers and books from home?

But she was mired in her dilemma. How could she satisfy the Mission Board without giving up MacKenzie and her own self-worth?

"Mika Kalona!" A little boy came running across the dunes, waving something over his head. Emily smiled. His name was 'Olina, which meant "joyful," and he was one of the brightest pupils in her class—on the days that he chose to attend school. "I find for Mika!" he shouted with a big grin, and when he reached her, Emily saw that he was holding out a beautiful conch shell, large and shiny and flawless.

"For me?" she said.

He held it out and Emily took it, saying, "*Mahalo*, thank you," and watched him run off to join his playmates.

As she ran her fingers along the smooth, inner surface of the beautiful shell, she returned to her ruminations. *Perhaps if I could somehow persuade the Board to see that MacKenzie is a Christian and an honorable man. . . .*

Her shoulders slumped. It wouldn't work. They would scowl and say that MacKenzie was an adventurer and a privateer, not devoted to missionary work and therefore totally unsuitable as a "proper" husband.

She gazed at the beautiful conch shell, realizing that the vivid pink was her sister's favorite color. *I will add it to my collection*, she thought, *to remind me of home.*

As the unspoken words echoed in her mind, she frowned. Something about the conch shell danced at the edge of her consciousness. As she struggled to capture the elusive thought, she saw youths running down the beach with their long boards, dashing into the surf to paddle out to the swells. She was envious. They were like MacKenzie's red kite. She had envied its freedom, and wished she could cut it loose. Emily briefly wished now that she had the courage to toss off her tight dress, grab a board, and paddle out to sea.

But young ladies brought up in New Haven do not paddle out to sea.

However, she thought in sudden decision. They can show that they have backbones and determination, and can be contributing members of a mission even if not married to a missionary.

That was it! She would ask the Board to make an exception in her case. She would invite them to Hilo and introduce them to the natives, to Chief Holokai and his son and daughter, Kekoa and Pua, and to Mahina and little 'Olina, and have the natives sing Christian hymns to show them all the good works she had done here. And surely when they met MacKenzie they would see what a good man he was and make an exception to the marriage rule.

Emily smiled, feeling greatly relieved. Surely a compromise could be reached. As she turned to walk back to her house, she felt the conch shell in her hands, and she heard again the elusive thought tease the edges of her mind. She stopped and looked at the shell. It was the exact shade of pink her sister always sought in fabrics and bonnet materials.

Memories of her sister led to thoughts of their father and a precious memory of him that Emily harbored. In all her growing up years, Emily had never known her father to hug her or kiss her or even offer a word of encouragement or endearment. But on the day she'd married Isaac Stone, not out of love but in order to serve the Almighty, her father had placed his hand on her shoulder, smiled, and said, "I am proud of you, dear daughter."

The memory now made her smile.

And then—

Merciful heaven!

She dropped the conch and pressed her hands to her mouth. Her family! In all her mental turmoil and ruminations about marrying MacKenzie and how to persuade the Board to give her a dispensation, she had not given a single thought to how her family would react.

She froze on the sand like a windblown statue, her heart thundering in her chest. She saw it all in an instant: her father's fury, her mother's retreat to the chaise longue, her sisters' embarrassment. *Emily leaving the Mission to marry a sea captain!*

It would cause a scandal. Her family would not be able to hold their heads up once news reached New Haven, as it surely would. They might never speak to her again. Her father would disown her.

Marrying an adventurer who visited ports of call that were notorious dens of vice and iniquity. The fleshpots of the Orient!

She hugged herself to keep from shaking. Tears stung her eyes. How could she have forgotten them?

And then there were the other missionaries on the island. Emily had not taken them into account either. What would they think of her "taking up" with a sea captain? She would be ostracized and more alone and isolated than ever.

How could I not have thought of these things? Am I so blinded by my love for MacKenzie, am I so selfish that I gave no thought to friends and loved ones? Thinking only of myself!

Looking down at the conch lying on the sand—she had thought it was a message from New Haven, as all her other "treasures" were, to remind her of home. But this time there was more to the message. It was a timely omen from God, a reminder of duty and responsibility, and where her priorities lay.

Retrieving the shell and resuming her trek back up the path, Emily sadly realized what she had to do.

He was at Clarkson's office on the docks, going over new navigational charts that had just arrived by another ship. "Emily!" he said, before he could stop himself.

"Captain Farrow, may I have a word with you?"

Clarkson's crafty eyes watched them as they left and followed the path up the cliff to the settlements overlooking the bay.

They reached a wide-spreading banyan tree, where Emily first looked around to see if anyone was within earshot. Then she said, "MacKenzie, though I love you with all my heart, I have allowed my feelings to corrupt my reason. Perhaps I have been influenced by the Hawai'ians, who are highly emotional people. I must remember myself, and how I am to conduct myself in this alien land. MacKenzie, my first duty in life is to God, and then to my family, and next to the Mission Board. Duty to myself and my desires comes last. I cannot marry you."

He searched her pale features, saw the pain in her eyes. She had spent the past hour in deep examination of her soul and conscience— he did not like what she had found. In a tight voice he said, "I will not accept that, Emily. I will continue to fight for you."

She squared her shoulders and straightened her spine. "I am going to strike a compromise with the Board. I will write to them and tell them I will take a husband by proxy marriage. But I will stipulate that he must be a man of my father's choosing. It is my final decision and I will speak no more of it—" Her voice broke and tears rolled down her cheeks.

"Good-bye, MacKenzie, and God bless."

Mika Emily," the sisters said, excited and giggling. "You make dresses? We watch?"

Emily was on her verandah, sorting through the fabrics MacKenzie had brought a week ago. She had not been able to look at them, so painful a reminder they were of what she had lost. And then her conscience had reminded her that idle hands were the Devil's instrument, and that it was a sin to wallow in self-pity. So she had decided she would bury her pain in honest labor and hard work.

She looked at Hannah and Mary, women in their forties, unmarried and without children because of an incomprehensible infraction they committed long ago—smiling, pleasant women who seemed to take life as it came to them. Emily had tried to get them to wear dresses, as she had the women in the village—clothing donated by congregants in New Haven—but the women didn't like them. After wearing nothing but a sarong and some flowers, they found New England bodices and full skirts too cumbersome and too tight.

But now, looking at the bolts of fabric that had yet to be fashioned into garments, an idea came to her. She would design a dress specifically for use in these islands. A project that would consume her thoughts and energy and hours, an undertaking that would bury the pain and sorrow of losing MacKenzie—bury all her emotions, because Emily was tired of sadness and anger and resentment and all the tides and eddies that drained a woman of her vital force.

From now on, I will feel nothing. Instead, I will make dresses.

But she wondered if that would be enough. She had thought that teaching by example would do the trick, but she understood now that simply wearing clothes in front of the natives was not enough. She must somehow entice them to want to wear clothes.

Wasting no time, she began her secret campaign at once. She quickly gathered up everything she would need, with Mary assisting her, and set off for the collection of grass huts on the other side of the meetinghouse.

When she arrived at the entrance to the village, which was guarded by two enormous effigies carved from lava—gods with large, wide eyes and angry mouths—Emily placed her stool on the grass, sat down, and invited Mary to sit with her. The village entrance was the perfect strategic spot, as this was the way the girls must pass when they returned to the village from their midday swim in the lagoon.

Emily methodically emptied the baskets and bundles she and Mary had brought with them, spreading out around them a display of: fabrics, threads, scissors, needles and pins, a tailor's measuring strip. Emily had also brought two parasols, three pairs of gloves, and two small drawstring handbags.

"We want to match colors," she said to Mary, paying no attention to the few natives who had stopped to watch. "One doesn't wear black gloves with a white dress."

She had cut cloth from four of the bolts MacKenzie had brought: red and white calico, green checkered gingham, salmon-pink cotton, and a new, lightweight fabric called "seersucker" which Emily thought perfect for the tropics. As she and Mary made a show of unfolding the fabrics, holding them up to the light, watching how they danced in the breeze, the girls from the lagoon came along, their bodies glistening with sparkling drops. They wore fresh flowers in their hair and they were laughing. They stopped at the strange sight outside the village entrance.

"Hello," Emily said. She knew most of them by name. Pua's daughter, Mahina, was among them, eyeing the objects on the grass with great interest.

"Please," Emily said, gesturing to the various items. "Take a look." She had never invited anyone to inspect her personal effects before. But now she encouraged them to do so, and when one of the girls shyly retrieved a folded parasol, Emily showed her how to open it and hold it over her head.

Presently, the giggling girls were passing the gloves and handbags and parasols around, walking to and fro to strike a pose, half-naked

79

girls wearing gloves and carrying little drawstring handbags. She knew
they were imitating her, but not in a mocking way. And then Mahina
squatted and ran her hands over the rolls of cloth. She picked up the
scissors and frowned at them. She picked up pins and put them down.
She held up the measuring strip—a length of cloth marked with inches—
and turned it this way and that. "What Mika Emily do?" she asked.

"I am going to make a dress. You are welcome to watch."

Soon the girls were sitting in a circle around her, while other
villagers had come to watch in curiosity. As artisans themselves, they
admired skillful handiwork, and Emily soon had their undivided
attention as she measured cloth, marked it, cut it, pinned the pieces
together, and commenced stitching.

When the sun went down, she and Mary collected their things and
said good-bye to the villagers.

She returned the next day, and the day after, and the natives saw a
garment slowly come to life. When it was done, Emily rose from her
stool and held up the dress for everyone to see. With puzzled expressions, they looked the dress up and down, they reached out and shook
it. They commented among themselves, because this was nothing like
what Mika Emily wore.

Emily had chosen her pattern from illustrations in a Mother
Hubbard nursery book, and the result was a loosely hanging dress with
a high-yoked collar and long sleeves, and a hem that reached the feet.

"This is for you, Mahina," she said, holding it out to the fifteen-
year-old girl. She knew that, as High Chiefess Pua's daughter, Mahina
was a leader among her own age group. The girl shyly took the dress
and, with Emily's help, slipped it over her head, her arms into the
sleeves, letting it fall to the grass. The salmon-pink cotton draped
over her tall, lithe form like a misty waterfall. To the cheers of her
friends, Mahina turned this way and that, swishing her skirts, unaware
that her arms were covered, her breasts and neck were no longer bare,
not even her ankles could be seen.

And then the girls were clamoring to take turns trying it on, and
as they dressed and undressed, and modeled the garment for the other
villagers, with everyone laughing and commenting, Emily saw something in Mahina and the girls that she had not been aware of before:
they were truly innocent. They laughed a lot. They were kind and

generous. And strangely enough, they were modest in an unexpected way. Although they went about in a state of undress, they were as shy and maidenly as New England girls. *They do not know their nakedness is a sin.*

As Emily brushed out her long hair in preparation for retiring for the night, she heard masculine laughter drift through her open window. MacKenzie was sitting outside his hut, entertaining a sea captain and his officers.

Emily had been invited to join them but it was too painful for herself and MacKenzie, and so she had dined alone in her own house while Hannah and Mary waited on her.

As she began to braid her hair, she heard, on the night breeze, a distant wail. It was a woman, crying in a high keening voice, *"Auwe! Auwe...."*

Emily shot to her feet. It was coming from the village. A moment later, there was a sudden, loud banging at her front door. Sliding her feet into slippers—she was in her nightgown and robe—she went to see who it was.

Hannah stood there, wild-eyed and frantic. "You come, Mika Emily!"

"What is it, what's happened?"

Hannah flung her arm toward the forest behind the native village. "They bury baby!"

"What?! Take me at once."

Emily had heard of the ancient practice of live infant burial, but she had been told that the custom had been stamped out. She followed Hannah through the night, past the village, and into the trees, where they reached a handful of women just as they were patting down the earth on a tiny grave. Emily pushed them aside and dropped to her knees to dig frantically.

"Dear God, help me," she said as she drove her hands into the moist earth. She pulled handfuls of soil out as quickly as she could, careful of not hurting the infant buried underneath. In the distance, the wailing continued, and Emily now understood the cause of the plaintiff cry.

As she got deeper, she probed the dirt and felt with her fingertips something warm and soft. She desperately dug further until she exposed the lifeless infant with umbilical cord still attached.

"Merciful Father, please don't let this child die," she whispered as she held the newborn to her breast, carefully scooping dirt out of its mouth. She sucked on the little nose, bringing out more earth, and then she blew into the tiny mouth with small, rapid puffs.

Finally the infant whimpered and its body quivered with life. Emily rose to her feet and gave the baby to Hannah, instructing her to return the child to its mother. Emily then turned to the women who had buried the baby and said, "It is wrong to do this! Life is sacred! Only God can take a life. Do you understand?"

But Emily saw, in the moonlight, that not only were they not contrite over what they had done, they seemed bewildered by her tirade. She knew these women. A couple of them were wearing her new Mother Hubbard dresses. Women who came to the meetinghouse on Sundays to hear Emily's sermons.

"Listen to me!" she shouted. And then MacKenzie was breaking through the trees, saying, "What is going on here? Emily, I saw you run from your house. What happened?"

The women spoke to him in rapid Hawai'ian, all at once, so that he waved them off and told them to go home.

"They buried that poor baby alive, MacKenzie!" Emily said, her eyes flashing with anger and tears. "What is the matter with them? Why can't I make them understand? Why can't I understand them? One minute I think I have made friends, and the next they are so alien to me that they almost frighten me."

He took her by the arms and when he felt how violently she trembled, he said, "Come away from this place." With his arm around her shoulders, MacKenzie led Emily back to his hut, where he sat her down beside the front opening. He went inside and returned with a bottle and glass. Decanting a small amount, he handed the glass to Emily and said, "Drink this."

"Is it—"

"Just drink it," he said tenderly and pressed it into her hand.

Emily took a sip, made a face, then took another, feeling the burning liquid slide down her throat. After a third sip, she set the glass down and felt her nerves begin to calm.

"Hawai'ians have practiced infanticide for centuries," MacKenzie said, his voice soothing in the sultry night. "It keeps the population in check. This way, there is no starvation, no poverty. When there are too few men, girl babies are killed. Too few women, boy babies are killed. Because old Kamehameha's bloody battles in the last decade resulted in the slaying of warriors there is now a population imbalance with there being more women than men."

Emily shook her head. "It's wrong. Only God has the right to balance out the population."

She turned large, woebegone eyes to him. "MacKenzie, I thought I could bury my emotions in hard work and thereby readily accept the rules of the Mission Board. But I cannot be an unfeeling creature. Only women who bury babies alive have no feelings! I need you, MacKenzie! I need your strength and love and trust. Build me a house, my love, and a school pavilion. I will establish my own mission here in Hilo. I will let the natives know that I am still here to help them and that even though I am no longer sanctioned by the other missionaries, I am no less their friend. And I will work all the harder to convince them that I am not an outcast."

He wanted to shout out with joy, but he wanted her to be certain of her decision. "And your family? What about them?"

"I can't worry about what my family will think—they have no idea the strange and frightening world I have come to, how badly I need a man who knows these people and will help me with them. But most of all, because I can't live without you."

MacKenzie was suddenly rocked with desire, but was helpless to move. He saw how her long hair caught the flickering light of the tiki torches. The night was silent except for the sound of waves crashing on the nearby beach. The wails of "Auwe" had died down, and he knew the child was back with its mother. He sympathized with Emily's plight. He, too, sometimes felt frustrated in trying to understand these people. But he hadn't come here to change them.

And then he wasn't thinking about the Hawai'ians at all but this beautiful young woman who had been left alone in a strange wilderness without any help or support, who made do as best she could, maintained her cheer and her optimism, and who had helped him to reopen a communication with his father.

"My God, Emily," he said in a husky voice. "My God. . . ."

She looked up at him. He was bareheaded, the night breeze stirring his wavy hair. His jaw was unshaven. He wasn't wearing a jacket, and his vest was unbuttoned over his white shirt. He must have removed his cravat earlier, so that his collar lay open to expose a sunburnt throat. She thought she was going to die with desire.

When he reached out to touch her, she didn't move. When he drew her to him, she went willingly. And when his lips met hers, she pressed her mouth to his, and swept her arms around his broad back to hold tightly as if to never let go. Scooping her into his arms, MacKenzie carried her inside, his mouth still on hers, and he lowered her gently to the mats and bark cloth that served as his bed.

Emily was startled at the slowness of his movements. She closed her eyes and savored every caress, every kiss. She ventured on her own to explore his hard, muscular body and found wonderful strong sinew and rough skin. He was gentle when he lifted her nightgown over her head and tossed it aside. Emily was shocked to find that she had no shame lying naked before him as he removed his clothes.

And then he came back to her and the feel of skin against skin was startling and delicious and suddenly she understood something new about the Hawai'ians—that they were right to believe that the sex act was good and natural and that taking pleasure in the intimacy between a man and a woman was not a sin at all.

Afterwards, she cried. She wept against his chest and let everything come out with her tears—her homesickness, Isaac's tragic death, her frustration with the natives, her desire to love them and understand them, and finally she wept because she was leaving the Mission, which she had so loved.

As she lay in MacKenzie's arms, Emily thought about her success with Mahina and the dresses, her influence over Mary and Hannah, and she saw that MacKenzie was right, she didn't have to be a member of the Mission to continue her work there.

But more than that, having known MacKenzie's love, she knew she could never leave him. That God had brought her to this hour, and this was where God meant her to be. The decision had already been made. She was going to marry Captain MacKenzie Farrow.

CHAPTER FIVE

High Chiefess Pua stood beneath a flowering lehua tree and watched the wife of the haole sea captain as she hung wet clothes on a line.

Pua liked Mika Emily. She was kind to the people of Pua's village, taught them to read and how to make dresses. Mika Kalono was dead two years now, and no preacher had come to take his place. Pua saw this as a good sign. No more trying to tell the kanaka how to live. And Mika Emily's new husband was a good man. He ate with the kanaka, he treated Pua's people as friends and never told them they should pray to haole god.

And now here was another good sign. Mika Emily was large with child. The baby should come any day. A special child. First white baby born in this sacred land. An auspicious birth. Pua knew that white babies had been born to the missionaries in Kona and Waimea, but those villages were not as special as Hilo and Puna and Kau. This southeastern part of the island was where the First Ones had landed many generations ago. White babies born elsewhere on the island were special. But Mika Emily's baby was most special of all.

Leaving the shade of the lehua tree, Pua went to the sacred heiau on the far end of the village and laid mangoes and bananas at the base of Lono's Penis. Raising her arms, she chanted to the giant phallus, asking the god of healing and fertility to make more babies for the kanaka, to keep their numbers strong.

Removing a stone knife from a string around her waist, Pua sliced open one of the mangoes and studied the seed within. To an untrained eye, it was merely a large, yellow moist pit. But Pua saw patterns in its rippled surface, understood the meaning of the frail threads that attached the seed to the fruit's meat.

The message was a prophecy.

Since Mika Kalono died, there had been no permanent missionaries living at Hilo, just those who passed through. Occasionally, a preacher came from Kona to spend a few days with Chief Holokai's people, and while he was here, their Sabbath attendance was impressive. But once he left, they drifted back to their old life.

This pleased Pua. She and her brother, Kekoa, worked hard to remind the villagers of their culture and traditions, telling them not to turn their backs on the old gods or something terrible would happen. The man from Kona had come and preached a month ago. He had coughed and sneezed all through the service, and after he left, many people in the village came down with a sickness that Pua, for all her magic and prayers and herbs, could not fight. Several died. Mika Emily had called it "a cold," and said it was something that did not kill white men.

Reverend Michaels' sermons frightened her people. He shouted at them that the almighty unseen God of the white man had more power than all of Hawai'i's thousand gods combined, and that if the islanders did not abide by God's commandments, they would perish. The haole preacher told them the rules and her people listened. He said that sexual promiscuity was a sin that God would punish them for. He spoke of eternal fires in a place called hell, and Pua's people pictured the fires of Pele when the goddess got angry and sent fountains of lava spewing into the sky. And because Pele's fires frightened them, hell frightened them, and so the people tried to abide by the preacher's rules.

Pua read the message in the mango seed. It said that fewer kanaka were going to be born this year, fewer babies to replace those who died of the "cold." In the years to come, fewer kanaka in the islands of Havaiki. Pua knew that it was her purpose in life to see that this prophecy did not come true.

And so she knew what she must do. She was going to give Mika Emily's child to Lono, as a gift.

As Emily hung washing on a line, she kept looking at the bay. She had sent a message to Mrs. Michaels in Kona, saying that her delivery time was close. Months prior, when the Reverend had come to preach, he had said that his wife would come and help in the child-birth. Emily watched every day for the arrival of the large outrigger canoe the islanders—both Hawai'ian and white—used for traveling to coastal settlements. It was propelled by a distinctive triangular sail made of bright yellow bark cloth.

She was also watching for the *Kestrel*.

In the six months following their simple wedding ceremony conducted by a preacher passing through, MacKenzie would go out onto the promontory and gaze out to sea. Emily would watch him and think: I am his kite string. I tether him to the earth while his heart yearns for the open sea.

Finally, she went to him one day and asked him to embark on a voyage. He had protested. He loved her, he declared, and wanted to be with her. But she had said to herself: If I cannot overcome my own fears, I should at least not make MacKenzie a prisoner of them.

So she had said, "Go, my darling, and bring me back stories of the places I can never see."

He had surprised her then by asking her to voyage with him. "Lots of ship captains take their wives along. I can have a special cabin outfit-ted for your comfort. We can be together for months at sea, my love, and visit islands and exotic places."

Emily had desperately wanted to say yes, but she worried about what would happen to the natives without her constant vigilance and influence. More infants might be buried alive!

But after his departure, her emotional state had worsened. Ocean travel was perilous; ships were frequently lost at sea with all on board. Whenever Isaac had been away, he was still on the island. But whenever MacKenzie set sail, it was out to the open sea where he was at the mercy of currents, typhoons, and pirates. Emily never knew for certain that he was coming home, and the worry ate away at her.

I could have gone with him, she thought in a rare moment of bitterness, but the natives need me. If I voyage with my beloved husband they might revert to their savage ways.

To her further dismay, she had not yet received a letter from her family. She did not yet know how they had received the news of her marriage to Captain Farrow. And so the need to go down to the beach had grown in her, as she spent more and more endless hours obsessively combing the sand and dunes and driftwood for any sign that her family and friends in New Haven had not forgotten her.

And especially that they had forgiven her for marrying a sea captain.

Perhaps their disapproval would be tempered by good news.

A week after MacKenzie's departure for Alaska, Emily had awakened one morning nauseated, and noticed her breasts were tender. She was pregnant. Her parents would rejoice at this news.

She paused in her labor to stretch her back and gaze with pride at her new home.

When the Mission Board told her that she was no longer a part of their organization, Emily had moved out of the small house Isaac had built and MacKenzie commenced to build a larger one for the two of them. He had organized the natives, and with the help of sailors from ships that had stopped to take on water and food, they built a house of coral blocks cut from reefs offshore. The house had two stories, an attic, and a cellar. The windows were large, numerous, and shuttered against the sun. He planned to add a covered porch and balcony. Many of the appointments (the fireplace mantle, the glass panes in the windows, the door latches) had been added gradually to the house as they had to be shipped from New England. Furniture had also come piecemeal, but Emily's house now boasted polished floors with scatter rugs, an upholstered settee with matching chairs, a hat stand, an armoire, a dining table with straight-backed chairs and a sideboard, a large bed and linen chest, a writing desk, and a grandfather clock.

In the time during which MacKenzie had stayed with Emily after Isaac's death, he'd built more trade ties and contracts with the royalty, the farmers, and the new cattle men. He had purchased two more ships and hired captains to carry his cargo. And then after Emily had told her beloved MacKenzie he could return to the sea. she reassured him that she would be all right, praying that the house Isaac built for her would not remain empty for long, that the Mission Board would send a new couple to live there and to minister to Chief Holokai's people.

Even though she was no longer a missionary, she was more determined than ever to bring these people to Christ. It had been almost four years since she'd first arrived here and she felt that, aside from getting the women to wear dresses, she had accomplished little. She blamed herself for Isaac's premature death. If Pua had been a Christian during Isaac's illness, she most likely would have cured him with her native medicines. But as he would not allow heathenish chants under his roof, he had died.

Emily understood more now about the Hawai'ians' view. They believed in the power of words. Not in the same way that Westerners thought of the power of prayer—that it was not the words themselves or the prayer that had the power, it was the fact that the prayer was directed at God, and the power was God's. But the Hawai'ians believed that the actual spoken word possessed power—to hurt or heal—and so they were very careful about what they said. This explained why Pua could not administer a medicine without the proper words, for those were what really did the healing.

Emily was determined to free Pua's people from the yoke of a superstition and belief in magic that prevented them from using medicine in a positive way.

When she saw Pua coming up the path to the house, she dropped the last wet dress into the basket and, placing her hand to her lower back, gave it a stretch.

"Aloha," Pua said with a smile.

"Good day to you, Pua." Emily was always glad to see the High Chiefess. Pua's smile never failed to lift her spirits. Emily didn't know much about the healing mistress's personal life. Pua was gone from the village almost more than she was there, being needed around the island for her services. Especially as, lately, there had been increasing outbreaks of illness among the islanders—ailments brought by white men to which the natives had little resistance. Emily wondered why Pua wasn't married. She was still young—early thirties—and quite beautiful. As far as Emily knew, sixteen-year-old Mahina was Pua's only child.

"How Mika Emily?" Pua said, placing a brown hand on Emily's swollen belly.

"I am ready to have this child. It should be any day now. Hopefully, Mrs. Michaels is on her way."

"Pua help."

"Thank you, but Mrs. Michaels has experience delivering babies." The truth was, Emily didn't know the extent of Charlotte Michaels' experience. But Pua had offered many times in the last few months to act as midwife, and Emily most adamantly did not want the High Chiefess to deliver her child. There would be magic involved, she knew, and all sorts of heathenish and Satanic rituals. Emily had no idea how it would affect her newborn's immortal soul. She could not risk it. If she had to deliver the baby on her own, she would.

Pua held out a small bundle wrapped in a large green leaf. Emily eyed it with suspicion.

Pua laughed. "Good food!" she said.

Emily took it and, peeling back the leaf, found fresh chunks of lovely yellow mango nestled within. "Oh, this looks delightful, Pua. Mahalo."

Emily sank into one of the chairs by the front door of her house, and invited Pua to join her. But the medicine woman said she had patients to visit.

The mango was sweet and refreshing, and Emily closed her eyes as she savored every bite. It was not until she swallowed the last piece that she noticed an odd aftertaste.

And it was only an hour later that the labor pains began.

Emily struggled to her feet and, holding on to the side of her house, walked to the end of the porch, from where she could see the harbor. No bright yellow sail was anywhere in sight. She tried to think. She had expected Charlotte Michaels to be here in time. There were no other white women around, and there certainly wasn't time to send for one.

She turned and looked down the path at the native village. As another knife-sharp pain swept over her, she thought of the baby. She needed help with the delivery. Emily knew she could not do this on her own.

Not Pua! her mind cried. She will use witchcraft on my child.

But there was no one else. And Pua would see to it that the baby survived.

She sent a frantic prayer to God. Send me help! If only MacKenzie were here! Or other missionaries! I am alone and giving birth to my first child! God help me!

Another pain encircled her and as it subsided, Emily saw, coming up the path, High Chiefess Pua and her daughter Mahina. When another pain struck, Emily could not think straight. Were these two natives an answer from God? Was this His wish? Or was it Satan sending these two heathens to lay hands on her newborn?

Tell me what to do, O Lord!

They were smiling as they drew near, brown-skinned half-naked women in sarongs with flowers around their necks—and who worshipped obscenely shaped stones and fornicated and committed incest and were doomed to perdition because of their sins and ignorance.

Emily staggered forward, clutching her abdomen. Pua and Mahina rushed forward, each taking her by the arm. "You come," the girl said gently. "We help."

"What—?"

They guided her down the path, away from the house.

"No, wait. Take me inside." But another pain made her legs go weak and she could only stand up with the help of Pua and Mahina.

"You come," the girl urged gently. "Mika Emily have special baby. We take care of special baby."

"Special?" Emily said breathlessly as she staggered with them to the village. "What do you mean . . . ?"

As they passed between huts, people came out to watch, and then they followed until, by the time they reached the far end of the settlement, a large crowd accompanied Mika Emily. "Birthing hut," Mahina said with a smile as they approached a large clean grass hut with carved wooden effigies of gods guarding the entrance.

"No," Emily said, trying to resist. She would rather have her child out in the open than in a heathen hut. But she was weak, and she wanted her baby to be delivered safely. She knew Pua was a skilled midwife.

But she wasn't a Christian. And as they helped her into the grass shelter, Emily saw in horror that the birthing hut was but a short distance from the entrance to the heiau where she'd seen the offensive phallus on the pagan altar—with priests in capes and sarongs standing on either side, looking at her, waiting.

"No!"

Mother and daughter helped her down onto the mat, which was covered in clean bark cloth. Pua spoke soothingly in Hawai'ian while Mahina stroked Emily's forehead and hair and said, "You good now. We help special baby. Lono help. We pray to Lono now."

"Please don't. . . ."

They gave her water and dried her perspiring face. Mahina stayed at her side while Pua took a position in readiness to catch the baby. Emily heard the drums begin, and then the chanting—high, rhythmic, wailing sounds. She panted and tried to hold back, but the baby insisted on coming. The pain tore through her. She had no sense of time, if it was minutes or hours of labor, aware only of pain and Mahina's soft voice reassuring her.

In terror Emily thought of the two priests, waiting at the altar. Waiting for what?

Finally, after an eternity of pain and exhaustion, the baby came. "You have son!" Mahina cried with joy, while Pua busily separated the child from its mother.

"Give him to me," Emily said breathlessly, holding her arms out.

But Pua rose to her feet, cradling a bloody, mewling infant in her arms, and without a word, hurried from the hut.

Emily screamed and cried while Mahina held her down, smiling, telling her that Lono will be happy with his gift. Emily tried to see through the door of the hut. She saw Pua stand before the pagan altar, before the depraved idol, and lift the baby high in the air while the priests chanted and shook bundles of *ti*-leaves. Then Pua laid the baby on the altar, on a bed of flowers, and held her arms out to chant into the night while the village thundered with drums and human voices raised in heathen song.

Emily was sobbing and begging Mahina to spare her son when Pua returned. Through her tears, Emily saw the baby in Pua's arms. He was covered in petals. The High Chiefess knelt and placed the baby at Emily's breast, stroking the infant, stroking Emily's hair. Pua smiled and said, "Baby now son of Lono. Very lucky boy."

And Emily's tears turned to ones of joy as she saw the little arms and legs move, the tiny wrinkled face roll from side to side, and love such as she had never known possible washed over her in a wave of peace and happiness.

Four weeks after the birth of her son, whom Emily christened Robert Gideon, the new missionaries arrived.

Two married couples and their children were cheerfully welcomed on the beach by Mr. Clarkson who escorted them, along with a boisterous native crowd, to meet Chief Holokai and his esteemed son and daughter, Kekoa and Pua. The newcomers were questioned and then treated to a fabulous feast with entertainment, and then brought through the village to the lagoon, where a new grass hut had been built for them. Emily watched from the front door of her two-story home, with Robert in her arms. She had not wanted to attend the luau. She would never forgive Pua for what she had done.

As the four missionaries deliberated on who would live in the grass hut and who would live in the house that stood on the land the Mission Board rented from the Crown, natives broke open crates of goods the haole had brought, and found hundreds of Bibles and prayer books, hornbooks and slates, paper and pens.

Emily heard the excitement in the new preachers' voices, saw the energy in their bodies, recognized the zeal she had seen in Isaac four years ago. Those two men of vision and conviction were going to see to it that these natives were converted to Christianity. Emily had no doubt of it.

Just as she had no doubt that, after today, the natives of Hilo were never going to be the same.

CHAPTER SIX

Emily watched her husband as he came up the path with a young gentleman from California, a geologist named August Tidyman. He had come to Hawai'i Island to study the volcano and map the lava flows. Captain Farrow was going to escort him around the Kilauea area, pointing out old, black lava beds, newer ones still warm, and those so ancient that they were overgrown with lush vegetation. The natives remembered when those flows took place while Mr. Tidyman made a detailed map.

With them were Emily's two boys, six-year-old Robert and four-year-old Peter. It was MacKenzie's custom, each time he came into home port, to come ashore as quickly as possible to see his family, leaving his crew and officers to see to his few passengers and cargo. After a joyous reunion with rapid talking and much embracing, he would go back to his ship. This time he had taken his sons with him. But while Robert now came running to excitedly tell his mother that he was going to be a ship's master when he grew up, Peter was crying. "He hated the ship," MacKenzie said. "I guess we can't all have the sea in our blood."

As he left to show Mr. Tidyman the native village, with little Robert in tow, Emily lifted Peter in her arms and held him until his crying subsided. She remained on the verandah to watch her husband as he walked and talked with their visitor.

Emily was pleased that MacKenzie's sailing route had changed. Although his other ships continued to make the Alaska-China run, he himself took the *Kestrel* to South America and Mexico, which made his voyages shorter. This change had occurred because of an accident.

Thirty years ago, Captain George Vancouver had presented King Kamehameha the First with five black longhorn cattle. The animals were in poor condition after the long sea voyage and Kamehameha immediately put them under kapu and freed them to range the island. But the wild cattle quickly multiplied and proved a nuisance and a danger as they trampled farms and gardens and terrified the natives.

So an American advisor to Kamehameha, named John Palmer Parker, was given two acres of land and permission to wrangle the maverick cows. With the help of Hawai'ian workers, Parker quickly established a booming beef, tallow, and hide business. Captain Farrow had entered into an arrangement with Parker, carrying these goods to Spanish colonies in Chile, Peru, and Central America.

There had been other changes in Hawai'i as well—a new king, for one. When King Kamehameha the Second, whom Emily and Isaac had met, had toured London with his sister-wife five years ago, in 1824, visiting Westminster Abbey, the Royal Opera House in Covent Garden, and the Theatre Royal in Drury Lane, they'd contracted measles and died. The young king was succeeded by a son of old Kamehameha the Great, an eleven-year-old boy named Kauikeaouli who became Kamehameha III, although the real political power was in the hands of his stern stepmother and regent, Queen Ka'ahumanu, who had abolished the kapu system ten years prior and embraced Christianity.

Emily now looked around at their growing little settlement, seeing even more changes.

The two preachers who had arrived six years ago had built a flourishing congregation. Now that the Hawai'ian language finally had a standardized alphabet, thanks to the efforts of Isaac's fellow missionaries, the Bible and prayer books had been translated into the native tongue and dispersed among the people.

These new missionaries were also less intransigent on the issue of baptism than Isaac had been, seeing the value in bringing the heathen into the fold and *then* enlightening their souls to the truth. As a result, divine service was well attended every Sabbath. Hawai'ians who had been baptized—and the numbers were growing—liked being part of the "family of Jesus" and felt that their new names—John, Mary, Joseph, Hannah—gave them higher status in the village.

Emily found herself also enjoying a high status of a kind, as the new arrivals had come to her for help, asking many questions, requiring her advice, and employing her as a diplomatic go-between with Chief Holokai's people. As a result, the new missionaries had a much easier time adjusting than Emily had, and in a way she envied them. But she was pleased to have white women for neighbors, to have white children for Robert and Peter to play with.

Demand for the Mother Hubbard dress was high among the natives, and so Emily now held weekly sewing classes for women, many of whom came from miles around to learn the craft. She had heard that Pua was not happy about it. The Hawai'ians had a saying: Nakedness is the attire of the gods. But Emily insisted that God commanded his children to cover their nakedness.

A strange relationship had evolved after Robert's birth. Emily could not find it in her heart to forgive Pua for placing her baby on a pagan altar, and yet Pua had brought Emily safely through a difficult childbirth. Pua had grown distant as well, as if something had not gone right or according to plan. Emily didn't know what it was, but suspected it had to do with the baby and the obscene idol. Whenever she encountered the High Chiefess there was an arch politeness between them, and Emily had to confess that she missed Pua's warmth and smile.

She went inside and consoled Peter with biscuits and milk, and then returned to the parlor. Before laying out pieces of cloth and baskets of needles and thread in preparation for her afternoon sewing group, she paused before the glass-fronted cabinet—a Chippendale piece brought in a crate of straw from Boston—and looked lovingly at her collection of beach "treasures." The collection was growing. Only last week, when her heart had ached for MacKenzie and she watched the horizon every day for his ship, Emily had taken Robert and Peter down to the beach to search for a memento. When they found a cork float from a fishing net, they brought it back to the house, where they ceremoniously placed it on the shelf with the other beach treasures while Emily had said, "Never forget where you come from, my dear ones. You might have been born here, in these islands, but your roots are far away in New England. Your blood is there. Your home is there. This fishing float traveled all the way from New England to remind us that those at home still think of us."

She had pointed to the other items and said to Robbie and Peter, "This piece of wood came from my mother, Rose, who is your grandmother. This piece of glass came from the ale bottle my uncle, your great-uncle, drank from. This conch shell was sent to us by my sister, your aunt."

As she listened to her sons recite words she had taught them— "New Haven is our true home."—Emily closed her eyes and thought: Yes, these things were especially chosen by my mother and uncle and sister, and set upon the ocean currents with instructions to come directly here, around Cape Horn, directly here to Hilo that I might find them.

Added to the collection was the letter she had finally received from her family, four years ago, in which her mother had written, "The master of a fine vessel is an honorable profession, one that requires courage, integrity, and stamina. We are certain that MacKenzie Farrow is a good man."

Turning away from the collection of links to home, Emily laid out the sewing supplies. She also laid out pamphlets she had asked Reverend Michaels to print on his small press in Kona. They were tracts outlining God's loving plan for His children. Like Isaac Stone, the two ministers in Hilo preached fire-and-brimstone. They thought that fear was the best way to bring new souls to God. But Emily's faith was about love. And so her sewing groups were less about making garments and more about a way to deliver a gentler, more positive sermon.

She understood the Hawai'ian view of the power of the spoken word. They had been convinced of the existence of hell, which they wanted to avoid at all costs. But so, too, should they be convinced of God's love for them. So she told them about a Father in heaven who cared for his children, and a son whom He sent to earth that he might die for their sins and thus save them. She was slowly bringing her own small flock around to seeing their new faith in a more positive light.

If only she could convince Kekoa and Pua of her good intentions. Yet it seemed that as missionaries grew stronger and gained more sway over the islanders, the more entrenched in the old ways Pua and her brother became.

But Emily was making inroads with Mahina.

The High Chiefess's twenty-two-year-old daughter, who had helped bring Emily's precious Robert into the world, had come to Emily in secret to ask questions. Mahina had been hearing from her friends and other village women how Jesus loved them and how the haole God was really a father who wanted to take care of his people instead of punishing them. Mahina wanted to know if this was true. And if, by praying to this loving father, she could stop the sickness that continued to claim lives among her people.

This afternoon, at the sewing group, Emily was going to tell Mahina and the others the story of the Crucifixion and how Jesus asked his Heavenly Father to forgive the soldiers, even as they were nailing him to a cross. She suspected this would bring Mahina into the fold.

In a secret cove a few miles down the rocky coast from Hilo, a large outrigger canoe, fitted with a sail and twenty oarsmen, waited for the High Chiefess's daughter, Mahina. They were to take her to Honolulu.

Pua and her daughter followed a worn path down an ancient cliff made of lava, and when they reached the small beach, Pua turned to say farewell. It caused her great pain to send Mahina away, but she had no choice. Too many Hawai'ians were embracing the haole god. The old ways were going to vanish if she did not act. When she had dedicated Mika Emily's new son to Lono, Pua had thought it would have pleased the gods.

It did not.

Now she must save her daughter.

Nearly all the villagers had been converted now. Some of the women had shortened their long haole dresses to make it easier to work in the fields or to gather kelp and seashells in tide pools, nicknaming the garment muumuu, which meant "cut off." The Sabbath sermons were in English and Hawai'ian, as were the prayers and the hymns. Pua saw this as a bad thing—when a haole sermon was in the people's own language, they took to heart what the preacher said. In the schoolhouse, where daily attendance was strong, lessons in reading and writing and arithmetic were taught in both English and Hawai'ian.

Pua had witnessed the gradual change in her people. She had also witnessed the shrinking of their numbers. They sickened and died from diseases that did not harm the haole. Fewer babies were born. And so she was sending Mahina away, to a village outside of Honolulu, in Nu'uanu Valley, where there was little taint from the white man. And then Pua was going to pray to the gods, and make sacrifice, and work her magic to bring her people back to the old ways.

Turning to Mahina, she said, "The haole tell us that our ancient traditions are wrong. They say that no longer can brother marry sister, or sister marry brother. No longer can one wife have many husbands, or one husband many wives. No longer can our women swim out to the ships and enjoy the pleasure of the foreign sailors. No longer can we circumcise the *piko ma'i* of our sons so that their sexual pleasure is enhanced. No longer can we form the *kohe lepelepe* of girl babies so that when they come into womanhood, their sexual pleasure is great. The haole say we must keep these parts hidden and not speak of them even though they are sacred to us. They have filled my people with shame about the old ways, the ways of our ancestors and our gods."

Mahina started to cry and Pua said, "The gods of our ancestors watch over you. Never forget the prayers to Lono, the sacred chants to Pele. Remember the sacred days and the holy festivals. Do not stop dancing the hula or someday no one will remember it. Be respectful of the spirits wherever you walk. Remember that you are an ali'i, you are a direct descendant of the great King Umi. *Aloha nui,* my daughter."

Pua removed a lei made of red ginger blossoms and white orchids from her shoulders and placed it over Mahina's head. Then she prayed and chanted in a loud, mournful voice as Mahina entered the canoe and the oarsmen shoved off, chanting in unison as they dipped their oars into the water.

Pua remained on the beach until the canoe was long gone.

CHAPTER SEVEN

"You have done a splendid job here, Mrs. Farrow." Reverend
Michaels paused to blow his nose. "Pardon me, but I have had a
persistent cough that I cannot seem to shake." He pocketed his handkerchief. "Splendid indeed. Isaac would be proud. I am afraid we have
had less success in Kona."

"I taught the women by example, Reverend Michaels," she said,
noticing that his face was flushed and shiny. She wondered if he had a
fever. Perhaps she should invite him to stay in the guest room until he
felt better to travel. "It isn't enough to say that they must not engage
in their native dancing. I find that informing them that Jesus does not
want them to dance the hula has more effect. The women themselves
destroyed their skirts and all the accoutrements of the dance. In the
same way that the men removed all the carved idols from their village.
By teaching them about Jesus's love and compassion, they are more
inclined to see their old ways as offensive."

Reverend Michaels sneezed and out came the handkerchief again.

He was a corpulent man, with his stomach straining at his waistcoat. Michaels and his wife had come out on the *Triton* with Emily and
Isaac ten years ago and now ran a successful mission in Kona. They
had adapted to the island more easily than Emily had. Where she
tried to keep New England in her home, including the servings of

lean beef, boiled, with turnips and cabbage, the Reverend Michaels had taken to Hawai'ian food, which consisted of sweet potatoes, fatty pork, bananas, and taro, in such quantities that he had grown obese on them.

But he was still a New Englander in appearance and now sat in her parlor wearing the latest in men's styles—gone was the cutaway coat with tails over tight breeches. Long black frock coats that came almost to the knees over loose trousers were now the fashion. Cravats were narrower, more modest, with less flair. And he sported a wide-brimmed, flat-crowned straw hat, better suited to the tropics than tall, beaver-skin top hats.

"It has been a very fruitful decade for us all," he said. "The natives wear decent clothing, they no longer bury infants alive or practice human sacrifice. They attend divine service on the Sabbath, they keep the Lord's Commandments. They no longer dance the hula or practice their old witchcraft. Many now read and write, in English as well as Hawai'ian. I am very proud of what my brothers and sisters have accomplished here."

"Mr. Clarkson, the dock agent," Emily said, "would have us believe that the old practices haven't been stamped out at all, they've merely been driven deeper into the jungle."

"Mr. Clarkson is a drunk and his word cannot be believed."

"I quite agree." But Emily could not share Reverend Clarkson's immense satisfaction with the work accomplished on the island of Hawai'i. There were still old traditionalists who refused to accept God as their only path to salvation. Emily was particularly disappointed that she had not been able to win Mahina to the faith. For reasons unknown, Pua's daughter went to the island of O'ahu and had yet to come back. Emily had heard that, in the year since her departure, Mahina had married the son of an ali'i and had given birth to a daughter, whom they named Leilani.

"Thank you for your hospitality, Mrs. Farrow," Reverend Michaels said, rising from his chair and giving his nose one last honk. "I must be joining my traveling companion, August Tidyman, whom you have already met. He has come back to continue his work on mapping the island's lava flows, although to what purpose is beyond me. Good day to you."

Emily stood in the shade of her verandah and watched him shamble down the path to where his horse was tethered. The geologist was just emerging from the village, where he had made inquiries among the natives about the history of this region. Having had no form of writing for over a thousand years, the Hawai'ians had created a remarkable oral history, passed down from generation to generation so that those living today could speak accurately of events in the distant past.

He looked pleased and Emily supposed his map was filling up with lines and dates. She waved and watched the two men ride off.

She looked up at the green cliffs that towered over the settlement, mists gathering against the verdant slopes, creating rainbows. In ten years, she had not grown tired of the sight. Then she brought her eyes to the nearby lagoon where her two boys, seven-year-old Robert and five-year-old Peter, were playing with the children of the other missionaries.

Hilo was growing and prospering. It was starting to look like a little town. There was talk of erecting a proper church with a steeple and pews. The wharf had more docks and warehouses, and Mr. Clarkson had competition from other merchants. It was a satisfying life, Emily thought. But it would be more perfect if she could persuade MacKenzie to stay home and let other ships' masters skipper his fleet of eight vessels. She thought he could do very well by running his small shipping line from Hilo. But the sea called, and he had to go.

As she turned to go inside, Emily saw that Reverend Michaels had accidentally dropped his handkerchief. Retrieving it from the ground, she carried it inside to add to her weekly washing.

S he didn't know what woke her.

Emily opened her eyes and stared at the dark ceiling. Her throat hurt. Her skin burned. And a strange throb sounded in her ears.

She sat up and the bedroom swam around her. She had never known such thirst. Staggering to the wash stand, she poured water from the pitcher into the basin, dipped her hands in and drank deeply. Then she splashed water on her burning face.

She paused. A strange thunder rolled over the town. Rain?

She went to the window and looked out. The stars were visible in the sky. The bay was dark and calm and quiet.

The thunder didn't stop. Where was it coming from?

She left the bedroom, holding onto the wall, and looked in on Robert and Peter, who were two slumbering angels.

She started to go back to bed but she knew she wouldn't sleep with the thunder. Forgetting her slippers, she cautiously made her way downstairs and went to the front door. Why was she burning up? Then she remembered: two days of sore throat, congestion, and a cough. She had gone to bed thinking she would be better in the morning.

Flinging open the front door, she was treated to a cool night. Stepping down from the verandah, her nightdress billowing about her in the breeze, she looked around. There were a few cottages scattered around the bay now, but all were dark. The homes of the missionaries were also silent and dark. Everyone was asleep.

Where was the thunder coming from?

Emily turned toward the native village, staggering barefoot over grass and gravel, oblivious to the pain in her feet. She saw no lights, no one outside. She went to the women's huts, looking in. But they were deserted.

Where was everyone?

In the light of the full moon, she turned this way and that, her skin on fire, her head throbbing, trying to locate the source of the sound.

And then she knew—it was coming from deep in the rain forest.

She plunged into the trees. Her mouth was parched, she felt dizzy, but she had to know why thunder was coming from the forest. She caught her nightgown on bushes, snagged her long hair on branches, sharp leaves brushed her face. The forest grew denser. Moonlight was blocked out. But the thunder grew louder.

She knew she was getting near.

Suddenly, an opening. A broad clearing where moonlight and stars shone. And tiki torches.

She stopped and swayed unsteadily. Perspiration dripped into her eyes, blurring her vision. She couldn't identify what she was looking at. The thunder filled her aching head. Her throat burned like fire. And the thirst was unearthly.

And then she saw—

She cried out and nearly fainted.

Demons. Evil spirits. Minions of Satan. Words flew through her head like screaming bats. Beelzebub. Lucifer. Asmodeus. Azazel.

Sodom and Gomorrah . . .

And then memories flashed like lightning in her feverish head: the obscene idol, Isaac on his deathbed, her baby on a heathen altar, the infant buried alive . . .

Thoughts now flew, long-buried, festering. *I could have gone to sea with MacKenzie! I could have visited exotic ports of call and seen the world with my beloved husband. But I had to stay behind because of you people! I suffered extreme loneliness because of you!*

I was homesick, I was heartsick because of you. I wanted to befriend you. I wanted this to be an adventure. I wanted to be brave. But you made me feel weak and cowardly. You reminded me that I don't belong here. That I am a New England woman born and bred. I hate you for that. You stole my dream and tossed my flaws back in my face.

Emily threw back her head and screamed.

And screamed again.

"There you are, my dear," came a cheerful, familiar voice.

Emily blinked and looked up at the ceiling, which was illuminated with sunlight. She rolled her head to the side and saw Cynthia Graham, wife of Reverend Keath Graham, who had come to Hilo seven years prior and who lived in the house Isaac had built. Cynthia rose from her chair and came to the bed. "How are you feeling?"

"What happened?"

"You were found three days ago, wandering at the edge of the forest. You have burned with fever since. Mrs. Millner and I have taken turns nursing you." She laid a cool hand on Emily's forehead and smiled. "The fever is definitely gone. How do you feel?"

"Hungry," Emily said, struggling to sit up. She was astonished at how weak she was. And her feet hurt. "I don't remember," she said, pressing fingers to her eyes. "I woke up in the middle of the night and I heard thunder. It was coming from the forest . . ." She shook her head. "I don't remember anything after that."

"Well, never mind, my dear. You are on the mend now. I shall bring you some soup. Your boys will be happy to hear that you are better. They have been quite worried about their mama."

Resting back against the pillows, Emily closed her eyes and tried to remember what had happened in the rain forest that night. But she could not.

Emily was content to sit idle on the verandah as she watched Robert and Peter play on the lawn. She was still weak from her recent ordeal. Captain Hawthorne, who had been trained in medicine, made port the day after Emily's fever broke and when he came to the house to visit, had told her she had suffered a particularly virulent bout of influenza. People in Kona had been stricken as well, but Hilo seemed to have been spared the worst of it. He advised Emily that she take it easy for a few days, and so she was, hoping that MacKenzie would be home soon.

Being sick and alone with two small children was not something she wanted to experience again. More worrisome than that, however, was that the ground had been shaking for the last few days and people were saying that Kilauea was preparing to erupt.

"Hello there!"

She looked up from her knitting and saw Reverend Keath Graham coming up the path. A handsome man in his forties, Graham had done a great deal of good in the Hilo area, helping the natives to build sturdier huts, teaching them how to trap wild fowl, showing them how to make improvements in their ancient agricultural techniques. Robust and energetic, Keath Graham was making a name for himself in these islands and it was rumored he was on his way to the chairmanship of the Mission Board.

"Good day to you, Reverend."

"I'm on my way to the docks," he said, "so I can't stay." He removed his wide-brimmed straw hat. Like Reverend Michaels, Graham had adopted the new long frock coat fashion. "I just wanted to tell you that something alarming is going on in the native village."

Emily glanced down the road at the native settlement. She had been surprised that, during her convalescence, no one from the village had come with food and flowers, as they normally did. "Alarming?" she said.

"The Hawai'ians are dying, Mrs. MacKenzie. And we can't fathom why."

"Dying! What are the symptoms?"

"There are none. It is as if they have given up. They lie on their mats moaning. They refuse to eat or drink."

"Is it the influenza?"

"No, it's nothing I can determine. Even the kahuna lapa'au can't help them."

An illness that not even Pua could cure?

"Anyway, I have to get down to the docks. I'm hoping Captain Hawthorne is still in port. Perhaps he can help. Ten villagers have already died, with many more close to succumbing."

She watched him hurry away, then she turned her eyes back to Chief Holokai's settlement. What on earth could be ailing the natives? Emily frowned. Perhaps she should go and see if there was something she could—

She gave a sudden cry. She shot to her feet, sending yarns and needles across the porch. Emily pressed her fists to her temples and swayed. "Oh God!" she called. "Oh God, oh merciful heaven!"

She had remembered.

It all came back in a rush—staggering through the rain forest, coming upon a clearing, seeing demonic images and a bestial ritual.

Emily collapsed into her chair, her face in her hands, and she burst out weeping. Great bitter sobs racked her slender body as she cried from the depths of her soul. Dear God in heaven . . . what did I do? The Hawai'ians dying from no apparent cause. . . . *Did I cause that?*

Emily prayed, and then she cried some more, and after a while she grew calm. A coldness settled into the pit of her soul, a dark pool of self-retribution and guilt. And she knew it would never leave her for the rest of her life.

She knew something else, too, that she could never tell a living soul the truth of what happened in the rain forest that terrible night. She couldn't even tell MacKenzie. And so she made a vow before God that, for all her days, she would live with what she had done, and she would never speak of it.

And that was to be her punishment. . . .

Mahina would have liked to stop in the village and visit her old friends, but when her mother had sent word to her in Honolulu that she was to come at once, Mahina knew she must hurry.

In the message, Pua had been explicit about where they were to meet, at the head of an ancient trail in the rain forest. The ruins of an old heiau still stood there. Mahina remembered the place. And there was her mother, waiting.

They had not seen each other in a year, but Mahina immediately saw the sorrow on her mother's face and sensed the gravity of the situation. They embraced and then Pua told her daughter to undress. Wondering what they were about to do, and why, Mahina removed her muumuu while Pua removed her sarong.

And when they were naked and alone, mother and daughter delivered themselves into the verdant primeval rain forest. Mahina understood that they wore no clothing to show their humility before Pele, the goddess of fire and volcanoes. But they wore garlands of flowers around their necks, and flowers in their hair, to show respect. Mahina did know one thing: they were bringing Pele a gift.

Lono's Penis.

All through the night they trudged, through koa and ohia trees, under great canopies of branches and vines and leaves, over rough rocky ground that was spewed out of the volcano centuries ago, cold and hardened now and covered with grass, ferns, flowers. The air was thick with the stench of sulfur and smoke. Kilauea had been belching lava for days, sending great plumes of steam to the sky, causing the ground to rumble and shake and make people run for their lives. In the towns of Hilo and Kona, natives and white men alike prayed loudly to God Almighty and to Jesus Christ to save them.

But only one person knew how to appease Pele. High Chiefess Pua, noble Hawai'ian ali'i and kahuna lapa'au—mistress of healing—who was bringing a sacred stone to Pele's Womb. Pua knew that the virile erection of the god Lono, when placed inside Pele's Womb, would appease the goddess and make her stop the earthquakes and lava flows.

But the stone was not going to be the only sacrifice to Pele on this solemn night. Pua's beautiful daughter, Mahina, twenty-three-years-old, copper-skinned, and voluptuous, walked behind her mother in terrified silence.

Finally they arrived at a place in the jungle that was filled with smoke and heat. The ground shook. Steam vents burst all around them and Mahina knew the lava would soon come. She thought they were lost. But then her mother parted dense vines to expose the entrance to an ancient lava tube.

While Mahina waited outside, Pua carried the penis-stone inside. When it was securely placed against a rocky wall, Pua raised her arms and cried, "O Madam Pele, the haole tell us it is wrong for men to give pleasure to women, and women to give pleasure to men. They have filled my people with shame about the old ways, the ways of our ancestors and our gods. And now the people are dying. Their spirits cannot fight white man's disease. O Madam Pele, accept this gift that came from far-off Kahiki and show mercy to your people who love you. *E h'oi, e Pele, i ke kuahiwi, ua na ko lili . . . ko inaina. . . .* Return, O Pele, to the mountain, your jealousy, your rage are pacified."

She listened for the Goddess's response.

While Mahina waited outside, the ground shook violently, the air grew hot and dry. Mahina's terror mounted. She thought the trees were going to catch fire. She thought that she herself was going to catch fire.

Pua was so long inside the cave that her daughter feared Pele would send another tremor, causing the cave to collapse with Pua inside.

But the High Chiefess finally came out and said, "Daughter, the days of kanaka are numbered. After the passing of a hundred moons, babies will be torn from mothers' arms. Husbands and wives will be torn apart. Brother will be taken from sister, and daughter will be taken from father. They will go across the water and we will never see them again! Auwe! That is when Pele will destroy all the people. That is the end of Hawai'i Nui."

Taking her daughter by the shoulders, Pua pressed her nose on either side of Mahina's, in the traditional kiss, and she whispered, "Aloha."

Pua paused to hold her daughter's beautiful face in her hands. Tears flowed. Pua thought of the day, ten years ago, when the haole had brought their god to Hawai'i. Pua had welcomed them. She had embraced Mika Emily as a sister. She had given her *aloha nui*—her true *aloha*. But now her people were dying.

She turned and trudged up the slope, toward the lava flow.

Mahina followed and saw that her mother was getting too close to Pele's blood. It glowed hot red and yellow beneath the black sky. The air was filled with smoke and a sickly stench. Mahina stopped at a safe distance and watched in horror as Pua came to a standstill before the slow moving flow of lava. She began to chant. She held her arms out, threw her head back so that her long black hair trailed out in the night wind. Mahina's eyes grew wide as her mother did not retreat from the river of lava, as she stood rooted, never breaking her chant, looking up at the stars. When the lava licked at her bare feet, she did not flinch. As it moved around her and rose up her calves, she chanted. Mahina could see her mother's perspiring skin in the glow.

And then her long hair caught fire. And in an instant she stood as a flaming statue, her chanting turning into a wail.

"Auwe!" Mahina cried. She cried again and her wails rose to the sky. She turned and dashed back to the cave. She ran sobbing, filled with fear. When she reached the cave she ducked inside, as if the lava could catch her, even though it was moving in a different direction, away from this sacred place. She sobbed and covered her face. She banged her forehead against the cold sharp lava of the cave's wall. And then something came over her. A feeling. A sensation.

It was forbidden for her to go deeper into the vaginal cave, but she could not resist. She wanted to know if Pele was accepting the sexual gift, she wanted to witness Pele's pleasure with Lono's manhood. Light from the moon illuminated the walls of the narrow cave. She saw the stone penis. But then, farther inside the tube, she saw something else. She *felt* it. . . .

She ventured deeper and came to a stop, and as her eyes adjusted, she made out a shape.

"Auwe!" she whispered, pressing her hands to her mouth.

Mahina slowly backed out, her eyes wide with terror. She had laid eyes upon the most supreme kapu. The gods were going to strike her dead for having witnessed what she had just seen. She knew she must never speak of this. Never tell a living soul of the kapu thing she had seen in Pele's Womb. . . .

As she commenced the sorrowful trek back to Hilo, Mahina thought of Lono's Stone, which had been with her people for generations, had kept them healthy and fertile and multiplying. What was going to happen to her people now, with the sacred healing stone buried forever?

PART TWO

WILLAMETTE VALLEY, OREGON TERRITORY

1851

CHAPTER EIGHT

Anna ran through the grass as fast as her legs would go, her hands pressed to her chest as she screamed, "Mama! *Mama!*"

But the cabin was too far away. Her mother could not possibly hear. In a panic, Anna ran faster.

The Barnett farm in the Willamette Valley in the Oregon Territory was a beautiful spread with crops and corrals and a handsome barn, the mountains rising tall and lavender. Ten-year-old Anna spent her days down by the creek, while her mother spent her days worrying about her daughter.

"Anna's a wild thing," Rachel would complain to her husband. "The minute she is out of the house, she removes her shoes and bonnet to run like a forest creature. And her head always in the clouds! Leaving me with the washing and the ironing and the cooking. I can't even get her to weed the vegetable garden because no sooner is my back turned than her dreamy thoughts have lured her away to the meadows again. You have to smack some sense into her, Mallory. I cannot live like this!"

But Mr. Barnett never got a chance to knock any kind of sense into his daughter because he had heard the call of gold and off he'd gone to California with half the farmers in the Willamette Valley. Anna's mother was by turns furious and weepy, and frightened all the time. That had been a year ago, in 1849. They had lived at that home-stead for six years, after arriving by way of the Oregon Trail in 1843. They were among the first white people to settle the Oregon Territory. Other than their little group there were just French fur traders and Indians. Anna's mother often said the Methodist missionaries got there not a minute too soon.

"Mama!" Anna cried, bursting through the door, startling her mother so that Rachel nearly dropped her cake pan.

"Goodness, child! Haven't I taught you better—"

Anna held out her hands. "He's hurt."

"Oh Lord," Rachel Barnett whispered when she saw the injured bird. And of course her daughter was barefoot and had left her bonnet behind again.

"I found him by the creek," Anna said with tears on her cheeks. "His wing is broken. We have to fix it."

Setting pan and spoon on the rustic table, which was made, like the cabin, of logs, Rachel held out her hands. "Give it to me, child."

Rachel had been a mill girl in a cotton factory in Massachusetts where Mallory Barnett was an overseer. The mill girls worked eighty hours a week and their days were strictly regimented. They woke to the factory bell at four in the morning, reported to work at five, had a half-hour breakfast at seven, worked until a half-hour lunch at noon. At seven in the evening the factory would shut down and the workers would return to their company houses. This was six days a week with Sundays off.

It had been very hard work. Each room had eighty women work-ing at great big power looms and the constant noise was deafening. The rooms were hot but windows were kept shut during the summer to preserve the delicate thread work. There were company boarding-houses near the mills, but you had to share, with up to six girls to a bedroom. It was cramped, tiresome living and Rachel had dreamed of getting away.

She'd caught the eye of her overseer, Mallory Barnett. They had courted and fell in love and confided in each other their secret dream to get away from crowded and regimented living. They had heard about all the free land out West, in Oregon and the Mexican province of California. Some argued that it belonged to the Indians who had lived there thousands of years. But louder voices pointed out that the Indians didn't use the land—they didn't build on it or grow crops—therefore it was free for the taking. When the Barnetts heard about this, they saw it as their chance for a new life.

They had thirty acres, but for Anna's mother it wasn't enough. She hankered after the vacant holdings on either side of the farm, although her husband often said, "Haven't we enough?" Rachel Barnett went into the mills when she was nine and she was twenty-two when she left, so he reckoned it was thirteen years of working and living in such cramped conditions that made her greedy for space, and he didn't blame her.

She had once said to her daughter, "We young ones were doffers, that is, we 'doffed,' or took off the full bobbins from the spinning frames and replaced them with empty ones. We were paid two dollars a week, and we worked fourteen hours a day. I don't think my need for space has anything to do with walls. It has to do with time. And freedom, which might be the same thing. We came West so that our children wouldn't be slaves to bells and clocks and other people's rules."

"Can you fix him?" Anna asked with big, tear-filled eyes.

Rachel sighed. Where had the child gotten this obsession with fixing things? She had once even brought a trembling butterfly home, hoping they could cure it. The creature was simply dying. A part of nature. She had tried to explain to Anna that not all injuries and illnesses could be fixed. Some just had to be accepted and endured. Maybe God would cure it; if not, you died.

"Child," Rachel said, "there's nothing we can do. It's nature, you see. This bird was injured so that another animal could eat. God's plan is foolproof. We can't go meddling."

"But when Mr. Miller broke his leg, Papa fixed it. And when Mrs. Odum was down with influenza, you and the other ladies gave her medicines and plasters and she got better."

"Yes, the good Lord saw fit to leave some troubles in our hands, he gave us solutions. But other things, well, I just don't know." Rachel laid the quivering sparrow on the dirt floor and stomped on it with her boot.

Anna cried out.

"It's all right, child," Rachel said, picking it up by one wing and flinging it far out onto the grass. "We couldn't have saved it and now we've put it out of its misery." Rachel bent to meet her daughter's eye. "Sometimes, killing is a mercy. At least, when there's no other solution. Now help yourself to a cake and then go back to the creek and collect your things. Say a prayer for the bird if you want."

As she tearfully left the cabin, Anna looked back and saw her mother shaking her head.

Anna had known from an early age that she wasn't like other children. She wasn't born in a proper house for one thing. She was born in 1841 in a covered wagon. Her mother liked to say how Indians were shooting at them with bows and arrows while she was delivering Anna. But she couldn't help the need in her to fix what wasn't right. When her younger brother Eli was down with the measles, Anna was at his side night and day, applying salve to his rash, and when it eased his torment, it pleased her. That's all it was, she just wanted things to be right.

Papa would understand. She had heard him say to her mother, "She's just got a tender heart, Rachel. Leave her be."

But Papa wasn't there. He had left to find gold in a place called Sacramento, so now it was just Anna and her mother and Eli. They got letters from Father, describing the hardships and disappointments in the gold fields, how dangerous it was, men stealing from each other, killing for the gold, while disease claimed a lot of lives. Anna's mother would weep for days after each letter.

He kept promising to come back once he had made a fortune in gold. And he was finding some—he drew pictures of the nuggets in his letters. "We'll buy the next parcel over," he wrote (Rachel read his letters to Anna and Eli after supper, as they sat by the fire in their log cabin). "We'll build us a real fine house and maybe have a woman in to help with the washing. I'll hire some hands and we can run cattle. It will be a grand homestead that people will talk about for miles around."

In the meantime, Anna's mother had to rely on help from neighbors when it came time to harvest the corn or when the spring lambs came. Winter was the hardest. The cabin was cold and drafty, and the nights were long.

But Anna had found her warm place in the sun. Down by the creek where her mother was always cautioning her not to go. But she could not resist. It was almost as if the gurgling water were calling to her.

Anna was blessed with thick beautiful wavy hair. Red-gold, it caught the sunlight like fire, so you could always spot her wherever she was, running barefoot through the grass and sitting on her favorite boulder that was smooth and scooped out so it fit like a chair. She would look up through the leaves and branches and set her mind free to soar with the hawks. She would dangle her feet in the water and feel the sun's heat radiate through her dress. Whenever a storm came to the valley, she heard the thunder and could feel it rumble through the rock upon which she sat. She relished rain as it fell into the stream, raising its level, causing it to rush and roil over the pebbles. All of nature in a glorious dance. And Anna Barnett, ten years old, at the center of it all.

She daydreamed about what lay on the other side of the mountains. Where did the river begin? What were the people like there? She read geography books and looked at maps, but they were a dry and silent testament to a colorful and noisy world that beckoned to young Anna. She was restless, eager to grow up, to know things, to see the rest of the world.

Anna's schooling came from her mother and a box of books she bought from a traveling man who went from farm to farm selling household things from his wagon. Anna learned her ABC's and how to do sums. Her mother said that someday she was going to learn how to write in a fluid, graceful style, which she said was the mark of a lady. Anna didn't know why she needed to be a lady when she lived on a farm, but her mother was adamant about those things, always making sure the girl had a handkerchief and said "Please" and "Thank you" and was polite to strangers.

Anna's heart was heavy. She found the dead sparrow and decided to bury it. But as she was digging a hole, the sky grew dark with thunder clouds and they were rolling into the valley with alarming speed. When a violent wind came up, Anna heard a man's voice calling out. She recognized it as Mr. Turner's, from two farms over, pulling up in his wagon. Collecting her shoes and bonnet from the creak, she ran back to the cabin to see her mother standing at the front door holding something in her hands.

It was a letter. Anna thought: It's from Father, saying he's coming home!

She knew her mother thought the same thing because she was smiling as she looked at the envelope. In his last letter Mallory Barnett had said that he was done with the gold fields and was looking to come home.

Anna was excited. She hadn't seen him in three years. She remembered loving the smell of his tobacco, the sound of his deep laugh, the feel of his warmth as he held her on his lap and called her "Egg."

She hurried inside as the first cold raindrops hit. Rachel purposely made Anna and Eli wait as she put a kettle on the stove for tea and stoked the embers in the fireplace. She used some precious whale oil to give them light—they used so many things sparingly because they were "farm poor."

After tea and biscuits and finding warm spots at the hearth, Anna and Eli sat in eager anticipation of their father's news.

Anna noticed how the light from the oil lamp cast a halo around her mother's hair. Folks thereabouts often remarked that Mallory's wife was pretty, and how could he leave her like he did. Rachel told folks she didn't mind, because he had gone to the gold fields for her and the kids. And when he came home, she said, they would continue to expand their farm and have more space than ever.

But as she silently read the letter, her shoulders slumped. "We are to join your father in San Francisco," she said softly. "He has put this farm up for sale. He is sending a man to help us load everything into a wagon and take us to Oregon City from where we will buy passage aboard a Hudson's Bay steamship." She lifted her head and looked at her children, and Anna saw the light of hope and future plans fade from them. "Children, we are going to live in a city."

Bowing her head, she whispered a strange prayer: "I promise you, Mallory, I will never be happy there. . . ."

They arrived at San Francisco after weeks of cramped living on a vessel that primarily carried furs to China. For Eli and Anna, it was a grand adventure and they loved the sea and the sailors, but their mother spent much of the time hanging over the rail. It was a happy reunion with Mallory Barnett, with laughter and tears and sincere embraces (although Rachel was somewhat silent and stony-faced). Barnett lavished them with gifts—many things Anna had never seen before, such as perfume and a fabric called silk, and sweet chocolates imported from a place called Holland. And then they rode in a proper covered carriage through muddy streets lined with towering brick buildings that made Eli and Anna crane their necks.

Their new home, which Barnett had had built while awaiting his family's arrival and which had just finished completion, stood on Rincon Hill.

As they rode from the docks, he told them that the Gold Rush of 1849 had made San Francisco's population explode. An entire town seemed to be raised from the ground as if by magic, he said. Within a year from when he had left the gold fields and had come here to make his fortune, the town had grown from two hundred inhabitants to twenty-five thousand. The forty-niners, as they called themselves, pitched tents or built canvas-covered shelters on the lower slopes of Telegraph, Russian, and Nob Hills, and in the sand dunes down by the harbor. But by the time Rachel and her children arrived, in 1852, the overgrown mining camp had disappeared. Officials estimated that San Francisco had fifty thousand inhabitants, and they said that eight thousand of them were women.

A lot of families lived in three- and four-room cottages scattered here and there along dirt streets, but well-to-do San Franciscans like Anna's father wanted substantial houses in stylish neighborhoods to show off their money. Rich people chose Rincon Hill because, Barnett said as they rode along, being higher than the flat land, the hill had warmer and sunnier weather than the blocks north of Market Street. It had views of the bay and city, and it was removed from the city proper and its nuisances such as saloons, gambling dens, and, as he put it, houses of ill repute (although Anna and Eli had no idea what those were).

They passed dozens of large, comfortable homes surrounded by gardens, with vacant lots in between, or houses under construction. Theirs was on Harrison Street near the top of the hill around Second Street, but as the carriage climbed the gentle hill, rolling past beautiful houses with trees and lawns, Rachel Barnett refused to look around. She was tired and angry and determined to hate this new life. She already hated San Francisco—from what she had seen so far: "This city was built by men *for* men. Gambling halls and saloons! Gunfire in the streets. A lawless town unfit for women and children. And you brought us here, Mallory! You'll have that on your conscience. We were safe and happy in Oregon."

But when the hansom cab pulled up in front of a three-story house with balconies and verandahs, and wrought iron work and a roof that had spires and slants and a lookout tower like a palace, and Barnett said, "Here we are!" Rachel's eyes widened and Eli and Anna gave a cry.

He was right about the views. They could see the harbor and ships with hundreds of masts making a forest, and northward, not far, they saw tall buildings made of brick and stone all crowded together in what he called the business and shopping district. They could even see, way out in the bay, an island that he called Alcatraz. "Hard to believe," he boomed as the wind threatened to snatch bowler hat and bonnets, "that just four years ago this place was an adobe village and only Mexicans lived here! Gold's a funny thing."

They went inside the house and Anna saw at once that her mother was awestruck at the opulent interior. Nonetheless, she pursed her lips in displeasure and said, "I will need help. Maids, at least."

"We will have a cook and a butler, too," Barnett said, grinning proudly. He had done well in San Francisco, and wished to reward himself and his family for his hard work and cleverness.

It was because of the ships.

He had struck it rich in the gold fields, but soon they were packed and the life there was hard. Hearing of opportunities elsewhere, he had come to San Francisco, searching for ways to increase his fortune, when he saw his answer out in the Bay. The sight was astonishing, as he told the story. As far as the eye could see, abandoned ships clogged the channel and were so choked together that one could not see the water. Ships from China, Australia, and the Sandwich Islands, bringing goods to sell and trade, rotting in the harbor with their cargo still aboard because the captains and crews had jumped ship and headed for the gold fields.

Barnett had used his gold to purchase and remove the abandoned cargo and arrange for the goods to be shipped upriver to Sacramento—shirts and trousers, boots and hats, axes and shovels, lanterns and whale oil, sugar and coffee, and, his most popular import, liquor of all kinds. What was left over he stored in a warehouse for local sale. He sold everything at ten times what it cost him, and the demand was growing.

"Our own carriage and horse," he said in their new living room that smelled of fresh paint. "Anything your heart desires, my dearest."

Rachel's eyes went over the velvet drapes, flocked wallpaper, satin upholstery, crystal lamps, and fine marble fireplace. "Maids, definitely," she said again as she removed her bonnet. "A governess for the children, of course. We are going to have to keep up appearances, now that we are rich. New clothes for Anna and Eli as soon as possible. New gowns for myself. I will send for a seamstress. The best that San Francisco has to offer."

It amazed Anna how quickly her mother adapted and forgot her promise to be unhappy there.

"As for the governess, I will settle for no less than a well-educated lady of class and quality. If I have to send all the way to Boston for one . . ."

I think this is enough for one day, chérie," Cosette said to Anna. "We barely have room for our packages! And I do not know about the dog."

"But he's hungry," Anna said, "and I think he's sick. I'm going to take care of him."

"Your mama will not take in a stray."

"We'll see," Anna said, holding the skinny mutt on her lap.

The two girls were riding in their private carriage, a landau with the hood folded down so that they rode in the open air.

Cosette had been Anna's governess for the past two years. Rachel Barnett loved the new house and had adjusted almost overnight, buying new clothes and more furniture, and hiring staff (including a French governess). Although the lot their house stood on was, as Rachel put it, "no bigger than a cracker," she was resilient. What she lacked in acres she made up for in gowns. Rachel quickly made friends with other rich wives and together they formed a tightly knit elite society comprised of the wealthiest families in San Francisco. Rachel Barnett, former farm wife, hostessed elegant teas and dinner parties, invited writers and poets to her "salon." Held literary discussions in her parlor and soon was happily caught up in the center of a glamorous world she had never even dreamed of before.

But while her mother thrived and flourished in ways one would never have expected, once Anna's wonder at seeing a city wore off, she had begun to sorely miss the farm and the animals, the creek and the boulder where she spent her days. There was very little "nature" in this new town that was so wild and lawless that a Vigilance Committee had to be formed and public hangings were commonplace.

Anna found the house, though large, confining. Streets with their wooden sidewalks and buildings made of brick and stone and wood, and congested traffic with horses and carriages and wagons and pedestrians—these were also confining. But worst of all was the new clothing her mother insisted she wear. No more calico farm dresses, no more going barefoot and without a hat. Rachel Barnett now had a new image of her family—one that must suit the grand new house and their new wealth.

And so the old restlessness invaded Anna's bones again, the yearning to see what lay beyond the horizon.

As their driver turned a corner to head up the hill to their house, the mongrel in Anna's arms suddenly let out a yelp and, before she could react, jumped out of the carriage to run down the street. "Wait!" she called. "Come back."

"He chases a cat, you see? No no, wait, chérie, you cannot go after him."

But Anna already called the coachman to stop and she jumped down to run in a very unladylike manner after the dog.

The cat veered suddenly and flew up a flight of stone steps of a large building standing between two empty lots. The dog scampered after it, with Anna charging up the stairs and Cosette behind her, wondering what a sight they must be!

The cat sought refuge on the other side of a towering door that stood open at the top of the stairway, and the mutt followed. "Wait," Cosette said, reaching Anna and seizing her arm. "You cannot go in there."

"Why not?"

"This is a hospital, chérie. You do not want to go in there."

Growing up among log cabins and Indian teepees, Anna was still adjusting to a city of brick and stone. She looked at the building's façade. It was made of brick, two stories tall with narrow windows spaced at intervals. She craned her neck to read the inscription on the stone lintel: MARINER'S HOSPITAL. "What's a hospital?"

"It is where poor people go to die. We have one in New Orleans. Poor people, when they are sick, come to a place like this."

Despite Cosette's protestations, Anna felt a compulsion to look inside. The entrance opened onto a central hall with doors leading to long rooms on either side. Anna saw rows of beds containing men who were moaning loudly, or crying out in pain, or retching into basins. The stench was overpowering. The two girls pressed their fur muffs to their faces to block out the smell.

"Come, chérie, we must leave at once."

Anna watched in grim fascination as a man in a bloody frock coat moved from one bed to another. At one, he paused to draw a sheet over the patient's face. An old woman followed him, her back bent, her gray hair escaping a dirty mob cap. Her dress and apron were likewise filthy. She carried a bucket into which the man threw bloody bandages. "Who are those two people?" Anna said, pointing.

"The man is a doctor. The old woman is a nurse."

Anna frowned. "What is a nurse?"

"Women who cannot find employment elsewhere. How do you say, the dregs of society. When no one else will hire them, and they need money, they come here to mop floors and feed the dying men. Or they become prostitutes. Or they do both. They aren't paid much. In New Orleans they were not paid at all. They made their living taking the possessions of patients who are brought in off the street, and sad little that is, too."

"Why aren't the men's families taking care of them?"

"They have no families. They have no homes."

Anna's eyes widened. Surely . . . there was always *someone*. A mother, wife, daughter who could care for these poor men. Like broken birds, she thought, and lame dogs. No one to take care of them except strangers.

And strangers—Anna saw now as she watched the nurse pull a bottle from her skirts, uncork it, take a healthy swig from it, wipe her hand across her mouth and hide the bottle again—who worked while drunk!

While Cosette plucked impatiently at her sleeve, Anna could not move. Across the entry hall, a door opened and two men came in carrying an unconscious sailor on a stretcher. "Hello! Got another one!"

Two women appeared from the other ward—shabbily dressed like the older one. "Fell from a yardarm," one of the men said. "Ain't come to since."

The women rushed to the new patient and rapidly searched his clothes, pulling out his pockets, taking his shoes. "Ain't got nothing on him," one of them groused. "All right, there's a spare bed that way."

Anna watched them carry the poor fellow into the other ward and lay him on a bed that had clearly just been vacated, as the sheets were rumpled and stained with blood. The nurses disappeared and the two men left.

"Come chérie, we must not be seen in this establishment. And I should imagine we will have to fumigate our clothes!"

"But they can't just leave that poor man."

"Come along, your mama will be wondering where we are."

Anna reluctantly left, greatly disturbed by what she had seen— men lying in their own filth, calling out for help but getting none, dying alone.

What a terrible place a hospital was. . . .

J ust one more stop, *chérie,*" Cosette said as she and Anna handed packages to their carriage driver, who waited patiently at the curb while his young mistress went shopping. "I must visit the drugstore."

San Francisco had just recovered from a devastating epidemic of Asiatic cholera and it was their first foray out of the house in weeks. Fifteen-year-old Anna and her governess had come to the business district with a list of things to buy and they were making the most of the excursion, visiting the shops, looking at the people, wondering if they could take tea in the dining room of Claridge's Hotel (they had only recently begun allowing unescorted ladies for luncheon).

Their latest visit was to Gleeson's Book Emporium, where Anna had purchased Mr. Nathaniel Hawthorne's latest work, *The House of the Seven Gables,* and now they were busily off to the chemist's shop.

For their shopping trip to Montgomery Street, Anna and Cosette were accompanied by a manservant and a maid, who carried their packages. The manservant acted as a bodyguard, as the girls were clearly from a wealthy family, in their wide crinoline skirts, fashionable shoulder capes, and matching muffs concealing their gloved hands. Their bonnets sported ribbons and flowers bunched to one side, which was the height of current fashion.

Rachel frequently reminded Anna what a lucky girl she was. She was already planning her daughter's coming-out party for next year, when she turned sixteen and would be introduced to the sons of wealthy families. Anna was going to make a "brilliant match," she would say.

Anna and Cosette followed a wooden sidewalk that was crowded with gentlemen in long frock coats and tall hats, miners wearing denim and suspenders, trappers and traders in buckskins and fringe, sailors and cowboys and merchants, while the muddy street was congested with wagons and carts and drays and carriages. All under the watchful eyes of their household staff.

They hurried along to Schott's and Colby's, chemist-pharmacists who dealt in drugs, medicine, perfumes, toilet soaps, and mineral waters, as well as prescriptions. They advertised in newspapers: "For sale both wholesale and retail, French Quinine, Opium, Morphine, Bull's Sarsaparilla, English Cod Liver Oil, Extract of Colocynth and many other items."

Anna couldn't say why, but she loved visiting the drugstore. It wasn't anything she could put a finger on, or put into words. It was just a feeling—strong and warm—whenever she came through the door and saw the shelves rising to the high ceiling stocked with jars and bottles and boxes and books. If she were pressed to describe what she felt, she would say, "It's just *right*, that's all. It's right to be here, among all these wonderful cures and remedies. The drugstore, with its cupboards and shelves filled with medicines and powders and tonics, is a place of hope. Somehow," Anna would say, "your pain or ailment is diminished a little, just by being here."

They were there for Cosette, who suffered from painful monthly cramps and was seeking a remedy. She had gone to three different doctors, the first of whom had told her to stop reading romance novels. The second had told her to abstain from using too much perfume, and the third had staunchly commanded her to find herself a husband and get herself with child as quickly as possible.

"The problem," she said to Anna as they waited their turn to see the chemist, "is that men can't understand women's problems and so they cannot help us."

"But a lady doctor would, right?"

"There are no lady doctors."

"Why not?"

Cosette shrugged. "They just don't allow women to be doctors."

Thinking that it didn't seem right, because women could benefit greatly from women doctors, and wondering just who "they" were that made such rules, Anna started to reach for the large glass jar of peppermint sticks, when the bell above the door jingled and a most extraordinary creature entered the shop.

Anna gasped and her jaw dropped open, and Cosette whispered, "Don't stare, it isn't polite."

But she could not stop staring. There, in the middle of a modern drugstore, coming down the aisle right toward her, was a woman in long flowing robes and a black veil with a white cloth framing her face just like Jesus's mother in *Hingham's Illustrated Bible For Children*. "Is she an actress?" Anna asked, although she had no idea what sort of play would involve a lady garbed in many layers of black cloth and having her face pinched by a white, stiffly starched garment, which Anna thought was called a wimple.

"She is a religious Sister. We have them in New Orleans."

Cosette Renaud was an educated lady of French descent. When her husband had come down with "gold fever," she had accompanied him on the journey from New Orleans to San Francisco Bay. They had not been in the gold camps long when an unfortunate fall from a wagon claimed Pierre Renaud's life, leaving his widow on her own and without a protector. Many women in the camps, finding themselves in similar circumstance, took up employment to survive, as cooks, laundresses, or prostitutes. But Cosette Renaud was a young lady of breeding and quality, and so with the small amount of gold Pierre had found, she took a steamer down the American River. When she arrived in San Francisco and found a rough town of wooden sidewalks and muddy streets and men everywhere, and knowing she would not find a hotel that would give a room to an unchaperoned lady, she hired a cab and asked to be taken to the nearest Catholic church.

The pastor was Father Riley, and upon hearing her plight he was able to find accommodations before the day was out, with a good Catholic family who gladly took her gold nuggets in exchange for room and board. Cosette advertised herself as a governess in San Francisco's many newspapers and within days received more offers of employment than she could handle—with so many newly rich wanting to add a "real French governess" to their status symbols. Cosette liked the Barnett's big roomy house on Rincon Hill, and she later told Anna that she had taken an immediate liking to her and Eli, and so she had accepted the post.

In the five years since, Anna had learned a lot from the refined Cosette, and today Anna learned yet another lesson, as they waited for assistance from the druggist, about women who joined religious societies in which they wore strange attire and devoted their lives to serving the church. "They make altar cloths and priests' vestments," Cosette said quietly, "and the bread for Communion. The Sister you are so rudely staring at is a member of the Sisters of Good Hope, who are dedicated to taking care of the sick."

"Most religious Sisters are nuns," Cosette added when she saw Anna's puzzled frown. "That means they live behind high walls and never leave. So you rarely see them, even in New Orleans, which is a very Catholic town. But these are what we call 'walking Sisters,' which means their work is outside the convent. They visit hospitals and private homes and nurse the sick and dying."

Anna was stunned. "She goes *into* a hospital? But she looks so respectable."

"That is precisely *why* she visits the sick in hospitals. Because they need her help most of all. You saw how useless nurses are."

The Sister carried a black leather satchel, and her waist was cinched with a thin rope from which a curious string of beads was suspended. When she handed a list to one of the drugstore clerks, Anna heard the soft-spoken Sister inquire whether the arsenic had come in. Anna watched in open interest as the clerk placed items on the counter that he retrieved from shelves, and she put them in her bag, paid him, and thanked him in a gentle way.

After the Sister left, her long black veil and black skirts billowing out around her as she opened the door to the street, Anna stood spellbound, suddenly gripped by the most intense curiosity she had ever experienced.

She wanted to know more. "Let's follow her!" she said impulsively.

Before Cosette could protest, Anna was flying out of the drug-store in an unladylike manner that would have earned a scolding from her mother. Their carriage was standing outside, with the maid and manservant waiting patiently. Anna looked to her right, down the street, and saw the Sister climb into a small carriage, take the reins, and drive off.

"Miss Anna!" Cosette said breathlessly, holding onto her bonnet as she caught up with her charge.

"Quickly," Anna said as she climbed in, so that the maid and manservant took their seats and the driver picked up the reins.

Anna kept her eyes forward while Cosette protested and the two servants exchanged puzzled looks. She watched the little buggy creep along Montgomery Street, the Sister deftly weaving through traffic like a seasoned cabby. How brave! Anna thought.

She turned the corner onto California Street and presently Anna's carriage did the same, the wheels making a loud noise due to the planking which the city had begun laying down to prevent great muddy quagmires when it rained. While Cosette complained that they were going in the wrong direction from home, Anna was intent upon her quarry.

The Sister turned off California onto Stockton and drew the buggy to a halt in front of a large stone building, two stories high, with many windows.

"Goodness!" Anna cried, recognizing the place. It was the awful Mariner's Hospital.

She frowned. The engraving on the lintel now identified it as Good Hope Hospital.

"Please stop here," Anna said to their driver and watched as the black-robed lady alighted from the buggy, carrying her black bag, and walked up the steps of the hospital's entrance.

Anna stared at the double doors, tall and imposing, to the right of which stood a white statue of a lady in robes similar to what the Sister wore. Anna wondered who it was it was. The statue hadn't been there three years ago.

While their carriage driver eased his shoulders back into a comfortable slump, and the two servants looked at Anna expectantly, Cosette said, "We should be going. Your mother will be wondering where we are. And I still have to go back to the drugstore and buy my medicine."

"I'm sorry, Cosette," Anna said in genuine regret, knowing she was acting selfishly. "We *will* go back. But first I must have a quick peek inside."

"*Sacré bleu!*" Cosette cried.

"It's changed, Cosette. I want to see. I shall be but a moment," Anna said and stepped down from the carriage. Cosette followed. They mounted the steps and Anna grasped the great iron door handle.

They found themselves in the familiar entry hall with many doors. But the place had changed. The smell was far less pungent, and two gentlemen in long frock coats and top hats, with whiskered jowls and stern expressions, who were conferring on a medical matter, were *clean*. There were paintings on the wall that Cosette said were of Saints Peter and Paul. Male attendants wearing gloves and rubber aprons walked by with buckets and armloads of blankets.

"We must leave," Cosette whispered, and reached for Anna's arm.

But Anna wanted to see what else had changed. She walked through the door of the sick ward, her eyes adjusting to the dimness. Just as it had been three years ago, the interior of the hospital was dark. The windows were closed, with curtains drawn. Smoky oil lamps burned beside each bed. But now she saw that the patients slept between clean sheets and were no longer ignored. Male attendants removed chamber pots, pushed wooden carts filled with supplies, brought trays of food to the patients. And now there was a cross above each bed, and black-robed Sisters silently glided about their unpleasant labors as if they were picking roses, bending over the suffering men, the black veils and robes flowing and fluttering like spirits from another world.

Anna did not know about counting pulses, or how to feel for a fever, or any of the myriad technical tasks the holy Sisters were performing in that sick ward. She could only watch spellbound as a strange and wondrous joy filled her. It was inexplicable. Cosette whispered, "This is a terrible place!" While Anna's heart said, No, it is a wonderful place.

Her eye was drawn to the patient in the nearest bed, a boy of perhaps ten years, lying beneath clean sheets, laboring for breath. His face shone with perspiration, his cheeks were bright. His large, staring eyes were shadowed and sunken. His arms, lying upon the sheets, were like twigs.

Anna moved toward the bed while Cosette hissed, "*Sacré bleu*, Miss Anna! Are you possessed?"

Anna stood at the side of the bed and smiled down at the feverish boy. "Hello," she said.

His eyes met hers. Their gazes locked for a long moment, then he parted dry lips and whispered, "Water, please."

There was a little table by the head of the bed, bearing a water pitcher and a glass. Filling the glass, Anna slipped her arm under his pillow, lifting him up, and he took a few sips before closing his eyes and saying, "Thank you."

Anna froze for one brief instant. She could not move. Her arm stayed beneath the pillow, the glass remained at his parched lips while inside her chest, behind hard breastbone and rib, she felt something soft and sweet flutter. Tender feelings filled her. He was so frail and helpless, like a little sparrow. And her heart was so moved with compassion in that moment that her tears fell on the child's face.

She thought: You have no mama, that's why you're here. All these sick people have nowhere to go and no one to take care of them. You were a little baby once and I'll bet your mother kissed your little pink head and told you that you were her sweet boy. Where did she go? Did she die? What sickness ails you, little boy? You're like a baby bird that's fallen from its nest. I can feel your tragic bones beneath your wasting skin. Don't worry, don't worry. These lovely Sisters with kind hands and religious smiles will take very good care of you.

Anna felt a change sweep over her, and her mind was suddenly filled with *understanding*. This was why she brought injured sparrows and stray dogs home. This was where she belonged.

Cosette took Anna's arm, as one of the Sisters was approaching them with a disapproving look on her face. She carried a broom as if she meant to sweep them out. Anna went willingly with Cosette, because she knew she was coming back.

CHAPTER NINE

"Your mother will never approve, *chérie,*" Cosette said as they followed the narrow brick walk to the white cottage that stood opposite Good Hope Hospital. A modest sign identified the residence as being the Convent of the Sisters of Good Hope. A brass plaque next to the doorbell read: "Hope for Those in Need."

"Already she is talking of sending away to Paris for your wedding gown! You are only fifteen, and already she is thinking of marriage. Your mother will be very upset. Religious Sisters do not have husbands or children. And membership is for life. Once you take the vows, you cannot leave."

"You've explained it all to me, Cosette."

The front door swung open and a girl not much older than Anna appeared in a modified habit: it was made of the same black serge as the full habits, but of shorter length. Her veil was white and short, without coif or wimple. Cosette spoke: "We have an appointment with Mother Superior."

It had taken Anna a week of cajoling and persuading to finally get Cosette to agree to help her find out more information about the nursing Sisterhood. Being Catholic, she knew about these things and had arranged an appointment for them—against her better judgment.

They were led along a narrow hall that was filled with many fragrances and aromas: the smell of tallow and beeswax, of laundry soap and bleach, of bread baking in an oven, of cloth under a hot iron—the smells of hard labor and industry.

They were taken into a surprisingly handsome parlor—surprising because the exterior of the house was plain and unassuming. Dark paneling covered the walls, with built-in bookshelves crammed with volumes. A painting hung over the fireplace. It depicted a young nun standing in a flower garden. In her left hand she was holding a prayer book, open to an illuminated page. In her right, she held a small blossom. Her robes fell so gracefully on her slender form that they looked like waterfalls.

"I see you like our new acquisition," a voice said and they turned to see a plump, middle-aged woman enter the parlor. She wore a full black habit, her face pinched within the starched white wimple. The long wooden rosary hanging from her belt made a clicking sound as she came forward with her hand extended. "I'm Mother Matilda. Welcome to our house." She had a firm grip and her eyes sparkled with intelligence and humor.

"She is beautiful," Cosette said of the painting. "Who is she?"

"It is a gift from a man whose daughter we nursed through the cholera. In gratitude he commissioned an artist to capture what he called the essence of our Order."

Mother Matilda took a seat behind the desk. On the paneled wall behind her was a framed needlepoint that said, "Before All Things and Above All Things Care Must Be Taken of the Sick." St. Benedict— A.D. 480.

She invited her visitors to sit in two straight-backed chairs and, looking from Cosette to Anna, she said, "Do I assume you have questions about our Order?"

Cosette began to speak, but Anna said impulsively, "I wish to join, Reverend Mother."

Matilda smiled and folded her hands on the desk. "I see. Do you have the vocation?"

"The what?"

"Did you receive a call from God?"

"Oh yes. He called me when I was ten years old," and as Anna spoke these words, she realized it was true. For what else could explain the compulsion that drew her away from the cabin and her chores, to be out among God's creations? And didn't it say somewhere in the Bible that God took care of sparrows?

"I so have a desire to take care of people, Reverend Mother. I would love to help in your hospital and ease the suffering of others."

"You need to know that nursing Sisters adhere to a higher standard of care than ordinary paid nurses who, I am sure you have heard, are usually women of very low morals and are often given to drink. And public hospitals are appalling places."

"Oh yes, Mother," Anna said in her excitement, forgetting the correct term of address. "Three years ago I went inside the Mariner's Hospital and it was a terrible place. But then the other day I went back, and it's all changed."

Mother Matilda gave her a look of surprise. "You noticed that? When our small group came to San Francisco five years ago, we confined ourselves to home visits. But then we saw the great need in the hospital and so we contracted with the County to take over its administration. Yes, we made a few changes.

"Our Order goes back five hundred years to our founding in England. With the dissolution of the monasteries under the Protestant Reformation, we were forced to flee to other countries, where we continued to flourish and grow. Our founder wrote two famous medical books, *Herbarius* and *Causae et Curae,* and she also experienced visions of Jesus and the Saints. . . ."

When the subject turned to religion, Anna's attention drifted. She couldn't stop thinking about the two old medical books Matilda had mentioned, and she imagined the wonderful wisdom they must contain. She hoped she would be allowed to read them.

Mother Matilda fixed Anna with a serious eye, taking in the expensive clothes, the rich, red-gold hair twisted into long braids. "I applaud your selfless ambition, Miss Barnett, but I must warn you that sacrifices will be demanded of you. You must be prepared to give up worldly things. And we are not idle here. The Sisters spend much of their time in the herb garden and manufacturing remedies. Do you think you are up to that?"

"We didn't have a doctor where we lived, so the farm wives shared their families' home remedies. We made our own cough syrup by mashing onions in sugar. Gunpowder dissolved in water made an excellent eyewash. Onion juice and warm tobacco leaves cured earaches. And a staple remedy for chest ailments was goose grease and turpentine. I would love to work in your herb garden."

Mother Matilda gave this some thought, straightening papers on her desk that were already straight. "We are a self-sufficient house, Miss Barnett. We do not rely on outsiders to provide for us. We do more than work in a garden."

"My family wasn't always rich, Reverend Mother," Anna said earnestly. "That came later. On the farm where I grew up we didn't have fancy shops like here in San Francisco. We made our own soap from animal fat and lye. We made our own cloth dye from bark and plants. If we wanted jam, we boiled carrots with sugar syrup. I reckon there's nothing needs doing in this house that I'm not up to. You might think you see sitting before you a pampered city girl, Reverend Mother, but I'm a country girl, born and bred."

Mother Matilda smiled. "Very well, you do not flinch from honest labor. But there is more to entering our Order than rolling up your sleeves. You will have to make sacrifices, give up things that you would otherwise have in the outside world. For instance, we all take a vow of chastity. Do you know what that means?"

Anna hesitated. She knew that chastity meant giving up a chance at motherhood, but the work of the Sisterhood was an even higher calling. "I am prepared for the sacrifices," she said.

"There is one more thing, Anna. In order to join us, you must convert to Catholicism."

It seemed an easy thing. Anna already believed in God and Jesus. She had read the New Testament and had attended Sunday services at the Methodist Church where missionaries were converting the Indians. "Gladly," she said.

But Mother Matilda said, "I want you to attend Mass on Sunday before you make this decision."

"I will take her," Cosette said happily, catching the spirit of Anna's new goal, and remembering her own love for her religion, which she thought was more beautiful than any other faith in the world.

"Should you be granted admission into our house," Mother

Matilda said, "there will be three years of intensive studies. Not only will you be instructed in catechism, but you must learn the history of the Church, you will read the lives of the saints and martyrs. You will read the Latin philosophers and theologians such as Saint Augustine and Saint Jerome. Besides your religious studies, you will be instructed in mathematics and chemistry, human anatomy and physiology. It will be a full course of studies besides your assigned duties here at the convent, as you will join your Sisters in cooking and cleaning, laundry and sewing, and when you are ready, you will go out with the Sisters into the city and visit the sick. Are you up to such a task, daughter?"

"Oh yes, Reverend Mother, I am!"

She tilted her burdened head to one side. "I want you to take a few days and think of what you will miss. No husband, no children. The Sisterhood will become your family."

"It seems a wonderful family to belong to."

"I will need signed permission from both your parents. Once that is taken care of, we will accept you into our little family, and your instruction will begin."

J ust follow my lead," Cosette said as they walked up the steps of the church, joining an eclectic crowd of rich and poor, Mexican and white. "There is kneeling and standing and sitting, and repeating what the priest says. You already know how to cross yourself. You learned that quickly."

Anna's parents were not devout churchgoers. They had attended services at the Methodists' mission in Oregon for the social aspect, and in San Francisco they occasionally went to Sunday services at a Lutheran church on California Street. They had no objection to their daughter accompanying her governess, "out of curiosity," as Anna had said, which was true. She had yet to tell her mother and father of her intentions to join a religious order.

She did everything that Cosette did, rising with everyone else, and then kneeling, and sitting back for the sermon. But she stayed in the pew when Cosette joined the line at the altar to receive Holy Communion. The Latin made no sense to Anna, but it sounded exotic and mysterious. She loved the fragrance of the incense and the profusion of flowers. The gentle sound of the altar bells. The colorful sunbeams streaming through tall stained glass windows. Catholicism, she thought, was a religion of the senses, delighting eye and ear and nose.

Fifteen-year-old Anna smiled to herself and thought: I shall very much enjoy being a Catholic.

It was raining. A cold and gloomy day. But Mr. Barnett came through the front door shouting out their names in the excited voice that always meant he had something special for them. "Generous to a fault," Rachel Barnett always said of her husband.

"Wait till you see what I've brought home for my precious ladies!" he boomed as he strode into the parlor where Anna and her mother had been sitting in silence. He didn't notice that his wife did not rise when he came in as she usually did, that Anna did not greet him. Shouting over his shoulder, "Bring it in here, boys!" he stretched his face into such a smile that it looked as if it might stick that way.

Anna and her mother watched as two men brought a heavy trunk into the parlor, setting it down on the carpet, respectfully tugging their caps before departing. "I was down at the docks early," Barnett said as he unlatched the lid of the trunk. "I bought these for a song! The captain was in a hurry to leave for Vancouver, he let me have this for half the asking price."

Flinging back the trunk's lid, he turned his beaming smile at them. "Well? What do you think?" Reaching for a bolt and drawing it out—a shimmering green fabric that cast the firelight back in emerald flashes—he said, "Fresh from China! The finest silk they make! Have you ever seen such yellows and reds? Look here, this one's embroidered. Imagine the beautiful gowns you will make from these. You will be the envy of every woman in California!"

He stopped, his smile vanishing. "What's wrong? I thought you'd be dancing a jig and smothering me with kisses. Not even a smile?"

Remaining seated with her hands clasped tightly in her lap, Rachel said, "Anna has something to tell you, Mallory. It would be best if you sat down."

Now he saw her pale face, how stiffly she sat. "My God," he said, rushing forward. "Are you all right, Anna? Are you sick?"

"No, Papa. I am very well. I have some news."

He frowned. "News? What news?"

She was nervous. She didn't know how he would take it.

Anna had no wish to hurt her parents. She knew her mother was a well-meaning woman who wanted only the best for her children, and that her father worked hard to give them a good life. She had suspected they would not approve, but in her naïveté and in the joy of her newly found place in life, she had been unprepared for her mother's extreme reaction to the news.

As Anna hesitated, Rachel blurted out, "Our daughter wants to convert to Catholicism!"

He wrinkled his nose. "What? Catholicism? You mean those folks over at St. Urban's? Lot of Mexicans and Irish, isn't it?"

"She wants to become a nun!"

His perplexity grew. "You mean like the ones back in Boston? Those women who go about in long religious robes? Why would Anna want to be one of those?"

"They are a nursing order here in the city," she said in a tight voice, as if she were delivering the worst news a person had ever heard. "They work at Good Hope Hospital. Your daughter . . . wants to be a nurse."

Anna's father frowned. Then his eyebrows arched. "Eh?" he said. "What are you on about? Nuns? Nurses? Our Anna's going to be married to the finest catch this city has to offer. Already me and Harry Connor who owns the ironworks, and is a good sight richer than me, have talked about what a fine couple his Edward and my Anna will make when the time's right." He waved a hand as if a gnat had entered the room and turned back to the trunk filled with silks. "Now look at this white stuff here. Tell me this won't make the grand-est wedding gown—"

"Papa," Anna said. "I want to join the Sisters of Good Hope. I want to do something important with my life."

He turned and put his hands on his hips, the gold watch chain festooning his paunch catching the fire's glow. "Now see here, little girl, you can put that nonsense from your head right now. Get married and give me grandchildren. There's nothing more important in a woman's life than that."

"Father," she said, rising from her chair. "I wish to nurse the sick."

"Nurses are little better than whores! It's an occupation for a woman in desperate circumstances, not for a respectable lady—"

"The Sisters of Good Hope are respectable, Father."

"I've seen inside a hospital and there's no worse place on earth!"

"But the Hospital of Good Hope is different."

Anna's father was a ginger-haired man, with a ginger moustache, ginger whiskers, and ginger eyes. When he stood in the firelight, he resembled an elf in one of her childhood picture books. He was stout, too, like he could sit on a toadstool. He had a merry nature and many friends. He was a hardworking man and if he liked to visit the saloons and gambling salons occasionally, no one blamed him (although Anna sometimes heard her mother weeping when he came home smelling of perfume). He had the amazing skill of agreeing with everyone around him while still maintaining his own opposite opinion, which made him very likeable.

He had called Anna "Egg" ever since she could remember. Back in Oregon, he would wade through the tall grass where she was playing, come to a stop, ham-hands on his hips, and say, "What's this? Some kind of bird's laid an egg in my field." He would bend down and scoop her up and carry her home on his shoulder calling for her mother, "Rachel? I've got a great big egg we can cook up for supper!" And Anna would giggle hysterically.

She wanted him to call her Egg now. She wanted him to knot his ginger brow and pretend to give this nursing issue a lot of thought and then say, "Egg, if that's what you want then that's what you'll get."

Instead his eyes took on a queer look and he seemed to withdraw into himself, this outgoing gentleman who bought beers for strangers and handed gold nuggets to beggars, who loved his daughter with everything he had, whose dream to strike it rich had nothing to do with his own comfort and everything to do with hers, his Egg, his little precious foundling in the tall golden grass of Oregon.

Nothing in the world could have prepared Anna for the pain in his eyes—the disbelief that she could betray him like this. He stood like an impotent old man in the middle of the carpet. Then he turned and left the room, kicking the trunk full of silk on the way, as if it had made him the biggest chump in the world.

After a week of uncomfortable silence in the house, with Barnett leaving at dawn and coming home well after dark, Anna worked up the courage to face him as he frowned over great ledgers in his study. A fire burned in the fireplace, lamps glowed softly, and the rain made a gentle sound against the windows. This was not a happy house. Anna knew that her joy had ruined everything.

"Father," she said, "there is a need inside me to take care of people. I can't help it. And I can't send it away. I've tried, but the need grows."

He didn't lift his eyes from the columns of numbers. "You can take care of a husband and children."

"It isn't enough."

He finally looked at her and the pain was still there; it hadn't even begun to fade from his eyes. More than ever she longed for him to call her Egg. "When you was little you was always bringing home birds with broken wings. You cried hysterically when a newborn calf died. You were inconsolable when a chicken disease took our hens." He shook his ginger-colored hair. "I told you a farm girl can't get attached to something that's going to be her dinner."

She started to cry. Painful, racking sobs came from her body. It was from frustration that she couldn't find the words, or paint the picture, or compose the symphony that would make him understand.

He sighed, and it was a sad sound, as if his soul were seeping out of him. "You want to give up love and romance and motherhood. You want to be poor and chaste and have to obey so many unnatural rules."

"It's the price I have to pay," Anna said softly, tears streaming down her face because, in her heart, she didn't want to give up anything. She wanted to be normal and live a normal life—she wanted to have children—but she also wanted to be a nurse. "A price I am willing to pay," she added in a broken voice.

The hurt in his eyes turned to disappointment, and that was worse than any anger. Then he shook his head and went back to his accounting.

Weeks went by and the hole in Anna's heart grew. The feeling of completeness that had filled her in the hospital went away and left a void inside her that was cold and unbearable. Rachel took her to parks, to the seaside. Barnett showered her with dresses and bonnets, but she was hollow. She yearned for Oregon, she yearned for the convent. She tried to forget these things. Yet try though she did to conform to her parents' wishes, to be the daughter they dreamed of, she could not.

Her mother took her to doctors. One said Anna was suffering from melancholia. Another said her problem was hysteria. They blamed her womb. They prescribed pills and tonics. Her mother scolded her. She cried. She asked Anna over and over, "Why?" She even tried guilt: "You don't care that I labored to give birth to you in a covered wagon in the middle of hostile Indian territory. For twenty-five long and agonizing hours I suffered excruciating pains and felt my flesh tear and the blood run out of me until I thought I would die. Never mind that your father thought he was losing me that day and he was helpless to do anything until you came screaming into the world, all wet and cold and as helpless as your father, but I sat up in my exhaustion and brought you to my breast and soon we were on our way again, even though I was in pain and still bleeding but we had to get away from the Indians. Never mind the hell and torture I went through to find a better life away from the choking cotton mills, to give my children a better life."

But in the end, all she could say was, "She's always been different, Mallory. You know that. She was wild as a little girl, and now she is a willful young lady. I cannot sleep, Mallory, we cannot go on like this. Let her join the convent. You know that things will not improve. And we have Eli to think of. His sister's mental state is affecting him, and he is turning into such a fine boy. Let her go," Anna's mother added in a bitter tone. "See how she likes living like a mill girl, crammed in with other girls and living by bells and whistles and other people's rules. She'll be running back home before it's time for those final vows."

But Barnett said, "My daughter will be no nurse, and that's the end of it."

And then one day Mallory Barnett came home a changed man. Calling Rachel and Anna into the parlor, he stood before the fireplace and said, "I was at the docks this morning, looking over a shipment of oranges and coffee from the Sandwich Islands. A large crate fell off a dray and landed on a man, crushing his leg. A group of us said we would take him home. But he had no home, having only just come to San Francisco. He said his name was Barney Northcote and he was all alone in the world. So we loaded him into a wagon and took him to the hospital on Stockton Street. The one that's called Good Hope. We said farewell to him because we knew he was a goner, but fear made him hold onto my hand as he begged me to stay by him until the end. So I did.

"A doctor came to examine him. He said he was a bone specialist and right there on the spot, he cleaned Northcote's leg, cut off some bad flesh and skin, set the bones straight, and put the leg between two boards. After that, the poor man was taken to a ward and put into a bed. I knew that such a wound was a death sentence, so I said good-bye to him and asked if there was anyone I could contact regarding his possessions.

"But before he could reply, one of those religious Sisters dressed all in black with a white apron came over and told me Mr. Northcote needed his rest. She was a clean woman, young I would say, and soft spoken. Her face was pretty, although pinched by that stiff white thing on her head. Her hands looked soft as she plumped his pillow and smoothed his blankets. She said she would be administering morphine and see to it that the leg did not become septic. She invited me to come back tomorrow to visit him, as he would surely be wanting to see his friends.

"I looked up and down the ward and saw neat beds with sleeping men. There were no bad smells. And these remarkable women, these Sisters, moving softly and silently at their labors, making me think they were heaven's own angels . . . don't ask me how I knew it, but I was certain Barney Northcote was going to recover after all and that what I was witnessing was nothing short of a miracle."

Barnett pressed a handkerchief to his eyes and said, "What man wouldn't be proud to know that his daughter was dedicating herself to such noble and selfless service? You may join the Sisters, Egg, with my blessing."

Anna was sixteen the day she was confirmed into the Catholic faith. She had spent a year in religious instruction under the tutelage of a lay teacher named Mrs. Sanchez. Once a week Anna went to Mrs. Sanchez's house where, with others wishing to convert, she learned the catechism and the liturgy of the Mass, and learned about sins and the sacraments. Father Riley baptized her, heard her first confession, and administered her first Holy Communion.

On the day of Anna's confirmation, when Father Riley beamed with pride as the bishop tapped her cheek, Mallory Barnett threw a huge party and made a generous donation to the church, bragging to everyone that his daughter was to become a "holy Sister."

Anna's mother had long since resigned herself to losing her, as she put it. But by then she had had another baby, a girl, so that between Anna's brother Eli and little Helen, she still had her perfect family.

Still, she stayed home the day Barnett delivered Anna to the convent, where she was to live as a postulant and then a novice until she took her final vows three years hence.

Barnett kissed Anna on the forehead and left her to ring the bell and go inside. She cried, both for joy and sadness. She was entering her "place" in the world, but she was leaving her girlhood—and the world of pleasures and luxury—behind.

Two other girls, Alice and Louisa, entered the convent with her and they were all taken under the wing of Sister Agnes, who was, at age forty, a senior Sister. They were escorted to the postulant's dormitory, which was a bedroom in the house with six modest iron beds, made private by curtains hanging from the ceiling.

Anna was now restricted by more rules than ever, and confined within walls. But she welcomed the lack of personal freedom because she saw it as the price she must pay in exchange for a life she knew she was born to live. And so the postulant's robes and veil and heavy shoes and tight stockings were not to be chafed at but to be welcomed, as a reminder of the great service into which she was soon to enter.

Anna did her best to mimic the others—Alice and Louisa, the saintly novices who were a year ahead of her, and the fully professed nuns. They all sang so serenely in chapel, and sat so perfectly still in meditation, and knelt seemingly without impatience. Whereas Anna found herself filled with impatience during chapel, her thoughts racing ahead to her next lessons, to her next visit to the hospital, where she was allowed to help serve the soup and bread to patients. They sang their Hail Marys and Anna thought of the day she would receive her own black medical bag and begin to nurse the sick in earnest.

Anna learned that the Order did not charge for charitable services. The members took vows of poverty, and so they relied upon the generosity of others to support their mission. The convent—which began as a modest cottage but which now consisted of a chapel, a dormitory, a kitchen, dining room, parlor, and classroom—had been donated by a wealthy San Franciscan who owned wineries in Napa and Sonoma. Food was given to the Sisters by local Catholic grocers, Mexicans who had not left when their country had lost the war to America and California had become a state. The Sisters did their own laundry and sewing, but the cloth for their habits came from Weston and Sons, owned by another Catholic businessman, on Montgomery Street. And when they must venture out farther than was feasible on foot, they had the loan of a carriage from a livery on Sansome.

Anna discovered that there were many Catholics in San Francisco, as Catholicism had been brought here by Spanish explorers and traders three centuries ago. And then, a hundred years ago, Franciscan Fathers had established the Missions up and down the coast, twenty-one in all, for the conversion and care of the native Indians.

Anna became friends with Louisa. She helped her with lessons, as Louisa seemed a little slow. She told Anna her mother had dropped her when she was a baby and she wondered if that was why lessons were so hard for her. She worried all the time that she would never make it to final vows but Anna told her she was going to make a wonderful nun.

Every night before going to sleep, Louisa would sit on the edge of Anna's bed and tell her how pretty she was and how glad she was that they were friends. Louisa's family wasn't well off. Her father alternated between being drunk or holding a job, so her mother sewed shrouds for a casket maker. They had six girls and no sons. "One has to go into the Church," Louisa's father had announced during a sober spell when he drove a milk wagon. "Don't care which one. Flip a coin." They had chosen Louisa because she was quiet and uncomplaining and wouldn't care where she went as long as people were nice to her.

In Anna's first year with the Sisters, she saw how they received a kind of respect that ordinary women did not, because nuns were important in a way no one else was. People (Catholics, mostly) were respectful and courteous and looked at the full-habit nuns with a mixture of awe and fear. Their mouths said, "Good afternoon, Sister," while their eyes said, "You are not natural. You work directly for God. You have hidden powers."

Upon entering a sickroom," Sister Agnes said as she stood at the head of her small class, with a black chalkboard behind her, "the first thing you do is make sure the windows are closed and the curtains drawn. You must not let sunlight or air from the outside get in. Sick people need darkness and still air."

The three postulants sat at desks with inkwells and writing paper. They took careful notes of everything Agnes said.

"Now watch me, girls, this is how we determine if a patient has a fever or the chills. Press the back of your hand to your cheek like so—no, Louisa, not to your forehead. Once you are professed, your forehead will be covered. Yes, your cheek. This tells you normal body temperature. Now press the back of your hand to the patient's cheek. Can you tell if the skin is warmer or cooler than your own? This skill will come to you after enough practice."

They spent a few minutes feeling their faces and each other's, and then Sister Agnes resumed her lecture. "Occasionally, if there is no doctor available, you will be called upon to suture a wound. You girls need no instruction in this skill as you have already learned sewing from your mothers." Sister Agnes tipped her chin. "Male medical students must spend hours learning to sew, therefore you have the advantage."

Louisa giggled and Agnes silenced her with a look. "When you are preparing to leave the sickroom, and you leave medicines with the patient, be sure to demonstrate how to take the medicine. Most of our patients are poor and uneducated and simple-minded. I once left a bottle of tonic with a man and instructed him to take a spoonful three times a day. When next I saw him, I saw that the bottle was still full. When I asked why, he said he couldn't get the spoon into the bottle."

The three postulants graduated from study in the classroom to internships in the hospital itself. At first they boiled the linens to kill the lice, scrubbed the floors with soda and lye, emptied chamber pots, kept carbolic acid and clean bandages, fed patients meals that were wholesome and nourishing, prayed with those in their charge.

They were soon given their own patients and were allowed to join the other Sisters in medical skills: counting pulses, checking color, checking wounds, listening for heartbeats, administering morphine, assisting the doctors when they came, and at the end of it, watching the patients leave, either through the front door or through the back to a hearse.

Anna retired each night on her cot feeling supremely satisfied with the job she had done that day. They were showing the outside world how civilized nursing could be. And she saw her life mapped out before her in a succession of days filled with prayer, Sisterhood, pious benedictions, and, above all, grateful, mended patients.

M other Superior wishes to see you."
Anna looked up from her work, folding linens, in surprise. She stared at Sister Bethany. "She wants to see me? Why?"

"I don't know, dear, I was just sent to fetch you."

Nervously wiping her hands down her skirt—a summons from Mother Matilda often meant a reprimand—she approached the office door and knocked. "Come in," Mother Matilda called.

"*Benedicite*, Reverend Mother," Anna said, using the form of convent greeting that was also a blessing. "You wished to see me?" Anna was seventeen and had graduated to the novitiate, but she had yet to learn to relax in Mother Superior's presence.

"Yes, daughter. I am sending you out on your first house call."

Anna stared at her. "What?" she said without thinking, quickly amending it to, "Oh thank you, Reverend Mother!"

"You will be accompanying Sister Agnes."

An uncharitable thought entered Anna's head. She did not like Sister Agnes, who never smiled and acted like she was closer to God than anyone. "Might I go with Sister Margaret instead?" she said. "Forgive me," she said, immediately retracting her words.

"You will go with Sister Agnes, my dear. *Benedicite.*"

They left an hour later, walking in silence down busy streets, ignoring stares and comments, until they reached the small wooden house on Kearny Street.

They didn't knock, but let themselves in, as Sister Agnes came regularly to this house. They entered a vestibule with archways on either side that opened onto other rooms, with a staircase directly ahead. Something out of the corner of Anna's eye caught her attention. She looked into the parlor and saw two people on a sofa. They were naked. The woman was on her back, her legs in the air. The man was on top, his plump white buttocks going up and down.

Anna was paralyzed, but Sister Agnes seemed unfazed. She tugged at Anna's sleeve and pointed to the stairs, reminding her of their duty. They climbed to the rooms above while the sounds of vigorous sex followed them into a dim bedroom where an elderly woman lay beneath the covers of her bed.

She smiled when she saw the nuns. Anna was only to watch on this occasion, while Sister Agnes took the woman's pulse, checked her eyes, tongue, color. Then Sister Agnes drew back the covers, lifted the lady's nightgown, and discreetly inspected her backside, where Anna saw three sores that appeared to be healing.

"Does your daughter turn you four times a day as I instructed?" Sister Agnes asked in a soft voice of which Anna would not have previously thought her capable.

"Yes, Sister. She does everything you tell her."

And a little more besides, Anna thought uncharitably as the sex grunts rose up through the wooden floor.

While Sister Agnes applied cream and administered an oral medicine, Anna looked around the room. The family was poor, judging by the homely, mismatched furniture, threadbare carpet, and curtains that admitted light through holes in the cloth. While the Sisters of Good Hope ministered occasionally to a rich patient, their devotion was to the poor and homeless. Their patients were all Catholic, not that the Sisters discriminated but Protestants didn't want Catholics touching them.

A large mirror stood over the wooden dresser and Anna caught a glimpse of herself. She was a novice now and wore a longer veil (though still white) and a short black cape over her shoulders. Her dress was black with a "day" bodice and no petticoats or crinolines so that it hung straight as an arrow. But she was coming closer to the image of the full-habit nun, and she liked what she saw.

They prayed with the lady in the bed (there was a large crucifix on the wall over her head) and lastly Sister Agnes sprinkled holy water on her forehead and blessed her. When they left, Anna saw that the downstairs parlor was empty. She wondered about the couple, who they were, where they had gone. She realized that she was going to enjoy home visiting, going inside people's houses, into their private places, seeing how they lived, seeing their secrets. It reminded her of her days as a girl, when she had wondered what lay beyond the horizon, what people were like in other countries.

She tried not to think about the sex she had witnessed. This was part of life that she was never going to experience. She couldn't wait to take final vows because she knew that once she was a fully professed nun, carnal thoughts would never again enter her head.

By the time of the day of Solemn Profession, there were only two, Anna and Louisa, as the other girl had dropped out. She had fallen in love with a young man who did carpentry for the nuns. They had run off to get married.

Mallory and Rachel Barnett attended the ceremony, along with Eli, now a tall handsome boy, and little Helen. Cosette was there, too. The ceremony was held in Saint Urban's church instead of in the convent chapel, and as it included the graduation of postulants to novices, a large congregation was gathered to celebrate the joy and sacred consecration of seven young women.

Anna and Louisa sang and carried candles and wore white wedding veils. Over each of their veils was fixed a crown of thorns, because a Bride of Christ must resemble her Spouse and welcome the sufferings the Lord would ask her to bear. The thorn pricks received on the joyful day of Solemn Profession were but a foretaste of the sacrifices to be asked of a nun by the Lord in the years to come. Mother Matilda assured them that when they finally knocked all the thorns off, a halo would be left in its place.

They knelt before the bishop, who asked each in turn: "Daughter, having completed the period of first profession required by the Rule of your Order, what is your desire?"

They each replied, "I ask to be allowed to make perpetual profession in this community of Sisters for the glory of God and the service of the Church."

The bishop dipped his thumb in sacred oil and traced the sign of the cross on their foreheads, saying, "May God Who has begun the good work in you bring it to fulfillment before the day of Christ Jesus."

They were given new names. Anna became Theresa, and Louisa was Veronica. They were taken to a vestibule off the altar where Mother Superior and Sister Agnes cut off their hair using heavy shears that sent clumps of locks into a basket on the floor. Anna watched her thick, red-gold curls tumble like marigolds, and thought it a small price to pay for her new, wonderful life.

Mother Superior then fitted tight coifs over the new Sisters' heads, tying the starched bibs around their necks, and fitting them with the starched wimple and black veil that would keep them from looking to the side and only straight ahead on their chosen path.

They then knelt before the altar and spread themselves prone, forming a cross with their bodies, their faces on the floor to show humility before God.

It was the happiest day Anna had known since her last happy day nine years prior, on their golden farm in Oregon. She was, once again, where she was meant to be.

Father Halloran was a lanky young man with orange hair and pale, freckled skin. His eyes were kind, but his words were dire and cut through to the heart of every Sister, novice, and postulant in the chapel (which now numbered nearly twenty, the Order was growing so fast).

Father Halloran was the pastor of a Catholic church in a town called Honolulu on the Sandwich Islands, and he spoke of the terrible circumstance that had befallen the natives of that place. "Hawai'i's first epidemic of smallpox swept through the islands seven years ago," he extolled from the pulpit. "It lasted a year and claimed one sixth of the population. King Kamehameha IV and his wife, Queen Emma, are very worried about the startling decline of the Hawai'ian population. In the Hawai'ian king's own words: 'We must stay the wasting hand that is destroying our people.'"

The Sisters listened in appalled silence as he spoke about this savage race of "wretched heathens" in the Pacific islands who were suffering terribly from ignorance and disease. When he told them that measles had recently swept the islands, claiming the lives of ten thousand natives, they all gasped out loud. While there were Protestants in the islands (whom he called pseudo-missionaries) ministering to the natives, there were sadly few Catholics (and those were French) so the call for help was great. When he asked who among them would brave hardships and self-sacrifices to help those poor people, Anna and her Sisters rose as a body, offering themselves.

Anna had no idea precisely where the Sandwich Islands lay, or what to expect there. Father Halloran spoke of the natives' depravity and decadence a mere two generations ago, when white men had arrived to find the island inhabitants walking about naked and praying to stones and trees. Anna felt a great urgency to go there and rescue them.

When six of the Sisters were selected, Mother Matilda cautioned them that the convent in Honolulu was to be completely self-sufficient, with no financial assistance from the Church or the Mother House in San Francisco. They could pray for generous donations but otherwise must find ways to keep themselves going.

They were to depart in a week under the protection of Father Halloran, and for Anna Barnett, now Sister Theresa, it was the fulfillment of a cherished dream.

On April 29, 1860, they set sail on the clipper ship *Syren,* a three-masted vessel known for speed.

Her family came to see her off.

They stood on the crowded dock as their trunks were loaded onto the ship. They were bringing Bibles to the heathens, as well as catechisms, rosaries, candles, communion wafers, medical supplies, and a nearly life-sized ceramic statue of Our Lady of Hope, carefully packed in straw in a secure crate. Anna's father gave her a small timepiece that she could pin to her habit for her nursing work. "I asked Mother Superior what to give you as a gift, and she said it must be something practical."

And then they embraced one last time. He held Anna so tightly that she could not breathe, and she drew upon her father's comforting strength, clutching him as she felt his chest vibrate when he said, "Take care of yourself, Egg. I'm mighty proud."

She clung to him. When she had begun her training at the hospital, she had been curious about the man with the crushed leg her father had brought in—Barney Northcote. There was no record of him. And when Sister Agnes told her there was no bone specialist there, she realized her father had made it up because they were at a standoff about her entering the Sisterhood and there was no proud way out of it as neither Anna nor he would give in. Ultimately, his love for her and his desire to grant her every wish had persuaded him to accept the fact that giving her the gift of chastity, poverty, and obedience, and a life of taking care of the sick, was greater for her than showering her with rubies and emeralds could ever be. He would never see her in gowns, or being courted by young men, he would never walk her down the aisle or hold her first baby in his arms. That was his dream and he gave it up, he sacrificed his own dream for her happiness and in this way he gave her the greatest gift of all.

Anna's mother cried and said, "I am glad you are going to tropical islands, that you are escaping the 'mill life' after all. It sounds very pleasant in those islands, and I pray you will find time to enjoy the outdoors there."

Cosette was there, too. "How will you do it, *chérie?*" she said teasingly. "I have heard that the Sandwich Islands is a land of palm trees and blue lagoons and eternal sunshine. It must be very difficult to remember one's vows in such a paradise!"

Anna smiled. "There will be no seduction in the Islands. It will be easy, in Paradise, to keep my vows."

They embraced and shed tears, and said good-bye, for Cosette was returning to her native New Orleans.

And then Anna joined the other Sisters for Father Riley's benediction, and to pray one last time with Mother Superior. Also, Sister Agnes was officially given the designation of "Reverend Mother," as she would be the superior of their new convent in the Islands.

As Anna followed the others up the gangway, she felt the warm Pacific sun penetrate the dark cloth of her habit, felt the heat go through her skin and into her bones and soul. And she knew the *Syren* was carrying her to her appointed destiny.

PART THREE

HONOLULU, OʻAHU

1860

CHAPTER TEN

here's an island in Pearl Harbor," Mr. Marks said as they stood on
the deck to look out at the busy harbor, "called Moku'ume'ume,
which means Island of the Sex Games. Back before the white man
came, if a married couple had trouble conceiving a child, they went to
that island, where they'd sit with other childless couples around a fire
and a kahuna would randomly select a man and a woman—not married
to each other, mind—to go off into the bushes for a bit of the old slap
and tickle. If the woman got with child, that child was regarded as the
son or daughter of the husband, not the man who did the diddling. If
no child resulted, they'd go back and try again! Quite a pleasant solution to the problem, eh, Padre?"

While Father Halloran muttered a response that the others could not
hear, Sister Theresa tried not to picture an island where licentious activities took place. Already her ears, and those of her Sisters, burned with
having heard many bawdy tales about the natives of Hawai'i. Mr. Marks was
a newspaper correspondent familiar with the Hawai'ian islands, and he
regaled his fellow passengers with colorful but sometimes shocking tales.
As the Syren glided across the water, with the crew getting ready for dock-
ing, Mr. Marks said, "The custom was, when a ship came to the islands,
maidens would strip off their clothing and swim out to take pleasure with
the sailors. The Protestant missionaries put a stop to that."

Moving out of earshot, Sister Theresa joined her Sisters at the ship's rail as they filled their eyes with the sight of their new home.

That morning, when land was sighted, they had come out on deck to watch the distant mountains grow larger on the horizon. As the *Syren* made steady progress over the rolling blue sea, Sister Theresa's eyes had widened at the astonishing sight—emerald green peaks shrouded in mist and rainbows, the shore fringed with tall palm trees bending in the breeze, the sky deep blue and infinite with rolling white clouds. Her new home.

"There's Honolulu!" the captain had cried. And now they were able to see wooden and grass huts with verandahs nestled under palms and banana trees, and church spires and a few gray roofs appearing above the trees.

They saw many ships, some under sail, others at anchor. Large blocky buildings—warehouses and shipping offices—crowded the waterfront. Flags of many nations snapped over rooftops or from ships' masts, the American flag dominating. How strange, Sister Theresa thought, to come so far and to such a foreign place, and still see the familiar stars and stripes of home.

Beyond the waterfront, she saw the buildings of Honolulu's mushrooming settlement—buildings of white stone, three and four stories tall; modest churches with tall spires; private houses, some humble, some grand, lining dirt streets. Beyond, a lush green plain ran away and up to the mountains in a graceful sweep.

The day was warm. Already Father Halloran, in his black cassock and wide-brimmed black hat, was sweating beneath his white cleric's collar. Sister Theresa and her companions felt the heat of the sun penetrate the thick fabric of their black habits, perspiration sprouting beneath starched white wimples. She turned her face this way and that, seeking the breeze for a bit of relief. Facing the wind, she saw a strange sight along a far beach: what appeared to be men walking on water. She blinked. She squinted. They were out on the surf, standing on the crests of waves, riding the waves like ancient sea gods risen from the ocean deep. And then she remembered what Father Halloran had said about the natives' passion for surfboard riding. It was one ancient pastime the Protestants had not been able to stamp out.

As the *Syren* sailed through the narrow channel, they saw a coral forest under the water, its marine inhabitants gliding in and out of the spiky reef in sparkling serenity. Men paddling outrigger canoes raced about with incredible skill, calling "Aloha!" in warm welcome. On the docks, a band played "God Save the Queen," even though the new arrivals were Americans, and a colorful crowd cheered as the ship was towed in.

The harbor was filled with vessels of all types—from schooners and whalers to dinghies and rowboats. The *Syren* was towed toward the waterfront by two small steam-powered paddlewheel boats that belched smoke from their tall stacks. But the little steamers brought the *Syren* through the congestion with ease, crewmen threw lines ashore, and dockworkers scrambled to secure the large vessel.

Father Halloran called his small flock together for a prayer of thanks. The six knelt before him on the deck and bowed their heads for the benediction, and they thanked God for safely delivering them to their destination.

When they said Amen and rose to their feet, brown-skinned girls came aboard, dressed in the loose, baggy dresses that the Americans knew were called "muumuus," in all the colors of the rainbow. The giggling young ladies swarmed around them, said "Aloha," and draped flower garlands around the newcomers' necks.

Mother Agnes clapped her hands and said, "Let us stay together, Sisters. We are now in unfamiliar territory with unknown pitfalls and perils before us. Remember what Father Halloran cautioned us about— to reach the convent we must pass through an unsavory section of town."

They knew she was referring to the many saloons and grog shops that lined the streets beyond the harbor. Father Halloran had warned them that with Honolulu being such a heavily trafficked port of call, sometimes as many as four thousand sailors could descend upon the town during a day of liberty in the harbor.

But Sister Theresa was eager to disembark. After so many weeks at sea, never standing still, battling sea sickness and often fearing they would all be washed overboard, she picked up her black bag, went to the railing, and looked longingly at the gangway. She knew she should wait for the others, but the solid pier beckoned. Lifting her voluminous hems, she delicately stepped onto the gangplank and hurried down, the black veils of her habit billowing out like a ship's sails.

When her feet touched the solid, unmoving planks, she closed her eyes and sent a prayer of thanks to God. She also prayed that she would never again be called upon to voyage in a sailing ship.

A loud crash disrupted her prayer. She looked around and saw that a large crate, being offloaded from a brigantine, had broken free of its harness and fallen to the dock. Workers shouted insults and blames at one another, while people walked by or stood in groups talking. In front of an office with glass windows and a sign that said Dealers in Sperm, Lard and Oil, two men appeared to be engaged in a friendly disagreement, with the short pudgy one wagging his finger and saying to his taller companion, "I'm telling you, Farrow, you're making a big mistake passing this up!"

Sister Theresa heard the other man say, "Whale oil is soon going to be a thing of the past, I'd be a fool to carry it on my ships," when she felt a sudden tug on her veil. Thinking it had caught on something, she turned to see a brutish man standing before her, a hank of the black material in his beefy fist.

He shocked her by stepping closer and giving her a leery grin. He stank of rum and his eyes were bloodshot. "What're you supposed to be?" he growled.

She was so stunned that she was without speech.

Another fellow appeared next to him, likewise dirty and unshaven and swaying on his feet. "Blimey!" he said with a toothless mouth. "She looks like she could do with having her porridge stirred, and I've got the stick to do it!"

They roared with laughter and the first pulled on her veil again, gathering more fabric between his fingers as if reeling in a fish. "Reckon you'll be good sport," he said. "Just unwrapping the package will be entertaining. What do you suppose is underneath, Frank?"

"Please," she said, trying to draw back. "Let me go."

A third joined them, men in tattered trousers and ragged jackets over striped sailor's shirts. They reeked of alcohol and closed in on her while people hurried past, intent on their own business.

"Please—" she tried to cry out but the breath caught in her chest. Where was Father Halloran? Where were her Sisters?

The third man wrinkled his nose as he reached up to her face. "What's this you're encased in? I seen an Egyptian mummy once. Is that what you are?"

But before he could touch her, a cane materialized from out of nowhere, cracking down on the man's arm so that he cried out and jumped back.

"Get back to your ship," the intruder said in a commanding voice. "You're cluttering up the pier."

Two of the men turned and scurried off, while the first who had accosted her dipped his head and mumbled, "Yes, sir. Sorry Cap'n Farrow, sir." And he then shambled off.

"Thank you, sir," she said breathlessly to her rescuer as she hastily restored her veil.

He fixed her with a disapproving frown. "This isn't a safe place for a woman on her own." He looked her up and down in curiosity, his eye lingering on her black bag and then on the rosary hanging from her belt. "It's dangerous here. You should have a gentleman escorting you."

She pointed up to the gangway, where Father Halloran was bidding farewell to the *Syren*'s master. When she saw her bare hand at the end of her sleeve, she quickly brought her arm down and, grasping her black bag with both hands, restored her exposed skin to the protection of her sleeves.

"Oh," the stranger said, looking at Father Halloran, "I see."

He was a handsome man, in his thirties she guessed, wearing a clean white linen frock coat over white trousers, the coat opened to reveal a pale green silk waistcoat over a white shirt. His head and face were shaded by a wide-brimmed straw hat with a silk hatband that matched the vest. She was briefly arrested by the eyes shadowed by the hat—dark and deep-set, holding her for a moment with a piercing gaze. Then he turned and strode away, and for another brief moment, Sister Theresa could not tear her eyes from his broad back and wide shoulders.

As Father Halloran came hurrying down the gangway, he said, "We're set to go! I saw what happened, Sister Theresa. You shouldn't have come down on your own."

He followed her line of sight and added, "Captain Farrow's a decent fellow, if a Protestant. Tragic family, though. His mother was one of the first missionaries to come to these islands. You'll hear her name mentioned. Emily Farrow. They say she went insane one day about thirty years ago, and no one knows why. Farrow's son is sickly, too, doctors don't know what's wrong with him. Very well, our luggage is loaded, let us get on to the convent, shall we?"

Father Halloran led his charges down the dock. Sister Theresa decided they must have formed a curious procession because they drew stares from people on the dock—sailors, longshoremen, porters, dock workers, people visiting the ships or preparing for a voyage. The Sisters followed Father Halloran in pairs, while behind them came a mule-drawn wagon filled with their luggage and boxes of supplies.

They walked past two-story wooden buildings with tall glass windows and signs that said, "Folsom Ship's Chandlery," "Geary & Sons Sailmakers," "Best Prices For Turpentine, Tar & Pitch,"— merchants plying a busy trade.

Fort Street ran parallel with the waterfront, with wooden side-walks, awnings, and, to Sister Theresa's surprise, gas street lamps. As they walked, Father Halloran boomed out in his pulpit voice, "What you see, Sisters, is the very proof of God's works in these islands! A scant forty years ago, these hills and plains and valleys were occupied by naked, ignorant savages committing human sacrifices in pagan temples. Now look! In this town alone, where hideous idols were once worshipped, six Christian churches now stand! On the neigh-boring island of Hawai'i, where godless natives surrounded a doomed and helpless Captain Cook just eighty years ago, and ruthlessly blud-geoned him to death, their descendants now attend church!"

People along the wooden sidewalk stopped and stared—ladies in fashionable crinolines and bonnets, gentlemen in frock coats and top hats, sailors in the various costumes of their navies, native women in long, loose dresses, and native men in all manner of curi-ous mismatched attire (white men's cast-off clothing, Sister Theresa assumed).

"There are four Congregational churches here," Father Halloran said, "the clergy and members of which are said to run the Hawai'ian government. Not only do their members compose the majority of the legislature and the king's cabinet, the present monarch devoted a lot of time to translating the Prayer Book into Hawai'ian. Therefore the New England Puritan influence is very strong here. So you see, dear Sisters, our work here is cut out for us. We must not only defend the Catholic faith in these islands, we must see to it that the

True Faith prospers and grows and makes its own influence felt."

But they had come prepared. During the voyage they had studied the Hawai'ian-language Catholic catechism and familiarized themselves with it. Although the goal was to have all Hawai'ians speaking English, thus eventually eradicating the native tongue (in the schools, children were forbidden to speak Hawai'ian), nonetheless, many natives were not proficient in English and so Theresa and her Sisters memorized the Lord's Prayer in Hawai'ian.

As they neared the church, a handsome structure of white stone, Father Halloran said, "Seventeen years ago, the Cathedral of Our Lady of Peace was consecrated." He pointed out the Chancery, a small wooden building from which the Bishop of Honolulu administered his executive powers. Next to it was the rectory—the office and residence of the rector and other priests serving the Cathedral of Our Lady of Peace. And then they came to the convent and school established by an order of French nuns.

"Last year, ten Sisters of the Congregation of the Sacred Heart arrived from France. Two months later they opened this convent boarding school and a day school. But they are teaching Sisters and rarely leave the convent and school. You Sisters of Good Hope, on the other hand, will go out into the community to administer nursing care and spiritual assistance for the housebound."

As they walked past the church, Theresa heard girls' voices raised in song, drifting through open classroom windows. She wondered about the ten French Sisters, what their lives were like, what their habits looked like. They had come from Europe, she thought, which meant they had made the horrific months-long voyage around Cape Horn, a voyage which often claimed lives.

"Through the generosity of local Catholic benefactors," Father Halloran said as they arrived at a two-story house with front verandahs on the ground and upper floors, "the Archdiocese was able to purchase this boardinghouse. It will serve as your convent until a permanent building can be arranged."

They were greeted by the housekeeper, Mrs. Jackson, who, despite her American name, was not, according to Father Halloran, in the least American, but half-Mexican, half-Hawai'ian. She had fallen in love with an American adventurer named Jackson and married him.

But he'd left for the gold fields ten years ago and hadn't been heard from since.

The house had two upstairs bedrooms, partitioned off by curtains fixed to the ceiling to form three compact cubicles, each with a plain cot, a night table, and a crucifix on the wall over the bed. The three Sisters in each room were to share a common washbasin, pitcher, and towels. Downstairs was Mother Agnes's small office, a kitchen, and a communal parlor where they would gather for evening Chapter, prayers, sewing, and singing.

Mrs. Jackson saw to the housework and the cooking. Once a week, two local girls would come to help with the laundry, starching, and ironing. The Sisters had come with a small allowance for the purchase of food and other necessities, but they must start growing a medicinal herb garden right away. A covered lanai off the back door, with woven screens that could be lowered against sun and rain, was furnished with tables and two spirit lamps—this was where they were to manufacture their medicines.

After a dinner of pork chops, potatoes, and salad, they settled into their new home and prayed and sang hymns together before spending their first night under the Hawai'ian moon.

As Sister Theresa laid on her cot in the darkness and looked ahead to her first day of service to the community here, she cherished the feel of a bed that did not move. And the silence of the house was a blessing. No trying to fall asleep to the ceaseless throb of waves beating the hull, the snapping of sails, the constant creaking and groaning of a ship. And no fear of the vast and deep ocean that lay beneath her. Just sweet silence and darkness and a bed that did not roll.

Her bones ached. She had never felt so weary. But this grand adventure made her feel, at nineteen, already mature, worldly, and wise. She thought of her parents back home, her brother and sister. She wished they could see her now, beginning a vocation of glorious purpose. She thought of Cosette, who must be in New Orleans now. And of the Sisters and novices left behind.

And then she looked into the future and saw bright hope and promise in this wondrous new land! Her soul expanded to the stars. Her heart embraced the cosmos in a joy she had never felt before. Tomorrow and all the tomorrows that followed were going to be nothing less than a brilliant destiny. And she could not wait to begin!

But as she drifted into sleep, her joy was dispelled by the sudden intrusion of a stranger, with dark piercing eyes that had looked at her with—what? Puzzlement? Disapproval?

Why had he come to haunt her thoughts as she was drifting off to sleep? Try though she might, she could not push Captain Farrow from her mind.

"This is a dangerous place for a lady on her own," he had said. What had he meant by that? The waterfront? Honolulu? Hawai'i?

And dangerous how? she wanted to ask. She drifted into dreams and imagined herself back on the pier, calling him back, wishing to ask him about the danger. "Tell me," she said to the handsome captain who had rescued her from brutes, "tell me about the danger, Captain Farrow. . . ."

CHAPTER ELEVEN

T hat's Captain Farrow's house," Father Halloran said as they
waited on the wooden sidewalk for the royal procession to pass.
"The natives call it Ka Hale Pallo. They can't pronounce 'Farrow' so
they call him Kapena Pallo."

They were on the corner of King Street when Kamehameha's
carriage and retinue suddenly came along, forcing traffic and pedestrians to halt. It fascinated Sister Theresa that, although the monarchy were
native Hawai'ians, with copper skin, round Polynesian faces, and thick
curly hair, their outer trappings were European. King Kamehameha
the Fourth, twenty-six years old with a sparse beard, riding in his open
carriage, wore a military uniform covered in medals, with a plumed
helmet on his head, while at his side, the beautiful and much-loved
Queen Emma wore a blue silk gown such as the wealthy ladies of San
Francisco wore, with a bonnet on her swept-up hair.

Hawai'i's royal couple was so enamored of all things British that
their two-year-old son was even named Prince Albert.

Sister Theresa turned around to see the residence Father Halloran
was speaking of. On the large corner lot, surrounded by wide green
lawns, was a white wooden house two stories tall with a peaked red roof
and deep verandahs, and shaded by magnificent tamarind trees. One
could see it was the home of a wealthy family.

Barbara Wood

"The Farrows have been here for forty years," Father Halloran said. "Hardly an enterprise in the islands that they don't have some sort of financial stake in. Made their initial fortune in the sandalwood trade, shipping wood to China in their own ships. I wouldn't be surprised if the ship we came from San Francisco on was owned by the Farrows. The captain sits in the legislature."

Theresa had learned that the government of Hawai'i was a hereditary and constitutional monarchy. There was a House of Nobles and a House of Representatives. There were cabinet ministers, an attorney general, a chief justice, circuit and district judges on all the larger islands, as well as sheriffs and police. Most of those lofty posts were held by Americans and Englishmen, and all were Protestant with great influence over the monarchy.

She scrutinized the grand house, wondering if she would glimpse its owner. She had not seen Captain Farrow since her arrival three months prior, when he had rescued her from brutish sailors, but she had heard a great deal about him, and read of his political activities in the newspapers. The *Honolulu Star* carried his likeness, executed by an artist who had captured Mr. Farrow's attractive features.

"There's a brother named Peter," Father Halloran said, as a contingent of mounted soldiers—Hawai'ians in European uniforms—cantered proudly behind the royal carriages. "He owns a cattle ranch in the northeast of the island, at Waialua. That's where the mother, Emily, who came here in 1820, lives. They say Peter keeps her locked away, out of the public eye."

Although Father Halloran preached to the congregation about the ills of gossip, he himself quite indulged in it. "But Robert lives here," he said, "and runs his shipping company from Honolulu. He used to go out to sea but he's land-bound now. Still, every day at precisely noon you will see him out on the verandah of the second story, looking out to sea through his familiar brass telescope."

On the lawn in front of the verandah, a child was reclining on a wicker lounge chair and covered in a blanket, despite the warmth of the day. He was about ten years old and sported a thick mop of black hair. His skin was olive, leading Theresa to suspect he was Italian or perhaps Portuguese. At his side, a young woman sat in a straight-backed chair, reading out loud from a book. "What a beautiful boy," she remarked to Father Halloran. "Is he a ward of the captain's?"

"He's Captain Farrow's son, Jamie." At her look of surprise, Father Halloran added, "The boy is *hapa haole*—half-white. Farrow's wife was Hawai'ian."

She had learned that Europeans were called *haole,* while Hawai'ians referred to themselves as *kanaka,* which meant a person or human being. "Was?" she said.

"She died a few years ago."

"I wonder what ails the boy."

"He's been sickly for as long as I can remember." Father Halloran frowned. "Although, it seems of late that the boy's condition has worsened. None of the island doctors can find out what's wrong with him, but he has a new physician, an Englishman who arrived in Honolulu just before we did."

She guessed that the young woman was not much older than herself, around twenty-two she would say, and judging by her plain gray dress, the prim little lace cap on her head, the way she read to the boy, she was his governess.

Father Halloran and Sister Theresa were forced to wait out the slow procession. They were on their way to the house of a family whose patriarch was ill.

The past three months had not been easy for Theresa and her Sisters. Hawai'i was suffering from a severe economic depression. Money was scarce and they had yet to find ways to generate income. The French Sisters next door were able to sustain themselves on fees received from the students in their school. But the Sisters of Good Hope as yet had no patients, had not begun their nursing duties.

Luckily, Mother Agnes convinced a parishioner to donate a milk cow, and with the few eggs they could purchase at the market—after much haggling—they were able to make the custards for which they had been known back in San Francisco. After an appeal from Father Halloran in the pulpit, members of the congregation were soon buying the custards every Sunday after Mass.

It was not yet enough, but it was a start.

To help, Father Halloran had delivered a sermon informing the congregation of the Sisters' arrival and the home nursing care they offered. Any family in need of help was to send a request to Mother

Agnes at their residence. Sister Theresa had expected a torrent of requests. But none had come. "They are suspicious of Western medicine," Father Halloran said of the Hawai'ians. And as for the Europeans, they preferred to be seen to by doctors.

They waited as the procession of royal carriages and mounted guards passed by. Sister Theresa tried to curb her impatience. Not for the procession, but for the lack of acceptance of her Sisters and their work. *We are supposed to be invisible, and yet we must make ourselves visible. We are never to draw attention to ourselves, yet we must draw attention to our work. How are we to accomplish this?*

She had come up with the idea that perhaps they could accompany Father Halloran on his charitable rounds among the parishioners, visiting the sick and dying, to make their mission known. And so there she was, on her first trial outing with Father Halloran, who was well known among the Catholics of Honolulu.

A gentleman approached Father Halloran, raising a hand and booming out a hearty greeting. "What nonsense, eh?" he cried. "Holding up all commerce and industry for an outing in a carriage!" The man spoke with a British accent and Sister Theresa assumed he was one of Honolulu's prosperous foreigners.

While the two men launched into a dialogue about politics— "Here we are in the middle of an economic depression, and Queen Emma has another new carriage!"—she turned her attention to the boy on the lawn.

The prim young woman rose and went into the house, leaving the boy alone. Sister Theresa decided to approach him, since Father Halloran was otherwise engaged.

"Hello," she said as she came across the grass. His eyes widened at her appearance. "My name is Sister Theresa. What's yours?"

"Jamie," he said in a thin voice, and she saw him wince in pain.

"Are you feeling poorly, Jamie?"

"Dr. Edgeware said I have a hot belly."

"Oh my. That can't be very pleasant. May I touch your forehead?" His skin was cool and dry. She thought for a moment, then asked, "Do you throw up?"

He nodded.

"When?"

"After I eat."

"What do you think you are doing?"

She turned and saw the young woman returning with a glass of milk and a wedge of cheese on a plate.

"What are you doing?" she repeated archly. Theresa sensed hostility, saw defensiveness in her eyes. She was guarding her territory. Cosette had been like that with her two charges.

"I was merely trying to see what ailed him, and if I could help."

The young woman made a point of staring at the rosary on Theresa's belt. There was contempt in her tone when she said, "We don't need your help."

In her three months in Honolulu, Theresa had learned about the anti-Catholic prejudice among the Protestants. A mere twenty-nine years ago, New England Congregationalists had persuaded the Hawai'ian monarchs to ban Catholicism in these islands, driving the priests off and forcing them to sail away. Eight years later, France, as a defender of the Catholic Church, had dispatched a warship to Honolulu. The captain was ordered by his government to use all force necessary to exact reparation for such wrongs and to ensure that the Hawai'ian government never again insult the Church. To the dismay of the Protestants, King Kamehameha III, fearing an attack, had issued the Edict of Toleration in 1839, declaring freedom of Catholic worship in the Hawai'ian Islands.

Twenty-one years had since passed, but resentment still ran deep.

Sister Theresa bid good day to the governess and her ailing charge, and as she joined Father Halloran, she glanced back and saw the young woman coaxing the boy to drink the milk.

The royal parade finally passed and traffic, both pedestrian and equestrian, was allowed to resume.

Theresa never failed to enjoy their walks around Honolulu. The streets, though not macadamized, gave the appearance of having been specially constructed. She had learned that this was due to the composition of the soil: a firm foundation of coral, built up from the bottom of the sea, and on top of it, a light layer of cinder and lava that was belched into the air eons ago by a long-dead volcano.

Residences and commercial buildings presented an interesting variety. Unlike the brick mercantile buildings of San Francisco,

Honolulu's business establishments were constructed of white coral harvested in blocks from nearby reefs. Private homes were airy cottages, neat and white, sitting on spacious lots with green lawns on all four sides, and great branching tamarind and mango trees casting permanent shade.

No two residences were alike, and occasionally one came upon a native grass hut in the middle of a field. These dwellings were shaped somewhat like the modest cottages, but were gray in color, with higher, steeper roofs, and constructed of weeds strongly bound, together in bundles. Surrounding these traditional Hawai'ian homes were cultivated patches as the families within grew local crops to sell at market. In Honolulu, one did not have to venture far to purchase groceries. Every sidewalk had its vendors.

One ubiquitous product was poi, sold on nearly every street corner, where natives squatted on their haunches overseeing great vats of the Hawai'i national dish. Poi was made by boiling taro root, mashing it to a paste, and letting it ferment until it was palatable. No cups were handed out. A customer paid for his portion, then dipped his finger directly into the vat of thick stuff, stirred it around several times until the finger was thickly coated. He then tipped his head back and thrust his finger into his mouth to strip off the poi. As he was doing this, other customers were likewise dipping fingers into the same vat. Once the finger was licked clean, it went back into the mixture for seconds and thirds.

Sister Theresa had yet to try it, and might do so, but it would have to be under more sanitary circumstances. Nonetheless, the natives swore by the nutritious benefits of poi, and swore also that for some diseases it restored health after all other medicines had failed.

But she had no money for food experiments. Besides which, the money here was extremely puzzling!

The only paper currency was treasury notes in large denominations—hardly practical. The coinage was basically the same as that of the United States, but the dollars were Mexican, or French five-franc pieces. A dime, or ten cents, was the lowest coin, and copper was not in circulation. An envelope, a penny bottle of ink, a pencil, a spool of thread, cost ten cents each; postage stamps cost two cents but one must buy five of them, so that dimes slipped away quickly. There were also English half-a-crowns, shillings, sixpences, and twopences.

Besides the vendors of poi and freshly caught fish, one also saw natives sitting on street corners selling bananas, strawberries, mangoes, and guavas. The only apples on the islands, however, had to be imported from Oregon and she refrained from indulging in them, as one bite brought such a bittersweet reminder of home that she would be filled with melancholy for the rest of the day.

Sister Theresa had not voiced this homesickness either to her Sisters or to Father Halloran—it was not a homesickness for San Francisco, or even for Oregon per se—it was a searing longing for the freedom she sorely missed, when she had run free as a child.

It had been easy, back in the convent on California Street, to put such memories and yearnings from her heart. But here, the deep-chasm valleys ran with fresh sweet water, and the wind was like the wind that had screamed down the Willamette Valley so that a young Anna almost thought she could lift her arms and fly.

But that Anna no longer existed. In her place was Sister Theresa, who not only must never remove her shoes and socks, but never rip the starched coif from her head, the confining wimple, the bib and heavy veils that kept her head from turning left or right. Not even her hands were blessed by the sun but must remain hidden, and tamed, inside sleeves.

"Almost there," Father Halloran announced. They were away from the center of town and following a dirt road shaded by over-arching trees with dense leafage: umbrella trees, bamboo, mango, candlenut, and coconut palms—the exotic wide-spreading trees of the South Seas. They were surrounded by the heady fragrances of garde-nia, roses, lilies. They saw verandahs festooned with passionflowers and bougainvillea. In fact all the houses, humble or grand, made of grass or wood or coral, were engulfed in Hawai'i's perennial greenery, with lattices and balustrades grown over with lush vines and creepers.

As they neared their destination, Father Halloran pointed to a collection of huts that Sister Theresa could barely make out in fields rich with crops. The huts, though made of grass, appeared to be large and well-shaped and could almost be called stately. They were not the houses of poor people. "That village is ruled by an old chief named Kekoa who refuses to have anything to do with Christians or Westerners. He's a powerful old warrior who holds sway over a large faction of hold-outs. No amount of bribery or persuasion will convince the old scalawag to learn to read, to wear proper clothes, to attend church like every other enlightened native! Forty years ago, when other ali'i eagerly embraced Western ways, when Hawai'ian princes and princesses took American and English husbands and wives, old Kekoa steadfastly refused to be assimilated. He rules over this valley with his niece Mahina, the daughter of a legendary kahuna named Pua, who vanished mysteriously a long time ago. You won't find any top hats or crinolines in those houses!"

They turned off the main road and followed a narrow, muddy track toward a lone hut. Father Halloran explained that the people who lived there were Catholic, although one rarely saw them at Mass. Still, he had a duty to come and pray with them and to administer Holy Communion. In this instance, their visit was to look in on the ailing old grandfather.

"What is wrong with him?"

Father Halloran removed his black, wide-brimmed hat and mopped his orange hair with a handkerchief. "Although he won't admit it, I suspect old Michael's had a lifelong habit of drinking spirits. As you know, distillation of spirits is illegal in these islands, and a foreigner is fined heavily for giving alcohol to a native. But the Hawai'ians have a way of distilling a very potent liquor from the root of the *ti*-tree. I am sorry to say, Sister, that in spite of the notoriously bad effect of alcohol in the tropics, people here drink hard, especially among the sailors, and the number of deaths due to this is quite startling. You and your Sisters will come across many such cases, I fear."

Replacing his hat, Father Halloran said, "One further warning, Sister. There are no windows in this house so the air will be pungent. And because Hawai'ians believe that urine keeps evil spirits away, they relieve themselves in the corners of their homes, around the sick person's bed. They even wash him in it."

To reach the hut they had to trudge across a mucky field. And so she tried to lift her hems off the ground so as not to track the mud into the house. But when they entered, she saw that her effort was for naught. The floor of the hut was filthy.

And the air, as warned, was rank. Clothes hung on pegs, pots and dishes were stacked on a wooden shelf, sandals were heaped by the door, blankets lumped in a pile, and wooden crates contained fat taro roots, onions, ears of corn, and dried fish tied on strings.

Father Halloran introduced her to the family, who sat on the floor in the semidarkness, Hawai'ians with copper skin and black hair so that they blended into the shadows. "This is Miriam, the granddaughter. Jonathan, her husband. Samuel, his brother. And Lucy, a baby sister." Like most Hawai'ians who converted to Christianity, they had taken Western names.

"May I take a look at Michael, Father?"

"If he doesn't mind. He won't let a doctor touch him."

She knelt beside the old man on the mat, studying the wrinkled features beneath a head of white hair. His eyes were closed and he struggled for breath. She opened her bag and pulled out a stethoscope. Since the coif and wimple of their habit prevented them from using the newer, flexible rubber binaural stethoscopes, the Sisters of Good Hope relied on the traditional wooden tube that ended in a trumpet. Placing the wide end on the old man's bony chest, she listened while the family watched in fascinated silence.

She looked up at Father Halloran. "His lungs are terribly congested. How long has he been like this?"

"Weeks."

"On his back? Father, could we turn him onto his side, please?"

He asked the family to roll the old man over, and what Theresa found shocked her. Three large, oozing sores on his buttocks, one of them so deep that she could see his white, exposed tailbone.

She said quietly, "This poor man must be turned every few hours, or the sores will get worse. He is more in danger of dying of infection from these wounds than he is of his lung condition. Can you tell them to turn him, Father? First on his left side, then on his right, every six to eight hours?"

"They understand and speak English. You can tell them directly. Although, I have to warn you, these people have no concept of time the way we do. You won't find a clock in here."

She thought for a moment, and then, turning to the granddaughter, said, "In the morning, you must turn your grandfather on his side to face the rising sun. Then he can go onto his back to look up through the roof at the noon sun. Then place him on his other side so that he can picture the sun going down in the sea. He will need to stay on his side through the night. He will need to be propped so he doesn't roll onto his back."

The young woman smiled and responded, but Sister Theresa didn't understand a word.

"Their English takes some getting used to," Father Halloran said. "Part of what she said just now was 'Kika Keleka.' That means 'Sister Theresa.' It's the only way they can pronounce your name. You'll get used to it in time. Miriam said they will place grandfather's favorite pig at his back so he won't roll over."

Father Halloran and Sister Theresa said a prayer over the old man, with the family joining in, and as they got up to leave, Sister Theresa said to Miriam, "I will come back tomorrow with ointment for the sores and medicine of camphor and eucalyptus for his congestion."

On their way back to the convent, she mentally mapped out a better plan of nursing care for the grandfather, but her thoughts returned to Jamie Farrow, the sickly little boy she had seen that morning, and she wondered if something could be done for him.

S ister Theresa, what on earth did you *do* yesterday?"
     She looked up from her garden work to see Mother Agnes looking agitated. "Just as I told you, Reverend Mother. I visited a kanaka family with Father Halloran."

"Well, it started something. Come with me."

There was a crowd at the front of the house—old men on crutches, young men with dirty bandages on arms and legs, mothers holding babies, children crying. All Hawai'ians in muumuus or ill-fitting Western trousers and shirts. A few of the men wore top hats that had seen better days.

Father Halloran was trying to quiet them down and bring order to the crowd. Passersby stopped to watch in curiosity and amusement. Theresa heard a sailor quip to his comrade, "What d'you suppose the Sisters are giving away for free?"

Sister Veronica brought a blank ledger, pen and ink bottle, and took a seat on the verandah to record names and addresses as Father Halloran dictated them. Next to each, she listed the ailment or injury, so that later Mother Agnes could arrange the visiting assignments.

A native woman in a loose muumuu was holding a listless child in her arms. Moved by her tears, Sister Theresa withdrew into the house and returned with a cup of milk. But when she offered it to the child, the mother shook her head and backed away, as if Sister Theresa had offered the child poison. As she pondered the woman's strange reaction, she recalled their visits to the local native market where they purchased fruits and vegetables. She thought of Mr. Van Dusen on Merchant Street, a Dutch cheese maker from whom they purchased their weekly cheddar. She thought of the European congregants who purchased the Sunday custards while the native parishioners passed them by.

And the solution to a problem suddenly came to her.

The next day, they were given their assignments. Theresa was to pay a follow-up visit to the old man with the congested lungs, and Sister Veronica was to go with her. When they passed by the Farrow place, she saw the boy in the sun with his governess. Telling Sister Veronica that she would be right back, she crossed the lawn and knelt next to the boy. "Hello, do you remember me?"

"Really!" the governess said, shooting to her feet. "This must stop." She turned and strode back to the house.

"Tell me how you feel," Theresa said to the little boy. As she took his thin wrist and counted his pulse, he told her about pains in his abdomen.

She drew down the blanket—he wore a linen shirt tucked into short tweed trousers—and asked if she could touch his tummy. His abdomen was very tender, and as she palpated it, Jamie expelled a good deal of gas. Even without the aid of a stethoscope, Theresa could hear the gurgling in his intestines.

"What the devil do you think you're doing?" Captain Farrow came striding across the grass, a thunderous expression on his face. He was without a jacket, and his shirtsleeves were rolled up. But he wore the familiar wide-brimmed hat.

She rose. "I'm Sister Theresa. We met three months ago and—"

"I know who you are. What are you doing with my son? His governess tells me you have been accosting him."

Sister Theresa saw a smug expression on the young woman's face.

"Mr. Farrow, what your physician described as a 'hot belly' is an intolerance for dairy products. Your son exhibits the classic signs. I understand that he is part Hawai'ian and I have observed that the natives have an aversion to anything made from milk. I believe that if you—"

She was unaware that Sister Veronica had joined her until the governess said, "You see, Mr. Farrow? You'll have to be putting up a fence to keep these people out."

"I'll be putting up no fences, Miss Carter." To Sister Theresa he said, "I'll thank the two of you to leave my property and my family alone, or I shall be forced to lodge a complaint with the bishop."

It was the Hour of Recreation, the time between supper and Compline—the final prayer service of the day—before the Rule of Silence for the night. While Sister Margaret and Sister Catherine sat in the convent parlor with sewing baskets on their laps, and Sister Veronica crushed chamomile leaves with a mortar and pestle, and Sister Frances quietly read Father Butler's *Lives of the Saints*—and the housekeeper Mrs. Jackson finished cleaning up in the kitchen—Theresa sat at a small desk, recording the day's events in her diary. She and Sister Veronica had seen three patients that day, and she now entered her observations, vital statistics, progress, and the expected outcome of each.

Her concentration was broken by the sound of sharp footfall across the polished wooden floor, a sound which she recognized as Mother Agnes's authoritative gait. "Sister Theresa, there is someone at the front door wishing to speak with you. It is a *gentleman*." Her tone was full of disapproval.

Wondering who it could be, Theresa went to the small reception entry and saw the front door standing open to a sultry evening.

And Captain Robert Farrow.

He filled the doorway with his stature and masculinity, making her think of Barbarian invaders on the threshold of a feminine cloister. He wore the usual long white frock coat over white trousers tucked into leather boots reaching his knees.

When he removed his wide-brimmed straw hat to reveal thick dark wavy hair, she saw a high forehead and well-shaped brow. But his eyes, although illuminated by the lamp on the verandah, were as dark and deep-set as before.

He handed her a calling card with his name engraved upon it in cursive script.

"I wanted to apologize for my behavior," he said in a baritone. "After you left, I gave your recommendation some thought. Jamie has been sickly for quite some time and none of the doctors on the island could help. And then a new man came and he recommended a diet rich in dairy fats. But it only made him worse. And then I remembered what you said about an intolerance for dairy products."

He cleared his throat and struck her as being ill at ease. Perhaps Captain Farrow was not used to apologizing, or talking to Catholics, or standing at the doorway of a house to which men were forbidden.

"I had Miss Carter take away all milk, butter, and cheese," he said, "and put Jamie back on fruit juice. In only a few hours, he is already showing improvement. The pains from his abdomen are gone and his appetite returns. It appears you were right, Sister. I should have thought of it, knowing the native diet as I do, but I think of Jamie as a Farrow, and Farrows have always been hearty consumers of cheddars, custards, and cream. But he is half-Hawai'ian. I will remember that in the future."

He reached into his trouser pocket and she heard the jingling of coins. "I would like to pay you, Sister."

"We do not accept payment. But we welcome donations to our charity fund."

"I'll take care of that," Mother Agnes said suddenly from behind. "Sister, if you would be good enough to step inside?"

Theresa turned from Captain Farrow, slipping past Mother Agnes who snatched the calling card from Theresa's fingers. Without a word the Mother Superior thrust the charity box toward the captain, and he dropped three gold coins into the slot. "Thank you," she said crisply. "Good evening to you, sir. God bless."

And she closed the door in his face.

CHAPTER TWELVE

*B*enedicite, Reverend Mother. May I have your permission to accompany Sister Theresa on home visits today?"

Mother Agnes barely glanced at Sister Veronica in the doorway.
She was embroiled in taking inventory in the kitchen, with a fretting
Sister Catherine. There was a shortage of lard—again!

"I have finished ironing the linens," Sister Veronica added.

Mother Agnes looked up with an impatient expression. "I assigned
Sister Margaret to go with Theresa."

"Margaret is down with her monthly time."

"Oh, I see," Agnes said, returning her attention to the nearly
empty lard tin—now she must decide whether to use the last of it in
badly needed salves and ointments, or to help make their evening
potatoes more palatable. "Yes yes, of course you may go. *Benedicite.*"

As Sister Veronica left, Mother Agnes called after her, "And
it wouldn't hurt to remind your patients today that we welcome
donations."

Sister Veronica packed her black bag slowly and methodically,
double- and triple-checking her supplies. She knew she didn't have
a fast mind. Just as she knew she wasn't pretty. She had once overheard her father say to her mother, "She favors your side of the family.
Same broad face and low forehead. We'll never pawn her off on a

husband. Give her to the Church. Solve two problems at once—what to do with the girl and gain some favor in heaven."

Her family hadn't wanted her, but she was happy. Her Sisters took care of her. If she was a bit slow at her chores, one of the others could be counted on to help. Especially Sister Theresa. Theresa was so pretty. Veronica watched her when she cut her hair. It was thick and naturally wavy with a golden sunset color. It was a shame to cut it, but they had to in this climate of heat and humidity.

"Ready, Sister?" Theresa said in the parlor, and Veronica felt her heart leap with joy. Sister Margaret wasn't really down with her monthly time—Veronica had begged her to switch assignments. Veronica didn't know why she so loved being in Theresa's company, but she sought an opportunity every time she could.

They struck off into the sunny Hawai'ian day.

"Did you ever notice, Sister Veronica," Theresa said as they walked along the sidewalk, "that there is more to Hawai'i than waterfalls and mists and rainbows and foamy surf?"

"What do you mean?" Although Sister Veronica often didn't understand what Theresa was saying, she just loved hearing her voice and walking at her side. *I could be like this forever with Theresa, and never ask for another thing.*

"It seems to me that, beyond the blue skies and warm rain and dazzling flowers," Theresa said, "invisible powers might be at work. The natives who thrived on these isolated volcanic summits did not consider themselves to be the owners of the land, the overseers of the animals, or kings of the waters and fishes. Hawai'ians believed they were part of a complex web of nature that was ordained by the gods back in the mists of time. Which makes me wonder if invisible forces exist here still, despite the arrival of white men with their guns and printing presses and macadamized roads."

"There are rumors," Sister Veronica said, "that the old ways have not been stamped out. The hula dance has been declared illegal, but people say it still goes on. I have never seen the dance but I hear that it is lewd and lascivious and worse than any abomination the Biblical Canaanites could have committed. Yet it is whispered that on outlying farms, in isolated districts, people gather for the dance, and to worship the old gods, and even to engage in worse, more unspeakable practices."

Sister Theresa sighed. Sister Veronica didn't understand. In the five months since their arrival, Theresa had felt an enchantment all around her, but there was no one she could voice this to. Mother Agnes, Father Halloran, her Sisters—they would not understand what she was trying to say, they might even call her blasphemous and Father Halloran would have her saying ten rosaries a day.

"Sister Theresa, what is that up ahead?" A crowd had gathered near the grounds of the Royal Residence.

There was a bandstand at the edge of the sweeping lawns where the king's band played every Sunday afternoon under the talented baton of the bandleader, a Prussian from Weimar. It was said that King Kamehameha III wanted to emulate European royalty and so he had put together a "royal band" for military marches and to enter-tain visiting dignitaries from Britain, France, and Germany. In their smart white uniforms with gleaming brass buttons, and tall hats with plumes, the musicians looked like any town band seen in America. The only difference was their distinct Polynesian features.

"Perhaps there is going to be a musical performance," Sister Theresa said, but as they drew near, they saw festoons of red, white, and blue bunting, denoting a political event of some kind. Closer in, they heard a commanding voice rise above the silent crowd, which was made up mostly of Europeans, but a few natives, and even fewer women.

As they moved in for a better view, Sister Theresa was startled to see Captain Robert Farrow standing on a wooden crate. He wore the familiar white linen frock coat over white trousers, the wide-brimmed straw hat shading his handsome features. He was gesturing and speaking most eloquently to a captivated audience.

"We are isolated!" he cried. "We are vulnerable! We are at the mercy of the rest of the world. Therefore we must build strong ties to a mainland. It just so happens that America is the nearest mainland. It doesn't make sense to join with a distant homeland such as England or France that could not sail to our defense should we need it. We need strong allies. *Nearby* allies."

"You just want to annex Hawai'i to America," came a grousing shout from the crowd.

"No, not annexation. I speak of an *alliance* between this kingdom and that republic. Hawai'i should always be self-ruling. I do not call for masters, I call for friends. But such ties must be strong and swift. An ally who cannot come to our aid for weeks is not a strong ally."

Sister Theresa was less interested in what Captain Farrow had to say than she was in Captain Farrow himself. As Father Halloran had reported, every day at precisely noon Captain Farrow could be seen on the second story verandah of his home, looking out to sea through his familiar brass telescope. It seemed to be a private ritual, for he was always alone. What did he think about, she wondered, as he held his eye to the spyglass? What was he hoping to see? Or was it simply the captain's way of sailing on his beloved ocean, if only in his mind?

She returned her attention to his speech. Captain Robert Farrow, she found, was a compelling speaker. His oratory was dramatic. His diction was like art. He gave every word earth-shattering importance. If he were talking about drinking a glass of water, it would be as if drinking a glass of water were a new idea and no one had ever thought of it before.

He looked over the heads of the crowd and, when he saw her, he paused in his words to lift his hand. She turned to see who he was signaling to, but there was no one. When she looked at him again, he sent her a small smile and resumed his speech.

"Why did he do that?" Sister Veronica asked softly.

"I have no idea. Perhaps he wishes a word with me. Let us wait."

Behind Captain Farrow on his soapbox lay the emerald grounds of the monarch's residence. The royal palace was called the *Hale Ali`i* (House of the Chief). Although resembling a stately mansion one might find in America, the building was constructed as a traditional ali'i residence, which meant only ceremonial spaces, no sleeping rooms. It just had a throne room, a reception room, and a state dining room. It was the grandest house in town and was largely meant for receiving foreign dignitaries and holding state functions. The young king, Kamehameha the Fourth, preferred to live in a grass hut on the palace grounds.

His speech over, to the reception of hearty applause, Captain Farrow stepped down from the box and was immediately surrounded by supporters, whom Theresa took to be men of commerce and industry—men in dark frock coats and top hats, with bellies like wine barrels and smoking thick cigars, slapping Mr. Farrow on the back and saying, "We like what you say, Robert, we like your energy and vision."

With Mr. Farrow agreeing to meet with certain parties, settling on dates and appointments and promises to "look into the matter," he finally made his way through the crowd, shaking hands along the way, and when he arrived at the two nuns, he said, "Thank you for waiting, Sister. I know you are very busy and your time is limited, but I was wondering if you could spare a minute to look at Jamie. He isn't doing well today."

"Is it the dairy intolerance?"

"He hasn't had so much as a sip of milk since you dispensed your excellent advice. No, Sister, this is something more insidious."

She said that she would gladly look in on the boy, whom she had only glimpsed on occasion in the past weeks, as she walked by his house and saw him on the lawn with his governess.

"My son was a robust infant and an energetic boy. You couldn't get him to stay put. Always running or climbing. And then about four years ago, he began to get sickly, he lost weight, he lost his desire to run around, he lost his appetite. He's been seen by every doctor in Honolulu and they are all at a loss to find what ails him. This morning, his governess couldn't get him to leave his room. He lies listlessly in bed. I am worried, Sister."

"And Dr. Edgeware has no idea?" She had heard more of the reputation of the Farrows' family doctor. He was held in high esteem in the islands.

"Dr. Edgeware has gone to Hilo for a few weeks."

When they arrived at Farrow House, she asked Sister Veronica to go on ahead to their home visit, assuring her that she would be along shortly.

Veronica hesitated, looking from Theresa to the captain, then back to Theresa. Reluctantly, she said, "Very well," and continued along the sidewalk.

Captain Farrow escorted Sister Theresa into his home, where she had never before set foot. A spacious entry led to a staircase and rooms opening off to either side. The wooden floor was highly polished, and a chandelier fitted with candles and crystal ornaments hung from the ceiling. It reminded her of her home back in San

Francisco, and the grand mansions where she and her parents had attended parties.

Except that Captain Robert Farrow's house, she saw as they passed by doors that opened onto a parlor and a library, was filled with all kinds of foreign oddities and curios—black lacquer Chinese cabinets, red Chinese lanterns, statues of what she assumed to be Chinese gods carved out of pink and green jade. Tiger skins covered the floors, and the stuffed heads of lions and antelope graced the walls.

When she saw a totem pole, guarding the foot of the staircase, she was drawn to it.

"It's Tlingit, from Alaska," Captain Farrow said.

She stepped closer to inspect the carvings. The carved pole consisted of four human figures, each squatting on the head of the man beneath him. They had huge round eyes and fierce mouths with bared teeth. All four had bird beaks and wings. The topmost wore a cone-shaped hat on his head.

Theresa said, "When I was ten years old and living in Oregon, my father sent for us to join him in California. We traveled by wagon to the Willamette River, and from there traveled by a small steamer to the coast, where we boarded a Pacific Mail Steamer for San Francisco. There were two totem poles at the harbor where the boats docked. Smaller and simpler than this, but similar, too. They had been carved by Chinook Indians, but no one knew what they stood for. I think they are beautiful. . . ."

"Unfortunately, they're becoming a rarity because missionaries are converting the Northwest Indians to Christianity and persuading them to stop making effigies, and even to destroy the ones already in existence. I reckon this one, which I got from a Tlingit tribesman in Alaska, will be valuable someday." He paused. "I would donate it to a museum except that I picked it up on my final voyage. When I got back to Hawai'i I learned my father had died and I had to take over the business. This totem pole is a remembrance of my days at sea."

As they turned to ascend the stairs, she glanced through one of the open doorways and saw a portrait over a fireplace. The subject was a young woman in a fashionable gown, with a boy around the age of five at her side. What arrested Theresa was her beauty. She was dusky and doe-eyed, with thick raven tresses. The combination of such foreign features with European attire captured not only one's attention, but one's imagination as well.

"My late wife," Captain Farrow said. "Her name was Leilani."

The boy in the painting was clearly Jamie. He had beautiful eyes, large and round and with a slight fullness to the lower lid that gave him a melancholy look—a trait which he had inherited from his mother. When she commented on this, Captain Farrow explained that it was island tradition to mold a child at birth, that as soon as the baby came out, the midwife pressed in his eyes at the corners and molded other parts of his body until he was fully formed. "It is to achieve ideal island beauty," Captain Robert said, staring at the painting.

After a moment, he gave a sigh and said, "Jamie was born in the month of *Welo* under the *Ku-pau* moon, a time of low tides and gentle winds. Supposedly this gives him a sweet and warm manner." The captain turned to look at her and she saw the worry in his eyes. "I'll take you to him."

They reached the top of the stairs, where a door stood open, revealing a bedroom within. Jamie lay fully dressed on the counterpane, the governess in a chair at his side. "Miss Carter," Captain Farrow said, "I have asked Sister Theresa to take a look at Jamie."

She rose stiffly, hands clasped at her waist. "Certainly, Mr. Farrow."

Although Theresa was taller, the governess gave the impression that she looked down at her. Theresa wondered what she had done to offend her so.

While the captain stood at the foot of the bed, Theresa examined Jamie with her stethoscope (his heart fluttered like a trapped bird) and felt his skin (it was cool and dry), examined his tongue (a pale color) and finally his eyes (more paleness). She asked him a few questions, then asked him to squeeze her hand as tightly as he could. He had barely any strength.

Jamie saw the wedding ring on her left hand and asked her if she was married. "Yes, I am," she replied.

"Where does your husband live?"

"Well, he's in heaven."

"Then are you a widow, like Grandmother Emily?"

Before she could explain, they were interrupted by a woman whom Theresa took to be the housekeeper, and who bore a remarkable

resemblance to Miss Carter—mother and daughter, she surmised—
who informed Mr. Farrow that he had visitors. Excusing himself, Mr.
Farrow left her alone with Jamie and the governess.

Miss Carter resumed her seat and let Sister Theresa know, by
her watchful posture, that she did not trust her. The governess was
an attractive young lady, with a heart-shaped face framed by auburn
ringlets. Although her gray gown was plain, she wore a fashionable
crinoline, and the tight bodice showed off a fine, slim figure. Theresa
wondered why she wasn't married.

She asked Jamie about his sleeping patterns, what he ate, did he
have good days and bad days. He had a beautiful face, round and exotic
with the expressive Polynesian eyes one saw all over this island. His lips
were full and his skin a lovely olive color, hinting of the handsome
man he would one day be.

But first they had to get to the source of his mysterious malaise.

A thought came to her. "Miss Carter, may I have a word with you?"

She frowned. Then she rose and they stepped toward the French
door standing open to admit fresh air. Out of Jamie's hearing,
Theresa said, "Miss Carter, when did the boy's mother die?"

She stiffened and pursed her lips. For one so young, Theresa
thought she seemed terribly old. "It is not something we discuss in
this house."

"I am wondering if Jamie's poor health stems from grief over the
loss of his mother."

She tipped her chin. "I thought you were the expert on illnesses."

"I was merely inquiring—"

"It is time for his noon snack," she said, and when a breeze stirred
Theresa's veils, Miss Carter recoiled, as if their touch might somehow
poison her. "I will be back momentarily," she said, and turned and left.

Theresa remained by the window, wondering why the governess seemed to see an adversary in a Catholic nun. Then her thoughts
returned to the listless boy on the bed. She was wondering what was
wrong with him and how he might be helped, when a small voice interrupted her musings: "What are you?"

A boy of about ten had come into the room. He wore a proper
little tweed suit with trousers that buckled at his knees, and a straw
derby on his head.

Jamie stirred on the bed, pushing up on his elbows, and saying with a smile, "Reese! You came."

The visitor approached slowly, keeping his eyes on Theresa. At the bedside, he said, "Hullo, Jamie. Are you all right?"

"I'm all right," Jamie said. "Sister Theresa, this is my cousin Reese."

"How do you do?" she said.

He frowned as he pointed to her veil. "What's all this?"

"It is the costume of a religious Sister."

"Does it hurt?"

She assumed he meant the coif and wimple, which confined the face. They were tight, but not painful. She shook her head.

His interest vanished as he turned to Jamie and said, "When can you come to the ranch? We have six new foals. And the river must be a mile deep!"

Theresa recalled Father Halloran saying something about Peter Farrow having a son named Reese. The cousins did not much resemble each other. She supposed that was because Reese had no Hawai'ian blood.

"It's not up to you to make that decision, Robert!"

The shout startled her, and as she turned toward the French door, she heard Reese say, "Aw, they're at it again, Jamie. I wish they wouldn't fight."

Theresa moved closer to the door and saw, on the rear lawn, two men walking away from the house. One was Captain Farrow, the other was shorter and stouter, and walked with a limp and the aid of a cane. She assumed he was Captain Farrow's brother, who was said to have over a hundred head of cattle on his Waialua ranch.

Their voices rode on the wind, and while the two young cousins got caught up on each other's news, Theresa could not help but listen to the brothers. "I will not talk about it, Robert!" Peter Farrow cried. "She was your wife! If you wish to continue to commemorate her birthday, then do so, but leave me out of it."

"For God's sake, Peter, why is it always 'she'? Why can't you honor Leilani's memory by at least speaking her name?"

When Peter refused to respond, Captain Farrow looked around. "Where is Mother? I thought you were bringing her to see Jamie."

"She got out of her room—how she unlocked the door I'll never know—and I found her wandering on the beach in the moonlight, wearing just her nightdress. She woke this morning with a chest cold. I made her stay home, although she protested loudly."

Captain Farrow removed his hat, ran his hand through his hair, settled his hat back on his head. "She was doing so well. What happened?"

"I have no idea. The last spell was months ago. She's been calm and quiet. And then suddenly a violent rage." Peter took his brother by the arm. "Robert, we can't take care of her anymore. Charlotte is pregnant and she doesn't want Mother around the baby. She will have to come here and live with you."

"Charlotte's pregnant again? Are you out of your mind?"

"Robert, I am not like you. I refuse to let fear rule my life."

"It's a foolish gamble, Peter!"

"It didn't stop you from having a son."

"A decision I now regret, believe me!"

At such startling words, Theresa quickly glanced toward the bed, but Jamie was so excited to hear Reese's talk of the ranch that he hadn't heard his father's explosive statement. But did he know it anyway? *How can a father say he regrets having a son?* And was that perhaps the source of his malaise?

"Robert," Peter said on the lawn below, "Charlotte has taken to her bed and threatens to stay there for the length of her pregnancy if Mother is not removed from our house."

He turned and, limping a few steps back toward the lanai, leaning on his cane, Peter Farrow raised his hand to the side of his mouth and shouted in Theresa's direction, "Reese! Come on down, boy! It's time to go!"

"Gee willikers," Reese said at the bedside. "Guess I have to go. I hope you get better and can come stay at the ranch."

After Reese left, Theresa went back to Jamie, who had closed his eyes. Her heart moved for him. Ten-year-olds were meant to be climbing trees and chasing rabbits. Laying her hand gently on his forehead, she made a solemn vow to bring him out of this mysterious torpor.

As she picked up her bag, she heard heavy footfall on the stairs, and was prepared to see Captain Farrow in the doorway. Instead, her eyes widened at the sight of quite possibly the largest woman she had ever seen.

Dressed in a bright-yellow cotton muumuu that covered her

entirely from neck to ankles and wrists, she was not only tall but of considerable girth. Dusky-skinned with long frizzy hair standing out from her head and tumbling over her shoulders, she rushed past Theresa and reached down for the boy.

"He's sleeping," Theresa said, wondering who this woman was. A servant, surely, as she was Hawai'ian and speaking to him in her native tongue. But, to Theresa's further surprise, Jamie opened his eyes and broke into a smile as he said, "Tutu!"

She collected his small body into her enormous arms and brought him to her breast. "My little Pinau!" she cried, rocking him.

"That's Sister Theresa," Jamie said. "She's come to help me. Sister Theresa, this is my *Kapuna-wahine*. Tutu Mahina, my grandmother."

Gently lowering her grandson to the bed, the woman turned to Theresa. She seemed to take up the whole room, not just physically, but she exuded a large personality as well. "You come help my little Pinau?" she asked. Her voice was remarkably soft and melodic. "Only three, four year ago, he run like *pinau*—dragonfly. He go here, he go there," she flung her beefy arms every which way. "Impossible to catch, like *pinau!* But now," she looked down with a sad expression. "He poor little boy. He sickly. The son of my daughter . . ."

So this was Captain Farrow's mother-in-law, mother of the beautiful Leilani in the painting—whose name Peter Farrow refused to speak.

She asked Theresa to say her name again, and Theresa waited while she struggled with it. Mahina finally blurted, "Kika Keleka!" and beamed with pride.

More of a struggle for her, however, was fathoming the mystery of Theresa's garments, which she examined with unabashed liberty, lifting the veils, tugging at the white starched bib, swishing the skirts. The rosary caught her attention.

"Ah, you believe Kirito?" she asked, looking more closely at the crucifix.

"Yes, I believe in Jesus Christ."

"You believe Akua?"

"Yes, I believe in God."

She frowned. "Not like Kapena Pallo."

"No, Captain Farrow and I are a little different. But still Christians."

"Ah!" she cried, and suddenly engulfed Theresa in a most startling embrace. Mahina's mountainous flesh utterly surrounded her and she felt the warmth of her enormous bosom through the layers of their clothing. "Aloha!" she said. "Aloha."

The way Mahina said "aloha" was like a lullaby. She stretched out the second syllable, dropping her voice, almost in song. It was a balm to the ears. So much breath behind the word that Theresa knew she was offering more than a greeting. She was offering love.

Mahina said, "Little Pinau, him so sick because bad spirits in this *hale*. Demons in his blood. Got to chase demons out. Father and uncle have terrible fight." She gestured with fists punching the air. "Uncle, him fall down stairs." She tumbled her hands over. "Broke the leg. Auwe! Bad blood now, Kika Keleka," she said. "Make boy sick. They need ho'oponopono but will not do it."

Theresa had no idea what *ho'oponopono* was, but she knew of the native superstition that unhappiness in a home could cause illness. While she talked, Theresa noticed that Mahina kept scratching her upper arm. She asked her to roll up her sleeve, and she exposed a nasty rash. The hives reached from Mahina's shoulder to her elbow and were raised in large, swollen patches. She had scratched the skin raw in places, so that it had bled.

Theresa offered treatment.

Although Mahina gave her a dubious look, she nodded, and Theresa had her sit down and hold her sleeve up.

The Sisters grew their own echinacea in the convent garden— primarily, purple coneflower and yellow coneflower—from which they made extracts, tinctures, and ointments. Echinacea was a wonderful and universal remedy for a variety of ailments and so the Sisters stocked it in their black bags along with the other supplies that formed their basic medical kits.

Bringing out the tin, Theresa gently applied the ointment and then covered it with a bandage, after which she instructed Mahina not to remove it or get it wet for seven days. Theresa told her that she would reexamine the rash in a week.

"You might be allergic to something," she said. "We've learned that some of the things Europeans have introduced to the islands don't agree with Hawai'ian blood. Perhaps something you ate."

But Mahina shook her head. "There is a curse on me."

"Why do you say that?"

She gave Theresa a calculating look, her large brown eyes roving the veils and skirts, to rest a moment on the rosary. She seemed to reach an understanding; Theresa felt that the woman had judged her and found her qualified to be brought into a special confidence because she said, "Long ago, when I was young, I go with my mother to Pele's Womb. Kapu to go inside. My mother tell me stay outside. But I go in. Goddess Pele take my mother and I go into Pele's Womb."

She paused and Theresa waited as she watched the large, round eyes wander over Jamie's bedroom, then she said, "I go inside and because it kapu, Pele curse me. Kika Keleka, how can I lift curse from me? I try ho'oponopono but it not work."

"*How* are you cursed?"

She lifted round, dark eyes. "Mahina not know! Many years ago Pele curse me, and in many years I wait to be struck down by the gods, yet they wait and I do not know why."

She rose from the chair and went to the bed, where she bent over a sleeping Jamie. "Poor little Pinau. Maybe this Mahina's curse. Gods make boy sick because Mahina broke kapu."

Theresa consulted the little timepiece pinned to her habit and saw that she had stayed much too long. She must catch up with Sister Veronica.

She left Mahina with her grandson and found Captain Farrow in a sunroom at the rear of the house, scowling in front of large windows that overlooked the garden.

Theresa cleared her throat and he turned. She saw dark melancholy in his eyes, the look of one who was lost. She thought: A strange sadness seems to hang over this house. The lonely little boy. The father, a man of passions and visions.

It was as if a secret kept them prisoner here. She suspected there was more to the boy's illness than a physical affliction. Troubles of the soul haunted this family.

As she was about to report on Jamie, Miss Carter appeared suddenly through a side door, holding a cup and a plate. She stopped short when she saw Theresa, and an annoyed look passed over her face. "Your snack, Mr. Farrow," she said, and he responded by gesturing to a table.

As she set the things down and turned to leave, she shot Theresa a look that spoke volumes: It was not the boy Miss Carter was possessive of, but the *father*.

"What can you tell me about Jamie, Sister?" he said.

"I believe he suffers from anemia."

"Other doctors have said that. I tried different tonics, but nothing works." He wrung his hands. "I love my son more than words can say. When his mother was taken from me, I nearly went out of my mind with grief. I cannot lose Jamie, Sister, I cannot."

A little taken aback by the sudden display of such naked emotion, she said, "I believe he needs iron. Have your cook boil a vegetable broth with a rusty nail in the pot. Let it simmer for an hour. Remove the nail, allow the broth to cool, then give it to your son to drink. Do this for as long as is necessary. If that doesn't work, my Sisters and I manufacture a variety of tonics."

The captain rewarded her with another of his long, thoughtful looks, and then startled her by saying, "You're very young."

"But my remedies are very old. And proven," she added with a smile.

Captain Farrow surprised her by returning the smile, and as she thought how handsome it made him look, her heart skipped a beat.

"Good day to you, Captain."

He watched her go, a curious figure in black and white. Sister Theresa was very pretty, Farrow thought. She had an oval face with a small nose and delicate mouth, and large brown eyes that were very warm. He couldn't see her hair, but her eyebrows were a fetching red-gold that made him imagine wild tresses under the black veil. Despite the religious habit that totally engulfed her, she was very feminine, he thought, and her hands, when she exposed them, were like escaping doves, pale and slender as they fluttered over medicine bottles and bandages, and he would imagine that their touch was like a kiss when she applied salve.

"Captain Farrow?" The housekeeper came in. "Young Jamie is asking for you."

He went through the house to the main stairs and was halfway up when he stopped. The day, which had begun with promise, was now clouded over. Peter's visit, the argument, the news that his mother, Emily, had had a relapse, Charlotte pregnant again . . .

Farrow gripped the bannister and wrestled with his emotions. He tried to act rationally, as he did when he was in the shipping offices, or in the government legislature. But this was too much. The boy in the bed upstairs . . .

The son he should never have allowed to come into the world.

The son that frightened him.

Robert Farrow, son of a sea captain and a missionary, couldn't face what lay in that little boy's bedroom. With a ragged sigh, he turned around and went back down the stairs.

CHAPTER THIRTEEN

The house on the outskirts of town, along the road to Nu'uanu Valley, built of wood with a sloping tin roof and a verandah festooned with bougainvillea, was owned by an Irishwoman named Mrs. McCleary, who lived there with her five "adopted daughters."

Mrs. McCleary was known to take in gentlemen "travelers," but only men of high quality, clean and well-behaved. She served sherry and claret in her parlor while a large Irishman, no relation to herself, acted as bodyguard and piano player. Her five "daughters"—young Hawai'ian women—entertained Mrs. McCleary's gentlemen guests with "conversation." These conversations took place in small bedrooms behind closed doors.

When Dr. Simon Edgeware was finished with what he called his "dirty business" behind one of those doors, he slipped through another to avail himself of the hot bath that awaited him.

Mrs. McCleary charged a high price—not for the services but for her silence. Dr. Simon Edgeware, who had come out from London two years ago, and who had political ambitions, knew he could count on her discretion. And she always provided a hot bath afterward, a service the fastidious doctor insisted upon, scrubbing himself raw with soap and hot water before returning to his rooms at the American Hotel.

After the bath he dressed with care. Simon was a tall, long-boned man of forty, with a narrow face and a long nose. The prematurely white hair and fluffy white side-whiskers made him appear older. His eyes were pale blue, his skin was pale—to Hawai'ians he looked like a ghost—a true haole.

What he did with the girls in this house wasn't pleasure, it was *necessity*. Simon Edgeware despised his carnal needs, trying for months to stem his base desires until he was driven to Mrs. McCleary's in the middle of the night.

Women couldn't help their natures, he told himself as he tied his cravat while strains of "The Ballad of Annie Lisle" drifted down the hall. They were governed by their wombs and had no choice in their actions. But surely a man, superior to women, rational and educated, should be able to rise above his baser nature? Every time he left Mrs. McCleary's he vowed never to come back. But the urge always came over him again until it was like a cancer. It had to be cut out of him. He thought of the release he found here as a kind of lancing of a boil. One could only hope that the pus did not rise again.

After paying Mrs. McCleary, who sat on the verandah looking, he thought, like a spider, Edgeware rode his mare back to his hotel. Dawn was breaking. After changing his clothes and taking a few minutes for hot chocolate and toast, he would leave on foot for an appointment at the Royal Palace.

The Council Chamber was the heart of the large, spacious *Hale Ali'i* and had been designed by a German architect to resemble the palaces of Europe—with crystal chandeliers, marble floors, Doric columns, and elegant furniture upholstered in rich silk and satin. The walls were hung with the life-sized portraits of various European monarchs, presented to Hawai'i's king, Edgeware surmised, as a symbol of the esteemed regard that existed between kings everywhere. He also surmised that portraits of Kamehameha and Queen Emma had likewise been given to the rulers of the Western world, although he wondered how many of those portraits saw the light of day. On either side of this central chamber were the reception room, where

Kamehameha held daily audiences, and a grand library which had a more intimate atmosphere.

It was into the latter that Simon Edgeware was ceremoniously escorted, where he found a small group of men with whom he had lately become acquainted—British and American men of commerce and law, who had climbed in government ranks to gain the royal ear. He was greeted by the minister of foreign relations, the minister of the interior, the minister of finance, and the minister of education—King Kamehameha's advisory council, of which Simon Edgeware hoped to soon be a member.

Edgeware had come this morning with a proposal. "For the benefit of native Hawai'ians," he was going to say, to win the king's favor. Simon Edgeware thought they needed a minister of health, and he thought that he should be that man.

King Kamehameha the Fourth, twenty-six years old with a sparse beard, was dressed in a black frock coat that reached his knees, and a white waistcoat over a white shirt. He might have been a gentleman from Paris or Berlin were it not for a vaguely diamond-shaped face with round eyes, dark skin, and a woman's mouth. Edgeware had heard the young king described as handsome. He himself did not think so.

The king and his cabinet sat in brocaded chairs and sipped tea from porcelain cups as morning light streamed through the windows. The king spoke excellent English, his accent betraying his boyhood years under the tutelage of American Calvinist missionaries (although it was well known that he did not wish to create ties to America and was cultivating mutual interests with Britain and France). The monarch was quite accomplished, Edgeware had learned, playing the flute and piano, and enjoying singing, acting, and cricket. He was more worldly than his predecessors, having toured America and Europe, meeting many heads of state.

Edgeware bowed, hiding his contempt for this primitive man who presumed to be the equal of Europe's royalty. You think the monarchs of Europe respect you, he silently said to the king. I would wager they find you a curiosity when you visit their grand palaces and all the aristocrats come for a gander at the monkeys in suits, for that is how they see you. As freaks, Your Majesty, belonging in a traveling circus, whom no one takes seriously. Sixty years ago, you would have gone about naked and committed human sacrifice and worshipped trees. And you have the gall to believe yourself the equal of kings whose lines go back to the mighty Caesars.

"Thank you for granting me this audience, Your Majesty," Dr. Edgeware said with convincing sincerity, while in his mind he sneered and thought: You do not know that all these white men who call you 'friend,' behind your back call you 'wog' and 'nigger.' You think they want your friendship but all they want is your rich land and the militarily strategic location of your islands. You do not know that they have not come here to stand shoulder to shoulder with you, but to steal from you. And when they—we—have accomplished that, you will not know what happened.

Nonetheless, Dr. Edgeware would not underestimate the young king. Kamehameha did indeed know that foreign interests viewed his kingdom as a prized catch.

Taking a seat, Edgeware accepted a cup of tea from a butler in yellow livery and white gloves. He smiled to himself. It had taken months of personal campaigning, toadying, dispensing free medical advice, and slowly climbing Honolulu's tight and elite social ladder to gain this somewhat private audience with the king. It was going to be but the first step in what he was sure was going to be a stellar rise to power.

Simon Edgeware had grown up in a small village where the only educated man was the local doctor. For miles around, people depended on him. When that man rode down a country lane, farmers doffed their caps. When he entered a house, women grew quiet and meek. The doctor's word was Gospel. No one questioned him. He could have said the sky was red and everyone would have agreed. Simon Edgeware, living alone with a bitter, domineering mother, was twelve years old when he had made this observation, and when he had decided he was going to be such a man.

With the help of a local doctor who had taken him as an apprentice, Edgeware had worked hard and managed to get himself into a London medical school. But he had discovered that he didn't like science, and that he liked sick people even less. That was the problem with being a physician, he had discovered. He reveled in the power but loathed the duties expected of him. He had searched for ways to elevate himself in status and power while distancing himself from the unpleasant aspects of medicine. A hospital administrative position, perhaps. But the problem was, Britain was entrenched in the caste system, with plum posts going to the sons of men who had previously held them. The son of an impoverished dressmaker had little chance of climbing that prized ladder.

He had cast his eye across the Atlantic and wondered if he would fare better in America, where a more egalitarian system existed, where a pauper could lift himself up. And then he had heard about the opportunities in the Pacific Islands where, literally, a nobody could make a somebody of himself. Where scalawags and malcontents, he had heard, were making money and names for themselves.

The night before his departure from Southampton, a messenger from his boyhood village had come to his London hotel to inform him of his mother's passing. "Good riddance," Simon Edgeware said, and never looked back.

But after a few months in Honolulu he had realized that patients, especially the wealthy ones, those who had the king's ear, such as the sons of early missionaries like the Farrows—practically a kind of royalty themselves—were his road to power.

"I say, Edgeware," the Minister of Finance (a pompous man who was himself the son of Congregationalists who had come to the islands thirty years prior) said, "tell His Majesty the proposal you outlined for me the other day. I believe it has merit."

The town's wealthy Protestants were pressuring the king to do something about the squalid red light district at the docks, where attempts to close the brothels were like stemming the ocean tide with a broom. The authorities no sooner raided one house and shut it down than two more cropped up.

"We all know, Your Majesty," Edgeware said, "that something must be done about the rampant prostitution in this town. It must be eradicated altogether. I believe I have the solution. Instead of merely making the practice illegal, instead of eradicating prostitution through *morality* laws, I suggest we place such laws under the domain of public health. Your Majesty, we run the risk of an epidemic of venereal disease. Isn't it bad enough that the native population is decreasing through measles and influenza? Must we allow another white man's disease to add to the alarming statistics? Perhaps if Your Majesty were to create a new cabinet post, minister of public health, for example, we could create sufficient authority to close down those establishments once and for all."

And kill two birds with one stone, Edgeware thought in satisfaction. If the temptation weren't there—if he didn't know about the existence of Mrs. McCleary's house—then he could fight his baser nature by having no outlet through which to succumb to it.

W ait," Mahina said softly against his ear. She stroked his muscular back, his thick hair, his firm buttocks.

They had been making love for hours, with Mahina bringing the young man to the brink of climax many times, and then halting it, like a warm tide, back and forth, stroking, caressing, pinching. He had left his hot breath on every inch of her vast, naked body. She had tasted every perspiring spot of his skin.

He was twenty years old and filled with the impatience of youth. It was up to Mahina, thirty-three years his senior, to teach him the ways of skillful lovemaking—a tradition her people had enjoyed for many generations. And the way the gods had meant for it to be between men and women.

It was time now. With the strong internal muscles of her *'amo hulu* she squeezed his *piko maʻi* until he finally gave a shout and shook and quivered in her fleshy arms, while Mahina rode her own wave of pleasure that felt as warm as a rainbow.

They laid together on the mat, damp and tired, but refreshed as well. They had just performed a sacred ritual. They both knew the gods were smiling. He whispered "Aloha, Tutu," and left the hut. Mahina waited awhile longer, relishing the feel of her body. Then she slipped into her muumuu and went out into the bright morning sunlight.

She was ravenous. She always was after a night of vigorous sex. Too bad the haole did not indulge in such pleasure. Although she had lived among white people since she was thirteen years old and Mika Emily and Mika Kalono had arrived on their ship at Hilo, Mahina still did not understand them. The haole said sex was bad. They stopped the girls from swimming out to the ships where the sailors happily embraced them. Instead, they built dirty little houses and the white men came in the night and paid for what they had once gotten for free.

She looked around at her people, going about their day as their ancestors had. Which was also a good thing. There had been no sickness here in many years, not like in Honolulu, or coastal villages where white men frequently visited. This place at the base of the Pali where the Nu'uanu Valley began was called Wailaka and the village, a collection of huts, pavilions, and its own sacred *heiau*, was hundreds of years old. Her uncle, Kekoa—her mother's brother—was its chief. Between him and herself, they saw to it that their people lived the traditional life and did not get seduced by haole ways.

She decided to collect herbs to make a tonic for her little Pinau, her *hapa-haole* grandson who was sickly.

As she carried her ponderous body through the village, waving to her friends, smiling, offering aloha, she thought about her ailing grandson, and about the kanaka who were dying each year of white men's diseases, and she thought back to when she was a little girl and her mother, Pua, had told her there never used to be disease and sickness among their people. High Chiefess Pua credited her people's good health to Lono's Penis, which had stood for generations on the altar in the sacred *heiau*. But her mother had hidden the healing stone in Pele's Womb, and no one knew where it was.

Mahina stopped when she came upon the *kapa*-cloth pavilion, where the women worked on pounding mulberry bark, cutting it into strips, laying it out in the sun to become cloth. Three girls were helping. They were close friends, fifteen years old, and always seen together. What made Mahina stop suddenly was that each of the girls had a lady's bonnet on her head. All three were small-brimmed, but one was made of straw and the other two of fabric. All three were trimmed with lace and ribbons.

The sight sent a chill through Mahina.

She pursed her lips, scratched her shoulder, rubbed her nose, and gave the situation a great deal of thought.

Finally, she went to the entrance to the pavilion, which was nothing more than a thatch roof supported on tall posts, and called to the three.

As the slender, smiling girls in colorful muumuus came up to her, Mahina chose her words carefully. She herself had accepted the muumuu long ago, when she had been a girl like these three and Mika Emily had let her and her friends try out her parasols and gloves and handbags, and they had wanted them all. The haole dress was a way of life now, and Mahina knew they could not go back to the sarong. But the bonnets represented more than simply something to put on your head—they were a lure. The haole threw out bait and when the kanaka took it, the haole pulled them in like fish.

"Very nice bonnets," she said to the girls in an admiring tone. "Where did you get them?"

They glanced at each other and shifted on their feet. "In town," one replied.

Mahina smiled. "Was it at a haole church?"

"There were ladies out front, handing out clothes. For *free*, Tutu Mahina, no money!"

"Did you go *inside* the church?"

They were reluctant to answer, but knew they had to. "They say their god is very powerful," one of them blurted defensively.

"Ah," Mahina said, nodding. "Did you see him there?"

"He is invisible. Just like the old kanaka gods."

Mahina knew they were speaking from innocence rather than disrespect, and so she was patient with them. She lifted her eyebrows and gave them a surprised look. "You think kanaka gods are invisible? You have never seen one? Auwe!"

The girls looked at each other. "Tutu, have you seen a god?"

"Even better. I have seen a goddess. Would you like to see?"

One gave her a skeptical look. "Is it a wooden idol?"

"No no, I mean real goddess, with hair and eyes and a smile. I take you to see."

They followed her into the forest, hands clasped to their precious bonnets so that branches and vines would not snag them away.

They came to a lagoon, calm and still with a glassy surface. The girls looked around with wide eyes. "Is the goddess here, Tutu?"

"Here, closer to the water. She lives here."

When they reached the grassy bank, she told them to kneel. "Now look."

They did, and as they watched their reflections in the water, she said, *"I ka wa mamua . . ."* which meant, "In a time past . . ." And she began her story with the double-hulled canoes that had come a thousand years ago from legendary Kahiki. She told them the story of Papio the shark goddess. She reminded them of the legend of the Menehune, the Dwarf People who lived deep in the forests. She talked about the time ancient Chief Puna was held captive by the devious Dragon Goddess. Mahina spoke of legendary heroes of long ago, their battles, their romances, their larger-than-human feats. In a soft, melodic voice that was almost a chant, Mahina spun tales in the air over the tranquil lagoon, while the three girls were held in thrall by their own reflections.

Finally, when she had so cleverly woven her stories together that one could see the great fabric that was these islands' noble history, Mahina said, "What you see, my daughters, are real goddesses. Not invisible. Not wood, not stone. Made of life. With power, with *mana.*"

When she was finished, and they had looked long and hard at the three beautiful goddesses in the lagoon, the girls pulled the haole bonnets from their heads and tearfully embraced their giant, loving "Tutu," asking for her forgiveness and promising never to go inside the haole church again.

Mahina watched them run back to the village, her heart troubled.

Today, she had saved those girls. But what about the days to come? Her people were being slowly seduced. They wanted haole hats. They wanted haole gloves and umbrellas and shoes. Mahina could not be everywhere at once. Slowly, these things were going to come into her village. Slowly, every girl and woman of her village was going to own a hat and gloves and umbrellas and shoes. There was a need for constant vigilance, to keep the old ways alive but in secret. To remind them, as she had reminded the three girls. But the day would come when Mahina would no longer be here and her people would stray and be lost forever.

She must do something to save her culture and her gods. But what?

Mahina lifted her eyes to the green cliffs that embraced the hidden lagoon. Covered in lush verdant growth, they rose straight up from the water like warriors on guard, watching, ever vigilant. The haole had a strange need to measure things, and they had come to these cliffs and climbed and counted and they had declared these peaks to be two thousand feet high. Many days, the tops could not be seen, when mists descended and shrouded the sacred summits in silence. That was when the gods visited the mountaintops, and they did not wish to be seen by the people.

There was no mist today. The craggy mountain summits stood against a deep blue sky. And so there were no gods up there.

She looked at the lagoon, a bowl of green-blue water embraced by forest and flowers. There were gods in the water.

Lifting her arms, Mahina began a holy chant, calling out the names of the spirits, praising them, promising them that they would never be forgotten. She moved her arms and stamped her feet. Her massive hips swayed like an earthquake. But she was graceful and light. Her hands told the stories of the gods and the ancestors, and while she danced the sacred hula and sang her ancient chant, Mahina sent a silent prayer for help.

Our ways are vanishing, our people want haole things. Tell me what to do.

And from far away, perhaps as far away as ancient Kahiki, came a whispered reply: The haole have pushed their ways on you for many years—it is time to push back.

Mahina's dance came to an end and she stood alone, with a frown on her face.

"But how?" she asked the silent, deserted lagoon. "How Mahina push back?"

CHAPTER FOURTEEN

The screams could be heard from the street.

"God have mercy," Sister Veronica whispered as she crossed herself.

"Poor Mrs. Farrow," Sister Theresa said as she looked toward the closed French doors on the upper verandah of Farrow House. "She is having one of her difficult days."

Other pedestrians glanced at the house on the corner of King Street. She saw pity on their faces. Honolulu was a small town where everyone knew everyone else's business. Ever since Captain Farrow's mother had come to live with him, rumors were rampant—that Emily Farrow was raving mad and her son kept her chained up in an attic. It was said that Farrow had already gone through three private "nurses"— robust women meant to keep Mrs. Farrow locked in her room—and judging by the screams and sounds of objects being smashed, Sister Theresa suspected that number four would soon be giving notice.

As the two Sisters were about to continue on their way, Captain Farrow suddenly appeared from a side street, on a galloping chestnut mare. Grooms came running from the stables and took the horse as the captain jumped down. When he dashed into the house, Theresa said to Sister Veronica, "We must see if we can help."

"But Missy Miller is expecting us."

"You go on ahead then. It doesn't require both of us to change Missy Miller's bandages. I will join you shortly."

With a dubious expression, Veronica hurried on and Theresa went down the path to Farrow House.

No one answered her knock so she let herself in, calling out. But there was a terrible commotion on the upper floor, and no one heard her. She took the liberty of closing the door behind herself and went to the foot of the staircase, from where she heard a frantic exchange at the head of the stairs.

"She refuses to take the medicine, sir. I think you should keep her restrained."

"I'll do no such thing. I will not tie my mother up like an animal."

"She's done a lot of damage to the room this time. Tore things up. Smashed 'em. Next time she might do serious harm to herself."

"Locking her in her room is sufficient, Mrs. Brown. Now please go and be with my mother. And try again to get her to take the medicine. Tell her it is what Dr. Edgeware ordered."

Theresa heard the rattle of keys on an iron ring, a door opening and closing, and a moment later, Captain Farrow came down the stairs with a dark look on his face.

He stopped when he saw her. "Sister," he said. "What can I do for you?"

"I thought perhaps I could do something for you."

"Ah," he said. "You heard the screams." He sighed as he came the rest of the way down to stand directly before her. She had to look up, as he remained one step up, and he was tall to begin with. "I suppose all of Honolulu heard it. Is there anything I can do to help?"

"Every doctor in town has seen her, and they all say the same thing. Give her laudanum." He removed his hat and descended the final stair. "But it is only to get her to sleep. It isn't a cure." He looked tired. There were shadows beneath his eyes, new lines around his mouth.

She followed him into the drawing room, where the portrait of beautiful Leilani hung over the fireplace. The spacious room was furnished with Chinese sofas and chairs coated in shiny black lacquer, inlaid with mother-of-pearl, and strewn with silk cushions and pillows.

"What's wrong with her, if I may ask?"

He strode across the room and opened a pair of French doors to admit the soothing trade wind. "She suffers from a nervous disorder that the doctors can neither identify nor cure. It started thirty years ago, actually." He turned to face her. "I was seven years old and my brother was five. Mother was alone with us because my father was at sea. Something happened that summer—I have no idea what. Mother refused to speak of it then and certainly will not now. My father questioned neighbors and local natives, but no one could tell him what happened. Whatever it was that my mother experienced or witnessed, it weakened her constitution and continues to give her nightmares to this day."

They heard shouting overhead, the sound of someone stamping a foot. "It must be hard on your son," Theresa said.

"Jamie is at Waialua, staying with his cousin Reese. I can't have him around Mother."

"Is she capable of hurting him?"

Captain Farrow went to a mahogany sideboard set out with bottles and glasses. Uncorking a crystal decanter, he poured brown liquid into a glass. "We don't know," he said as he took a bracing swig. "But we can't risk it. Sister Theresa, when we were still living in Hilo and my father was between voyages, he woke one night to find my mother gone. This was eleven years ago. I wasn't home, but Peter was. My father got up and went in search of our mother and found her on the cliffs overlooking the sea. Father climbed out on the rocks to bring her back to safety, lost his footing, and plunged to his death. Mother doesn't even remember it. To this day she believes our father went out to sea and never returned."

"I am so sorry."

"I don't know what to do, Sister. Mother can't live at Waialua, because there will be a new baby. But if she stays here, I can't have Jamie." He released a weary sigh. "And I miss my son."

"Captain Farrow, what triggers these episodes?"

"I have no idea. She goes for weeks being completely normal. She reads her Bible, works at embroidery, attends church. And then, she will wake up one night and be unable to fall asleep. Nights of insomnia follow, one after another until it affects her mind."

"Do you know the cause of the insomnia?"

He stared into his glass. "She says ghosts gather around her bed. They keep her awake with their screaming. So she screams back to scare them away."

"And she won't take laudanum?"

"My mother is a staunch supporter of temperance. She will not have anything to do with alcohol. No spirits, no drugs. Which leaves us with nothing." He looked into his drink and frowned, as if it had somehow offended him. Lowering his voice, he said, "The thing that troubles me, Sister, is that a sane person doesn't just go insane over-night, does she? There has to be something there already, doesn't there? Surely my mother was destined to lose her faculties, even if she had stayed in New Haven. And if there is insanity in my family, then my son stands a chance of inheriting it. I have heard that mental illness skips generations. Since Peter and I appear to be of sound mind . . ."

Now Theresa understood why an air of tragedy seemed to hang over this house and this family. She also understood the comment Mr. Farrow had made to his brother weeks ago, about deeply regretting fathering a son. She had thought it a cruel statement. But now she saw it in a different light. "I cannot answer you on that subject, Mr. Farrow, but I would like to try to help your mother. There is an herb, valerian, that has mild sedative effects and helps a person to sleep."

"Valerian? I've never heard of it."

"It is not found in Hawai'i. My Sisters and I cultivate the plant in our garden with seeds we brought from home. We concoct a very effective tea from the root."

He stared at her with his direct eyes. As it unnerved her, she smiled and said, "I know, I am very young."

He smiled and seemed to relax a little.

"I would like to meet your mother." Sister Theresa wondered about Mrs. Farrow's strange condition, if the insomnia came first and caused the hallucinations, or if it was the other way around. It seemed possible that, if they could stave off the sleeplessness, the spells of mental instability might be averted and the cycle broken.

"I don't think that's wise." He lifted his eyes to the ceiling. "Mrs. Brown seems to have calmed my mother somewhat. It happens. Her insane episodes occur mostly at night. Today her hysteria was brought on by Mrs. Brown trying to give her the laudanum. Perhaps we should wait until the episode has passed."

"But it is possible I can help her *now*."

"I must warn you, her reaction to you might be strange. I doubt Mother has ever seen a nun. There were very few Catholics in New Haven when she lived there. There wasn't even a Catholic church built there yet. So if she stares at you or makes a remark . . ."

She smiled and said, "I am used to it."

He set the glass down. "I am sure you are. Very well. We can go up now."

When they reached her door, they heard muffled shouts on the other side—one tone pleading, the other furious. "I guess Mrs. Brown doesn't have things under control after all," Captain Farrow said.

"I would still like to meet her."

"It will have to be brief," he said as he knocked on the door. They heard keys rattling, and then Mrs. Brown looked out. Her face was florid and her gray hair stood out under her mobcap. "It's not a good time, sir," she said, but Captain Farrow insisted, and the nurse stood aside.

They found Mrs. Farrow standing on the far side of the bedroom, brandishing a poker from the fireplace. Other than her threatening stance, she appeared quite normal. Slender and white-haired, she wore a green day gown with long sleeves and a high collar with a cameo brooch at the throat. "Robert," she said, "will you please tell this maddening creature to stop forcing her devilish alcohol upon me—"

Her eyes fell on Theresa and she stared with parted lips. "What are *you*?"

"Sister Theresa is a religious nun, Mother."

Mrs. Farrow wrinkled her nose. "Surely not one of ours."

"Sister Theresa is Catholic."

"Ah, that would explain it. Funny people, Catholics."

"She wanted to meet you, Mother."

"Why?" she snapped, still brandishing the poker.

Theresa spoke, keeping in mind three important facts about this woman: that she was a devout Christian, that she had come here as a missionary, and that she was above all a *lady*. "I have only recently come to Hawai'i as a missionary, Mrs. Farrow, and I would be most fascinated to hear your story. I thought it would be pleasant to have a chat over a nice cup of tea."

Mrs. Farrow stood in silent indecision while sounds from the streets—the creaking of wagon wheels, the clip-clop of horses' hooves, children shouting—drifted through the doors opened to the verandah. Presently she said, "A nice cup of tea would be most welcome right now," and lowered the poker.

When Mrs. Brown said, "First your medicine," and started forward with a bottle and a spoon, the poker went up again.

Sister Theresa turned to Captain Farrow and said, "Would you please arrange to have tea service sent up? Hot water in the pot, two cups. A plate of biscuits if you have any." He transferred the request to the nurse, who set the bottle of laudanum down and, grumbling, left the room.

"I'll take that, Mother," Farrow said, removing the poker from her hands and leading her to a rocking chair by the open doors. "You've exhausted yourself. You need to rest."

She looked up at him with sadness in her eyes. "I cannot sleep, Robert. They keep me awake. They haunt me to madness."

Theresa helped herself to a chair, bringing it to face Mrs. Farrow, who seemed content to let her sit. Theresa looked around the room—at the broken things, the disarray—and wondered at the "ghosts" that threw her into such frenzies.

"Do you know, young lady," Emily said as she looked out at the trees in the garden, "when I left New Haven it was with such dreams and visions, and with so much love for God in my heart that I thought I should be able to fly here on my own. But the voyage was hard. We had to make many attempts to round Cape Horn, as we kept being driven back by storms and swells. Three crewmen were washed overboard. I thought we were going to perish. And then when we finally arrived here and stout sailors carried us ashore, I found naked savages babbling in an incoherent tongue. I was suddenly filled with terror and wondered why God had brought us to this terrible place. Perhaps that is why He is punishing me. For my faithless heart so many years ago."

She looked at Theresa with eyes filled with pain. "Do not be fooled by the smiles and by the way they wear European clothes, and call themselves by Christian names and sit in the church every Sunday. The old ways are still here. The superstitions, the ghosts, the evil. They are all around us, the powers of Satan have not been driven from these islands. I tried forty years ago, the Good Lord knows, I tried. . . ."

The tea service arrived and Mrs. Brown placed it on a small table. Theresa opened her black bag to bring out the packet of valerian. As she spooned some into the pot, leaving it to simmer, she said, "This is a special tea we make at the convent. It has a strong aroma and taste, but it is hearty and restorative."

Emily smiled and offered her visitor a biscuit, taking one for herself, and spoke about those days long ago when she went for weeks without seeing another white woman, while her husband, Reverend Stone, traveled about the island of Hawai'i preaching and baptizing. While they spoke, Captain Farrow had retreated to a corner, in watchful silence. When the tea was ready, Mrs. Farrow poured and gave Theresa a cup.

Her hands shook and Theresa saw that her eyes were bloodshot, and she wondered if it was those very days, long ago, that were now causing the sleeplessness. Theresa remembered what Mahina had told her about believing she herself was cursed because of something that had happened thirty years ago. She wondered if perhaps there was a connection.

Theresa watched Mrs. Farrow as she brought the cup to her lips. Valerian root tea had a powerful, unpleasant aroma—there was nothing she could do about that. But she had disguised the strong taste with a spoonful of sugar. Emily started to take a sip, then paused. With a frown, she lifted the cup to her nose and sniffed.

Theresa glanced at Captain Farrow, who stiffened. He gave her a questioning look, which she interpreted as: Did they have anything else in their garden that cured insomnia? Unfortunately not. Like the Honolulu doctors, the Sisters administered tincture of opium for sleeplessness and other ailments. Valerian root was their only hope.

Mrs. Farrow wrinkled her nose and said, "This tea has a terrible aroma."

"It's a bracing brew," Theresa began.

Emily turned to her guest, fixing her with an irritated look, and Theresa feared for a moment that Emily might throw the cup at her.

Then Mrs. Farrow said, "Why is it so familiar? Ah yes!" she said, her face clearing. "It is unmistakably valerian root. My mother used to drink it every night. I had forgotten about that. I wonder if it will help with my insomnia." With that, she took a healthy sip, and then another. When half the cup was gone, she said, "This reminds me of home! My grandmother grew summer herbs. I loved helping her plant the seeds in the springtime. . . ."

She refilled her cup and continued to speak nostalgically of halcyon days in New Haven, over forty years ago, and then closer in time—something about a red Chinese kite and a lovely pink conch shell—and when the tea was gone she thanked Sister Theresa for the visit and suggested that she might try for a nap.

Theresa said good-bye and, out in the hall, she said to Captain Farrow, "It sometimes takes a few days of drinking the tea before one feels the affects. I will leave this packet with you. Make sure she drinks a cup every evening before she retires."

He took her hand, which shocked her, and looked deep into her eyes as he said, "I can't thank you enough, Sister. Yours was certainly a new approach."

"Sometimes kindness works better than bullying."

"I am even more surprised at how easily she accepted you. I would have thought she wouldn't tolerate a Catholic in her presence."

"I was relying on her ladylike upbringing and that she would place manners before prejudice. We shall see if this works. In the meantime, Captain Farrow, my Sisters and I will add your mother to our prayers."

"Will you come back?" He stood very close, and the hallway grew warm and intimate. She wanted to say that it was best he have Dr. Edgeware look in on his mother, she wanted to say that she would happily send one of the other Sisters, she wanted to say that Mrs. Brown would be best suited to look after her. But she said, "Of course I will come back."

Theresa was on her own, as Sister Veronica was down with the croup. Mother Agnes only reluctantly allowed her to go—she did not like the Sisters going out alone. But Mrs. Liddell urgently needed medicine, and Theresa promised Mother Agnes she would take only "safe" streets, one of them being King Street, which brought her at noon, upon her return from the Liddells, to the Farrow property.

Two women were sitting on the lawn, Mrs. Farrow in a straight-backed chair, working a needlepoint, Mahina on the grass, stringing a lei from baskets filled with flowers. Sister Theresa could not help comparing the two—Emily Farrow, slender, diminutive, a dainty lace cap on her white hair. She had brought a new religion to these islands, new morals, new traditions. And Mahina, dusky-skinned, voluptuous, full of life, keeper of Hawaiʻi's gods and culture, with her bare feet so grounded in Hawaiʻi's volcanic soil that she made one think of Gaia, the Earth goddess of the ancient Greeks. Two more dissimilar women could not possibly exist, and yet they were the two grandmothers of Jamie Farrow.

Theresa called out as she walked across the grass. Mahina rose to her feet and engulfed her in her generous arms, while Mrs. Farrow said, "Hello, dear."

Captain Farrow's mother was improving. After Sister Theresa had given her the valerian root tea, it had taken several days before she'd begun to enjoy better sleep. But it was only a matter of time, Captain Farrow warned Theresa, before something set her off and she would need to be confined to her bedroom again.

Theresa came around to look at the needlepoint canvas stretched on a standing frame. Emily Farrow was working a landscape scene with trees and flowers and blue sky. "It's beautiful," she said.

"The Devil loves idle hands, my dear."

Despite giving an air of fragility, there was vigor in the arm that drove the needle into the canvas, the hand that pulled it out behind and stabbed it up again. For an instant, Sister Theresa was given a glimpse of Emily Farrow as she must have been when a young woman, bringing civilization to a foreign shore. Theresa recalled how her own mother, running her farm up in Oregon, had put the same robustness into everything she did.

Mahina tried to drape a garland of fragrant ginger blossoms around Theresa's shoulders but she laughed and thanked her and said she could not accept it. Mahina's leis were famous all over the islands, and although she could sell them for a profit, she insisted on giving them away.

Nearby, in the shade of a tamarind tree, Miss Carter was giving Jamie a history lesson. He smiled when he saw Theresa, waving his hand and calling out. His constitution was improving, for which she accredited the rusty iron nail in his soup. He was still a frail boy, and she wondered what more could be done to build him up.

"Hello there!"

She turned and, shading her eyes from the sun, looked up to see Captain Farrow at his telescope—reminding her that it was the hour between noon and one, and that he was at his daily ritual. "Come up, Sister. The view is beautiful from up here."

When she hesitated, Mahina said, "You go, Kika! See plenty ships. Plenty water. Maybe Mano. Good luck see Mano."

As Theresa excused herself from their company, she caught a venomous look on Miss Carter's face, and she wondered again why the young woman disliked her so.

When she came out onto the second-floor verandah, two things struck her: the breathtaking view and the refreshing wind. She could see the harbor, the docks and ships' masts and, beyond, the ocean. But it was the wind that captured her soul. It swept against her face as she closed her eyes in welcome. She could only imagine it blowing through her hair and she wished in that moment that she could tear the heavy veils from her head and feel the cool caress of the blessed breeze.

"To what do we owe this visit, Sister?" Captain Farrow asked. He seemed to be in good humor, as he was grinning and smoking a long, narrow cigar.

"I was merely passing by. Your mother seems to be doing very well."

"She hasn't had a spell for days. And it's good to have Jamie home. Have you ever looked through a spyglass, Sister? It's like looking at a whole new world."

He stepped aside and gestured for her to come forward. So she set her nursing bag down and bent to place her eye to the scope. As she peered through the glass, Captain Farrow said, "That's one of our ships coming in now. The *Kestrel,* named for my father's vessel that was scuttled ten years ago."

She watched the majestic clipper ride on the bosom of the sea while Captain Farrow said, "My father got his start sixty years ago, trading metal goods to the natives of Alaska in exchange for furs, carrying them to Hawai'i to pick up sandalwood, taking it all to Canton province in China where there was a huge demand for sandalwood."

He puffed on his cigar and the manly aroma of the smoke drifted her way. "By the end of the 1820s the forests were almost entirely denuded, and my father had to find other cargo to carry, such as sugar and coffee and beef. He built more ships, expanded routes, and diversified, so that my family prospered."

Another draw on the cigar, more smoke coming her way, and she realized she would be carrying the scent with her back to the convent. "I'm proud of the Farrow shipping line today, but now I want to connect Hawai'i to the rest of the world. Improved shipping is the answer. The days of a three-week or four-week passage on clippers are over, Sister Theresa. The age of steam is upon us, an age when we can make that same passage in as little as ten days. Can you imagine such speed?"

"It sounds wonderful," she said, straightening up from the spyglass, "especially to one who suffered miserably on the crossing from San Francisco."

"Right now, Sister, Hawai'i is too far away for the average traveler or businessman. But an established steamer line would see to it that Americans come in hordes, bringing with them capital, enterprise, and prosperity. And then we will see Hawai'i grow into a kingdom worthy of the title."

The view from up there was wonderful. She could see over rooftops, see the distant beaches and Hawai'ians riding on their amazing surfboards. "It is apparent you love the sea, Mr. Farrow."

"I first went to sea when I was eleven years old. I could read and write by then, and do my sums. My father took me on my first voyage. I was a cabin boy. But I was not idle. My father was a well-read man and prided himself on his ship's library. He gave me books to read— Plato, Aristotle, Voltaire. He saw to it that I was an educated man as well as one who knew how to read the stars and run a ship. I received my master's ticket when I was twenty-two."

He shook his head as he turned toward the busy harbor. "But Hawai'i is in the grip of an economic depression, and I am certain I have the answers. The problem is getting men to listen."

She had already read, in local newspapers, of Mr. Farrow's campaign to build faster, safer ships, and that he was looking for investors. "Many more people would come to these islands," she said, "if the voyage were shorter and more pleasant. But faster sea travel would also connect people to home much more quickly. Think of the mail, Mr. Farrow. It takes weeks for a letter to come by clipper, but only days by steam. Many people here are homesick. They are eager to hear from loved ones back home."

Captain Farrow gave her one his characteristic looks, long and thoughtful, and then his lips lifted in a faint smile, as if a fine idea had just occurred to him.

They were distracted by a squeal of laughter on the lawn below, and they saw Mahina tickling Jamie, making him squirm with delight. She reminded Theresa of a bear with her cub.

"What about Jamie's Hawai'ian grandfather?" she asked. "Does he come around much?"

"Eighteen years ago, Mahina's husband, and two of their sons, had the misfortune of being down at the docks when press gangs were searching for unwary victims to nab. It was a real problem in those days, when nearly a thousand whaling ships a year stopped at Honolulu. Used to be, these waters were filled with whales every winter, when they came to Hawai'i to bear young. The whaling ships would come and wait, and hunting was easy. But soon there were no more whales in Hawai'ian waters, so the ships had to go farther north, all the way up to the arctic. As a consequence, the sailor's life was a hard one, so as soon as a whaler dropped anchor, crews would abandon ship and disappear into the forests. The captains had to force anyone they could into service."

"And Mahina has never heard from them since?"

He shook his head.

She looked down at the laughing child. "It's a shame Jamie cannot see his cousin more often," she said, thinking that small boys need play companions.

Captain Farrow's demeanor changed, his face darkened, and she suspected he was thinking of the rift between himself and his brother. All of Honolulu knew of the break between the brothers, although Sister Theresa had never heard the cause of it.

"Does Mahina have other family?"

"Her daughter, Leilani, who was my wife, died in a chicken pox epidemic. And one son still lives on a family farm. Her uncle, Kekoa, is chief of a village in Wailaka, at the base of the Nu'uanu Valley, just three miles from here."

Mahina's melodic laughter reached them. "Their history fascinates me, Captain Farrow. Would it be all right if I asked a few questions?"

"The elders don't mind sharing their knowledge as long as you are respectful and don't ask in an offensive way. But I somehow think you could never be offensive."

"I will be politely curious. I think, Mr. Farrow, that if I can learn more about the natives' history and culture, I can better understand how to approach their nursing care." She thought for a moment, and added, "My curiosity has rewarded me with the life I am now living. Had I not wondered about a religious Sister I saw in a chemist shop, had I not followed her and wanted to see inside a hospital, I would not have received the revelation that this was the life I am meant to live."

He looked her up and down, not in a rude way, but in a detached manner. "It seems a difficult life, Sister," he said. "It seems, forgive me, *unnatural*."

"The rewards outweigh the sacrifices, Mr. Farrow. To take care of people is all I have ever wanted to do."

"Still, you're quite young to give up so much."

"I have turned twenty," she interjected with pride.

He looked down and, to her utter shock, took hold of her left hand. He lifted it to examine the ring on her third finger. "It looks like a wedding ring," he murmured. "Especially as it is worn on the left hand."

She felt her face burn. Mr. Farrow stood uncomfortably close and, despite the breezes that swept across the balcony, he gave off masculine scents: shaving soap, tobacco, whiskey. They should have offended her, instead she found them alluring. "It is a wedding ring," she said, barely finding breath. "When we take final vows, we are considered 'brides of Christ,' symbolic of our union with our Savior in heaven, a sign that we have dedicated our chastity and virtue to Him."

"Is that so?" Captain Farrow said softly, continuing to hold her hand, his eyes delving into hers so that she suddenly couldn't breathe. For an instant, she felt they were the only two people on earth. She was lost in his magnetism. And then he released her hand and returned his attention to the vista that lay before them—the lush vegetation, the palm trees, and in the distance, the extinct volcano called Diamond Head.

Theresa sensed agitation in the captain. He seemed suddenly impatient with her, and she wondered why. Presently he said, with his back to her, "A woman can be dedicated to God and still lead a normal life." He turned and fixed stormy eyes on her. "To be so young and to have given up all possibility of having a husband and children isn't right. My mother served God in the most self-sacrificing way, and yet she had a husband and two sons."

"My calling is to nurse the sick, Mr. Farrow," she said softly. "The Sisters of Good Hope opened that door for me. And you are right, ours is not a natural life. But it is a small sacrifice for the privilege of taking care of those in need."

He gave her a long look, then said, "Forgive me, Sister. I did not mean to criticize you or belittle your way of life." He looked down at the lawn below. "I have always admired my mother for coming here to an unknown land, facing terrible hardships. And I admire you. You are very brave, Sister. I would wager that nothing frightens you."

She retrieved her bag, straightened her veils, and said, "I must be going now. Thank you for showing me this view. I see now why you come up here every day."

"I suppose the whole town knows about my noon break. It's a luxury in a way, but I also like to monitor the ships in the harbor."

"I think it is a ritual that refreshes your soul, Mr. Farrow."

He gave her a startled look. "I'm not one for ritual, Sister."

"Everyone is. Rituals anchor us. They afford us moments of reflection. Rituals have a way of making time stand still and making us aware of our surroundings. Our life in the convent is comprised of rituals, and my favorite is an hour of silence every day in the herb garden. It is there that I listen to the symphony that is Hawai'i."

He gave her a curious look. "I've heard Hawai'i described as everything from a paradise to a hellhole, but never a symphony!"

"The music of the mists fills my heart with joy, Mr. Farrow. I delight to hear the songs of the flowers. Even birds in flight create melodies." She smiled self-consciously. "When we lived in Oregon, I had a favorite spot I visited every day, where I would sit and enjoy the sun. Nature sounded like music to me."

He lowered his voice. "'You only need sit still long enough in some attractive spot in the woods that all its inhabitants may exhibit themselves to you by turns.'"

At her questioning look, he said, "It's a quote from *Walden*, by a fellow named Thoreau. Have you read it? It was published six years ago."

She shook her head.

"Come, Sister, I will show you out."

In the downstairs hall, he paused and disappeared into his study. When he came out, he handed her a small book. "You may borrow this for as long as you wish."

She read the cover: *Walden* by Henry David Thoreau. Although she thought she should decline it, she slipped the book into her black bag and thanked him.

As she left Farrow House, she told herself that she would ask Mother Agnes if this was permitted reading. But as she walked beneath shady tamarinds, feeling the day embrace her, she felt the book beckon to her.

She came upon the verdant lawn spreading before the Royal Palace. Here were quaint benches for the weary pedestrian, or for those simply wishing to while away the hours and watch the parade of Honolulu society go by. She sat and brought the book out into the sunlight. It looked as if it had been read many times. A much-loved book. Inside the cover was written: "From the library of Robert Gideon Farrow."

Theresa ran her fingertips over his name. Robert Gideon. It sounded so commanding. She turned to the first page and began to read: "When I wrote the following pages . . . I lived alone, in the woods."

She soon became lost in the narrative. "Let us first be as simple and well as Nature ourselves . . . I would rather sit on a pumpkin and have it all to myself, than be crowded on a velvet cushion . . . A lake is the landscape's most beautiful and expressive feature."

Theresa hated to close the book. Mr. Thoreau had transported her back to her beloved Oregon, but the hour was growing late and she needed to get back to the convent.

Mother Agnes met her in the front parlor, a look of fury on her face. "I'm sorry I'm late, Reverend Mother, but—"

"You were *seen*, Sister." She trembled with anger. "Seen alone in the company of a man. Looking through a telescope with him. And I am told you were laughing!"

Theresa bowed her head and admitted that this was true. "Forgive me, Reverend Mother. Captain Farrow invited me to look through his spyglass. I saw no harm in it."

"The harm is that you are still too worldly, Sister. You must work harder to keep your mind on spiritual matters. And you must curb your curiosity, Sister. By being curious about others, you open yourself to earthly matters and you put yourself in danger of straying from the religious path to the carnal one."

Agnes clasped her hands at her waist, drew herself stiff and straight, and said, "You may not return to Farrow House. Under no circumstances are you ever again to set foot on that property or to have anything more to do with that family."

"Yes, Reverend Mother," Sister Theresa said. And she knew then that she was going to keep her new book a secret.

CHAPTER FIFTEEN

O h Sister," Veronica said with a sigh, "look at these colors. Have you ever seen such purples? It says here that mauve and purple and magenta are all the fashion this year. Crinolines are wider than ever and perfectly bell-shaped." Sister Veronica let her eyes linger over the colored illustrations in the ladies' magazine, recently arrived from America.

She and Sister Theresa were in Klausner's Emporium on Merchant Street, an enormous store that offered everything from pins to hand-operated washing machines with attached wringers. As the two nuns pored over the newest arrivals in publications for women, the sales clerk, a pasty-skinned young man fresh from New York who had come to the islands in hopes of finding opportunity, scowled openly at them. They came in once a week to read the periodicals and newspapers, and they always left without buying anything. He didn't know that the two young religious Sisters would have loved more than anything to purchase some lavender soap from him, or chocolates, or linen handkerchiefs. Or even just some lard for the kitchen, needles for sewing, or something as prosaic as a pencil. But they had no money. Their little convent was struggling and even the cost of a one-penny boiled sweet was beyond their means.

"Look at the yards of lace and bows on this evening gown," Veronica said, holding the magazine up for Theresa to see. "You would look so lovely in this, Sister. You would be the belle of the ball!"

Theresa looked at the color illustrations and smiled politely. She was not interested in fashion, something Veronica seemed to have a passion for. Her interests lay in the latest newspapers. Not those imported from America and England, months out of date, but island news—*The Honolulu Star, The Polynesian, The O'ahu Herald*—and she wasn't interested in just any stories, her focus was very specific.

Local news seemed to always carry mention of Robert Farrow, as he was politically active and very vocal about the government. Since she was forbidden to return to Farrow House, she found herself in need of seeking other means to remain connected to the family, although she could not say why.

"Look at this cloak, Sister," Veronica said, showing her another magazine illustration. "You would look so pretty in this."

Theresa laughed. "Sister, the cloak is scarlet!"

Veronica laid a light hand on Theresa's arm, her eyes bright as she said, "You are so very pretty, Sister, you should wear beautiful clothes."

Before Theresa could suggest to Sister Veronica that she temper her enthusiasm for material things, the glass doors of the front entrance opened and a familiar voice boomed, "Ah, there you are, Sisters!"

Father Halloran came in, mopping his face as usual. The long black cassock was not suited to the island climate, yet he and the French clergy all wore the close-fitting, ankle-length clerical attire of their home churches. "Mother Agnes suggested I might find you here."

"What can we do for you, Father?" Theresa said, laying down her newspapers.

"I set out on one of my evangelical rounds, which I attempt every few months but without success, and as I was heading toward my destination, it occurred to me that I might have more success if I had two nursing Sisters with me. In offering free medical care, we might open a roadway into a dark den of sin."

The two Sisters gave him a startled look. "Father," said Sister Veronica. "Where on earth would that be?"

"Come along, Sisters. We are paying a visit to the houses of ill repute along the docks."

It had been several weeks since the spirits of the lagoon had spoken, instructing Mahina to "push back." And in that time, she had not been able to fathom the meaning of their words.

As she moved through the forest with her basket, searching for perfect blossoms, she knew she would not be able to decipher the gods' commandment on her own. She needed their help again. But this time she would not simply ask. She would give them a gift.

"Ah," Mahina whispered as she pushed through the trees and came upon an isolated clump of bamboo orchids standing in a patch of sunlight. They grew here wild, untended by the hand of man, so she knew they were special. She smiled as she examined the pink blossoms that crowned the tips of the tall stalks. Some came up to her waist, some were over her head. Each flower was blessed with a deep, pink heart that faded outward to white petals. They were newly bloomed, fresh with *mana*. They would be perfect.

She carefully pinched each blossom from its stalk, gently depositing them into her basket. When she had enough, she said a prayer to the spirits of this place, saying *"Mahalo,"* and pushed back through the dense trees to the lagoon, where she sat down in the sun and spent an hour stringing the fragile orchids into a lei.

She chanted as she created the garland, and as she did so, her thoughts drifted back to the days of her girlhood, when the first haole had come to Hilo. Recalling the sermons in the meetinghouse, the lessons in the school, sewing classes in Mika Emily's house, Mahina realized that Mika Kalono and his wife had not really *pushed.* They had seduced, just like the haoles were doing today with their church hats for girls.

They offer something and wait for us to take it, she thought as she threaded the fishing line through the stem-end of each orchid and pulled it through. Like catching *palila* birds with green mamane seeds and flowers and *naio* berries. You place the bait on a tree limb, and when little yellow bird come down to feed, drop net. Poor *palila* bird is trapped. Just like kanaka is trapped in haole ways.

She paused to squint at the sun-dappled lagoon. Two bright red dragonflies flitted across the surface, moving quickly in search of food, darting this way and that, just like her grandson, Jamie, her little *pinau.*

Maybe not push, the spirit of the lagoon whispered. *Maybe . . . teach. . . .*

Mahina's smile widened. She strung the final orchid on the line, tied the knot, then hefted her bulk to her feet and as she stood at the edge of the water, she called out a prayer of thanks and praise and tossed the lei onto the surface. As she watched the ripples fan out from the flowers—a sign that the gods of this place appreciated her gift—Mahina felt less troubled. The ancient spirits had told her what she must do.

Now they needed to tell her *who* it was that she must teach.

The women in these establishments are woefully without spiritual guidance," Father Halloran explained as they made their way down to the docks. "The government tries to shut down such establishments, they nonetheless keep cropping up. I am told that many of the girls suffer from diseases brought by the sailors, and are victims, too, of attempted abortions using poisons and instruments."

"Merciful heaven," Sister Veronica whispered as they followed a wooden sidewalk fronted with saloons and barber shops that advertised hot baths for five cents. There were also shops that sold ship's supplies, sailor's uniforms, nautical maps, tobacco, and newspapers. All the buildings were two and three stories tall and made of wood. Behind them, great warehouses loomed, and the sounds of a busy, bustling harbor drifted over flat rooftops.

The grog shops were quiet at this noon hour, although sailors staggered in and out and the occasional upright piano could be heard as someone banged out a tune. The so-called "hotels for men only" were also quiet at this hour of the day, but Father Halloran had visited this notorious street at night, where painted women with low décolletages and exposed stockings stood in doorways, and the grog shops were filled with customers, and light poured onto the sidewalk from windows. A dangerous place where a stranger had to watch his pockets and his back or he might wake up in an alley with a lump on his head and his money gone—or worse, find himself on a ship miles out to sea, pressed into working as a deckhand until the next foreign port.

Sister Theresa imagined that at night, with the lights and music and gaiety, this was another world, possibly even enchanting. But under the noon sun, she saw only drab buildings with dark doorways. Customers came and went through the doors of legitimate shops, but there was no mistaking the smell of vomit and urine, stale beer and rum.

The first place they stopped at was next door to a tailor shop that offered special discounts to "Officers of the American and British Navies." It was a plain-fronted, three-story structure with a sign that said, "Hotel" (one of many along the street, Sister Theresa saw). But a lantern made of red glass hung next to it. Father Halloran tugged on the bell pull and a moment later, the door cracked an inch and a bloodshot eye peered out. "We ain't open yet," came a gruff female voice.

"We are not here to conduct business, my dear woman, we are here to bring the message of Jesus Christ and salvation through His name."

The door went all the way open and a stout, gray-haired woman in a wrap-around kimono squinted up at the tall, young priest. "I told ya before, we don't want none of your preaching here. If it ain't the blasted Calvinists, it's you lot now! Why can't you leave us alone?"

But Father Halloran remained cheerful as he said, "Let me introduce these two dedicated Sisters, who—"

She started to close the door but he put a hand on it and said, "Sister Theresa and Sister Veronica are health practitioners, trained in all manner of ailments and cures. They follow in the footsteps of the Good Lord who worked miraculous cures in Galilee long ago. They specialize in female complaints," he added with significance, and she looked at the two nuns in curiosity.

Sister Theresa and Sister Veronica saw that the woman, whom they surmised to be the landlady of this "hotel," was considering Father Halloran's words, no doubt weighing the value of calling upon such services for her girls against having to listen to the sermon afterward. "Do you have any catnip?" she asked.

Father Halloran frowned. "What sort of a question is that?"

But before she could answer, they were interrupted by the arrival of three men who marched up the steps to push Father Halloran out of the way as they crowded onto the small verandah.

"My name is Dr. Edgeware, madam," the intruder said in an authoritative voice. "And I have come to execute a health inspection." The two men with him were soldiers in the Honolulu Rifles, a police force formed by Kamehameha the Fourth.

Sister Theresa sized up the tall, crane-like man in a long black frock coat. Dr. Edgeware was around six feet tall, thin and bony, with long, ungainly arms. He stood so erect that he leaned back a little. Whiskers on his cheeks framed a narrow face and long nose. So this was the physician who was taking care of Emily and Jamie Farrow. She had heard his name all over the island, and now she had a face to put with it.

He looked at Father Halloran with blatant contempt, but when his gaze moved to the Sisters, the contempt turned to a look of disgust, as if, Sister Theresa thought, she and Veronica were something he must scrape off his shoe.

He turned to the woman in the doorway and held out a piece of paper. "I have here a warrant signed by the king. It gives me the right to conduct a health inspection of any residents in this establishment."

"Ain't got none at the moment."

"Are there any women currently in residence, besides yourself?"

"Just my housemaids."

"Housemaids indeed. I will need to examine them."

"They're asleep right now."

"Really? In the middle of the day? Shouldn't they be about their housework? I suggest you wake them up." He nodded to the two soldiers, who pushed past the landlady and stomped into the entry.

Edgeware turned to Father Halloran and his companions. He paused to give them a contemptuous look, then he waved a hand, as if to shoo them away. "You'll have to move along. I cannot allow you to interfere with my *governmental* duties."

"Now see here," Father Halloran said. "I have every right to be here. This is a public establishment. A hotel, sir."

"That's currently under my jurisdiction, so I say move along or I shall have you forcibly removed."

Father Halloran locked eyes with the doctor, who was slightly taller than himself, then he glanced inside where the two red-coated soldiers stood with muskets.

Finally, he turned to the landlady and said, "Good day to you, madam, I promise I will come back."

"Don't bother!" she called after him. "You ain't wanted here."

As they continued along the sidewalk to the next "hotel," Sister Theresa said, "Why did that gentleman treat us so rudely?"

"Simon Edgeware is a self-important, over-inflated balloon of a man who lets it be known that he hates Catholics," Father Halloran said.

As Sister Theresa looked back, Edgeware turned and fixed an eye on her. It sent a chill down her spine. Something told her that Catholics weren't the only people Dr. Simon Edgeware hated.

For the rest of the day, Father Halloran and his two companions had doors slammed in their faces. They also heard some colorful expletives, but the priest would not be deterred. "Next time," he said, "we shall come armed with literature, which we will leave with the landladies. And perhaps the Sisters can make up some small, free samples of medicines we can hand out?"

Sister Theresa wasn't sure about that. They were having a hard enough time making medicines for their needful patients. "We shall see, Father," she said. She was glad he had not brought up the strange catnip question. It would have been embarrassing for her to explain that catnip stimulates contractions of the uterus, and the landlady of a brothel could only want the herb for one reason.

As they left the district, Sister Theresa noticed that Dr. Edgeware was still conducting his rounds, gaining admittance through every door he knocked on. "Dr. Edgeware is having better success, Father," she said. "I suppose it's because he has the power of the king behind him."

"Take heart, Sister. *He* might have the king, but *we* have God."

CHAPTER SIXTEEN

Sister Theresa had to go back to Farrow House. It was impera-
tive that she return Captain Farrow's book, and in so doing must
disobey Mother Agnes

But she had no choice.

She had had the book for a few months, reading in stolen
moments. But each time she opened to a page in *Walden* and read
Thoreau's words, she heard Mr. Farrow's voice inside her head. She
also pictured him in her mind, and it was not her own hands she saw
holding the book, but Mr. Farrow's. She loved Mr. Thoreau's words,
but she wondered at the wisdom of continuing to read them, for they
brought Mr. Farrow into her thoughts more often than was proper.

She could have asked Mrs. Jackson, the housekeeper, to return it,
or Rodrigo, their handyman. But it seemed ungrateful. She had so
enjoyed the book that it struck her as disrespectful not to return it in
person. And anyway, she planned only to knock at the front door and
give the book to the housekeeper, Mrs. Carter. And she had a good
excuse. It was her turn to visit the drugstore on Merchant Street for
supplies, and the route would take her past the Farrow property.

As she walked down King Street, she so relished the blue sky and
gentle breezes that she did not at first notice all the carriages lined
up in front of Farrow House. And then she heard the music and

laughter, and realized that there was an afternoon garden party in progress.

She knew by now that Captain Farrow was famous for his social events. To be invited to Farrow House was to be Somebody in the Islands. She took the path to the rear garden, where she saw a hundred or so finely dressed people enjoying the flowers, sunshine, and gentle breeze. She hovered on the edge, searching among the elegant crowd for the host.

Musicians played violins beneath swaying coconut palms while smiling young Hawai'ian women in long white muumuus moved among the guests with silver trays bearing delicacies or glasses of wine. The guests were dressed in such finery that Theresa knew they were the Islands' high society—judges, lawyers, bankers, men in the legislature. Many had wives brought over from America and England, but a few had married Hawai'ian women, dusky ladies in fashionable gowns and crinolines, wearing shoes and gloves and carrying parasols.

The guests sat at tables covered in white tablecloths, or stood in small groups beneath the pandanus and mango trees. Theresa saw Emily Farrow sitting in the shade, flanked by two housemaids in black dresses and white aprons.

She appeared to be presiding over the party like an entitled dowager, graciously receiving guests with smiles and personal comments as men and women filed past to pay their respects to a woman who, in her own fashion, was Island royalty. Dr. Edgeware stood behind her, as if he were some sort of secret power behind the Farrow throne. Theresa saw him bend down and say something to her. But Emily impatiently waved him off and Theresa heard her say, "Stop fussing over me, young man."

As she crossed the green lawn to pay her respects to Emily Farrow, she caught pieces of conversation. Everyone was talking about the war in America. Hostilities in the United States had begun in April, when Confederate forces had fired upon Fort Sumter. President Lincoln had called for each state to provide troops to retake the fort; consequently, four more slave states had joined the Confederacy. The majority of Americans in Hawai'i passionately supported Lincoln and were rooting for the Union (some families had even sent sons to enlist in the Northern army).

Theresa joined the line of guests, and when she reached Emily, was rewarded with a glowing smile and an enthusiastic, "Hello, my dear! I am so glad Robert invited you. We haven't seen you in ages. Are you well?"

Theresa smiled. "I believe I am supposed to ask you that. It looks like a wonderful party."

Emily waved her hand over the Hawai'ian women in modern gowns and said, "It took the power of the Lord to clothe these people, but He won in the end." She laughed. "And all it took was a parasol and a pair of gloves!"

"I've come to have a word with your son. Would you know where he is?"

"Standing on a soapbox somewhere, I have no doubt," Emily said with a laugh, and it made Theresa feel good to see Robert Farrow's mother in such high spirits.

As she turned away to search for the captain, she saw people quickly avert their eyes, as they had been staring at her. Theresa was familiar by now with such looks. And yet, amid the curious expressions, scowls, frowns of disapproval, and blank stares, Theresa found a welcoming smile. "Well, well," he said as he came up to her. "I have not yet had the pleasure! I have heard of your group, of course, most admirable!"

He spoke English with a thick accent that she assumed was Prussian. He was a prosperous-looking gentleman, with a gold watch chain festooned across his ample belly. In his late forties, Theresa guessed, with thinning gray hair. His face was ruddy, his cheeks jowly. But it was his eyes that arrested her, as they were blue and bright and quite merry behind rimless spectacles. "Frederich Klausner," he said, bowing. "At your service."

"How do you do?" she said, a little nonplussed at his behavior.

He quickly explained, "We have religious Sisters in Germany, who work in hospitals. Remarkable ladies, so devoted! I know you feel out of place here, but I assure you visitors from Europe would not find you an oddity at all."

She smiled. Mr. Klausner was clearly Lutheran, as Theresa had heard of such nursing orders in his country. And his manner did indeed put her at ease in so elegant a setting and one in which she certainly did not belong.

"How is it you know the captain?" he asked.

"I took care of his son a few months back. And yourself, sir, how are you acquainted with Captain Farrow?"

"I am one of his business investors! I am very eager to see steamship service commence between Hawai'i and the rest of the world. Progress is important if we are to prosper, is it not?"

"Klausner," she said thoughtfully. "There is a Klausner's Emporium on Merchant Street."

He beamed with pride and bowed at his corpulent waist. "I have that honor. You see, my dear Sister, I never learned to read and write. The only work I could get was sweeping the floors of a newspaper office in Frankfurt, Germany. When the publisher found out I was illiterate, he fired me. Can't have an illiterate man working for a newspaper, he said! But my brother and me, we heard of gold in California so we pooled our money and sailed to San Francisco. We panned for enough gold to get me to Hawai'i, while my brother stayed in California. I opened a little tobacco shop here on Merchant Street and did well enough to expand my merchandise. I added sweets, petticoats, suspenders. Soon I was selling hats and boots. I opened a shop next door and imported textiles, needles and thread, knitting yarns. Whatever folks wanted, I got for them. I expanded on the other side and made it a book emporium. I now own the largest general store in Honolulu. You need a sewing machine, you come to me. I am the only purveyor in Hawai'i of the new chain-stitch single-thread machines! I offer everything from German chocolates to Irish walking sticks."

Theresa congratulated Mr. Klausner on his amazing success. "Imagine," she said, "where you would be if you could read and write."

"Mein Gott," he said, "I'd still be sweeping floors at the Frankfurter Zeitung!"

She smiled, finding herself taken with the affable merchant. "I came to pay a quick visit to Captain Farrow, but I can't find him. I suspect that he is very busy with his guests. Would you please tell him I dropped by?" And she turned to leave.

But Mr. Klausner, who had apparently taken a mutual liking to Theresa, would not hear of it. "Our host is in the house, drumming up more investment money. Look for him in his study. There you will find him!"

Upon Mr. Klausner's insistence, she went inside the house and, hearing men's voices, found Captain Farrow in his study, entertaining guests whom she recognized as prominent men in Honolulu. Large swaths of paper were spread out on his enormous desk, on which she glimpsed what appeared to be architectural designs of some sort. When Captain Farrow said, "Here is my new engine," Theresa realized he was showing his guests blueprints for his new steamship.

"People don't want to wait weeks to hear from loved ones back home," he was saying. "And think of the swiftness of getting the latest news."

Theresa smiled. Captain Farrow was repeating her own words to him from months ago, almost verbatim.

"Not just the mail, gentlemen!" he expounded. Captain Farrow strode to the cabinet, where he kept a stock of various liquors and crystal glasses. He was bare-headed, but formally dressed in white linen coat and trousers. Theresa could not help but notice that he stood a head taller than his companions, and cut a finer figure than any of them.

"We must think in terms of passengers, too! We need to lure more people here. Make sea travel more pleasant, enjoyable even. My new ship will have a 'harp' engine, laid horizontally so as to be entirely below the water line. This engine takes up less room, leaving the ship with a good deal of extra space for the passengers."

"It's a big expense, Farrow," said a man whom Theresa knew to be the president of Honolulu Bank.

Robert came back to the desk carrying a decanter and glasses. "I know only too well who my opposition are—"

"I say!" declared one of the men when he saw Sister Theresa in the doorway.

Another turned and said, "Good Lord!"

But when Captain Farrow saw her, his face broke into an attractive smile. And her own heart gave a painful leap. He broke away from his guests and strode toward her, his hands extended, forgetting that her own hands were forever hidden in the folds of her sleeves. "Where have you been, Sister? We have missed you!"

"We are blessed with a lot of work," she replied, although the work was their herbal garden and making medicinal lotions and tonics and powders. Their actual patient care had slowed, after the initial rush months ago. In fact, the convent was struggling to make ends meet.

"To what do I owe the honor of this visit?"

"I came to return your book. I fear I have had it overly long."

When one of the men cleared his throat, rather loudly Theresa thought, Captain Farrow took her arm and said, "I could do with some fresh air," and he led her through the French doors and out to the garden party.

In her year in Honolulu, Theresa had discovered that Captain Farrow was what was referred to as "eligible," and it was obvious that every widow, spinster, and mother of marriageable daughters had their eye on him—a few married women, too, she noticed. Miss Carter, the governess, still watched him with doe eyes when he wasn't looking, but in the past weeks her manner toward Theresa had warmed, perhaps because she realized by now a religious Sister was no threat.

Robert helped himself to two glasses of punch from a passing servant and, handing one to Theresa, led her to the far edge of the garden, where they found cool shade beneath a banyan tree. "Can I fetch you something to eat?" he asked. "The cook has outdone herself with a delicious rare roast beef. Perhaps a dessert is more to your liking?"

Theresa would have loved to make a plate for herself from the buffet. The aromas drifting on the breeze were making her stomach growl. But money was tight at the convent, resources were stretched thin. How could she fill her stomach when her Sisters were going to bed hungry?

"I am not hungry, thank you," she said.

"What news do you have of your family?" he asked as he leaned against the tree and seemed to savor the respite from the demands of being a host.

"My baby sister is growing up healthy and pretty, my mother says, and my brother Eli is about to go off to college. Father will settle for nothing less than Harvard, although Mother expresses dismay at the three-thousand-mile separation, and the fact that a war is now going on. Eli expressed a desire to enlist with the Union Army, and Father forbade it. And how is your son, Captain Farrow?"

"Jamie is in Waialua, at my brother's cattle ranch. His health always seems to improve when he visits his cousin Reese. I think it might be the native influence. My brother Peter is fond of Hawai'ians and hires the local natives to work his cattle ranch. Jamie and Reese, and Peter as well, spend a lot of time in the local village."

Mahina appeared at that moment, waddling across the lawn in a bright yellow muumuu and bellowing "Aloha!" as she encompassed Theresa in her enormous arms. Then Mahina held her at arm's length and said, "Where you be? Mahina not see her little Keleka many month now!"

Before Theresa could reply, Mahina said, "Where you *hale?* Where you house? Keleka no come here, Mahina go Keleka *hale!*"

"Our house is at the corner of Fort Street and Beretrania."

She frowned. "*Our?* You have husband?"

"Not in the sense you mean. I live with Sisters."

"I come. You show."

"Now?"

Captain Farrow grinned. "Mahina is impulsive. And when an ali'i is impulsive, there is no putting her off. Keep *Walden,* Sister, re-reading it is even better than the first reading. And remember not to be a stranger here."

As Theresa accompanied Mahina across the lawn, she turned to wave good-bye to Emily Farrow and found herself, once again, the object of a very dark, direct look from Dr. Simon Edgeware.

Mahina was chatty as they walked along King Street, with people greeting her respectfully and giving Theresa an odd look. They were a strange pair—a young Catholic nun in black-and-white habit at the side of a renowned Hawai'ian elder in a canary-yellow muumuu.

When they arrived at the convent, Theresa brought Mahina into the small parlor, where Mrs. Jackson was polishing the floor. She blushed and welcomed their esteemed guest with great humility.

Mahina looked around and said, "Who live here?"

"Just the Sisters."

Eyebrows arched. "No men?"

"Men are not allowed in here."

"Kapu?"

"I suppose you could say that."

She smiled and nodded. "Men's house and women's house." She seemed to approve. Mahina was old enough to remember the days of idol worship and kapu, and Theresa wondered if, in her uncle's village in Wailaka, they still practiced the old ways.

"You show me church."

Theresa gladly took her down the street and through the front doors of the cathedral. There were no services going on. It was cool inside, with the colors of the stained glass windows pooling on the marble floor.

Mahina's round eyes swept over every detail. "Not like other haole church. They have no flowers, no fires, no gods."

"The 'fire' is incense and those aren't gods, Mahina, they are simply statues. That one is the Virgin Mary, Christ's mother. And there is Joseph—"

"Virgin *and* mother?" she said in a loud, echoing voice. "How that possible?"

Theresa started to explain, but Mahina fixed her eye on the crucifix above the altar. "Poor bleeding man hanging on tree! You believe in human sacrifice, like kanaka?"

"This is different, Mahina. He sacrificed *himself*."

At that moment, she saw Father Halloran watching from the doorway leading to the sacristy, and by the look on his face, she wondered if he was angry that she had brought Mahina here, wondered if she was about to be chastised.

Mahina thanked Theresa for showing her her life, and as soon as she left, Father Halloran came down the aisle and approached Theresa with a very serious expression.

"I can explain—" she began. But he held up a hand and said, "Ever since I first came to these islands, Sister Theresa, I have prayed for the lost souls of those natives who do not accept Jesus Christ as their Lord and Savior. It has weighed heavily upon me as I have sought a solution to this terrible state. How can we, as good Catholics, live our happy and healthy lives while a mere three miles away, there exists a den of demon worshippers, a dark forest teeming with unimaginable sin and promiscuity. In Chief Kekoa's settlement, he holds sway over the families who live there, forcing them to cling to old, satanic practices, and it has pained my heart to know of their existence yet I cannot find a way to save them! But now, Sister Theresa, you have brought that solution to my doorstep."

"I have?"

"Mahina is very influential among the non-Christianized Hawai'ians. And the chief is her uncle. You can be their salvation, Sister Theresa. You can lead the misguided heathens into God's light."

"But—"

"They will listen to you, because you have befriended the family of Mahina's grandson, Jamie Farrow. And I know Captain Farrow is grateful for the way you cured his son of an inflamed abdomen. I encourage you to foster this friendship, as well, Sister. Pay visits to Farrow House. Befriend Mahina and tell her about the Gospel."

She doubted she would be successful. Nonetheless, she promised Father Halloran she would do her best. At the same time, she was secretly pleased that she was once again free to visit Farrow House.

S ister Theresa was surprised to receive a note from Mr. Klausner, whom she had met at the garden party, imploring her to come and see his wife.

When Mother Agnes gave her permission to go, Sister Veronica met her in the parlor and asked if she could go with her. Now that they were a more familiar sight in Honolulu, and were themselves familiar with the town, the rule of traveling in pairs had been eased. "I would so love to see how the Klausners live," Veronica said in her usual enthusiasm. "They are so rich, they must have beautiful things in their home. And Mrs. Klausner must wear the latest high fashion."

"But I don't know why I'm being summoned, Sister. It certainly isn't for tea."

Veronica impulsively grabbed Theresa's hand and squeezed it. "Oh *please*. I simply must go with you."

Mother Agnes gave permission, and so they went on foot, with Sister Veronica talking the whole way. The Klausner residence was a handsome two-story house off Nu'uanu Road, and a very distraught husband met them at the door and brought them into a richly furnished parlor. "Thank you for coming, Sisters. My wife, she is very sick, in a bad way. Please help her. I know you are not doctors but my Gretchen throws them out!"

They could hear the poor woman screaming upstairs. "She is

hysterical," Mr. Klausner said, wringing his hands. "She has, how do you say? A big *lump* in her abdomen and now it is bleeding. She is so terrified that she has driven three doctors away. She will not let them touch her. She insists she is dying. My son from Hilo is here with his wife. We are in a panic. We do not know what to do. And then I think of you kind ladies and I think maybe she will listen to you."

"How old is your wife, Mr. Klausner?"

"She is near fifty. But always in good health, until yesterday. Then the pain and the blood!"

"But she went to no one about the growth in her stomach?"

"My wife is, how do you say, very plump."

"I understand," Sister Theresa said. "We will go and look in on her now. I suggest you and your family spend this time in prayer."

As they went up the stairs, Sister Veronica gave Theresa a worried look and said in a soft voice, "There is nothing we can do about a mass in the abdomen. Especially as it has started to bleed. That is always a sign the cancer has gone too far and she will soon be dead."

"Then we will give her something for the pain and pray with her."

They found Mrs. Klausner in bed, screaming at two maids who were attempting to straighten her rumpled bedclothes. As her husband had said, she was quite plump. Her face was flushed and glistening with sweat and her graying hair stood out from under a white nightcap.

Theresa and Veronica approached the bed and, to their surprise, as soon as Mrs. Klausner saw them, she calmed down. "You are the new Sisters," she panted, "from the Catholic church. I have heard of you. Please help me."

"You do it, Sister," Veronica whispered. "You are so much better at this than I am."

Mrs. Klausner was very fat, but when Theresa palpated her abdomen, she was able to feel the rigid mass. Theresa was about to announce that all they could do was make her comfortable when she saw the abdomen ripple. Taking her stethoscope and placing it on the mound, she listened. When she detected a second heartbeat, faint and rapid, she whispered to Sister Veronica, "Mrs. Klausner isn't sick with cancer, she is in labor!"

Upon hearing that she was pregnant, Mrs. Klausner's eyes bugged out. "A baby? I am too old, no? When my monthly days ended, I thought it was over."

"Don't worry, dear," Theresa said, "we can fetch a doctor now. It's all right."

"No no." Mrs. Klausner grabbed her hand with a surprisingly strong grip. "Please. You are the servants of God. I know He is here because you are here."

"Then we shall do what we can."

But Sister Veronica was worried. "Sister, what will we do? We weren't taught how to deliver a baby."

"We will pray. And ask God to guide our hands."

Mrs. Klausner cried out, "Hurry!"

They hastily pinned their veils back and slipped their sleeves into protective white coverings, and lastly donned white bib-aprons. Between grimaces, Mrs. Klausner breathlessly told them they would need to order the cook to boil plenty of hot water. "You will need towels, thread, scissors. And I need schnapps!" They sent the maid for the supplies, and then washed their hands in carbolic soap.

Mrs. Klausner screamed and before they could prepare themselves, the new life came into the world—the glory of God before their very eyes. Theresa and Veronica wept with joy and laughed with Mrs. Klausner, who was likewise laughing and crying at the same time. She had an unexpected baby girl and wept with happiness. "I did not know!" she cried, her tears splashing like baptismal water on the newborn's head. "My children, they are grown. I do not see them. But now I have this little angel. I cannot thank you enough, good Sisters." She lifted shining eyes to them. "I will tell all my friends. They are like me, they do not like the doctors who are men and who do not understand the ailments of women. You are sent by God."

They left her to rest, and went downstairs, where a beaming Mr. Klausner unabashedly embraced them, praising their names and their good works, and assuring them that he was going to tell friends and customers in his emporium about their services. He pressed gold coins upon them and assured them that, from now on, they would receive discounted prices at his store.

As they were saying good-bye at the front door, a gentleman came up the path, wearing a top hat and carrying a black medical bag. Dr. Simon Edgeware.

"Mein Gott," Mr. Klausner said when he saw the man. "My son insisted on sending for another doctor, the best in Honolulu. We do not need you now, Herr Doctor!" he called out. "Sister Theresa has done a wonderful job! She will take care of my Gretchen from now on!"

As they passed on the stone path, and Theresa offered Dr. Edgeware a smile, he gave her such a look of disgust and hatred that it chilled her to her core. She thought of the venomous look he had shot at her in Captain Farrow's garden, and she knew that she and her Sisters now had an enemy in these islands.

It was October, what the Hawai'ians called *'ikuwa,* the time marking the end of the Hawai'ian summer and the start of its winter. It was the time of *Makahiki,* and while many of the rituals associated with this time had been banned, there was still a great deal of feasting, surfing, and general merrymaking. Mahina invited Sister Theresa to partake in a feast near their village in Wailaka, at the feet of the towering craggy mist-shrouded mountains. Theresa received permission from Mother Agnes, who voiced her disapproval, saying that it was Father Halloran's wishes that Theresa witness the celebration and report to him what she had seen.

"To know what we are up against," Father Halloran had said. "In our efforts to bring the recalcitrant family of Chief Kekoa to the Lord, we must learn their ways, and therefore find methods to combat them."

Because Captain Robert was related by marriage to Chief Kekoa's family, he too was invited, and so he and Theresa traveled together, going the three miles by carriage, with the captain handling the reins while she rode at his side.

As they followed the broad road that led out of the city and up the Nu'uanu Valley to the mountains, they watched the play of light and color on the mountains and the deep blue green of the valley, where showers, sunshine, and rainbows made perpetual variety.

Captain Farrow broke the silence by saying, "Have you heard of the telegraph, Sister? Just weeks ago, the first transcontinental telegraph system was completed! It spans the North American continent, connecting the eastern United States to California by way of Salt Lake City. The first telegram was sent by Brigham Young, the governor of Utah, and it said, 'Utah has not seceded but is firm for the Constitution and the laws of our once happy country.' Can you imagine, Sister? Within minutes, news is shot across three thousand miles!"

As they neared the end of Nu'uanu road and would soon be turning onto the track that would lead to Mahina's village, Captain Farrow said, "Queen Emma's summer palace is up there, near the pass."

"So many rainbows," Theresa said, filling her eyes with the deep, green ravines and low-hanging mists. "Look, I count three in the valley!"

"We can even see rainbows on the moon. Did you know that? We have rainbows at night, and when the moon is full, you can observe its face through a rainbow."

"Oh, I should *love* to see that."

"You should also take a ride up to the Pali. The view is like nothing else on earth."

"What is the Pali?"

"It's a mountain pass connecting the two sides of the island. We can't see it from here but it's full of history and legends. They say there *is a mo'o wahine*—a lizard woman—who lingers around the pass and takes the form of a beautiful woman who leads male travelers to their deaths off the cliff."

Theresa watched the shifting mists, rising and falling, drifting over the craggy ravines and chasms. A rainbow spanning two steep cliffs faded and another appeared a short distance away.

"The Nu'uanu Pali was the site of the most famous battle in Hawai'ian history. In 1795 Kamehameha the Great sailed from his home island of Hawai'i with an army of ten thousand warriors with the intention of conquering O'ahu. Up ahead, in Nu'uanu Valley, the defenders of O'ahu were driven back up into the valley, where they were trapped above the Pali. Kamehameha's army sent hundreds of the O'ahu warriors off the edge of the cliff to their deaths, a thousand feet below."

Theresa tried not to imagine that ill-fated day in 1795, so she changed the subject. "How is your mother, Captain Farrow? She seemed quite well at your garden party."

Robert looked at her. "The valerian has stopped working and the insomnia is back. Dr. Edgeware is giving her a sleeping powder. But I would welcome your advice, and I believe Dr. Edgeware would not mind if you paid my mother visits for her health."

She doubted very much that Dr. Edgeware would not mind but rather would resent her intrusion terribly, but she was concerned for Mrs. Farrow. Surely they could find a balance between her periods of hysteria and periods of calm, other than keeping her drugged.

Finally, they came upon a vast expanse of fields of taro. As they drove by, Theresa saw the village—a collection of large neat grass houses, with imu pits in the center, tall idols carved into fearsome creatures, and pavilions that were simply poles supporting grass roofs.

Captain Farrow brought the wagon to a halt and looked out over the quiet and seemingly deserted settlement. "My wife, Leilani, was born in this village," he said, "so these people are her family—what's left of them anyway." He sat in silence for a moment, then turned to Theresa and said, "Many died in the chicken pox epidemic a few years ago. These people, the survivors, are still her family and therefore they are mine, I do whatever I can for them." He smiled. "But Chief Kekoa is proud. He doesn't accept charity. He's all alone. His wife and children perished in that epidemic."

While their horse nibbled on grass, Captain Farrow sat with the reins loose in his hands. "At the start of the outbreak, the authorities came and rounded up all the infected ones and quarantined them in a makeshift pavilion on Kuhio Beach. But they didn't take into account that swimming is one of the natives' traditional forms of healing. Sick people were often taken to lagoons for water therapy. The authorities didn't take into account the torment of the intense fever and itching of the pox. They didn't realize that, as soon as night fell, the people would rush into the surf to soothe their torments and to let the sea cure them. They didn't take into account that there was a storm out at sea and the surf was high. The waves were fourteen feet and there were rip currents. Leilani didn't have chicken pox. She was with me at Farrow House. Jamie was five. But when she heard about the quarantined people, she went there to take care of them. When they ran into the surf she went in, with others, to pull them out. Over a thousand perished that night, including my wife."

Theresa didn't know how to respond to such an awful story. All she could do was say, "I'm sorry."

They did not enter the village, continuing on instead until the track ended at a wall of dense trees. They alighted from the carriage, and walked the rest of the way.

Before setting out, Captain Farrow said in seriousness, "I trust you will be discreet, Sister. What you are being allowed to witness tonight is forbidden by law. In their eagerness to prove to the rest of the civilized world that Hawai'ians are no longer savages, the royal family has made certain rituals illegal. The authorities would love nothing more than to find out what Chief Kekoa is up to, and especially where. Where I am about to take you is a highly kept secret. Were the police to find out, they would come here and cart Kekoa off in chains and put him in prison."

"I had no idea," she said, a little excited and a little afraid. But she gave Captain Farrow her promise that she would tell no one about tonight's event.

Sister Theresa had never been in this forested region of Honolulu, but often wondered what mysteries were hidden there. Now she carefully picked her way over ground covered in tall grass and moss and creeper vines. They could not see the sky, the trees overhead were so thick. Often, Captain Farrow had to hold back branches with his body so that she might pass without ensnaring her veils, and for the first time she saw the practicality in wearing little clothing in so "grasping" a landscape.

Before they reached their destination Theresa detected the aroma of roasting pig, and she knew the hog would have gone into the ground hours ago and would soon be dug up for a succulent feast. She also heard laughter and saw, through the trees, torches winking brightly, as night was falling and they would all soon be plunged into primordial darkness.

She had never been this far from civilization—even in Oregon she had never gone out of sight of their cabin.

When they came to a clearing, they found Mahina's people excitedly gathered for the coming festivities. Captain Farrow said, "This grove is dedicated to Laka, goddess of the hula. The spring here is sacred and the water can only be drunk during certain rituals. Otherwise, it is kapu."

A young lady came up, said "Aloha," and draped a lei around Theresa's neck. She left it in place so as not to offend. She also tried not to stare, for the young lady wore only a tapa cloth sarong around her waist. Theresa noticed that most of the women were bare-breasted, although Mahina and the older ladies wore muumuus.

Theresa was taken to meet their leader, of whom she had heard so much, the legendary Chief Kekoa, Mahina's uncle. He was a man of great stature and girth, like his father, Chief Holokai, who had years ago befriended Reverend Stone and his wife, Emily. A towering nobleman with his close-cropped white hair decorated with *ti*-leaves. Around his thick neck, a choker made of green leaves, and matching circlets around his wrists and ankles. Upon his bare chest lay a necklace of shark's teeth. He wore a sarong of brown tapa cloth, and carried a tall staff topped with a flower. A rope of yellow feathers encircled his waist—symbol of his high authority. His complexion was dark and glowed like bronze in the torchlight. His brow was thick and his eyes fierce.

Captain Farrow had explained to Theresa ahead of time that Kekoa was an ali'i of the highest blood and a *kahuna kilo 'ouli*—a character reader. "He was trained from early boyhood to 'read' people. You might think he's just staring at you, but his keen eyes are taking in a thousand details, analyzing, sorting, making equations of every minute detail about you and at the end he sums you up. He's very good."

The chief scrutinized her now as she stood mutely, his eyes going up and down her body, looking this way and that, while she wondered what on earth he could see of her when all that showed was her face.

She looked around the grove, at the men in skimpy loincloths and the bare-breasted women, and at the altar that was a large flat stone set upon tree stumps. The altar was covered in long green leaves, and upon that stood a tall stone, phallus-shaped, and draped in shell necklaces and fresh leis. Theresa thought of the Hawai'ians at Captain Farrow's garden party, people who had married Americans and Englishmen, who knew which fork to use for fish or meat, who had embraced Christianity and a new world, a new way of life. But for Chief Kekoa and his people, time had stood still. For them, it was the year 1777, and Captain Cook had not yet brought the Western world to Hawai'i.

Chief Kekoa startled Theresa by suddenly asking a question. Captain Farrow translated. "He wants to know what month you were born in."

Theresa replied and Robert translated. Chief Kekoa asked another question. Robert said, "What did your birth home look like?"

Chief Kekoa continued to ask her a series of baffling questions until Robert said, "He wants to know, does your god speak to you?"

Theresa hesitated. She didn't know how to answer.

Finally, Chief Kekoa broke into a broad grin and, seizing Theresa by the shoulders, shocked her by bringing his broad, brown face close to hers and pressing his nose on either side of her nostrils. "Aloha," he said, in the same way Mahina did, not just as a word, but a wish from the heart, a breathed word, with the middle syllable drawn out with emotion.

As they went to take their places for the feast, Robert said, "You impressed the old boy. He has declared you *kama'aina*. That means 'child of the land.'"

They passed, in the center of the clearing, a large, flat stone surface covering the forest floor, and Theresa saw engravings carved into it. "They're called petroglyphs," Captain Farrow explained. "Carved so long ago that the artists are unknown. But they are considered sacred, so the caretakers of this grove make sure this old patch of lava is kept clean of weeds and debris."

"What do they represent?" she asked, bending closer for a better look. The engravings made no sense to her, for all she saw was a hodge-podge of lines and circles.

"You don't really need to look at them," Captain Farrow said, taking her arm.

But as she started to turn away, the pictures suddenly fell into place. They were human beings—primitive stick figures, to be sure, but people nonetheless. And as she peered, she differentiated between men and women. And then—

She gasped and straightened up. Captain Farrow cleared his throat in embarrassment and led her away from what could only be depictions of sex acts. There was no mistaking the erect members of the male figures and the outspread legs of the females. What sort of grove *was* this?

And then Theresa wondered what sort of ritual she was about to observe.

They all sat at the edge of the small grove so that they formed a circle with the men on one side, the women on the other. Theresa was given a place next to Mahina, and while the women sat directly on the grass, Theresa was thoughtfully provided with a wooden log for her comfort. A coconut shell filled with fermented *ti*-juice was passed around, and everyone took a sip. But as none drank too much of the liquor, Theresa saw it as a sort of Communion wine, marking the sacredness of the ritual. To show respect, she took a sip, and had to stifle a body-racking cough.

While they waited, Theresa thought of the phenomenon she had heard about, of seeing rainbows on the moon, and she so badly wanted to see it. But although the air was heavy with mist, the night warm and humid, when she looked up at the sky, she saw no night-rainbows. The face of the moon was ivory and clear.

She looked at Robert across the circle, laughing with the men on either side of him, a handsome Westerner in a white linen coat over linen trousers, and a white shirt underneath. Boots on his feet. He was such a contrast to his companions, who were nearly naked, and yet their lack of clothing did not unsettle Theresa, for such a state seemed only right in this rain forest setting where Adam and Eve would have felt at home. In fact, she envied these free-spirited people who were comfortable in their nakedness, laughing loudly and freely, drinking and eating without worrying that their teacup might rattle in the saucer. She wished she could pull her shoes off and run barefoot.

She was looking forward to the performance. When Mahina had invited her to this feast, Captain Farrow had cautioned her that it might not perhaps be to her liking. But Theresa had seen hula before. On such occasions as when it was permitted—as entertainment, not religious ritual—she had delighted in the sight of the young ladies dancing in their muumuus, and applauded the graceful way they moved their hands and arms.

Finally, the crowd grew quiet, a singer began to chant while drumming on the double gourd called *ipu heke,* and then the girls came out. They were wearing very short grass skirts and were bare-breasted. And by the suggestive way they churned their hips and opened their knees, this seemed to be no ordinary hula. "Mahina, what kind of ceremony is this?" Theresa asked.

"Ask gods to bless us."

"Is that all?"

"No no. We dance for make babies."

Theresa stared at her. "It's a fertility ritual?"

Mahina nodded vigorously. "You see. Men and women make babies tonight."

"But I can't—" Before she could collect herself and depart, as surely she must, the other half of the dancers appeared from the forest, and they so stunned her that she was immobilized.

Young men, virile and strong, muscles glistening in the flickering torchlight, flew into the clearing with yelps and shouts, jumping and stamping their feet. They shouted in unison and slapped their chests and arms. They were painted most fearsomely, with startling facial expressions and angry slashes of color across their broad backs and taut abdomens. Their precision was astounding, with the young men executing the dance steps in great synchrony. They performed agile gymnastics, flying into the air, dropping to the ground to push themselves up and down on one hand and one foot, veins and muscles bulging, tight skin straining, while sweat poured of them.

As the tempo of the drumbeat increased and the singer's chant picked up, the men fell onto their backs and thrust their pelvises up and down. The girls then rejoined the dance, each choosing a man to straddle, bending at the knees so that the ends of her grass skirt brushed his pelvis. The pairs gyrated their hips in unison until the illusion of sexual union was achieved.

As Theresa felt the rhythm of the drums pulsate in her blood, smelled the loamy fragrance of the jungle, and felt the moist air envelope her, she was suddenly no longer shocked or scandalized by what she was witnessing. All in an instant, as she watched the dancers against a backdrop of dense forest and beneath a canopy of leafy branches and stars and moon, she thought: they are children of nature.

Just as I once was. . . .

In the next instant, she could not breathe. She had never seen such raw animalism. She told herself she was merely an interested observer, not a participant. Yet the rhythm of the drums, the movements of the dancers, filled her with a strange ache, an unfamiliar yearning, and it alarmed her. Captain Farrow's eyes were fixed on her as he watched her from across the circle. She grew hot. She wanted to tear off her veils and feel the night air on her skin. She thought her blood was going to boil.

And then the dancers vanished into the forest, running in pairs, laughing and shrieking, to finish the ritual in private. The boar was dug up and sliced and handed around on large green leaves.

When Mahina handed her a slab of savory meat, Theresa hesitated. She was hungry. Her stomach rumbled. But money was tight at the convent again and once more the Sisters were reduced to plain bread and turnip soup.

As Theresa stared at the roast pork in her hands, her mouth watering, Mahina said, "You no hungry? You too thin. Eat, Kika Keleka."

"I'm fine, thank you," Theresa said, wondering if she could conceal this delicious pork in her pockets and take it back to her Sisters.

Perspiration trickled between her shoulder blades. Her abdomen throbbed with the pulse of the islands as she imagined the ancient gods and goddesses and the ancestral guardians—the *'amakua*—all the ghosts and spirits of the rain forest gathering close to watch. And she was suddenly afraid—not of the forest or of these people, but of herself. Of the weakness of her flesh.

Robert escorted her up the steps to the front door and waited until she went inside. Theresa was immediately surrounded by her Sisters. "We were so worried! We prayed for you, dear Sister."

Veronica impulsively embraced her, saying, "I would never be brave enough to go into the jungle and watch a savage rite!"

Aware that she reeked of banquet aromas—Theresa knew that her Sisters could smell the smoky scent of roast pig on her clothes—she reached into the deep pockets of her habit and brought out two bundles wrapped in large, waxy leaves. In one, she had brought a moist chunk of pork; in the other, a few roasted sweet potatoes. Theresa handed them to Mother Agnes, who took a long look at the offering, and then said, "I will portion these out in the morning."

"Tell us about the feast," Veronica said, holding onto Theresa's arm. "Tell us what you saw."

But Mother Agnes held up a hand. "We will not be listening to talk of heathenish things. It is enough to know that the natives are stuffing themselves while *others* go hungry."

"But that's now how—" Theresa began.

"Did the natives give this food to you to bring to us?" Agnes asked. "Is this a gift from them, or did you hide this food in your pockets?"

"I'm sorry, Reverend Mother," Theresa said softly. "I thought you would be pleased."

"We'll make do," Agnes said with a weary sigh.

"What's that?" Sister Margaret said suddenly, going to the window.

They heard voices outside, and horses in the street. "It's a wagon," Margaret said. "Stopping in front. And natives on horseback. Why . . . they're coming up the steps!"

Mother Agnes opened the door and received a shock. Men were unloading baskets out of the back of the wagon, to hand them to native women who then brought them up the steps.

"What's all this?" Mother Agnes said.

Mahina came up onto the veranda and grinned. "This for you. We bring inside?"

Nonplussed, Mother Agnes stepped aside to let the women in, and as she did so her eyes grew big at the sight of the sweet potatoes and bananas, the fresh eggs, the heaps of salted fish, and great chunks of warm roasted pork. Even a wire basket of chickens, squawking in protest.

Mahina said, "We have plenty. You hungry. You too thin."

The Sisters stood in mute shock as more baskets were brought in, filling up the little parlor with more food than they had seen in a year. Yams and pineapples, oranges and mangoes. Even three squealing piglets.

When the women were done, they left. Mahina remained in the doorway. You need more food? You tell Mahina."

Mother Agnes's voice was tight as she said, "We thank you for your gifts. Mahalo, and God bless."

As Mahina left, to be assisted up into the creaking wagon by three sturdy men, she smiled to herself. Tonight was a good feast. Plenty men and women making babies. Plenty blessings from the gods.

And something more, something unexpected that made Mahina

grin all the way back to the village. She had been wondering to whom she must teach the old kanaka ways, to whom was she to entrust Hawai'ian secrets.

Tonight, the gods had spoken. Chief Kekoa had called Kika Keleka *kama'aina*—a child of the land. Sister Theresa was the chosen one.

A fter a night of troubled sleep and disturbing dreams, Theresa awoke in emotional turmoil.

She felt different, changed. But she could not say how. She bathed and donned her habit and prayed in the chapel with her Sisters, but something was no longer the same.

The fertility hula . . .

She was still in the grip of its hypnotic power. The energy of the dancers. The passion in the chanters' voices. The joy of the onlookers.

But, before that. Chief Kekoa, the character-reader, asking her so many questions. She had answered them all except one. Kekoa had asked her if God spoke to her and she honestly did not know.

As she knelt in the chapel, waiting for her turn in the confessional, hearing sins and faults being whispered behind a heavy curtain, she thought of the piety and devotion of her Sisters. They seemed to have sincere faith in God and their religion. While Theresa had balked at Kekoa's question, she knew her Sisters would say, "Yes, God speaks to me. He answers my prayers."

She wondered now if she herself really spoke to God, or if she recited prayers by rote, not with feeling or passion. They were just words to get through.

But whenever Veronica and Margaret and Agnes sang in church on Sundays, you could hear their joy and their love for God, just as the dancers in the sacred grove expressed their own joy and faith in their ancient gods.

I didn't join the Sisterhood to serve God but as a means to take care of people. I have only been going through the motions.

For the first time, Theresa was struck by how different she was from her Sisters. When she had first entered the order, she had simply stepped in, as if entering a stage, and had taken up her role as postulant without questioning her faith or her motives.

But now, a small part of her knew she was an outsider, and might always be.

She felt a tap on her shoulder. It was Veronica, indicating that the confessional was available. Theresa went in, knelt, crossed herself, and waited for Father Halloran to open the window.

"Bless me, Father, for I have sinned. It has been a week since my last confession."

He recognized her voice. "Good morning, Sister, I am eager to hear about your experiences last night. And I must say, getting all of that food from the natives is nothing less than a miracle! Praise the Lord."

You should be praising Mahina, she thought as she knelt in the hot, stifling booth.

Theresa listed her few sins and failings and then fell silent, as she knew she must confess something shameful and she didn't know how to begin. So she simply said, "Father, I am attracted to a man in an improper way. When I am around him, my thoughts stray."

"Are you ashamed of these thoughts?"

"I am, Father."

"Will you promise to fight them and not give in to temptation?"

"Yes," she said. And then she asked, "Would it be best if I saw to it that I was never in the man's proximity?"

To her shock, Father Halloran said, "God places temptations in our path as a way of testing us. To run away from temptation disappoints the Lord and shows a weakness in character and faith. You must face this temptation, daughter, as it is a test from God."

"Yes, Father."

"What did you witness at the ritual in Wailaka?"

His question took her aback. The confessional seemed a strange place for the subject. "The hula, Father." She dared not elaborate.

"Where did the ritual take place?"

She could not tell him, as he might send the authorities, and she had made a promise to Captain Farrow. "I don't know that I could find it again," not a lie exactly.

"What was its name? Hawai'ians name everything. A ritual place that important would have a name."

"I . . . I don't recall."

"What district is it in then?"

"I . . . I'm not sure."

"Very well. When you are invited again, go there. Mark its location, its name, and how one gets there. For your penance, five Our Fathers and five Hail Marys. And now make a good Act of Contrition."

She folded her hands and bent her head. "Oh my God, I am heartily sorry for having offended Thee . . ."

And please forgive me, Lord. The name of the grove is "Eia ka wai la, he Wai ola, e!" Which means, Here is the Water of Life. It is located in Wailaka District where the Nu'uanu Valley rises. . . .

And I pray most heartily that Robert Farrow never invites me to go there again, for I would say yes, oh yes. . . .

CHAPTER SEVENTEEN

Sister Theresa struggled with her forbidden thoughts.

She could not help herself. Captain Farrow haunted her dreams. He invaded her waking hours. During prayer, her wayward heart conjured up his voice, his smile. In the street, when she passed a man smoking the same cheroot as Captain Farrow did, her soul leapt. When she took tea and tonics to his house, she wanted to run to Farrow House. She also wanted to run *away* from Farrow House.

She looked back two and a half years to the day she and her Sisters had stood on the docks, waiting to board the *Syren*. Cosette had asked, "How will you do it, *chérie?* Hawai'i is a land of palm trees and blue lagoons and eternal sunshine. It must be very difficult to remember one's vows in such a paradise!"

And Theresa, in her naïveté, had said, "There will be no seduction in the Islands. It will be easy, in Paradise, to keep my vows."

Thus was her mind engaged on the morning it was her turn to do the shopping. She paused before turning down King Street, and studied the play of light and shadow, mists and rainbows on the craggy green slopes of the mountains. It had been a year since the night she had witnessed the fertility ritual in the secret grove at Wailaka, but its pulse and rhythm were still in her blood. Per Father Halloran's instructions, she continued to build a bridge between herself and the

253

Farrows. She looked in on Jamie and Mrs. Farrow, taking medicines and teas and tonics. And though she tried to time her visits during hours she thought Captain Farrow wouldn't be there, she frequently encountered him and he always wanted to stop for a pleasant chat. She even tried to avoid walking past Farrow House at noon, because he was up there every day on the hour, peering through his brass spyglass.

It was during those moments, as she paused to study him, the curve of his back, the intensity with which he looked through the glass, that she was struck by Captain Farrow's loneliness. She wondered if she was the only one who sensed it, for otherwise the captain was rarely alone, as his house saw the comings and goings of friends and business partners; he held parties and musical events; ladies dropped by with their unmarried sisters and daughters; politicians came to discuss new legislation or the war in America. And yet, despite such constant company, Theresa sensed loneliness in the man, as if he were with his visitors and guests in body only, while his thoughts, his heart were far away. Was he thinking about Leilani? At night, alone in that big house, did he pour a whiskey and go into the study to stand before her portrait and think about their short time together? Did he pine for her? Theresa had heard talk among the gossips of Honolulu, who wondered why he had not yet remarried, for surely he must. It didn't seem proper, a man of his standing and health and prospects to be without a wife, they said. It seemed . . . *suspect* somehow.

But Theresa understood. She knew how the heart wanted what the heart wanted, and nothing else would do.

She squinted at the deep V of Nuʻuanu Valley, where dense forests held ancient secrets. Here in the streets and lanes of Honolulu, Western commerce was conducted and white men signed contracts and congratulated themselves, church bells called Hawaiʻian Christians to Sunday service—dressed in their best gowns and suits, parasols and top hats—while there in the distance, at the foot of mist-blanketed mountains, commerce of another kind went on, forbidden, unthinkable. The missionaries believed the old gods had left these islands forty years ago. They had not.

They are here still. Watching. Waiting . . .

She tore her eyes from the might and power of Nuʻuanu and forced herself to set upon her errand.

A year ago, she and her Sisters didn't have many home patients, as the Catholic community was small and hadn't enough demand for the work of six nursing Sisters. And then Mr. Klausner had sent for them to help his wife, and Mrs. Klausner was so grateful that she had spread the word so that Lutherans and Episcopalians began requesting their services, and when Congregationalists heard that Emily Farrow was being seen by one of the Sisters of Good Hope, well, that was endorsement enough. Especially as they did not like to take their female problems to male doctors. So now the Sisters of Good Hope had their hands full.

There was only one chemist in Honolulu, a man named Gahrman, a pleasant fellow from Pennsylvania whose acquaintance Theresa enjoyed. She entered the drugstore as the druggist was telling a story to his only customer in the shop, Dr. Edgeware. "So this fellow comes to me and he's been blind for twenty years asking if I can do anything for him. I examine him and say, 'Yes, I can restore your sight.' So he pays me the money and I give him a special eye wash that I mix up myself, and he leaves with bandages over his eyes and instructions to remove them in a week, at which time he will have perfect sight. Well, doc, he came back a week later, storming into my shop and demanding his money back. Not only that, he wanted me to make him blind again. I asked him what was wrong. Wasn't he pleased with his new sight? 'The new sight is fine,' he shouted, 'but no one told me my wife was ugly!'"

As the chemist roared with laughter at his own joke, Theresa stepped up to the counter and politely cleared her throat. They had seen her enter the shop, they knew she was waiting, but the druggist ignored her. "Pardon me, Mr. Gahrman," she said. "I wish to purchase some calomel and ipecac."

Dr. Edgeware turned his back to her and said to the chemist, "There ought to be a law against allowing such unnatural females to walk the streets."

"There was a law once, y'know," the chemist said, as she stood in shocked silence at so rude a remark. "Twenty-some years back, when all the Catholics were thrown off the islands and none were allowed to set foot on our shores."

Dr. Edgeware flicked a speck of imaginary dust from the counter. "That law should never have been stricken from the books."

A rebuff stood on Theresa's lips, but she managed to keep her silence, waiting for Mr. Gahrman to finally acknowledge her presence.

Dr. Edgeware was notoriously anti-Catholic and known to be a bachelor who despised women. He wrote letters to the Honolulu newspapers, not bothering to couch his opinions in tactful terms: "Women are silly creatures, given easily to hysteria as they are governed by their wombs. They are put upon this earth for one purpose only—to produce children. Those who cannot bear children must be pitied, but those who deny this duty are unnatural and to be looked upon with suspicion."

Edgeware had circulated a petition demanding that the Sisters of Good Hope be restricted to the convent, as the French Sisters were restricted to their school. One didn't see them roaming Honolulu like women of loose morals!

"Pardon me," Theresa said a little louder, and was again ignored.

Trying not to show her indignation, she placed her medical bag on the counter and said, "Mr. Gahrman, if you please, we need ten bottles of calomel and five of ipecac."

"Don't have any," the druggist said without even looking at her. "Out a stock."

His gruff attitude surprised her, as Mr. Gahrman had always been cordial to Theresa and her Sisters. She suspected that with Dr. Edgeware now being in King Kamehameha's inner circle, men were scurrying to take sides, and Mr. Gahrman had clearly cast his lot.

"When will you have some in?"

"Don't know."

She thanked him and turned to leave. When she reached the street door, she heard Dr. Edgeware say, "I'll be needing some calomel and ipecac."

"Certainly! Just got in a new supply from Boston," Mr. Gahrman said in a loud voice. "How many bottles of each do you need, doc?"

As Sister Theresa neared Farrow House, her eyes, and her heart, searching for signs of the captain, her mind was a-jumble with worries and concerns.

It had been weeks since the Sisters had been able to purchase supplies from Gahrman's Drugstore. And neither Mother Agnes nor Father Halloran had had any success in resuming commerce with the druggist. Appealing to the bishop was of no use as he was in a delicate political situation himself, trying to strike a diplomatic balance with the anti-Catholic politicians. And she couldn't ask Captain Farrow for help as it might cause problems for him among his own people.

But if the drugstore continued to refuse the Sisters' business, what would they do? They were helpless without medicines. They could grow a few things in the garden, but they needed to purchase such drugs as morphine and laudanum, which must be imported.

She did not understand this resistance to their help among the doctors. The native population was shrinking at an alarming rate. When Captain Cook had first arrived there in 1778, it was said that one million Hawai'ians had inhabited these islands. By 1822, that number was reduced to two hundred thousand. Nine years ago, in 1853, a general census was taken and it was found that the natives numbered 73,000—and that figure continued to shrink! The Western doctors should not be fighting over Hawai'i like dogs over a bone. They should be welcoming the help of Theresa and her Sisters instead of boycotting them.

She turned off the street and went up the path to Farrow House, her heart racing, as it always did when she came to Robert's home. Miss Carter answered the front door and when Theresa saw her red, swollen eyes, and the handkerchief clasped in her fingers, she wondered if the governess had been crying. And then Theresa grew alarmed. Was Jamie all right?

The convent's herbal tonics were helping him, and the iron nails boiled in his soup. He had days of near normalcy in which he could run and play. But then he would slip back into malaise and Theresa would try a new treatment.

His affliction was indeed baffling. Mahina had once told her that Jamie was sickly because he'd witnessed a fight between his father and uncle in which they had come to blows, resulting in Peter being crippled. "Bad blood between brothers, Kika Keleka. This makes bad blood in boy."

"No one is home," the governess said archly and closed the door in Theresa's face.

Apparently she was back in Miss Carter's bad graces.

As Theresa left the verandah, she looked down the carriage drive that led from the side street to the stables, and saw them just arriving: Robert and Jamie, Emily Farrow, and Peter and Reese. This surprised her, as she rarely saw them all together. She watched as they alighted and saw the tension between Robert and Peter. Although she could not hear their words, she could *feel* their anger, see it in their eyes, their stilted manner. The brothers had had a fight in which Peter had become crippled. That must be the reason for the animosity between them. But what had the fight been about?

She saw, too, how it affected Jamie. How he walked with a dejected air as his grandmother leaned on his shoulder. Reese, too, was clearly unhappy, and Theresa understood the reason when they were close enough for her to hear Peter say, "Come along, son, we're going home." Without a word to Robert, Peter kissed his mother on the cheek and the two left for the ride back to Waialua on the western end of the island.

Robert released a sigh and offered his mother his arm.

"Sister Theresa!" he called when he saw her, clearly happy to see her.

"Sister!" Jamie cried, perking up, letting go of his grandmother's arm to run to Theresa. He seemed a little more energetic and she wondered why. She soon had her answer. "Sister," he said excitedly, "I'm to go to school!"

Theresa no longer had to stoop to meet his eye. In the past two years, Jamie had grown. She knew that someday he would tower over her, as his father did.

"School?" she said.

"O'ahu College! I'm going to study logic and rhetoric, mathematics, history, and philosophy. The boys play ball games with kukui bats. They have hiking and swimming and croquet, even track and wrestling!"

When Robert and his mother caught up, the captain said, "I am gone a lot, being needed at the docks and shipping office, which leaves Jamie in a house of women. It will do him good to be among boys."

"I believe it is an excellent move. What about Miss Carter?"

"I found a position for her with a family in Kona. She leaves tomorrow."

That explained why Miss Carter had been crying. She was being dismissed. And Theresa pitied her, as she knew how she herself should feel were she to be denied ever seeing Captain Farrow again.

"To what do I owe the honor of this visit?" Robert asked, presenting her with one of his smiles that always made her heart soar.

"I come bearing gifts," she said, lifting up her canvas carry-all bag. "Something for Mahina." She did not reveal that it was for constipation. "Something for your mother's insomnia, and a new tonic for Jamie—although prospects of attending school seem to be tonic enough."

She fell into step at his side. "I also have news. My mother wrote to say that my brother has joined the Union Army—The 20th Massachusetts Volunteer Infantry, which was organized at Readville in September. Mother has taken to her chaise and vows she will not rise from it until he is safely restored to the family."

When they reached the rear lanai, Emily Farrow let go of her son's arm and, turning to Theresa, said, "The war is a terrible thing, my dear, but it is necessary that we keep the country together. It is also necessary if we are ever going to abolish slavery. I wish my husband Isaac could have lived to see this day. He was a very outspoken abolitionist."

Mrs. Carter came out, wiping her hands on her apron. "I'll take the missus up, sir," she said, taking hold of Emily's arm and saying, "Steady, dear." Emily smiled and asked if she could have a cup of tea.

When they had gone inside, Theresa said, "Your mother seems to be doing well today."

"A visit to the beach always calms her, which was where we were today," he said. "She likes to comb the beach for what she calls her treasures. Shall we go inside?"

Inside, in this case, meant Captain Farrow's study and an immediate visit to the liquor cupboard, where he poured himself a stiff whiskey and downed it all at once.

Theresa saw the many papers scattered on his enormous desk. Ship's models. Designs. Contracts. "I am in a race against time, Sister. I am in negotiations with the Pacific Mail system, hoping to contract with them for the Hawai'i run. Once that route is mine, it will be a simple thing to start focusing on steamers designed especially for passengers. But I am not the only ship owner who wants that lucrative mail contract. I'm having to deal with some underhanded blackguards who are offering bribes and the like. I won't do business that way."

He poured another whiskey, but held off drinking it.

"The trick is not necessarily to be the first, but the best. And the way to do it, Sister, is to offer something more. Not just passage—all passenger steamers will offer that. I have to make my ships more desirable somehow. Like offering luxuries and extra amenities that the others won't. Entertainment, perhaps."

"Entertainment! On a ship? That would be different, and most desirable!"

He looked at her, and held her with those eyes again that retreated into deep thought. "You would know, wouldn't you? You said how you hated coming across on the *Syren*. If you were to take a voyage, and there were steamers to choose from, which would you choose?"

"I would choose the one that offered something the others didn't, something desirable." And as soon as she spoke the words, she had the solution to the problem of Mr. Gahrman's drugstore.

H onolulu's citizens had a voracious appetite for news, and they were already lined up in front of Klausner's Emporium awaiting delivery of the morning editions of the city's many newspapers.

As Theresa walked past the line of customers, she noticed that the numbers were fewer than in prior months, just as she knew Mr. Klausner's business had dropped off recently. Due to Hawai'i's economic boon, a result of the burgeoning sugar industry, the population had mushroomed as well, with newcomers arriving every day in the hopes of finding new prosperity in these islands. A few of those new arrivals were merchants who had opened shops that competed with Mr. Klausner's. Theresa saw customers lined up across the street and at the corner, where newspapers were also going to be delivered.

She entered the large store and the bell over the door rang. Klausner's establishment was always a delight, with its row upon row of tables and counters stocked with everything from bolts of silk to boxes of chocolates. The walls were lined with shelves all the way up to the ceiling so that clerks rode rolling ladders to reach the topmost merchandise. Frederich Klausner boasted that he sold "everything one could need or want in the islands."

Almost true. There was one commodity he did not sell.

Mr. Klausner greeted her with his usual enthusiasm. "My dear Sister Theresa! How good it is to see you!"

In the year since the baby's birth, she had been back to the Klausner house many times, to see Mrs. Klausner and to check baby Theresa, who was thriving wonderfully. And with each visit she was treated like a returning daughter. Thanks to their frequent generosity, plus the food Mahina's people regularly delivered to the convent, the Sisterhood was thriving again and enjoying prosperity.

Theresa and Mr. Klausner exchanged the usual pleasantries and then she went straight to business. When she asked him how the store was doing, he pulled an unhappy face.

But Theresa was cheerful as she said, "My dear Mr. Klausner, I believe I have a solution to your problem! Since your shop offers all the same merchandise that your competitors offer, there is no reason for customers to choose you over them. What you need to do, Mr. Klausner, is offer something *more*—something the others don't have."

He looked around his shop, wide-eyed, opened out his hands, and said, "What more could I offer? Everything is here!"

"You don't sell drugs, Mr. Klausner. You don't offer medicines of any kind."

"But that is Mr. Gahrman's specialty."

"He doesn't have to hold the monopoly. Anyone can sell drugs."

"But I am not a chemist. I cannot mix drugs."

"A chemist is a *convenience*, not a necessity. Doctors can mix their own formulas. And my Sisters and I can learn how to make prescriptions. Anyone can order products from a pharmaceutical company and sell them. Which is what you can do, Mr. Klausner. And since you will not be preparing any recipes or formulas, but selling directly, you can offer your drugs at a lower cost than Mr. Gahrman does. My Sisters and I will buy solely from you, Mr. Klausner, and when we prescribe medicines to our patients, we will tell them to go only to Klausner's. As you know, many people must take medicines for life, so you will have a steady customer stream for your morphine and tonics. And when customers come in for laudanum and calomel, they will see your newspapers and magazines and chocolates, and might even end up buying a sewing machine!"

He scratched his balding head. "I had never thought of that. But, my dear Sister Theresa, I would have no idea what to order!"

She smiled and opened her bag. "I have a list right here."

S ister Theresa, you are so clever!"

They were in the garden, Theresa and Veronica, harvesting herbs. A sharp sun shone down on the little enclave of medicinal plants and two nuns with veils pinned back, sleeves pinned up, and hems lifted, digging in the dirt and praising God for their labors.

"I would never have come up with such a wonderful solution to that awful drugstore problem," Veronica said as she dropped parts of a sage plant into her basket. Not only would the leaves go into their cooking, but the Sisters would make tonics to cure diarrhea and dry up phlegm, and a salve for cuts and burns. "You are so smart in everything you do."

"It was common sense and we were desperate."

Setting her basket down, Veronica put her hands on her hips and said with a grin, "You are always so modest, Theresa. You are the prettiest of us, and the smartest, and yet you are so quiet and humble. I wish I could be more like you!"

"Really, Sister—"

"Oh, Theresa!" Veronica cried. She suddenly reached out, took Theresa by the shoulders, declared, "I love you!" and kissed her on the mouth.

Theresa froze, and the kiss lingered until a sharp voice said, "Sisters! What is going on here!"

Veronica broke away and turned an astonished look to Mother Agnes, who had come out to the garden at just that moment. Now all three stood in shocked silence. And then Veronica burst into tears, and Theresa looked at her in confusion, and Mother Agnes muttered, "Oh dear."

Fifteen minutes later, their habits restored to modesty, the dirt of the garden washed off, the two young Sisters stood before a weary-looking Mother Agnes, who could only shake her head and wonder at the burden she had been asked to carry. She should have seen it coming. Sister Veronica always asking to go on home visits with Theresa, following her everywhere.

"Sister Veronica," said Mother Agnes as she sat at her desk. "You do know that what you did is wrong, don't you?"

Veronica stammered, "I . . . I don't know."

Mother Agnes turned to Theresa. "I know you are innocent in all this." And Mother Agnes could see by Theresa's perplexed look that she hadn't any idea what "all this" meant. For that matter, it appeared Veronica herself hadn't any idea.

Agnes liked both girls, had brought them up from postulancy and took care of them in this strange and savage land. She hated the decision she must make, but it was a stern rule of the Order—no special friendships. While this one didn't seem to have gotten very far, she needed to nip it in the bud.

"Sister Veronica," she said as gently as she could. "I'm sending you back to San Francisco."

"What? Oh no, Reverend Mother. I beg of you!"

"It is for your own sake, child. You were sent to the islands too soon. You are not yet ready for this calling. Mother Matilda is better able to take care of you and give you the proper training that you need. And then, perhaps, after a time, when you are ready, you can return to us. Go now and pray on this. *Benedicite.*"

They were at their evening mending, a quiet and somber group, sad over Sister Veronica's departure that morning, when Mrs. Jackson brought a very distraught visitor into the parlor. He was a young Hawai'ian dressed in trousers and a shirt, and he babbled incoherently. "My good man," Mother Agnes said archly. "Do you speak English?"

He nodded vigorously.

"Are you speaking it now?"

He spoke rapidly again until Mrs. Jackson stepped in and addressed the young man in their native tongue. She said, "He has been sent to fetch Sister Theresa back to his village in Wailaka. There is a very sick man there."

Mother Agnes's eyebrows rose so high on her head that it wrinkled her coif. She turned to Theresa and said, "Is this the village you visited last year?"

"Yes, Mother. It must be Mahina who has sent for me."

She watched Mother Agnes mull this over. The hour was late and one of her Sisters was being summoned to a hotbed of heathenism. Theresa assumed she would not give permission. To her surprise, Agnes said, "This is an excellent opportunity, Sister Theresa, to show those people what true Christians are like. Although they give generously of their food, we have never had a chance to offer our own charity in return. But now we are being invited! Of course you must go. Make sure your bag is stocked with as much as it can hold."

The youth had brought a wagon to transport Theresa the three miles, and they rode in haste, flying down Nu'uanu Road and thus startling evening pedestrians. The streets of Honolulu were uncharacteristically quiet and dark, as the city was in mourning for four-year-old Prince Albert, recently deceased. The king and queen were so grief-stricken that they had not appeared in public for weeks.

They finally arrived at Wailaka. A large crowd was gathered around one of the main huts. From within, Theresa heard the rhythmic beating of a drum, and a man's voice chanting. She slipped into the dimly lit interior and soon her eyes adjusted. She saw a man lying in the center of the floor on a woven mat. People sat cross-legged along the four walls, silent and watchful. A tall man in a brown tapa robe, with a crown of leaves around his head, stood over the supine fellow, shaking a bundle of wet *ti*-leaves, so that they sprinkled water upon the patient.

Mahina greeted Theresa with a sorrowful expression. "Aloha," she murmured and embraced her.

Theresa was surprised to see Captain Farrow there, but when she learned the identity of the man on the mat, his presence was understandable. The patient was Mahina's youngest son, named Polunu, and he was Robert Farrow's brother-in-law.

"What is wrong with him?"

"He got *'ana'ana*," Mahina said.

"What is that?"

Robert spoke up, "It's praying someone to death. A curse that kills."

Theresa stared at him. "Are you serious?"

"Very serious."

"So there's *nothing* wrong with him?"

"Only that he's dying."

"This is nonsense," Theresa muttered as she placed her bag next to Polunu. "No one dies just because someone puts a curse on him." Before examining him, she pinned her sleeves and veils back and out of the way, and then unfolded a clean white bib-apron, tying it around her neck and waist. Then she knelt and looked at Polunu.

She saw that his eyes shifted rapidly back and forth, as if watching a butterfly flitting about in the hut. The whites of his eyes were clear, the pupils neither pinpoint nor dilated. His skin was warm and dry, his pulse normal. When she listened to his chest, she heard no sounds of lung congestion, his heartbeat was strong and steady with no irregularities. His color was normal, his nail beds pink. She palpated his abdomen. It was not rigid, nor did she detect any abnormalities. There were no rashes, no wounds, no signs of any disturbances on his body.

The man appeared to be in perfect health.

She held spirits of ammonia under his nose. He did not react. When she said, "He needs to be bled, and that is something I am not trained to do," Captain Farrow shook his head. "Chief Kekoa will not allow a doctor to see his nephew. You and I are the only white people he trusts. Are you sure bleeding will help?"

She had to say no, for, truth to tell, Theresa had no idea what was ailing the poor man. "Can he be taken out into the fresh air? It is very stuffy in here."

Mahina appointed four strapping youths to carry their fallen friend out to lie in the clear air of the night. They placed him on a woven mat and when people crowded around, Theresa asked them to step back, then she knelt again at his side, fanning him with her apron.

His breathing grew labored. She listened to his chest and found his lungs clear. Why couldn't he breathe? His pulse remained steady and strong. His color was good. This man was perfectly healthy and yet he was slipping away!

She thought of Jamie Farrow who, according to Mahina, had "demons swimming in his blood."

Theresa looked up at Captain Farrow. "Have they tried to cure him?"

"For three days," he said grimly, and by the shadow on his jaw, she judged that Robert himself had been there for all three days. "When someone falls ill, Hawai'ians pray to the great god Kane, life-giver and restorer. They pray for days, appeasing the gods, before they treat the physical problem. They've done everything they can. That's why Mahina sent for you. Kanaka way didn't work, maybe haole way will."

"Captain Farrow," Theresa said in a low voice. "There is nothing I or my medicines can do. This man is under some sort of spell."

"Someone spoke a death prayer over him and now he believes he is dying."

"Nonsense," she said again, but felt the grip of fear. She had seen people die before, she had held their hands and prayed with them. But they were sick, injured, old. Not a strapping man thirty years of age who had not a stitch wrong with him!

Fear was suddenly replaced by anger. Turning to her patient, she gently tapped his cheek and called his name. Then she struck him hard, and shouted his name. She demanded that he respond. She commanded him to acknowledge her! She shook him by his shoulders until tears of frustration fell from her eyes onto his bare chest. "Dear God," Theresa cried. "Do not let this happen. Mother Mary, help this man! Show this poor, misguided man the way out of his darkness and into the light of your blessed grace. Touch his soul and open his heart."

She traced the sign of the cross on his forehead and then on his chest. She hastily unhooked the rosary from her belt and draped it over his breastbone, directly over his heart, and she prayed as she had never prayed before.

"Pele, Pele!" Mahina suddenly cried, lifting her arms and her voice to the stars. "Send sacred stone to Pua's people!"

Theresa looked up at her, to see her face twisted in agony, tears streaming down her cheeks. "Mahina sorry!" she shouted. "Mahina break kapu. Take me, no take Mahina's son! Send back Lono Stone!"

Theresa rose and put her hands on Mahina's shoulders. "Please," she said, on the verge of sobbing. "You must have faith."

"Mahina have faith," she said in a tight voice. Her fleshy chin trembled. "Stone save my son! Very powerful healing stone. Great *mana*. Come from ancestors long ago. Come from Kahiki!"

"Where is this stone, Mahina?" Theresa was desperate. If looking at a stone would stop this man from dying, then she would do it!

"My mother hide it in Pele's Womb! Kapu to go there! Kapu to go inside!"

Polunu gave out a strangled cry and Theresa rushed to his side. "Are you all right?" she asked, searching his face. "Can you hear me? *Polunu?*"

She felt for a pulse. She found none.

"Auwe!" shrieked Mahina, and the villagers took it up, sending their grief to the stars in an unearthly chorus of wails.

Mahina dropped her to knees, screaming, pulling at her hair. She seized Polunu and pulled him to her bosom, rocking back and forth as tears streamed down her cheeks and her wails of grief filled the night.

And Theresa watched her clutch the lifeless body of a perfectly healthy man who had died simply because someone had told him he would.

*T*he sun has died in the sky. There is no daylight. The fish have left the sea. Trees grow yellow, fall down. No more taro patches. Hawai'i Nui is dust.

Mahina paused in her labor to wipe the tears from her eyes. But as soon as she did, more tears came, blurring her vision. "Auwe!" she cried, feeling a sharp pain in her breast. *"Aloha 'oe, Polunu! A hui hou k'kou! Aloha au la 'oe!* Farewell, my son. . . ."

Her knees screamed with pain, she had been kneeling for so long. But she would not stop. The gifts for Pu'uwai had to be perfect.

Others in the village watched their beloved Tutu as she knelt in front of her hut, wrapping offerings for the most ancient god on the island. They knew that Mahina's heart was heavy over the loss of her son. They saw how she was losing weight. They knew of her sleepless nights. But no one, not even the *kahuna lapa'au* of the village, had been able to help. They knew she was going to appeal to the gods. And they knew why.

Mahina's people needed her; she could not let herself sicken and die.

As she wrapped the gifts in large green leaves and tied them with dried vines—flowers, colorful pebbles, fresh chunks of juicy pineapple—she thought: I will not go to Pu'uwai alone.

Since the night of the fertility hula over a year ago, when Chief Kekoa had declared Kika Keleka to be kama'aina, a child of the land, Mahina had been teaching her some of the island's medicinal secrets. She was doing it slowly and gradually, as Mika Kalono had done many years ago. Teaching and enlightening, sharing sacred knowledge.

It was only here and there, this day and that, sometimes at Farrow House, sometimes in the village, but not obvious lessons. Mahina would tell something to Sister Theresa, a tiny secret, something small—"Mashed *koali* roots heal wounds and broken bones"—and gradually, over the months, Keleka's mind became a storehouse of ancient kanaka medicine.

Now it was time for other secrets. Mahina was going to take Keleka to a place so sacred that no ordinary kanaka could walk there, only ali'i, a place where it was kapu for haole to walk.

It was going to be a test.

Finished with her work, Mahina lifted her eyes to her surroundings—the grass huts, the imu pits, the work pavilions, and a few villagers going about their daily tasks.

More of the women were wearing muumuus. Some of the men now wore trousers. Mahina saw bottles and newspapers. The haole ways were creeping in.

And so she must break kapu and take a haole wahine to O'ahu's most ancient and sacred place, so that the ways of the ancestors would not be forgotten.

As Theresa neared Farrow House, feeling the morning sun penetrate her black veils—wishing she could remove them just once and feel the ocean wind in her hair—she wondered whom she had been summoned here to see.

The messenger who had come the night before, a groom from Captain Farrow's stable, had said only that her services were requested and could she please come this morning? Was it Jamie, staying home from school? Had Emily suffered a relapse?

She was surprised to see Mahina standing at the head of the path that led to the house. She wore a beautiful blue muumuu and a lei of purple flowers. The wind stirred her hair, and when it played with the fabric of her dress, Theresa was shocked to see how much weight Mahina had lost.

They all still grieved for Polunu, and Sister Theresa was haunted by his mysterious death. How could mere words cause a healthy man to die? She had tried to discuss it with Father Halloran and Mother Agnes, even with her Sisters, but they seemed to have no interest in the arcane beliefs of the islanders.

When Mahina embraced her in aloha, Theresa saw the sadness in the woman's big brown eyes, the new lines of grief on her face.

Then Theresa looked around and had the feeling that no one was home at the Farrow house. "Did you send for me, Tutu?" she asked.

"We go," Mahina said, taking Theresa by the arm.

"Where?"

"You see. We go."

Mahina took her down to the beach, trekking eastward, away from the center of town, away from the harbor and ships and warehouses. Here, they skirted mudflats and wetlands until they came to a secluded strip of shoreline where few kanaka came, and no white man ever visited. The beach was pristine and deserted, and embraced the water in a deep curve. Mahina called it Waikiki and said it was the most sacred place in Hawai'i Nui.

Theresa thought it was a beautiful spot. Far from noise and the smoke of chimneys and steamships. The sand was almost white, stretching from grassy dunes to a calm surf where the water was lime green turning to turquoise and aquamarine farther out.

Sister Theresa followed Mahina into a cluster of slender coconut palms, where scarlet hibiscus bloomed among the narrow tree trunks. It was like a secluded paradise—one could think one was the only person on earth. She wondered why no one had constructed huts in this lovely setting.

And then she had her answer. "Very sacred ground," Mahina said in a reverent tone. "What I show you, only *kahuna* see."

Mahina pushed aside dense clumps of white ginger blossoms to expose, in the center, a moss-covered boulder, waist-high and irregularly shaped. Mahina didn't speak as Sister Theresa stared at the huge rock. She couldn't see anything significant about it. There were no carvings, no pictographs, no obvious places where sacrifices might have been made. Just an old mossy boulder.

"This most sacred place in all O'ahu," Mahina said. "Long ago, before white man, my people come here to celebrate the gods, to be thankful for life and fertility. We feast here. We hula. We have games. We ride surfboards and amuse the gods. We go back to our homes filled with blessings." Her sigh was filled with sadness. "My people start to forget. They go to church instead of come here. Now only Mahina come to remember the ancient gods."

When Mahina said nothing more, Theresa looked around, wondering what made a rock so sacred. There were only trees and grass and shrubbery along the flat beachfront. She looked back at the plain where Honolulu and myriad dwellings and structures were scattered. It, too, was flat. She recalled something Robert Farrow had told her, that it was believed that these islands were the tops of massive volcanoes rising from the ocean floor. The plain upon which Honolulu had been built was the result of millennia of volcanic ash building up beneath the sea, and coral growing and dying and decomposing, layer by layer until it rose above the sea. The plain had stopped growing when O'ahu's volcanoes became extinct. Now there was a flat expanse stretching from the ocean about three miles inland to where sheer cliffs, blindingly green, rose vertically in a towering backdrop of sharp ravines and steep waterfalls, all crowned in cobwebby mists.

Theresa returned her attention to the boulder and a question sprang into her mind: Where did this come from, on an earth so flat?

She looked back at the towering peaks that had once been violently active and she thought: this rock was spewed from the fiery belly of a volcano. She pictured its pyrotechnic eruption from the mountain, its flight through the air, its heavy landing here on this flat spot to spend the next hundreds of years in the protection of new palm trees and lush growth.

Mahina studied Theresa's face and then nodded. Theresa had passed the test. "You know. Kika Keleka understand. This come from the gods. This come from inside a god. We call the sacred stone, Pu'uwai, 'heart.'" Mahina placed her leaf-wrapped gifts at the base of the stone and said, "This is the heart of O'ahu, this is the heart of

Hawai'i Nui. Someday kanaka will forget. But Kika Keleka not forget."

"What do you mean? Why did you bring me here?"

Mahina laid a gentle hand on Theresa's arm. "Uncle Kekoa say you *kama'aina.* I teach you kanaka secrets."

"I'm hardly—"

Mahina smiled and nodded. "Uncle Kekoa know truth. Uncle Kekoa always right."

As she was about to protest that there must be some mistake, the ocean breeze picked up, bringing the sound of far-off laughter. Theresa turned in its direction and saw, far out on the water, tiny figures sitting on boards. She knew they had paddled out there on their stomachs. She reckoned they had to go at least a half-mile out to catch the waves. Sturdy souls, she thought.

She couldn't distinguish who they were, just tiny brown ocean nymphs kneeling on boards. Now she saw them rise up on one knee as they caught a fresh swell. They let out whoops and shouts as they got up on their feet, knees bent, arms out for balance. The ocean swell grew. It became a traveling wave with a frothy cap parallel to the shore. The riders were strung out, putting space between one another as the long line of snowy foam came steadily toward the beach.

Mesmerized, Theresa stepped away from the heart of O'ahu and walked through the coconut palms, her eyes on the riders.

The figures grew bigger. They laughed and called to one another as they performed feats of skill, turning their boards this way and that as the water carried them toward the beach. She marveled at their agility, the way they zigzagged and yet kept their balance. It was a race, she realized, and some were coming faster. A few fell off. The numbers shrank.

Closer they came, giddy boys intoxicated by the sun and the wind and their youth. Out of the laughter she recognized one. It was Mahina's grandson, Liho, a comical boy who made people laugh. He was Polunu's son, and also Captain Farrow's Hawai'ian nephew and Jamie's cousin.

Keeping her eyes on the surf riders, Sister Theresa left the cluster of palm trees and walked down the white-sand beach. She saw Liho wave his arms, heard him call out to her. She saw him make his board go faster, then he suddenly turned it to the side. In a curious optical illusion, Liho was traveling sideways while the wave continued to come toward her.

She felt Mahina come and stand at her side, at the edge of the surf where sandpipers ran into the tide. "You see?" Mahina said. "You understand? The boys not ride the waves . . . the waves *carry* the boys. The gods of the sea are happy. They share their joy. The gods of Hawai'i Nui still live."

Sister Theresa frowned. There was talk in town of banning surf riding just as the hula had been banned. One by one, the different aspects of Hawai'ian culture were being erased. What would be left? And what was the harm in dancing, in riding waves, in living the way their ancestors had lived?

Finally the froth grew thin. The wave's energy began to wane, as if weary from carrying so many happy boys. The swell gave up and joined the undulating green water. Liho jumped from his board and waded to shore.

"Kika Keleka," he shouted. *"E he'enalu kakou!"*

"What did he say, Mahina?"

"He say, let's ride surf. You go, Kika, Liho teach good."

She shook her head. "How ever did it first occur to someone to ride a board on waves?"

"The gods teach the kanaka. And now kanaka teach haole."

Theresa laughed. "I doubt you will ever see a white man on a surfboard!"

Liho drew near, grinning and sparkling with salt and water and sand. He wore a loincloth and a necklace of shark's teeth. He was missing a front tooth so that he sometimes whistled when he spoke, making people laugh. Laying his board down, he reached for Sister Theresa. "You come. Ride board with Liho."

She cried out and fell back, laughing. But deep in her soul, a part of her wanted to say Yes! *Tear off the veils and starched linens, swim out beyond the reef, and wait for the perfect ocean swell to carry me back to shore . . .*

And the small part within her, that made her feel like an outsider among her Sisters, grew.

As they watched Liho paddle back out onto the water, Theresa tried to absorb the importance of the moment. She felt honored that Mahina wanted to teach her kanaka secrets, and humbled and not up to the noble task. And conflicted now, too. I am supposed to be teaching you. I was ordered to instruct you in Catholic catechism and convert you to Christianity.

But even as she thought this, Theresa felt her excitement grow. She was not only going to learn something few white men knew, she was being brought into a secret Sisterhood of sorts. And Theresa felt a curious kind of love fill her heart. Love for this woman who trusted her, who asked no questions, made no demands, but who had simply chosen her for a very special task.

Turning to Mahina, she said, "Teach me more, Tutu."

CHAPTER EIGHTEEN

Once a week, one of the Sisters was assigned the task of taking a basket of freshly baked sugar buns down the street to the rectory, where Father Halloran resided with the other priests, most of whom were French. Sister Theresa thought to bring along the newspaper that had been delivered that morning. Mother Agnes always perused a newspaper, to see if there was anything going on in Honolulu that might affect her Sisters—an outbreak of an illness, perhaps. In one instance, she informed them of a reported case of what the Hawai'ians called *mai pake,* or the Chinese sickness. The Sisters called it leprosy. But it was only one case, and the man, a worker on a sugar plantation, was deported back to China.

It was Sister Theresa's turn to deliver the buns, and she carefully folded the paper and tucked it into the bag. The news, as usual, was about the war back home. The conflict between the North and the South had had another, unexpected impact on the islands: because the South could not export textiles, ladies in Honolulu who wished new gowns made of ginghams, muslins, and dimity were forced to turn old clothes into new. The result had been to create a great demand for sewing machines, so that Mr. Klausner could scarcely keep up with orders.

For Theresa, the war news was personal. Her mother wrote that Eli was still alive and "keeping up the good fight." But the citizens of

Honolulu heard of so many young men being cut down that Sister Theresa prayed daily that her brother be kept safe.

The rest of the news was about the new king, Lot, who had succeeded his recently deceased brother because King Kamehameha the Fourth had left no heir. The poor man had never recovered from the death of his four-year-old son, Albert. Fifteen months after burying the boy, he died. He was only twenty-nine.

While everyone wondered if the new monarch might shift the balance of power, it turned out that the anti-American, pro-British views of his predecessor were being carried on. And in fact, the new king so loved his predecessor that he changed the name of the royal palace to 'Iolani Palace in his honor. `Io was the Hawai'ian hawk, a bird that flew higher than all the rest, and *lani* meant heavenly, royal, or exalted.

Several medical men were campaigning for the post of Minister of Public Health, and Dr. Edgeware was working hard to ingratiate himself to the new king, hoping to get the appointment, and so his tireless anti-Catholic diatribes appeared almost daily in the press.

Theresa let herself in through the rectory kitchen and heard voices. She looked in and saw six men gathered in the parlor. Besides Father Halloran and another priest were four prominent Honolulu businessmen. She did not mean to eavesdrop, but when she heard Father Halloran mention Robert Farrow, she could not help but stay by the door and listen.

"The heretics still hold sway in the legislature," groused a newspaper man whom Theresa knew to be a wealthy Catholic from Boston. He had come to the islands with political ambitions and was pushing for more Catholic presence in the government. "Men like Robert Farrow are difficult to un-seat," he complained. "He has a great deal of wealth and political influence. I hear he has all but sealed a contract with the Pacific Mail Steamship Company. That will give him a monopoly on the Hawai'i run! And what you said, Father Halloran, about the secret meeting that took place at Farrow House last week, involving his shipping investors, indicates that his cadre of Protestant business partners is growing."

Sister Theresa could not believe her ears. She had told Father Halloran those things in the strictest confidence!

"What of the Sister, Theresa? Is she making any headway with the natives at Wailaka? To bring Chief Kekoa into our congregation would be to bring not only hundreds of Hawai'ians, but thousands of acres of rich land as well. Wailaka would support an extremely lucrative sugar plantation."

"So far," she heard Father Halloran say, "Sister Theresa is the only Christian that Chief Kekoa will allow into his village. She reports to me everything that goes on there."

Theresa barely stifled a gasp. As she stood against the door, fearing her knees were going to give way, she heard terrible words that pierced her to the core.

The wealthy Bostonian said, "If we can catch Kekoa breaking a law—or several, or urging his people to break the law—we would be able to go in and cart him off to prison. It could be a way to confiscate his lands. After all, he would be fomenting treason."

"I understand," came the voice of one of the other men, "that Kekoa's niece is the daughter of a high kahuna and has a noble bloodline. I also understand that the woman is fond of Sister Theresa. With her influence under our control, we'll have Kekoa and his thousand acres."

Theresa couldn't hear Father Halloran's answer as her pulse pounded in her ears. She could not believe what she was hearing. Robert Farrow's cadre of Protestant business partners . . . Chief Kekoa's thousands of acres . . .

Her words!

She pressed her hand to her stomach. She suddenly felt sick. Father Halloran, her confessor—a man in whom she had placed the purest trust and in whom she had confided her most personal thoughts—was using her as a pawn in a political game. He was using her as a spy. . . .

She had begged him not to push her into the path of temptation. He knew how hard it was for her to go to Farrow House and that it strained her morals and conscience. He had told her it was to save souls. But it was really to gain control of the government! Was Father Halloran truly willing to sacrifice her virtue, her morals, *her very soul* for the aggrandizement of a few greedy men?

She fled the rectory kitchen, dropping the pastries on the floor.

Robert read the letter four times, standing at his desk with a whiskey in his hand, until he finally threw the letter down to join the other papers scattered on the desk.

It was from Peter, asking for a loan so he could invest in a new sugar plantation near his ranch. Robert had heard that his brother had been in Honolulu last week. Why couldn't he have come by the house or the shipping office and asked for the money? Instead, an impersonal letter.

Of course Robert would give him what he asked, but it would be handled through Farrow's bank. As if Peter were just another business client.

He looked at his ship's designs scattered on the desk. This was what he had to be satisfied with. Drawings on paper. He remembered the day his father had first taken him and Peter out on the *Kestrel*. Robert was six at the time and had taken to it at once. The rigging, the sails, the great big helm where his father had held him up so he could grasp the spokes. But four-year-old Peter had cried and wanted to go back to shore.

Robert stared across the room at the painting over the fireplace. A fine clipper ship under full sail. The *Kestrel*—his father's, which Robert had taken over when MacKenzie decided to retire from the sea and run the family shipping business, which was rapidly growing, and also to take care of Emily, whose spells of mental instability were increasing in frequency.

And then, in 1849, MacKenzie had died while Emily was in the grip of violent hallucinations. Robert hadn't known about it until he came into home port and learned not only that his father had passed away weeks before, but that Peter was leaving the family business and moving to Waialua to raise cattle.

Forcing Robert to give up his passion.

That was fourteen years ago and he had been shackled to a desk ever since.

There was another letter among the papers that required his immediate attention. It was from the principal of Oʻahu College. A man named McFarlain who wrote in a fluid hand: "He daydreams, Mr. Farrow," the letter read. "I am not sure what it is. Jamie has spells. That is how his teachers describe it. He drifts out, if you get my meaning.

His marks are good and when he pays attention, he is a bright and gifted lad. But his mind wanders. You will have to have a word with him."

Jamie was home for a holiday break. He had brought Mr. McFarlain's report with him. Robert dreaded the conversation he must have with his son. He had kept his fears a secret. Jamie didn't know his father thought he might inherit his grandmother's mental illness. Robert didn't know how much longer he could keep his fears to himself.

The letter went on to say more about Jamie, but Farrow remained fixed on the word "spells." Emily had suffered several more spells in the past year—admittedly, they weren't as intense as they used to be, thanks to Sister Theresa's calming teas. She also had a way of quieting Emily just by being in the room with her. But Robert's mother needed constant watching, and he feared that her mental instability was starting to manifest itself in his son.

Were the boy's spells soon going to escalate into screaming fits? He tossed back the last of the whiskey and reached for the decanter.

It wasn't fair to Jamie. Robert had known at the time that he shouldn't father children, not with the risk of inherited insanity in his blood. But Leilani had wanted a baby and he couldn't refuse her anything.

Leilani. She was starting to become a distant dream. They had stopped visiting her grave—of course, Peter refused to go from the very beginning—and now she didn't enter Robert's thoughts as often as she used to. Instead, he found himself—when he was riding around the island, or inspecting one of his ships, or working in his office— thinking of Sister Theresa. He would be doing something that had no connection to her whatsoever, and suddenly she would be in his mind, filling his inner vision with her loveliness, her soft-spoken voice, and her practical wisdom and healing lore as well.

After Leilani, Robert had thought he would never fall in love again. But Sister Theresa worked a special kind of magic that troubled him. No woman could be more unreachable to a man than a professed religious Sister. It was illogical that he should even entertain thoughts about her, wondering about the color of her hair, what it would be like to kiss her. Robert Farrow had always prided himself on his strength of logic and will, but his heart was apparently another matter.

"Mr. Farrow?"

He turned to see Mrs. Carter in the doorway. "Yes?" he said, setting the decanter and his empty glass down.

"There's an urgent message for you."

What now? he wondered as he reached for his coat.

Three days had passed since Theresa had overheard the conversation in the rectory, and she was still in pain. She had never felt so betrayed.

For the first time, working in the convent garden did nothing to calm her troubled soul. Mother Agnes and her Sisters were out on various errands, and Mrs. Jackson had gone to the market. She was alone at the house, alone in the garden. It had rained during the night, flooding their newly planted furrows, so Theresa had lifted the hems of her skirts and tucked them into her belt. Then she had removed her shoes and stockings so that she would not ruin them as she walked through the mud. As she needed to rescue the seedlings, she'd also pinned her sleeves back so that her bare arms were kissed by sunlight.

Her mind was so filled with thoughts of Father Halloran—so sacred a trust had been broken!—that it was some minutes before she realized she was no longer alone in the garden.

Robert Farrow stood in the sunshine as if he had grown from the soil, straight and tall and perfect in his white linen suit that was always without the slightest smudge or blemish, the wide-brimmed hat casting a shadow on his face. But she saw the smile, the even, white teeth. "I'm sorry," he said. "I didn't mean to startle you."

She was suddenly aware of her bare arms and legs, the mud on her feet and hands. What a sight she must be!

"I rang the bell several times but no one answered."

"You're not allowed back here," was all she could think of to say. She was overjoyed to see him. After such disillusionment, it was good to be in the presence of someone she could trust. And in the next moment she felt terrible, knowing that she had passed his secrets along to a man who was sharing them with half of Honolulu!

"I am on my way to Wailaka and Mahina asked me to stop by and pick up some ointment for her rash. She said you would know what it was."

"I will get it for you."

"I'm to attend a *ho'oponopono* ritual for her grandson. It's Polunu's son."

She looked at him in alarm. "Liho? Tell me it is not another death curse."

"No no, the boy is sick with an unknown illness. They hope to cure him through *ho'oponopono*."

Although Mahina had been teaching her more of Hawai'i's healing and spiritual secrets, Theresa had yet to witness *ho'oponopono*. "Captain Farrow, could I possibly join you? I'm very fond of Liho and would like to be on hand in case my skills are needed."

Robert looked at her in surprise, and then delight. "I will wait for you out front."

By the time she had cleaned herself up and was presentable, Mrs. Jackson had returned and Theresa asked her to tell Mother Agnes where she had gone—and that she might be late.

The evening was balmy and perfumed. "You're very quiet tonight," Robert observed when they were halfway to Wailaka and the moon was rising over treetops to cast the landscape in an ivory glow.

She told Robert what she had overheard, and that Father Halloran's words troubled her. "He is more interested in putting Catholics in power than in saving souls."

"So you are disillusioned."

She could not tell Robert the whole truth of her disillusionment—that she had begged Father Halloran not to force her to go to Farrow House because she had feelings for Captain Farrow. So she told him a partial truth: "Father Halloran sent me . . . into homes I did not think I should visit. He . . . ordered me to have congress with certain persons that I had preferred to avoid. But he pushed me, telling me I was saving souls for Christ. But now I see that all he wants is to convert more of those with wealth and influence to Catholicism, to shift the balance of power in these islands!"

"He's no different from any other man on the island."

"But I told him private things about you, and he passed them on to other men. Doesn't that infuriate you? And aren't you angry with me?"

He smiled at her in the moonlight. "Sister Theresa, for one thing, I could never be angry with you. And for another, every man on this island is a spy."

They arrived at the village and, leaving the wagon on the road, they went to the main hut where villagers had gathered to hold vigil.

Theresa knew that, prior to treating a person for an illness, Hawai'ians prayed. And it was not a simple affair. It took hours, sometimes days, to render the area ritualistically cleansed and harmonious. Evil spirits must be driven out, bad luck and negative energies chased away while the gods and the family ancestors were summoned. Sacred water was sprinkled everywhere. Holy words were chanted. Good luck spells were spoken, and ancient objects containing great *mana* were placed about.

Theresa saw that, by the time she and Robert reached the large hut where the *ho'oponopono* was to take place, the spiritual and religious preparations had already been completed. The "cleansing" priest was gone, and now the mediating kahuna was with the sick boy. It was this man who would be conducting what Theresa had heard could often be an extremely painful, emotional, and sometimes utterly exhausting ritual.

But she had heard of miracles happening in *ho'oponopono.* She wondered if she would witness one tonight. She prayed that she would, because Liho was a sweet boy.

The hut was crowded inside, with everyone, from very young to very old, sitting quietly on woven mats. From what Theresa knew of *ho'oponopono,* each member was performing a personal search for whatever they might have contributed to the family's problem and therefore to the boy's sickness. Chief Kekoa, in his tapa robe and staff of office, sat in a place of honor, somber and dignified. Mahina greeted them with aloha, then she said, *"O ka huhu ka mea e ola 'ole ai,"* which meant, "Anger is the thing that gives no life."

Mahina had lost more weight, but she was still robust and large of stature. Her gray and black hair was now completely white and grew down to her waist. She had lost her husband, her sons, and her only daughter. All she had were her grandsons: Jamie and Liho.

"What is wrong with him, Tutu?" Theresa asked.

"You take look, Kika."

She knelt at the youth's side and saw that he was indeed sick. His forehead burned and sweat poured off his body. He clutched his stomach and moaned. As Theresa started to open her medical bag, she felt a hand on her shoulder. She looked up to see Robert shaking his head.

As he helped her to her feet, he said, "The *kahuna lapa'au* has already seen to the boy and has pronounced him sick of spirit. The family is hurting, out of harmony. Something is wrong with the whole family and that injury is manifesting itself in the boy. The only medicine that will work now is *ho'oponopono,* setting things right."

Theresa knew that the ritual was essentially a family conference. All members gathered to get things off their chests, to admit to things, to confess to grudges and maybe admit to secret punishments against others, and then they all asked for forgiveness, and in turn dispensed forgiveness. Basically, it was clearing the air and making things right again.

As there were no chairs, they found a space on the woven mats, and Theresa sat as modestly as she could in such an unladylike position, with Robert next to her.

There was a seaweed called *kala,* which meant "to forgive." Mahina distributed pieces of kala to the family members and while they chewed on the seaweed, they prayed. Then they began to speak up and it soon came out that part of the family disharmony was a battle between the older women and a younger one, the older ones making fun of her for having too many children too close together. "Every *waha ko'u* talk about her. Bad shame."

Theresa knew that *waha ko'u* referred to local gossips; it literally meant "clucking mouth." And she knew how stinging some tongues could be.

Another family member blurted out that he had promised to help Liho repair a canoe, but had gone surfboard riding instead.

One by one the confessions were recited, and as it was all conducted in Hawai'ian, Robert quietly translated for Theresa.

For hours they sat and listened. Sometimes tempers flared and accusations flew. Chief Kekoa would intervene and tell everyone to go outside. After a few minutes in the fresh night air, they would reconvene and the ritual would resume in a calmer fashion.

As the hour grew late, the air in the hut became warm and humid. The rhythmic chanting made Theresa sleepy. She leaned against Robert and he put a strong arm around her. But she did not fall asleep. She kept her eye on the supine boy who, Theresa realized after a while, was no longer moaning. She watched him carefully as confessions were recited, as one man apologized to another man's wife for improper advances; as a boy said he was sorry for stealing another boy's surfboard; as a wife asked her husband to forgive her for her sharp tongue. On and on the sins, offenses, transgressions, grudges, jealousies were aired and carried away by the ancestral spirits, to be followed by weeping and tears and loudly sworn oaths to be a better brother, wife, daughter, auntie, cousin, and then came the laughter and jokes and visible relief until Theresa saw that Liho was no longer perspiring. His skin no longer glowed with fever, and his respiration was normal.

As the kahuna lifted his arms and chanted prayers, Mahina helped Liho to sit up—he had not been able to sit or eat or drink for days—and she gave him a gourd of water, from which he drank thirstily. And then he looked around at everyone with a grin on his face.

Each family member knelt to embrace him, and to each he murmured, *"Aloha nui loa,"* which meant, "I love you very much."

Theresa held him tight, this water nymph who wanted to take her for a ride on his long board. She had thought he was going to die, like his father, but forgiveness had saved his life.

They returned to the dark lane, leaving lights and laughter behind. Robert held out his hand to assist Theresa into the wagon, and when she slipped her hand into his, she paused and looked up into his eyes.

It was the hour before dawn. The stars were beginning to fade and the moon hung low on the horizon, casting a silvery path on the black water. The wind was cool and refreshing, but Theresa felt bone-weary. Not just physically, but emotionally as well. "Robert," she whispered, looking up at his handsome face, which was ghostly in the pre-dawn. "I can't forgive him. I can't forgive Father Halloran for what he did. Those people back there . . . they have such strong faith. They have the power to forgive. I do not."

He looked down at her, searching for words. He saw pain in her eyes, heard it in her voice. Robert Farrow had just turned thirty-nine, and in all his years on this earth, he had learned that human beings can both protect and betray, that they can be trustworthy and yet deceitful.

He had learned never to place total faith in another man, a lesson that had finally come in this young woman's life.

"Mahina's people possess such strong faith!" she said again, and when the breeze blew the edge of her veil across her face, he reached up and brushed it back, brushing her cool, smooth cheek as well. "The very power of their beliefs," she cried, "brought Liho back from the brink. Where do you find such faith, Robert? I used to have faith in Father Halloran. Now I have nothing."

He took her by the shoulders and stepped close. She had filled his thoughts these past months, and now here she was, in the early hours of a new day, shrouded in the last remnants of night, shrouded in a ridiculous costume. "Why did you become a nun?" he said, demanding to know what had driven her to condemn herself to such an unnatural life.

"Because I wanted to be a nurse, I wanted to help people. My decision was not a religious one. Not like my Sisters who have true faith. I never had a true vocation, no religious awakening. I suppose that's why Father Halloran's betrayal is so painful. I looked to him for spiritual strength and guidance, but now that that has been shattered, I have no real foothold on spiritual strength. Robert, I resent the bells and the regulations of my convent life, I chafe against the monastic rules. And it gets harder with each passing day."

The wind shifted and brought a heady perfume from a nearby gardenia shrub covered in white flowers. Theresa stepped closer, placed her hands on his chest and said, "Oh Robert, don't you see? If the nursing should ever be taken from my Sisters, if the Mother House should change their mission, they would still have their devotion to God. But I do not have that."

His grip tightened. "Then leave the Order."

"And if I did, what would I do? Where would I go?"

He wanted to shout curses to the sky, to the ancient gods, to God Himself. The unfairness of it all! Never had he felt so helpless. Captain Robert Farrow, who commanded a fleet of ships, who debated politics in the legislature, did not have the words that would assuage her conflict. How could he encourage her to walk away from the impossible situation she had committed herself to, when he had nothing to give her in return? She was not free, but neither was he.

The letter from Jamie's school . . . "spells" . . . "his mind wanders" . . .

Like Theresa, Robert was trapped by circumstances beyond his control.

"Oh Robert, I am so confused! I look back at my fifteen-year-old self, when I was Anna Barnett and filled with idealistic dreams, and I realize that converting to Catholicism had seemed like a *game.* I only acted the part. In a way, I lied, and it is not something I am proud of. I mimicked the other Sisters. I memorized the prayers and recited them by rote. I used religion as a means to an end. My vows were empty words. And now I feel I must make it up somehow. Now, more than ever, I must be true to those vows, for if I do not, then what does that say for my character, my integrity?"

"You have character and integrity, believe me—by God, I loathe addressing you as Sister, for you are no Sister to me. I think of you as a woman—a desirable woman. Let me call you Theresa. Or better, Anna, for that is your real name."

She looked up at him, saw the fire in his eyes—and confusion as well, for this was something new for both of them, and for Captain Farrow, these must be strange, uncharted waters—and felt the strength of his hands as he held her. She wanted to succumb.

"If only it were that easy," she said with a sob as the eastern sky grew pale and the wind picked up and birds began their calls in the jungle surrounding them. The morning air was cool and sharp. Theresa felt her emotions sharpen, as if the *ho'oponopono* had changed her as it was rescuing Liho from the brink.

As if the faith of all those people gathered in the hut had touched my soul. Yesterday morning I was content to deliver pastries to the rectory. Now I want to deliver myself into the arms of a man I must never love.

"Anna," he whispered, bending his head.

She waited for an instant, her face uplifted to his. Then she broke away, stepping back to let the cold wind create a chasm between them. "Take me home," she said, the words feeling hollow in her mouth, for where, now, was home?

CHAPTER NINETEEN

Robert was worried. He had looked for a letter from Jamie in the past three days, and so far none had come. As he worked in his office, he glanced frequently through the window for the local postman whom, he prayed, was bringing the letter at last.

Farrow Shipping was headquartered in offices at the docks, where a steady stream of foot traffic—ship's captains, importers and exporters, people with mail and parcels for home, merchants and farmers, people booking passage or just making inquiries—came and went.

Robert Farrow's company owned thirty vessels that crisscrossed the world's oceans carrying goods, people, and news to the far corners of the earth. Robert himself headed a maritime empire that employed captains and officers and sailors, dockworkers, boatwrights, and, here in the main office, a staff of twenty who kept track of Farrow ships, balanced the accounts, maintained cargo lists and bills of lading, kept records of passengers—young clerks who sat on tall stools at high desks, scribbling with quills and ink while dreaming of striking it rich in the islands.

Robert maintained an enormous map of the world—it covered an entire wall and upon it he stuck markers that indicated the known locations, and possible locations, of every ship he owned. He was proud of the Farrow reputation for getting cargo and passengers to ports safely and on time. Around his office were the relics and mementoes of a maritime career. Robert had just turned forty and one of his most prized possessions was the miniature model of the John Fitch steamboat, the first ever that had plied a commercial business on the Delaware River. The archaic little prototype had been put together by Robert's father, MacKenzie, for his tenth birthday.

Robert missed his son. Jamie was summering with Peter's family on their ranch in Waialua. He wrote to his father describing days of fun and play. Jamie and his cousin swam in the Anahulu River, or rode wild colts in the corral. They enjoyed gardening in a yard that grew grapes, figs, guava fruit, and coconut. They swung from *kukui* trees in front of the house, or helped out on the ranch. Sometimes they played with neighbor boys, the sons of missionaries. And when the day was hot, they whiled away their youthful hours in a sugarcane patch, chewing on sweet stalks and laughing.

Jamie thrived on the ranch, his health returned when he was with Reese. Robert wished Jamie could live with Peter and his family indefinitely, but a son belonged with his father. Even though, each time he returned to Honolulu, so did Jamie's inexplicable malaise.

Sister Theresa—Anna—did her best, bringing new tonics and teas, searching her Order's archives for overlooked remedies. Their healing went back five centuries, with each generation of nuns adding to an already impressive archive of herbal lore and healing practices (although Anna had complained that many of their recipes were clearly useless but that Mother Agnes insisted they continue to use them simply because "we have always done so").

Anna . . .

Another reason he preferred to have Jamie in Honolulu. Robert saw more of her when his son was at home.

Neither of them had spoken of their pre-dawn moment of unleashed emotion, at the edge of the Wailaka village, the night Liho was cured through *ho'oponopono*. But he knew it was sharply in her mind, just as it was in his, every time he saw her. They were polite and guarded and, when others were around, he addressed her as "Sister." But when they were alone together, and in his own heart, she was Anna.

The bell sounded over the door and Robert turned to see the postman at last. While the man had brought a mountain of correspondence for Farrow Shipping, Inc. there were no personal letters. "I am so sorry, Captain," the man said with a sorrowful expression. "The skipper of the coastal steamer just told me that there is trouble at Waialua. That's why no mail is coming through."

"Trouble?" Robert said in alarm. "What sort of trouble?"

And when he heard, the color drained from his face.

Sister Theresa and Sister Catherine were crushing leaves in the little herbal workshop at the back of the convent house, while Sister Margaret and Sister Frances were making rounds about town, visiting patients, and Mother Agnes was in conference with the bishop.

"My brother, Eli," Theresa was saying, "survived the Battle of Gettysburg, but the last we heard, the 20th Massachusetts Infantry was engaged at North Anna, and then went on to lose heavily at Cold Harbor. Since then, nothing. Father wrote that my mother is a nervous wreck." As are mothers all across America and even here in the islands, she added silently, as many families had sent sons to fight for the Union. Everyone is hungry for news of the war and of home, she reminded herself.

They might be over two thousand miles away, but hearts knew nothing of distance. Americans in Hawai'i had applauded when President Lincoln issued the Emancipation Proclamation in 1862, abolishing slavery. And when he was recently re-elected, Americans in Honolulu celebrated with great enthusiasm.

As she worked at the bench, Theresa looked out over the convent garden and was reminded of the night, a year ago, when Robert had suddenly shown up to say they were on their way to a *ho'oponopono* ritual.

The cure had been miraculous. Liho was once again a healthy, vibrant youth who spent his days carving canoes and riding his surfboard. Theresa could not explain what had happened that night. Faith healing was nothing new. So she supposed it was the boy's belief in the power of family confession that cured him.

With each day that she walked the roads and lanes of this island, she saw contradictions. Hawai'ians seemed to possess a remarkable power over the flesh—a man could literally be talked into dying, while family confessions cured an illness—but at the same time, the native population continued to shrink. It was white man's diseases that were taking them, and it would seem Hawai'ians had no power over such illnesses.

But nor did white doctors. While more physicians came to these shores, they brought no cures against measles, influenza, chicken pox. And although Dr. Edgeware, now Minister of Public Health, had implemented island-wide sanitary and hygienic laws, each day there were fewer natives.

More cases of the *mai pake*, or Chinese sickness, had been reported. Health officials were asking citizens to report any sickness that they suspected might be leprosy so that immediate action could be taken to deport those persons.

Theresa heard the front doorbell and a moment later Mrs. Jackson came out to announce Captain Farrow.

She hastily brushed off her skirts, removed her apron, straightened her veils, and tried to walk slowly to the parlor. She expected to see his usual charming smile, but was taken aback by a look on his face she had never seen before. It could only be described as *bereft*.

"Is something wrong?" she asked, thinking of Emily and Jamie.

"There has been an outbreak of scarlet fever in Waialua. People are *dying*."

The road from Honolulu to Waialua was narrow and in many places composed of just a track with two ruts for wagon wheels. But it cut straight across, north-south, through the Central Valley, with the Ko'olau Mountains on the right, the Wai'anae on the left. It was a cool upland covered in forests of ohi'a, koa, and kupukupu ferns. This was said to be the birthplace of O'ahu's rainbows, and Theresa certainly saw many as Captain Farrow guided their wagon down the road. They saw the occasional cluster of grass huts, and once in a while the white wooden house of a haole family, with little farm plots here and there, but otherwise it was virgin wilderness.

The news from Waialua was alarming. Scarlet fever could spread through the native population like wildfire. And they didn't know whether Peter's family had been affected. Theresa was not worried about the more robust Farrow men, but she did not know if fourteen-year-old Jamie could weather a bout of scarlet fever.

And Charlotte was pregnant! This would be her seventh child. But she could not expose it or herself to illness. Of her previous six, only Reese and a three-year-old daughter still lived.

A cold wind came up and Theresa had to hold onto her veils while Robert slapped a hand on top of his hat so that he held the reins in one hand. He looked to the dark sky in the west. "There's a storm out there, off the coast, but it might roll in."

No sooner had he spoken than the first drops started to fall. "It's only a squall line!" he said above the wind. "It will soon pass."

Tree cover was nearby. Tethering the horse and wagon under the protection of overhanging branches, they found shelter under an acacia koa.

There was something intimate about sharing a dry spot under a tree while rain was coming down all around. Theresa was sharply aware of Robert's arm against hers, how he towered over her, his solid strength like the tree that sheltered them. The familiar, and unwanted, ache rose within her and she was once again thankful for the cumbersome habit she wore. Although there were days when she found the veils and starched linen uncomfortable and a burden, there were times she knew this black cloth was her armor.

She felt Robert's eyes on her. She looked up. His face held an unreadable expression. She was sent back four years, to the day she had thoughtlessly walked off the *Syren* and into the attention of surly seamen. A stranger had come to her aid, warning her of danger in this place. Did Robert ever think of that meeting, she wondered?

And then she thought of their last intimate encounter as dawn was breaking and she had poured out her troubles to him. His hands on her arms, standing so close, bending his head . . .

She had wanted to succumb. As she did now, as his eyes held hers for too long. Words needed to be spoken, but they were both speech-less. Theresa felt something strange and curious shift about them, as if it came in on the wind and the rain. She saw sorrow in Robert's eyes. It was a look she had glimpsed on occasion when he thought she was not watching.

He parted his lips and inclined his head toward her, ever so slightly and hesitantly, and she felt her heart rise in her throat. She tore her gaze away from his and forced herself to search for another object of attention, and she saw through the downpour a curious collection of large, oddly shaped stones jutting up from the earth. She could see petroglyphs carved into them, and when she saw what were clearly gifts left by local folks for the spirits of this place, she asked Robert, with what breath she could muster, the significance of this place.

"It used to be a heiau," he said, squinting at the rocks through the rain, his voice strained, as if he were wrestling with an inner conflict. "A sacred precinct. Those are birthing stones, where Hawai'ian royalty and nobility gave birth for generations. When a high-ranking woman neared her time, the whole family came here and performed a complex program of sacred rites and purification rituals. It went on for days, while special kahuna women tended to the laboring mother. Chiefs and other ali'i stood in a circle, dressed in their finest, while commoners stood at a respectful distance, no doubt in awe of the fact that a new god was coming into the world. Hawai'ian kings were thought to be divine, you know."

Theresa tried to imagine the high chief or king wearing his tall helmet of yellow feathers and the yellow-feather cape of his supreme office, the women in sarongs with flowers in their long hair, and garlands festooning their bare bosoms, the hula dancers and drummers, the chanting and intricate ceremonies that had to be followed perfectly, step by step. Ritual would have made the birth very special. It would have proven that the gods were in attendance. There would be pageantry and everything must be done just so, as the Sisters did during Mass and when the bells rang in the convent.

When the rain passed, she asked Robert if she might walk on that ground, and he said that she could, as long as she did not deface or remove anything.

Closer up, Theresa saw that the large rocks had surface depressions and fluted edges, most likely from natural weathering with a bit of help from human craftsmen. She could see how a woman would fit into the indentation, where her hands might go, where the newborn would be caught by the waiting kahuna midwife.

"Think of all the lives that began in this place, all the generations of kings . . ."

"Frankly, I've never given it much thought," Robert said, as he looked at the stones as if seeing them for the first time. "All the times I came to Waialua and rode past this place, I never gave it a thought. But you are right, it is fantastical."

Theresa reverently placed her hands on one of the stones and closed her eyes. She could feel the power emanating from it. She whispered, "Spirits of this sacred place, spirits of life, we ask respectfully that you use your beneficent life-giving powers on the people who are suffering from sickness at Waialua."

Farrow Ranch covered hundreds of acres, with fields and corrals, stables and barns. The house was two-story and painted white with a deep verandah all around, with vegetable gardens and flowers and shrubs and trees. As it stood on a hillock, Theresa could see the ocean a mile away. It was gray and rolling with whitecaps.

The wind was up and the day chilly. Ominous dark clouds were gathering as Peter came out to greet them. He walked with his cane and his limp was more pronounced, so that Theresa wondered if the ill-knitted bone was susceptible to weather. He was in his shirtsleeves and suspenders and looked as if he hadn't slept in days.

"The first case was discovered a week ago," he said. "We sent word to Honolulu and Dr. Edgeware himself came out by steamer. We have over a hundred cases now. Edgeware has quarantined them all in one place."

"You and Charlotte, Lucy and the boys?" Robert asked anxiously.

"We are all fine, thank God. But I'm worried about my people."

Peter Farrow had an affinity for the island natives and employed many *kanaka* to work his ranch. He was well-loved in return, such that he was frequently seen at celebrations, and treated by the Hawai'ians as an honored father.

"Come inside," he said, "I don't like the look of that sky."

Peter's wife greeted them with hot tea and a plate of warm scones. She kept a tidy house. Theresa marveled at this, as she was eight months along and had to watch over a three-year-old and two rambunctious fourteen-year-olds as well. Theresa had met Charlotte before on her rare visits to Honolulu. She was a quiet woman with a strong Christian faith and the resilient spirit needed in a wife living on a busy ranch.

"What can we do now that we are here?" Robert asked.

Adding logs to the large brick fireplace, Peter said, "I'm worried about the families across the river. The men who work for me. We haven't heard from them in days."

"Then let's not waste time." Robert stood and turned to Theresa. "Sister?"

"I will lend assistance to Dr. Edgeware. No doubt he has medicines, but I have brought additional." She turned to Charlotte. "Won't you please stay off your feet for a bit? We can make do for ourselves."

"I'll just go bring the boys in for their lunch. You'll find Dr. Edgeware on the beach. It's not far, you can't miss it."

Wondering why Dr. Edgeware was walking on the beach when, according to Peter, there were over a hundred quarantined patients that needed seeing to, Theresa struck off down a path that led from the house to the shore. She looked out at the angry sky over the ocean. A storm was sending a high surf to Waialua. The breakers were strong and crashed like thunder. Whitecaps rose and fell between the frothy waves. She knew there would be rip currents with such an angry, churning tide. Luckily, no natives were riding their boards.

She was halfway through the sand dunes, wrestling with her veils and skirts, when she received a shock.

Dr. Edgeware had set up a pavilion on the beach, consisting of poles stuck in the sand and roofed with palm fronds lashed down with rope. Countless numbers of men, women, and children—all Hawai'ian—were crowded beneath the fragile shelter. They lay on woven mats, or sat on their haunches at the side of a friend or loved one. Babies wailed, children cried, and adults moaned and groaned.

It was an outdoor hospital of the worst sort, having only one doctor and, from what Theresa could see, a handful of women who appeared to be overwhelmed by their duties.

She hurried down and when the wind shifted, she caught the stench of vomit, urine, and feces. Those people should not have been corralled like that, but should have been allowed to be cared for at homes, in their family huts.

Dr. Edgeware was at the far end of the pavilion, seated at a table, writing in a book. In his spotless black frock coat, gray trousers, and black top hat, he looked as if he were sitting in his own parlor.

As Theresa walked among the patients, many of them lying on their backs and groaning, she saw the classic signs of scarlet fever:

swollen neck glands, a rough-textured rash on chests and armpits, red faces with a pale area around the mouth. She knew that if she stopped to examine them, she would find a bright red tongue. The patients would also have aches, nausea, vomiting, and loss of appetite. A nasty enough illness for a white man, but deadly for a Hawai'ian.

She hurried to the far end, glancing out at the breakers crashing on the beach. It was a violent surf that she feared was only going to intensify.

"Dr. Edgeware," she said, and when he lifted his head, a look of disgust immediately came over his face. Not an attractive man to begin with, Dr. Edgeware's constant habit of looking down on others, giving himself airs, lifting his long nose in a superior fashion, made him even less attractive. Nonetheless, he had left his comfortable home in Honolulu to oversee the care of these poor people and Theresa had to give him that (although the less charitable side of her suspected this was more a political gesture than one of compassion).

He dismissed her with a wave of his hand. "We don't need you here. I've plenty of help from good Christian women."

Theresa looked at the white women helping in the hospital. They appeared to be exhausted and about ready to give up, their aprons stained, their backs bent as they tried to see to the needs of too many sick people. "I would say you need my help very much. But first I must tell you, sir, that it is vital you remove these patients to a place inland. If you insist on quarantining them together, then please find a meeting hall or a—"

He shot to his feet, sending his wooden stool over. "I told you to leave! I have a few stout fellows here, good Christians who have come to pray with us, and they will happily take you by the arms and throw you out."

"Dr. Edgeware, Hawai'ians believe the sea can cure them. They won't stay here. They'll run into the surf!"

He snapped his fingers and two natives rose from their haunches. "Get this creature out of here!" Edgeware shouted. "She is an abomination!"

She left the pavilion and hurried back up the dunes, praying that Robert and Peter would have enough authority to have those people rounded up and taken to safe shelter. But when she arrived at the ranch house, Charlotte met her in a most distraught state. "Reese is down with the fever! He is burning up!"

"Where are Robert and Peter?"

"They have ridden to Hale'iwa where several kanaka families live. They are cut off from us by the river. Please take a look at Reese."

"Charlotte, listen. Do not go into his room. And keep Jamie and your daughter away. Do you understand? This is a highly contagious sickness. And Charlotte, please let me know the minute Peter and Robert return. There is something urgent they must see to at the quarantine beach."

The boy did indeed have the sickness. Theresa helped him to gargle a spearmint wash to soothe his throat, and mixed willow bark extract into a glass of water to bring the fever down. Lastly, she applied eucalyptus salve to the rash on his chest. Once she saw that he was comfortable, she went downstairs to see how Charlotte was doing.

She had put the little girl down for an afternoon nap, and so they had a quiet spell, although Theresa's thoughts raced as she frantically sought of ways of persuading Edgeware to move the patients. "We can't lose Reese," Charlotte said, stroking her swollen abdomen. "I've already lost four. I don't know if I could take the grief."

She turned solemn eyes to Theresa. "Did you know that Peter witnessed his own father's death? The newspapers said MacKenzie slipped on some rocks and fell into the sea. That part is true. But what they left out was that he fell while trying to stop Emily from throwing herself into the waves below."

She looked around and, although they were alone in the kitchen, lowered her voice and said, "You know that Mrs. Farrow is mentally unbalanced. I don't know the details, just that she sustained a shock some thirty-odd years back and it deranged her. During one of her bad spells she ran outside in her nightgown. MacKenzie went after her. Peter was twenty-four years old at the time and still living at home. He told me he awoke in the night to hear shouts. He followed his father to the cliff, where he saw his mother teetering on the edge. MacKenzie reached for her and but she eluded him. Peter saw his father plunge to his death."

Charlotte absently stirred her tea. "That was when Robert came back and Peter said he was leaving the family business. Ships and the sea were never in his blood. He wanted to start his own ranch. So Robert stayed home to run the shipping business. He met Leilani and they got married. Well, you know the rest, the chicken pox, Jamie. But the two brothers . . ." Charlotte shook her head, "they never were close, and now they are enemies. It is so sad really."

They heard Reese's voice in the room above, calling for his mother. "I'll go," Theresa said.

She helped him gargle his burning throat again and gave him another dose of willow bark extract for the fever. But his skin was too hot. She drew back his blanket and told him not to cover himself, as he must cool his body.

She sat with him until he fell asleep, and then went to check on Jamie, who was sitting beside an oil lamp reading a book. He insisted he felt okay. Theresa checked his tongue and his temperature anyway, but when she heard the door to the rear verandah open and close, followed by the stomping of boots, she hurried back downstairs. Night had fallen, Charlotte was lighting lamps, and Robert came in looking weary. "Peter's putting the horses away," he said. "How are the boys?"

"Captain Farrow, it is urgent you go down to the beach and talk to Dr. Edgeware."

"Why?"

"That is where he has set up the quarantine pavilion."

"What!" He seized a lantern and, saying to Charlotte, "Send Peter to the beach as soon as he comes inside," ran out the back door.

Theresa followed with a second lantern, but they didn't need lights to know they had come too late. As the moon sailed in and out of passing clouds, casting ghostly light onto the shore, they saw the people swarming the beach and plunging into the surf, while Dr. Edgeware shouted for them to stop.

Men and women, carrying children and babies, crying out in fear and delirium, calling the names of ancient gods, falling to their knees, tripping, disappearing under the water. Waves crested over them and carried them away. Theresa was frozen with horror at the sight of it.

Robert dropped his lantern and, throwing off his coat and pulling off his boots, dashed into the surf. Edgeware followed, throwing down his top hat and coat, splashing into the frothy water, shouting at the people to come back. Theresa saw Peter plunge in and swim out. And suddenly she, too, was pulling off her veils and wimple and outer habit so that she stood in only her white under-shift and coif.

The tide was treacherous. Lifeless babies bobbed on the water. A boy, floating face down, bumped against her like a little boat cut from its mooring. She saw Robert dive under a wave but come up empty-handed. Peter was pulled down several times. Dr. Edgeware screamed something at her but she couldn't understand what he was saying. She saw a Hawai'ian stumble out of the water with his arm around a gasping woman, but before they made it to solid sand, water rushed in and pulled her down. She cried out, rolled over and over, until the tide took her out and she disappeared.

And then the tow had Theresa. It pulled her under. She was swirling, swirling. She couldn't breathe. She knew these were her last moments, and then a pair of strong arms clamped around her waist and she felt herself rising, rising. They broke the surface and she couldn't breathe. Her lungs wouldn't work. Her throat was choked.

"Not again!" Robert cried. "I will not let it happen a second time!"

He covered her mouth with his and blew breath into her lungs. She felt the air expand her throat. She gasped and coughed as they rode the choppy sea in a frightening embrace. "Stay calm!" he shouted. "Don't fight the tide!"

She held on to him as he propelled them toward shore, his arm around her as his legs kicked with great force. She was on her back, looking up at the stars. She searched for the moon and there it was. She wondered if she would see a rainbow there.

The waves washed over them. They coughed and sputtered but Robert kept swimming until his feet hit bottom and Theresa's heels touched sand. Robert crawled onto the beach, dragging her with him, until they collapsed, arms entwined about each other, breathless, sobbing with frustration. Robert lifted up and dashed water and sand from her face, he wiped her forehead and cheeks and tugged at her tight-fitting coif, but it would not come off. He said, "Stay here. I have to go back."

She was too weak to go with him so she stayed on the beach, shivering in her wet, clinging under-shift as she watched him and Dr. Edgeware and the few able-bodied swim out and bring people back. She understood the meaning of his words when he had cried,

"Not again." This was how Leilani had died during the chicken pox epidemic. Rescuing people from the sea.

Theresa sat on the beach in her wet clothes and wet coif, watching the horror unfold, seeing bodies wash up on the beach, seeing survivors search for loved ones and fall down weeping, hearing the screams and pleas for help as the current swept them out. She saw Robert carry lifeless babies and children out of the water. When she saw moonlight on the water, she looked up. Although there were squalls out at sea and heavily misted clouds hanging low, she saw no rainbows on the moon.

By midnight there were no more people to find, and some of those lying on the beach turned out to be dead. She wrapped a blanket around herself and, carrying a lantern, followed Robert as he walked along the line of bodies, counting them.

By the time it was all over, dawn was breaking and, having heard the news, people had come from nearby farms and houses and stood in silence as Dr. Edgeware reported the loss of forty-eight lives to the sea. He then announced that the new quarantine shelter was to be the Congregationalist meetinghouse and asked all who could to please bring bedclothes, food, and water.

He trudged back to the pavilion to pick up his pens and books and medical bag, restored his coat over his damp shirt and trousers, and replaced his top hat, and as he left, leading a tragic procession of people barely able to walk, he glanced back over his shoulder, and his look told Theresa that now, more than ever, she had an enemy in him.

Theresa and Robert and Peter wearily returned to the ranch house, where they gave Charlotte the terrible news. She wept into her apron while Theresa stood by the fire to get dry. After a few bracing cups of coffee and slices of bread, Robert and Peter struck out into the hostile night to see how they could help at the meetinghouse.

Charlotte made a bed for Theresa in the parlor, and then she herself went to sleep with her three-year-old daughter. But only the child slept.

The next morning, Reese continued to burn with fever. Theresa gave him the gargle and the willow bark, and joined the others downstairs. They made a solemn foursome around the kitchen table, barely touching the bread and cheese and toast with marmalade that Charlotte had prepared.

"Our greatest concern," Sister Theresa said, "is Jamie. He is half-

Hawai'ian and his constitution is not strong to begin with. I know the boys are close. We are going to have to make sure he doesn't go into the sickroom."

"We'll take turns sitting with Reese," Charlotte said. "It shouldn't be all on Sister Theresa."

"The main problem is keeping his temperature down," Theresa said. "It is fever that ultimately kills in the case of scarlet fever. We shall need to frequently bathe his body in alcohol and cold water, and fan him to bring his temperature down."

"That will be my job," Peter said grimly. His eyes were bloodshot and his jaw unshaven. "He's my boy—" His voice broke. "I brought him into the world. It's up to me to see he stays in it."

As Theresa rose from the table to go upstairs, Jamie came into the kitchen. His hair stood out. He looked as if he hadn't slept. "Sister Theresa," he said. "Please don't let Reese die."

"I'll do my best, dear," she said, laying a consoling hand on his shoulder.

While Theresa mixed the willow bark and the eucalyptus gargle, and made a stronger salve for the growing rash, Peter stayed at his son's bedside. Robert rode to a saloon down at the docks and purchased alcohol, as his brother had none in the house. On his way back, he stopped at the meetinghouse. It was a horrific scene. Friends and loved ones of the patients inside were camped on the grounds, wailing and calling on the gods, some gashed their faces and pulled their hair out. An overwhelmed Edgeware did what he could for the sick and dying, but it was clearly a losing battle.

It filled Robert with fear. What if Jamie came down with it?

When he returned to the house, Peter and Theresa were at Reese's bedside. The boy had slipped into a sleep from which he would not wake. His face was bright red and his breathing was labored. Charlotte was in the hallway, wringing her hands, while Jamie was relegated to the parlor downstairs, as far from the contagion as possible.

Robert handed the bottle of alcohol to Theresa, who proceeded at once to sponge it on Reese's feverish skin.

"Son," Peter called. He sat on the bed and held Reese's hands. "Son, don't leave me. Come on, boy, Annabel will be foaling soon and I'll need your help."

Theresa lifted Reese's eyelids to check his pupils. She opened her bag and brought out her stethoscope. She listened, while Robert and Peter watched in fearful silence.

"What?" Peter said when he saw the look on her face. "What is it?"

"His heart is weak."

"Reese!" he cried. Taking his comatose son by his shoulders, Peter gave him a gentle shake. "Reese! You can fight this!"

The boy's breathing grew shallow and rapid. Perspiration streamed off his face. His jaw went slack. He began to pant.

"Oh God," Robert whispered.

"Mr. Farrow—" Theresa began.

And then a strange rattle came from Reese's throat. He gasped. And his chest went still.

"Reese?" Peter said. "Son?"

"Mr. Farrow, I'm sorry."

"No!" He gathered his son into his arms and stroked Reese's head, caressed his face, shook him gently. "Wake up, son. You can do it. How will I live without you?"

Tears rolled down Robert's cheeks and his throat tightened, while Sister Theresa crossed herself and commenced a whispered prayer.

When Robert stepped to the bed, reaching out for his brother, Peter drew back, clutching his son's body. He leveled a bitter gaze at Robert and said through clenched teeth, "Your son lives while my son died. It is Leilani all over again. I will hate you forever for this."

It was time to go.

Robert had hitched the horse to the wagon and placed his and Theresa's bags in the back. She had left the house earlier, having said good-bye to Charlotte and Peter. Telling Jamie, who was already in the wagon, that he would be right back, Robert followed the narrow track through the dunes down to the beach.

He knew he would find her there.

The beach was deserted beneath the gray sky. The kanaka had spent days here, wailing and mourning, but now they had returned to their homes to mend their lives. All traces of the makeshift hospital were gone. Per Edgeware's orders, all bedding and personal items, even the wooden poles, had been burned to stop the spread of the contagion. The tide had then come in and washed away the ash.

She stood alone, a black-clad figure looking out to sea. Although the bay was embraced within the curve of lush, green cliffs, and breathtaking waves crashed in foamy majesty close to shore, he knew she wasn't admiring the view.

Robert couldn't get that terrible night out of his mind, how Anna had ripped off her habit and flung aside the confining fabrics that unsexed her and kept her in an unnatural prison. He had seen the true woman that she was then, courageous and selfless. There lay her liberation, he knew. Anna needed to find a way to throw off the robes once and for all and find her true place in the world.

But how could he tell her this when he himself was trapped, when he himself had no solution to his own dilemmas? Burdened with a mentally unstable mother and the fear of his son going the same way, what right had he to tell Anna how to conduct her life?

He came to her side. Her face was shockingly pale. "We're ready to go," he said softly.

Theresa couldn't speak. Their faces haunted her. Their cries filled her ears. She couldn't stop thinking about the ones they didn't save, who got swept out to sea in fever and delirium. She tried to recite an Our Father and Hail Mary, but they were empty words with no meaning.

"It was terrible, Robert. No matter what we did—" She choked back the tears. "We haven't the medicine. We haven't the skills. How can my Sisters and I be good nurses if we are so ignorant of sickness and the human condition?"

"It wasn't your fault, Anna."

"We have stethoscopes and scalpels and sutures and bandages and ointments and tonics, and nothing we did could save those poor souls!" Even the things Mahina was teaching her—the curative qualities of the kauna'oa plant, how to extract cleansing *noni* juice, the best time to harvest *kukui* nuts—could not have helped.

She turned to face him. She saw fatigue and exhaustion etched on his handsome face. She could only guess at the enormity of the grief that weighed upon his heart. Jamie losing his best friend, losing his holidays here on the ranch. The rift between Robert and Peter now so wide that it seemed impossible to mend. And what had Peter meant by "It's Leilani all over again?" Why had he been unable to speak her name the day Theresa had overheard their argument in the garden? She wondered if Robert's late wife lay somehow at the heart of the brothers' estrangement.

She wanted to console him. Place her hand gently on his face. Comfort him with her touch. But these things were forbidden to her. He wasn't a patient, whom she was perforce allowed to touch. He was a man—and a man she yearned to be with.

You were right, Cosette, it is very difficult to remember one's vows in such a paradise.

And Theresa knew that, from now on, holding to those vows was only going to get harder.

CHAPTER TWENTY

The terrible tragedy at Waialua a year ago, her utter helplessness to save those people, haunted her still. And she felt that same helplessness now as she sat at Jamie Farrow's bedside, defeated by an ailment she could not name.

Nor could anyone else. Each time a new medical man arrived in Honolulu, Captain Farrow sent for him. The man would conduct the same examination countless others had performed before him, with the same pronouncement at the end: "I have no idea what is ailing your son."

This particular morning, Jamie was not well. Mrs. Carter had sent for Theresa, who asked her to send for Captain Robert. He was at his shipping office by the docks. Jamie was incapacitated by severe stomach pains. Theresa dispensed a special tincture the Sisters manufactured for colicky babies, hoping the mixture of chamomile, licorice, and mint would soothe his spasms.

She stroked his hair as he lay on his side, knees up to his chest. Jamie was undersized for a youth of fifteen. His muscles had not filled out, and although his voice broke occasionally, he had yet to show signs of an early beard. Not a strong boy to begin with, Jamie's recent decline had begun with Reese's death. Captain Farrow believed he was pining for his cousin, and it was possible that that was the source of his new malaise. Just as everyone said Jamie's health had declined after his mother died.

Reese's death had caused an even greater rift in the family. The brothers hadn't spoken to one another in the year since the scarlet fever tragedy. Whatever had festered between the two to cause the rift in the first place had now received its final straw.

"How is he?"

Theresa turned to see Captain Farrow in the doorway. Robert had aged in the year since Reese's death. New lines framed his mouth, sorrow seemed never to leave his eyes. While he still fought for his principles and visions for Hawai'i's future, Theresa sensed that some of the life had gone out of him.

They left Jamie to sleep and went downstairs. "Anna," he said, and it still sounded strange to her ears to hear her former name. It pleased her to hear Robert say it, but it dismayed her at the same time, as it made her inner conflict all the more turbulent. They had never spoken the word "love," but Theresa knew it was there, knew that Robert shared her feelings. But it was an ill-fated involvement as it could go nowhere and must only end in tragedy. And so they played the roles they were assigned and lived a life of pretense.

"Anna," he said, "I have been invited to the royal ball in three days' time. It is a celebration of the king's birthday and promises to be the event of the year. I am allowed to bring a guest. Have you ever been inside the Royal Palace?"

She could not believe her ears. "No, I have not."

"Then would you do me the honor of accompanying me? Believe me, in my state of mind, I would rather not go, but it wouldn't be politically wise to stay away. I think I might be able to stomach the occasion if you were with me."

"I would have to ask permission." She knew Father Halloran would approve but she feared Mother Agnes would not. Nonetheless, her heart raced with excitement. It would be pleasant to attend a ball again. She hadn't been to one since before she entered the Order, nine years prior. Of course, she would not be able to dance but she would love to watch, and listen to the music.

In the company of handsome Captain Robert Farrow.

Mrs. Carter came into the study to announce the arrival of Miss

Alexandra Huntington. "Please ask her to come in," Robert said, and Theresa noticed how he raked his fingers through his hair and straightened his tie.

Miss Huntington had come to Hawai'i six months prior with her father, a wealthy lawyer from Maryland who had just been appointed to a judgeship by King Kamehameha the Fifth. She was around Theresa's age, twenty-four, and the fact that Captain Farrow was forty-one did not seem to deter her pursuit of him.

"Robert, darling!" Miss Huntington did not so much walk as glide, moving with the grace and aplomb of her station in life. She had extraordinarily beautiful hair, a blond that was so light it was called "platinum," and caused people to stare admiringly.

Miss Huntington's father had invested in Farrow Shipping and owned a coffee plantation as well. So Miss Huntington was wealthy. Theresa tried not to let jealousy and envy fill her heart, but it pained her to see Robert with Miss Huntington, to see her so freely laugh with him and, every now and then, touch him with a gloved hand.

While Captain Farrow and Miss Huntington chatted about the weather and mutual friends, and Theresa gave Mrs. Carter a bottle of the tonic, explaining how and when she was to administer it to Jamie, Emily Farrow came in, gracious and polite. Theresa noticed that Mrs. Farrow was enjoying one of her good days, in which she exhibited vigor and presence of mind. The ring of keys hanging from her belt indicated that she was mistress of the house today, not the invalid she otherwise was.

"Hello, my dear," she said warmly to Alexandra Huntington, who in turn addressed her as "Mother Farrow."

"Theresa, dear," Emily said, "might I impose upon you for a moment? I need help with something."

"Mother," Robert said, "are you sure you should be exerting yourself?"

"Please do not fuss over me, son. I have been exerting myself since before you were born. Don't forget that I came to these islands with no map and no help, just a lot of Yankee know-how. I would like to see young people accomplish today what Isaac and I managed to do forty-five years ago. Come along, Theresa. We need to go upstairs."

Mrs. Farrow's bedroom suite included a separate sitting room, nicely furnished in Chippendale pieces that had been in the family for years, and brought over in the 1820s. A green braided rug covered the floor. It was the living space of a dignified New England widow, with not a hint of Hawai'i or the tropics.

Although there was a collection of curios combed from beaches, which Emily somehow believed had been sent to her by her family, and among the oddities were a pink conch shell and a white sand dollar.

Theresa had been visiting Mrs. Farrow on a regular basis. Physically, she was frail, and sometimes needed to catch her breath. But otherwise, Emily did not need much nursing care. The spells of mental instability were under control, manifesting these days in nightmares only, without the nocturnal ambulations and frights. Even so, sometimes an attentive ear was the best medicine. Emily Farrow loved to talk to Theresa about the past, about her life in New Haven before marrying Isaac and sailing to the Sandwich Islands, as she still called them. She talked of her early days in the Hilo area, teaching the native women to sew, how she had explained to them that it was a sin to go about half naked.

Most of all, she loved reminiscing about the times when Captain MacKenzie Farrow was in port, either on his way to China or Alaska, to fill her lonely hours while her preacher husband was touring the island. "I learned so much from Captain MacKenzie," she said now as she led Theresa to a large sea chest that must have been brought from the attic. As she unlocked it, Emily said, "He took me to see a river of lava. Have you ever seen that, my dear? The molten rock runs right by you and cascades into the sea, literally boiling it, and sending up towering plumes of steam. It is a most horrific, and yet beautiful, sight.

"MacKenzie told me about the native customs. Do you know why Hawai'ians don't kiss on the lips, why they rub noses instead? They say it is taboo to steal someone's breath, or to let them steal yours. And they call the sex act 'making rainbows,' which I think is so lovely. Here we are," she said when the trunk lid was lifted.

Theresa saw that the chest was filled with packing straw. As Emily dug in and brought out a tarnished teapot, she said, "These were made by Paul Revere himself, commissioned by my father as a gift for my mother. They look like works of art, don't they?"

She tenderly handled each piece, picking off the straw, wiping it with a cloth: the teapot, on its stand, for holding hot water; the tea caddy, a lockable box, to contain loose tea; a matching cream pitcher and sugar bowl; tongs for picking up the sugar lumps; a small shell-shaped scoop used for measuring the tea; teaspoons and tablespoons and a punch strainer.

"They're beautiful," Theresa said, imagining the shiny silver under the tarnish.

"And worth a lot, too. Mr. Revere used coin silver for his works of art, melting coins and fashioning the liquid metal into functional items. In case of need, the owner could then sell the set for the value of the coins. My mother gave me this set when I married Mr. Isaac Stone." She paused, and a little frown knotted a delicate brow. "He died. . . ." She blinked and looked at the silver plates in her hand, as if wondering where they had come from. "MacKenzie died, too, on a voyage to Santiago. A storm at sea, I think. . . ."

She shook her head. "These were my best pieces, which I reserved for special days and for when MacKenzie and I had guests. I put these away after he was gone because it was too painful for me to see them. But now they can be put to good use."

"You are expecting special guests?"

Emily set each piece on a round table by the window. "Why no, dear, they are to be my wedding gift to Robert and Miss Huntington. I shall need to inspect each piece, but I was always careful with them."

Theresa reached for the back of a chair to steady herself. "Wedding?" she heard herself say. "I hadn't known. . . ."

Emily flashed her a conspiratorial smile. "They haven't set the date yet. But it will be soon. There should be a set of chinaware at the bottom," she said as she pulled out hanks of straw. "Imported from England. I want Robert and Miss Huntington to be able to host their guests in proper style."

Theresa suddenly needed air. She went to the French doors and when she opened them she saw, on the lawn below, Robert escorting Miss Huntington to her carriage. Before handing herself up to the footman, she kissed Robert on the cheek. Then she said something that made him throw back his head and laugh.

He watched her ride off and then he turned, paused, and looked up. Theresa knew he saw her in the doorway because he continued to stand there for another long moment before she turned away.

It was not for Theresa to have feelings of the heart. But under her robes beat the heart of a woman who yearned for a man she could never have. She was soon to celebrate her fifth anniversary in the islands—five years marking the day a tall, handsome stranger had come to her aid on the docks. It was a bittersweet celebration. She was doing the work she was born to do—she was happy in her daily labors, and she found great joy and satisfaction in helping others. But each time she came to Farrow House was another stab in her heart.

And now Miss Alexandra Huntington had arrived to pour salt into her wounds.

Although 'Iolani Palace was not far from the convent, Robert picked Sister Theresa up in a carriage. They were to arrive there "in style," as he put it. He was handsomely attired in a black evening tailcoat over black trousers, a starched white shirt with a white cravat. On his head, a black top hat. He remarked that, for once, he and she matched. Theresa tried to smile, but her heart was heavy.

As they joined the evening traffic on King Street, where noisy wagons and carriages and people on horseback competed for space, Robert looked at Theresa and said, "You seem very quiet, Anna. Is everything all right?"

"I am fine," she said. Theresa had had three days to adjust to the fact that Robert was marrying Miss Huntington. She knew that it was only a matter of time before she came to think of it as inevitable and perfectly normal, and she hoped that someday she could be happy for him.

They joined the parade of carriages pulling up to the palace, and when they reached the brightly lit entrance, young ladies in white muumuus draped floral leis over their heads. Inside, the orchestra was playing a Viennese waltz, and couples were sailing around the highly polished floor like lily pads on a lagoon.

Robert escorted Theresa to a small table and asked her what she would like to drink. Any nonalcoholic fruit punch would do, she said, although she did not care what she ate or drank. For this one evening in her life, she was with the man she loved. It would never happen again.

She was swept away by the glamour of the ball, the beautiful women and handsome gentlemen. She saw Robert Farrow get waylaid by three men, dressed in evening tailcoats and starched white shirts, who took his arm and engaged him in earnest conversation. He sent Theresa a look of helplessness and she smiled and waved. The fruit punch could wait.

She received a few strange looks, a few unfriendly ones as well, but on the whole the crowd seemed intent upon enjoying the evening and ignored the presence of a Catholic nun. Although there was one man who did not disguise his frank disapproval of her attendance at the ball. Dr. Simon Edgeware, who sat across the ballroom at a table with the Minister of Finance, the Minister's wife, and two prominent Congregationalists who held sway, Theresa knew, over the legislature.

Ignoring Edgeware's dyspeptic look, she turned her attention to the entryway and saw Miss Alexandra Huntington make a stunning entrance on her father's arm. Heads turned when the pale blond hair piled high on her head caught the lights of the chandeliers.

The talk in the crowd was mostly about the war back in the States. For Theresa, news from her brother, Eli, was sketchy. In February his regiment had seen action at Hatcher's Run, and in April had taken part in the assault on Petersburg. The last they'd heard was that the 20th Massachusetts had joined in the pursuit toward Appomattox.

When the king made his grand appearance, the orchestra immediately struck up the Hawai'ian National Anthem, which was set to the melody of "God Save the Queen."

Kamehameha the Fifth was thirty-three years of age but looked fifty. He had a heavy, massive face with dark, Polynesian coloring. Thick black hair, moderate moustache and large, imperial stature, inclining toward corpulence. He was not married, and it was said that if he died without leaving an heir or naming a successor, the crown would likely fall upon either his Highness Prince Lunalilo or David Kalakaua, the king's chamberlain. Both had distinguished pedigrees. Lunalilo was of the highest blood in the kingdom—higher than the king himself it was said—and Kalakaua was descended from the ancient kings of the island of Hawai'i.

Both could trace their ancestry back to the legendary King Umi—a claim that Mahina could also make, since her mother, Pua, had been eleventh in descent from Umi—a prestige no one else could claim.

The gathered guests stopped dancing or rose from their chairs as the monarch marched in stately fashion to a special throne on a dais. He was dressed in a handsomely tailored black evening tailcoat with a silk sash lying diagonally across his broad chest, along with a few other ribbons and impressive medals. He was accompanied by Queen Emma, his sister-in-law, with her attendants about her, simply but elegantly dressed in mourning black. As the royal pair passed, gentlemen bowed and ladies curtseyed, and someone nearby, whom Theresa could not identify, remarked to his neighbor, "Never thought I'd see the day when white people bow and scrape to coloreds!"

When they were seated, the festivities resumed, and people took up dancing again, or engaging in pleasant conversation, flirting, arguing politics. Robert finally joined Theresa with a much-welcomed glass of refreshing mango punch. "There's rather good-looking caviar on the buffet," he said.

She promised him she would look over the dinner offerings in a while. For now, she was breathless with the sweep and dash of the scene, the intoxicating atmosphere. The Barnetts used to hold such parties at their mansion in San Francisco, and Theresa felt the bittersweet pain of nostalgia in recalling those days. How she loved wearing gowns and being guided about a dance floor by a young man! But she was not that girl anymore. Nor was she really part of this gala event. It was as if she stood at a window, looking in.

Theresa rose from her chair, saying something about the buffet, and Robert rose with her, when a low rumble started to roll through the crowd. It began at the double doors that stood open to the entry beyond, and rippled through the ballroom as people fell silent or stopped dancing until finally the orchestra ceased playing and everyone was looking at the ballroom's entrance. Theresa and Robert widened their eyes at an astonishing sight.

Mahina stood there, statuesque and mute, staring down the length of the room to the man on the throne. She wore only a colorful sarong around her wide, fleshy hips, and nothing else. But her enormous breasts were covered by layers of leis, all the colors of the rainbow. On her head, a crown of flowers. Her wrists and ankles decorated with floral cuffs. Her feet were bare. Her long hair, now white, fell like a foaming waterfall past her waist. After a moment, when not a sound was heard among the gathered company, she started to walk forward, keeping her gaze ahead, her face set in a solemn expression.

Now the guests could see the man who walked behind her—a stately Chief Kekoa in the robes of his high office, a crown of spiky *ti*-leaves on his white head. He carried the tall staff of his rank, a *kahili* topped with feathers, emblem of his power. Behind him came four priests carrying bundles of sacred *ti*-leaves.

No one said a word as the dignified procession advanced slowly toward the royal dais. The king's expression was unreadable, but Theresa saw many shocked looks, especially on the faces of white women. The tension was palpable in the air as everyone wondered why Mahina had come here in this manner, what she planned to do.

When she reached the throne, she raised her arms and cried out in a shrill voice—words in Hawai'ian that few in the ballroom could understand. Kekoa joined in the chant, while the priests shook their *ti*-leaf bundles in all directions. Mahina moved her arms, she shouted, she cupped her mouth with her hands and called out words while the monarch remained impassive. Her voice echoed off the ceiling for a few more minutes and then she fell silent and the room was held in hushed suspense.

"What is she doing?" Theresa whispered.

Robert smiled. "She is blessing the king, for his birthday."

And at that moment, everyone in the frozen crowd saw King Kamehameha smile, as did Queen Emma, and the relief was palpable in the atmosphere. People released held breath, they relaxed their shoulders, they turned to their companions and murmured. And then everyone watched as Kekoa and the priests stepped aside to allow the great ali'i Mahina to pass, then fell into step behind her.

As they slowly proceeded to the entry doors, Mahina looked straight ahead, acknowledging none of the 300 or so guests, except for two: she stopped when she came to Robert and Theresa and made a great show of embracing each, pressing her nose to theirs and saying, "Aloha," in her significant, meaningful way. Then the curious procession left and Theresa saw that absolutely everyone in the ballroom, including the king and queen, were staring at her.

The music started up again, people remembered themselves, and the festivities resumed. "That was wily of the old girl," Robert said.

"What do you mean?"

"Did you notice how Mahina just upstaged Kamehameha himself? I always knew she had a flair for theater. She doesn't care a wooden nickel for the king's birthday. She just chose this event to remind everyone, haole and kanaka alike, and especially the king and his haole ministers, that this is still Hawai'i and that the old ways can't so easily be dismissed. She would make a good politician, I'd wager."

"I think I shall take a look at the buffet now," Theresa said, adding, "I think perhaps you hadn't noticed the arrival of Miss Huntington with her father."

"I saw them come in."

"I should think you would rather be with them than with a religious Sister," she quipped, trying to make light of a matter that weighed heavily on her heart.

"Why would I rather be with them?"

"Your mother gave me the news of your impending marriage to Miss Huntington."

Robert stared at Theresa in surprise. "Mother said that, did she? It's one of her fantasies. She *wishes* I would marry Miss Huntington, but the fact is I have no interest in the woman."

Theresa's heart gave a leap. "But she's very beautiful."

"Yes, I suppose she would be, after spending two hours in front of a mirror. Alexandra's looks are all Alexandra cares about, and if a man is lapse in giving her a compliment, say, letting five minutes go by without reminding her that she is the most beautiful woman in the room, she grows petulant. No man can keep up with her demands. Although, as you can see, there are plenty of applicants for the post."

And then Robert gave Theresa one of his long, intense looks and said, "Besides, Miss Huntington will never become like us, Anna. She'll never be Hawai'ian."

"I am hardly Hawai'ian."

He smiled and lowered his voice so that the ballroom and everyone in it vanished and they were the only people on earth. "You are more Hawai'ian than you know. Chief Kekoa said that you are *kama 'aina*, Anna. You are a child of this land."

She suddenly felt too warm and needed some air. Muttering something about getting a bite, she hurried away from Robert and when she reached the endless buffet tables spread with more food than she had seen in her life, she sidestepped the line and slipped into the glass and marble entryway that glittered and shone beneath a brilliant chandelier.

He isn't getting married!

She put her hand to her forehead, and felt the starched linen of her wimple.

"Are you all right, my dear?"

Theresa turned to see a redheaded lady in a beautiful lavender gown smiling at her. She wore long white evening gloves and had egret feathers pinned in her hair.

"I just . . . needed to get out of the crowd."

"I know what you mean," the woman said with a laugh. "Sometimes these affairs can be overwhelming." She opened her evening bag. "Can you use some smelling salts?"

"No . . . thank you. I'm all right."

"I always carry some with me, just in case." She extended her hand. "Eva Yates," she said, and Theresa politely shook her hand. "And you are Sister . . . ?"

"Theresa. Of the Sisters of Good Hope."

"Yes, I know. I'm familiar with your wonderful work. I've only been in Honolulu a couple of weeks, but I have certainly heard of your splendid Sisterhood. I was hoping we could meet. You see, I am also a nurse and will clearly be needing some assistance getting my footing in these islands. I understand your group has been here for five years?"

Theresa stared at her. "You're a nurse?"

"I suppose I come as a bit of a surprise to you," Eva Yates said. "Hawai'i is isolated and news takes a while to reach you here. I was in the first class that graduated from the new Nightingale School in London. I take it you haven't heard of the Nightingale School?"

Theresa mutely shook her head, too stunned to speak.

"You certainly heard of the Crimean War?"

"Yes, I think so." The Crimean War had occurred ten years ago, when Theresa was fourteen and hardly interested in world news, let alone military campaigns.

The woman's voice sounded as if it came from far away as she spoke of an Englishwoman named Florence Nightingale who, having heard of the horrific conditions of wounded British soldiers in a place called Scutari in the Ottoman Empire, had called for volunteer ladies whom she trained as nurses. Miss Nightingale had sailed to Scutari with thirty-eight nurses as well as fifteen Catholic nuns. Once there, they found deplorable hospital conditions and an overwhelmed medical staff.

The story was nothing less than heroic, and while Mrs. Yates happily filled Theresa in on the details of that epic, the only point that reached Theresa's rational mind was that nursing was suddenly an honorable profession, open to any respectable lady with a good background, upstanding morals, and dedication.

"I would eventually love to find a position at Queen Emma's Hospital," Mrs. Yates said, "but with two small children, I must stay at home. That's where my husband's surgery is, so I assist him with patients there, and I accompany him on house calls."

"Your husband," Theresa heard herself say. And two small children.

"Yes, he's inside, introducing himself around. He's a doctor and we've come to Hawai'i to make our home here."

Theresa stood as mute as a statue, feeling as if she had been struck by lightning. As Mrs. Yates's words sank in, the breath was knocked out of her. *She has a husband, children, she wears gowns and drinks champagne, and yet she nurses the sick. . . .*

Theresa thought of the steep price she had paid for the privilege of being a nurse—the chance to be a wife and mother, the chance to know a man's love. Just as Emily Farrow had paid a steep a price—giving up the company of her own kind in order to minister to heathens. The loneliness she had received in return, which perhaps had mentally unbalanced her. Have I done the same thing? Theresa now wondered. If I had waited even a year or two, I would have heard of the Nightingale nurses! But I was eager and in a hurry. So I threw away precious joys and now I am committed to vows I should never have spoken.

Now I can never know Robert's love. I can never be his wife, or the mother of his children!

What have I done? Dear God, what have I done?

CHAPTER TWENTY-ONE

T he superintendent of Queen's Hospital is here to see you, sir."
"Thank you, Milford. Send him in, please."

Simon Edgeware was in his office in the Capitol building where the legislature met, across the street from 'Iolani Palace. It was a spacious, nicely appointed chamber with portraits on the walls—of King Kamehameha the Fifth, and Queen Victoria—both portraits rendered in the latest photographic process. While he waited for his clerk to bring the visitor in, Edgeware looked out the window at the street below.

He was a man of power now. Soon, with his investments in the burgeoning sugar industry, he would be a man of wealth as well. Not bad for the bastard son of an impoverished seamstress who had blamed her ills on an unwanted child. Overbearing and given to drink, Miss Molly Edgeware would berate her son and tell him he was worthless, that he had ruined her life. When he tried to point out that it was his *father* who had ruined her life, the back of her hand would send him across the room.

Edgeware had accomplished a lot during his six years in the islands, cleaning up the towns, improving sanitation, overseeing the isolation of outbreaks of disease, and quarantining ships that had sickness on board. Next on his agenda, to convince the king to banish the meddling Catholic nuns from the kingdom. Not the priests, not Catholicism—that was never going to happen. But Edgeware wasn't afraid of the priests. The Sisters, however, were another story. They went into people's homes and took care of women who were sick and vulnerable and impressionable. The Catholic nurses dispensed popery along with their medicines, he was convinced, offering rosaries with their panaceas. They brought more than teas and tonics into sickrooms, they brought propaganda.

Which made them dangerous.

Edgeware was working on a plan to convince Kamehameha that, while Catholicism was a necessary evil to be tolerated in the islands, those women should be banished.

He particularly despised Sister Theresa. She had humiliated him in Waialea. She had shouted at him in front of others that he had made a mistake by moving the scarlet fever victims to the beach. And then she had been proven right when the sufferers delivered themselves into the raging surf. He would never forgive her for that.

There were deeper currents that drove Simon Edgeware in his hatred of the Sisters of Good Hope, and Sister Theresa in particular, but these ugly currents were unknown even to Simon himself. Sometimes, at night in his dreams, they came dangerously close to the surface, when his brain tormented his mind with images of Theresa in her black habit and he would wake up sexually aroused. But a pitcher of cold water would dispel any memories he might have had of those taunting dreams.

He was only vaguely aware, at times, of his discomfort around women of power. Those would include women who possessed tangible power, like Mahina, who was a legend in these islands. But there were other kinds of power. Edgeware didn't like being around pregnant women. They represented woman-power at its most extreme and, in a way he could not define, they frightened him. It was the whole sexual mystery part of women that gave him bad feelings. It was almost as if, should the women ever decide to unite and rise up, they could easily take over the world and men would be helpless to stop it.

But Sister Theresa and her unnatural companions, those he had the power to stop. And it was going to be all legal and legitimate, with no loopholes for them to slither through. Sooner or later, they were going to break a law or commit a crime, and Simon Edgeware was going to be on hand with his soldiers to have them taken before a court of law, where there would be no recourse for them or their Church.

He sighed and turned away from the window. He understood why the Good Lord had needed to create women, but couldn't the Most High have given them a more subservient nature?

The salve Theresa had applied to Mahina's urticaria on the day five years ago when they'd first met had become very much in demand in her family village, as the Hawai'ians suffered from a variety of skin afflictions. The balm that Theresa and her Sisters manufactured from herbs grown in their garden had gone a long way to easing some of the rashes.

Theresa was sitting in front of Tutu Nalani's hut, changing a bandage on a patch of dermatitis on the woman's left forearm. Nalani, whose name meant "quiet skies," was a white-haired elder, distantly related to Mahina and Chief Kekoa. The two women sat in the midst of village industry, where children and dogs and chickens ran freely, women sat in front of huts stringing leis or sewing muumuus, talking and laughing, while men worked at various labors among the many huts and pavilions.

Theresa smiled as she worked, but her heart was filled with pain. In the week since meeting Nurse Yates at the royal ball, she had walked with a cloud over her head. The mistake she had made! The impetuousness of her act! "Leave the order," Robert had said two years ago, and Theresa had replied, "Where would I go? What would I do?"

But now she had options! She could work as a respectable nurse, perhaps at Queen's Hospital, or with private patients of her own.

I could marry Robert . . .

But Theresa knew she could never leave. She owed a huge debt to the Sisterhood. They had taken her in and given her a valuable education. And now they needed her. While the white population of Honolulu mushroomed, the small Sisterhood had not. There were still just the six of them, and they were overwhelmed with demand.

As she applied a fresh bandage to old Nalani's arm, she recited a Hawai'ian prayer Mahina had taught her. Theresa had discovered that the kanaka took better care of their injuries if they believed they were protected by a sacred spell.

She used to question the efficacy of chants while making herbal medicines until one afternoon Mahina had opened her eyes. She was showing Theresa how to mash *noni* berries to make a poultice for boils. She had chanted while she worked and Theresa asked her if the words really had any effect. Mahina had thought for a moment, then she had reached into Theresa's black bag and brought out a clear bottle. "What this?" she asked.

"That's holy water," Theresa had said.

"What make it holy?"

"A priest sanctifies the water with prayer."

Theresa now knew various chants and their precise pronunciations. She had also learned a few steps of the hula, and she relished the feeling of freedom when she pinned up her sleeves and waved her arms. It was minimal, to be sure, not the sensuous, seductive dance that the statuesque Mahina performed, but it reminded Theresa of the night of the scarlet fever when she had thoughtlessly ripped off her habit to dive into the water. Tragic though that night had been, the freedom of the vigorous swim had exhilarated her and she yearned to experience it again.

The daylight was suddenly blocked and a cheerful voice said, "Aloha, Keleka!"

She looked up to see a wiry youth silhouetted against the sun. She couldn't see his face, but she recognized him as Liho, Mahina's grandson, who had been cured during *ho'oponopono*. She was pleased to see him.

"I bring mango for Keleka," he said, handing her a knotted tapa cloth filled with fruit.

"Thank you, Liho. If you would just set it down there, please."

He did so and squatted on his haunches to watch her finish the bandaging.

As she turned to reach for the scissors in her bag, she noticed Liho's left foot. He was barefoot, and she saw a nasty wound on the big toe. It had stopped bleeding and was crusted over. Still, she thought it should be cleaned and an ointment applied.

When she was finished with Nalani, she shifted her attention to

Liho, who proceeded to tell her about a successful fishing expedition he had just come back from. "Plenty mahi-mahi," he said with pride.

She bent to examine the foot. When she touched it to lift it into the light, she expected him to flinch. He did not. "Doesn't this hurt?" she asked.

"What?" he said. And when he looked down, he was surprised to see the gash.

She touched the wound with a fingertip. "This. Does it hurt?"

"Don't feel it, Keleka."

She gave this some thought. She pressed harder. He didn't react. When she looked up, Liho's face was now in the sun and she saw a scratch on the end of his nose. "Does *that* hurt?" she asked.

When he gave her a confused look, she touched his nose. He felt nothing.

Her stomach tightened as she looked more closely at his face. Now she saw, on his copper skin, what she had not noticed before: several flat lesions, slightly paler than his skin. She asked him to close his eyes. Then she brought out a suture needle and punctured one of the lesions. "Do you feel that?" she asked, already knowing the answer because he had not flinched.

"No, Keleka."

In rising terror, she examined his hands, testing the fingertips with the needle. Liho had no sensation in any of them.

"Merciful God," she whispered. There was no doubt. No other illness presented this way in the early stages. Although so far only twenty-five cases had been reported and contained, it was believed that many more were going unreported by frightened families.

She saw the boy's future. Leprosy was incurable and mutilated its victims by slow, agonizing stages. Liho faced blindness, severe facial disfigurement, kidney failure, and damage to nerves that led to a dangerous loss of feeling. One of the most horrific and tragic complications of leprosy was a creeping muscle weakness that twisted the hands into permanent claws.

"Liho," she said with a smile, keeping her voice as steady as possible. "Where is Tutu Mahina?"

He pointed to the other end of the settlement, where she knew the women had a pavilion in which they made tapa cloth.

As Theresa approached, she saw Mahina and her companions working in various stages: peeling the bark from mulberry stems, soaking the strips, and then pounding them. The women used sharp shells and flat stones in the manufacture of the cloth. They all looked up and smiled at her and called out greetings.

"Keleka!" Mahina cried, and hefted her bulk off the mat to waddle over and engulf Theresa in one of her famous loving embraces. She had gained back the weight she'd lost after her son, Polunu, had died of a death curse. Intense joy over the saving of Liho through *ho'oponopono* had restored her appetite and zest for living. She was more generous than ever, a familiar sight in the streets of Honolulu as she walked along, spreading aloha as she handed out her colorful leis.

But now Sister Theresa had terrible news and she didn't know how to break it to her.

By law Theresa was bound to report Liho to the health officials. Dr. Edgeware would come with soldiers and have his staff examine the entire village population. He might even go so far as to quarantine all of them, and burn the village down. For certain, Liho would be taken away and placed in a newly created quarantine camp in an isolated stretch of the island. His family would have to make special arrangements to visit him, and themselves be subject to frequent medical examinations. But it was necessary due to the highly contagious nature of the disease.

"Mahina, I need to talk to you."

She grew concerned. "Keleka look worry. What worry Keleka?"

Theresa glanced at the others. "Privately, please."

"My Pinau, he all right?" she asked in alarm. Mahina was forever worrying about Jamie.

They went to the edge of a sweet potato patch, where no one was working. Theresa quietly explained her examination of Liho and her diagnosis.

First Mahina stared at her in disbelief, then she cried, "Auwe! Not true, Keleka. Say not true!"

Theresa looked over at Liho, standing among the huts, throwing a stick for a puppy and laughing as it came running back. There had been a great deal of talk lately, led by Dr. Edgeware, of possibly creating a leper colony on another island. Families would be torn apart.

"Mahina, listen to me." Theresa took her by the arms. "Liho will not get better. White doctors cannot help, nor can *kahuna lapa'au*. No *ho'oponopono*. His sickness will get worse and he will make others sick. Do you understand? You must take your grandson into the forest, far away from other people and keep him there, hidden. He is kapu for others, do you understand?"

"Where we go?" Mahina wailed.

"Find some place. And never let him come back to the village. Never let him go down to the beach."

Mahina's eyes bulged. "No fishing? No making canoes? No riding surfboard?"

Dear God, Theresa thought. No more Liho riding the waves on his long board.

"Explain to the others that they must never tell the haoles." Theresa knew Mahina would need help from her family, that she would have to let them know what happened to Liho.

She nodded sorrowfully. "You tell Kapena?"

"Yes, I will tell Captain Farrow."

"Mahina, Liho must go into the trees," Theresa said in a tight voice, "and never, ever come out."

CHAPTER TWENTY-TWO

P lease," Nurse Yates had said at the Royal Ball, "come and visit us anytime you like. I would love to hear of your experiences here, and perhaps you could give me some advice. This is all so new to me."

So now Sister Theresa stood at the end of the path leading to the verandah of the two-story wooden house with a shingle that read: STEVEN YATES, PHYSICIAN & SURGEON—LADY NURSE AVAILABLE.

Lady Nurse, Theresa thought. It had an elegant ring to it. Respectable indeed.

The verandah was lined with benches, and Sister Theresa knew this was where patients waited. As the one nearest the door was called inside, everyone moved over a space on the bench, with newcomers taking the last spot.

The only patient at the moment was a Chinese man who sat by himself on the verandah. He was dressed in baggy blue pants under a padded blue jacket. His hair was twisted into a long braid down his back, and a black skullcap fit snugly on his head. Theresa knew that with the proliferation of sugar plantations in the islands, more and more laborers were being imported from China. She wondered where this man worked. His right arm was wrapped in a dirty bandage.

She smiled at him and took a seat across. After a few minutes, the front door opened and a woman with a child came out, effusively thanking Mrs. Yates for "clearing up Jenny's clogged chest."

"Sister Theresa," Mrs. Yates said. "What a pleasant surprise. Please come in." She turned to the Chinese patient. "Mr. Chen, please come in." He nodded and grinned and followed them inside.

The front door opened upon an entry hall. On the left were closed doors. Ahead were stairs to the upper floor. On the right, double doors opened onto an airy, sunlit room that Theresa surmised had once been a parlor or library but which had been converted into a physician's examination room. There were books on shelves, anatomical charts on the walls, a skeleton hanging from a hook, cabinets, a desk and chairs.

"My husband is at Queen's Hospital," Eva Yates said, gesturing to Mr. Chen to take a seat. "He will be sorry he missed you."

Sister Theresa couldn't help thinking that Mrs. Yates looked like any lady of the house entertaining a caller. She wore a lovely silk gown, pale green with lace collar and cuffs. Her hair was caught up under a white lace day cap.

As Mrs. Yates began to unwrap Mr. Chen's dressing, Sister Theresa thought: She does the same things I do. And yet she is unfettered. And she has a husband.

"Mr. Chen was brought to us last week by a friend who explained that he had injured himself while loading crates onto a wagon. It took Dr. Yates nearly an hour to remove all of the splinters and then to stitch him up."

Something fell out of the bandages, landing on the floor. Theresa picked it up. The object was flat and round, an inch or so in diameter, made of metal and stamped with designs. She handed it to Mrs. Yates who said, "The friend who brought Mr. Chen in told me it's a good luck coin charm for health. This one was specially designed to ward off something called sickness *chi*. It's called a *Tian Yi* coin because *Tian Yi* means Heaven Doctor."

Theresa watched in amazement as Mrs. Yates, using tweezers and small scissors, removed the black silk stitches from Mr. Chen's wound. It was almost mesmerizing to watch, her concentration was so great, her skill so keen, as Mr. Chen didn't flinch once. Theresa was envious. Suture removal was something she and her Sisters were not allowed to do.

Finally, Mrs. Yates rebandaged the arm, making sure to tuck the lucky yellow coin into the gauze directly over the wound.

Theresa was about to ask a question when they were interrupted by children suddenly bursting into the room—a boy of around six and a girl of three, well-dressed and squealing with glee.

Mrs. Yates gathered them into her arms, laughing. "Little ones! How many times have I told you not to come in when Mummy is in here? Go back to Nanny, my angels. Go on now. Biscuits and milk in a little while."

Mr. Chen bowed and said something in Chinese, and then he left. "Let me clean up here," Mrs. Yates said, "and then we can go into the parlor for tea. I am so glad you accepted my invitation. I have so many questions!"

"I have a few myself," Theresa said as she looked around the room. When she came to a cupboard with a glass front, she said, "For instance, what is this?" She pointed at a glass cylinder with a plunger at one end and a needle at the other.

"It's very new, a recent invention," Mrs. Yates said. "It's called a hypodermic syringe and it is used for the subcutaneous injection of medicine. It is more effective, in some ways, than medicine administered orally. It is also used to deliver local anesthesia to an injury."

"And that strange instrument next to it?"

"It's called a microscope. It magnifies things many times. My husband uses it in his research. He believes that some illnesses are caused by unseen organisms called germs."

Sister Theresa marveled at the wonderful instruments and modern inventions. Equally impressive was the stock of medicines lined up on the shelves, from castor oil and cocaine to liver salts and bunion removers. A remedy for every possible ailment under the sun. She wished she and her Sisters could afford such luxuries.

During a delightful conversation over tea and sweet mango tarts, Theresa enlightened Eva Yates on many of Hawai'i's customs and mysteries, and at the same time learned more about how Florence Nightingale, and an American woman named Clara Barton who trained nurses to take care of wounded soldiers in the War Between the States, had cleansed nursing of its disrespectable stigma that equated nurses with prostitutes, and made it an honorable profession to which respectable ladies everywhere might aspire. Schools were being established, hospitals were hiring the new nurses, doctors wanted nurses in their offices to help with children and female patients. It was a whole new era. And Theresa had missed it.

As she was leaving, Mrs. Yates handed her some books—her nursing school manuals and textbooks. "Take your time with them, Sister. There are some innovative ideas in there that perhaps you and your Sisters can use. And remember, my door is always open."

T he summons came while Sister Theresa was doing the weekly ironing.

Mother Agnes looked tired, Theresa thought, as if she weren't sleeping enough. "Sister Theresa, it is clear to me that you are struggling with spiritual issues, that your conscience is troubled. You are not putting your whole heart into your work here, and I fear you tend toward the secular rather than the religious. Therefore I am sending you back to San Francisco, where you will live sequestered from the outside world, as I believe you will serve God best within the safe confinement of a convent."

L iho sat alone outside his hut, his belly filled with sorrow.

He had a sleeping mat, bark cloth for bedding, a spear for fishing in the nearby stream, a knife to cut fruit from trees, and a carved wooden statue of Kane, the creator and giver of life, for companionship.

It wasn't enough. Liho missed his friends. Surfing. Fishing. Sleeping with his family. Now, he heard no voices, no singing, no drums, no laughter. Sometimes, he woke up in the night and thought he was the only person on earth. As if everyone had left Hawai'i for some reason. It frightened him. He didn't understand what had happened. Some places on his body had lost all feeling. It was not his fault. Why was he being punished? He tried to think. Had he offended a spirit? He had been trained since early childhood to respect the spirits and gods of every place he went.

When a kanaka set out on a trail through the forest, he was not just out for a daily stroll, as it was for the haole, he was following a sacred path where everything was touched by the gods, by magic. He must chant to the place he was passing through, and he would chant to the place he hoped to arrive at. The traveler kept himself aware of every flower, every stone he touched. Even the air was sacred. Everything must be respected, acknowledged. Kanaka were never without a prayer or protective saying on their lips.

But sometimes a boy could be forgetful. Liho racked his brain. If only he could remember where, and which spirit, then he could chant a song of apology and promise to make amends. If he knew where, and which spirit, he would go back to that place and ask for forgiveness and leave gifts and then he would be healed. Why couldn't the kahuna *lapa'au* cure him?

He had been banished from the family. No kanaka lived alone. Even an elder whose family and friends had all passed into spirit form, even such a one was taken in by others and made into a new family member. Liho had been surrounded by people from the minute he was born. It was the kanaka way.

But Tutu Mahina said he must stay here for the rest of his life and never see his family or friends again.

I will run away, he decided. I will swim far out to sea and ride on the back of *nai'a*. I will join Mano in his underwater kingdom and from far below watch my brothers ride their boards on the waves.

He looked up and peered into the trees. A sudden rustling sound. Someone was coming! It would be Tutu Mahina. She was the only one who came. She brought him food and words of comfort. But she never stayed long. She couldn't stay forever, which was what he wanted. To live forever with his grandmother.

His eyes widened as a large, lumbering figure emerged through the trees. A towering, brown giant wearing a skirt of long *ti*-leaves and a crown of *ti*-leaves on his head. Uncle Kekoa!

Liho's look turned to one of puzzlement. Uncle was carrying a surfboard.

Kekoa didn't speak as he propped the board on top of three rocks and then climbed on as if he were about to ride the waves. His thick, fleshy arms went straight out, to balance himself, and then he bent his knees and wobbled from side to side, straightening his legs to wave his arms until he fell off in a comical way.

Liho smiled. When Uncle fell off the board again, Liho grinned. A third time made him chuckle. When Kekoa fell off the board onto his back on the grass and his legs went up in the air and he made a funny "oof" sound, Liho laughed out loud. When his uncle recovered himself and bent over to straighten the board, he broke wind so loudly that Liho doubled over with laughter. Kekoa made a face, pinched his nose, and waved his hand behind himself.

While Liho laughed until tears rolled down his cheeks, Kekoa rushed to his nephew and gathered him into his arms. "My precious boy," he cried, as he wept into Liho's hair. "My precious, sick boy! Great-grandson of my beloved sister, Pua. *Auwe!*" They rocked together for some minutes and then Kekoa, releasing Liho, dashed the tears from his cheeks and said, "Come, you must ride the waves!"

Settling the board back on the rocks, he told Liho to climb up. While the boy held his arms out and kept his balance, his uncle knelt on the ground and moved the surfboard this way and that, up and down, while Liho shouted with joy as he rode the waves and his old, proud uncle stifled sobs within his massive chest.

It was with a heavy heart that Theresa walked along a crowded sidewalk in a busy street. She was going to Farrow House to say good-bye.

The population of Honolulu had increased dramatically since her arrival. There were more buildings, more traffic, more pedestrians. Everyone was profiting from the war in America, and especially from its ending. Hawai'i was still reeling from news both joyous and devastating. General Lee had surrendered to General Grant at Appomattox on April 9, and five days later, President Lincoln was assassinated.

For Theresa and her family, the news was wonderful. Her brother Eli had survived the war. His regiment had assembled for the last time at Readville, where the men were given their final pay and were discharged. Theresa didn't know what he was going to do next, return to Harvard or go back to San Francisco. All she knew was that her mother's four years of worrying were over.

Theresa knew that she herself should be filled with joy to be going home, to see her family again, but she had a family *here,* and with more cases of leprosy cropping up and Dr. Edgeware intensifying his campaign to make harboring lepers a crime, she felt she would be abandoning Mahina and her people.

"You did the right thing, Anna," Robert said when she had told him about Liho. "For now, at least. It gives us time to think, to come up with a plan. Were Edgeware to find out, he would storm the village, drag Liho and possibly others to one of his quarantine camps, and burn the huts to the ground."

And then he had added in a grave tone, "Anna, it is not yet publicly known—we have been debating it in the legislature, but members of both houses are coming close to passing an act that will stem the spread of leprosy. It entails establishing a leper settlement on the island of Molokai."

Theresa had begged him not to let that happen. The victims needed their families for support and to take care of them. To isolate the afflicted on a remote island was sentencing them to a living death.

"I'm just one vote, Anna," he had said, "but my voice is loud. I will fight it, I promise."

"And I will fight it with you," she had said.

But now she was being sent home.

A small, one-horse buggy stood at the gate leading to Farrow House. Theresa recognized it as belonging to Dr. Steven Yates. Mrs. Carter opened the front door and invited her to go upstairs. Theresa found Robert in Jamie's bedroom, watching as Dr. Yates examined the boy.

As she waited for the doctor to finish his examination, Theresa thought of one of the books Eva Yates had lent her: *Notes on Nursing*, by Florence Nightingale. In it, Theresa had read, *"Nursing is defined as the act of utilizing the environment of the patient to assist him in his recovery."* She thought of this now as she looked around Jamie's bedroom. Was it possible that something in his environment was hurting him? He always seemed healthier when visiting the ranch at Waialua. Or was she herself missing something in his environment that she could draw upon to cure him?

Finally, putting away his stethoscope, Dr. Yates said, "Your son needs a diet rich in dairy. Give him plenty of milk and cheese and butter."

"We tried that," Robert said. "Jamie can't tolerate dairy. He's half-Hawai'ian."

"Ah yes, I have heard that. Well then let us try . . ."

While they spoke, something began to flit around the edge of Theresa's mind. It came in the form of Mahina's voice, but she could not quite seize upon it.

"Captain Farrow," Dr. Yates said, "was Jamie born this way?"

"No, doctor, that's the maddening part. Until a few years ago he was robust, energetic. You couldn't keep him still."

"What happened to change things? A catastrophic illness, perhaps?"

"The nearest I can figure is that Jamie began to weaken after his mother died. He missed her terribly. He pined for her and I think that started the decline."

Robert had told Theresa this before, and she had thought that might be the reason for Jamie turning into a weak little boy. And then losing Reese had advanced his weakened state. But now, the elusive whispering of Mahina's voice made her take Robert's words in a different way.

And suddenly she heard Mahina say of Liho, her grandson: "He not haole. Haole medicine no good. He need kanaka medicine."

While Robert filled the doctor in on the particulars of Jamie's health history, Theresa thought: Jamie is half-Hawai'ian. What if his malaise were not from an emotional or physical source but a *spiritual* one? What if his weakened state did not begin when his mother died, but when Robert and Peter had had their fight in which Peter fell down the stairs and broke his leg? What if Jamie were suffering from the bad blood that had existed between his father and uncle?

"Captain Farrow," she said suddenly. "I might have a solution." The two men turned to her.

"I wonder if Jamie can benefit from *ho'oponopono*. The way we saw it performed over Liho two years ago."

"Ho-ho *what?*" Dr. Yates said.

"Captain Farrow, when did you and Peter—" She glanced at Dr. Yates, a newcomer to Honolulu. "When did Peter break his leg?"

"Eight years ago."

"Did Jamie witness it?"

"Yes, he was seven years old." Robert stared at her, and then she saw comprehension dawning on his face. "It was a few months after Leilani died. And now that I really think about it . . . Jamie was fine for a while. He was sad and he cried, but he was healthy and strong. Until Peter and I had our argument."

"I believe he needs kanaka medicine," she said.

When he hesitated, she added, "Mahina once said to me: *O ka huhu ka mea e ola 'ole ai*—anger is the thing that gives no life. Captain Farrow, it's possible Jamie is suffering from the anger that is poisoning this house."

Dr. Yates spoke up. "If I may say something? As a sub-specialty to my medical training, I also studied the field of mental illness, what we call psychiatry. I observed cases in which the patient convinced himself he was ill when no pathology was present. The scientific term is psychosomatic, and many medical men are beginning to believe there is a close interaction between mind and body, one that can manifest itself in observable symptoms. I confess, Captain Farrow, I can neither diagnose nor prescribe for your son. If he is part Hawai'ian, and if Hawai'ians have their own form of medicine, I would suggest you give it a try."

Robert did not need to think twice. "I will send for Peter at once." He stopped in the doorway. "What about Mother? Should we ask her to take part?"

"I don't think she is up to it," Theresa said, thinking of Emily's recent spells of extreme fatigue, and the blue tint of her lips and nails. "I suspect Mrs. Farrow is suffering from cardiac insufficiency."

"I concur," Dr. Yates said, and Theresa gave him a smile of gratitude. He was the first medical man to treat her with respect.

But then, his wife was a nurse.

Robert was in such an emotional state that Theresa could not, in that moment, tell him that she was leaving Hawai'i. And so she busied herself with preparations for the ritual. She went to the local market and purchased the *kala* seaweed. She also bought *ti*-leaves, rich green and blade-shaped, and sacred to Lono.

It was late when Peter arrived, tired and in ill-humor. "You said it was urgent. It had better not be about that blasted ship!"

Robert had purchased a decommissioned warship from the Union Navy—a two-thousand-ton propeller and one of the strongest built vessels afloat. It was being retrofitted with cabin accommodations for sixty passengers, and bunks for forty more. A fast, comfortable vessel that was going to be the next step in the evolution of shipping. But Robert needed a trusted agent to go to America and finalize the sale. He had asked Peter, who had flatly turned him down.

"It's Jamie. He is gravely ill. He might not last another two days."

They came into the drawing room, where Theresa had lit candles and incense. Peter looked terrible. She had not seen him in a year, but those twelve months had not been kind. Grief had stripped the flesh from his body, had turned his skin an ashen color, had thinned his hair. Not a terribly good-looking man to begin with, she thought, Peter Farrow now bore not the slightest resemblance to his handsome, more robust brother. His limp was more pronounced as well, reminding her of why they were here. To mend things.

He frowned when he saw her. "What the devil is she doing here?" She knew that Peter equated her with Reese's death, perhaps in some way blamed her for it.

"We're going to do *ho'oponopono* for Jamie. Sister Theresa is going to mediate."

Peter pursed his lips in thought, although Theresa saw a spark of interest in his eyes. She knew of Peter's friendship with his Hawai'ian ranch hands, how he joined them for celebrations. He had no doubt witnessed a few *ho'oponopono* rituals himself. Finally, he said, "I suppose it couldn't hurt. And after all, his mother was Hawai'ian."

"Captain Farrow," Theresa said, "will you please bring Jamie downstairs? Tell him what we are going to do. Remember, it's all about belief, the power of the mind over the body, as Dr. Yates explained. If you can convince Jamie that he will be cured if you and Peter perform *ho'oponopono*, then he will be cured." She thought of Mrs. Klausner, who surely would have been better off having her baby delivered by an experienced doctor rather than two inexperienced nuns. But it was her belief that, by their presence, they had brought God into the bedroom, which made what might have been a complicated birth an easy one.

Peter paced in the drawing room, glancing at Theresa now and then with a skeptical look. She would have liked Mahina there, but she couldn't be present. A few more villagers had shown symptoms of leprosy and now lived with Liho in his secret camp in the forest. Mahina was their only channel to the outside world.

Robert brought Jamie downstairs, carrying him in his arms, a youth of fifteen looking like a child. They laid him on a satin-uphol-stered chaise longue and, when he was comfortable, Theresa went to him, sat at his side, and said, "Jamie, you know what *ho'oponopono* is? You have watched the rituals at Tutu Mahina's village."

He nodded. His pallor had worsened. His lips were white. He tried to lift his arm but let it drop back down.

"We are going to do *ho'oponopono* tonight," she said, "to make you well."

When he seemed not to understand, Theresa said, "Look, see? Uncle Peter is here."

Jamie's eyes seemed to light up when he saw Peter in the room, and already Theresa could see that the ritual had a chance to work.

"Hello, son," Peter said in a tight voice, limping over on his cane. "Sorry I haven't seen you in a while, but—"

"It's all right, Uncle Peter," Jamie said in a voice that sounded light as a feather. "I know you've been sad."

"That I have, son, that I have. But listen now, this ritual that we're going to do, it will help you because you are half-kanaka."

Robert led them in prayer—first to God and Jesus, and then he called upon the ancient gods and spirits of the islands. Theresa dispensed the seaweed, which was crispy and salty, with an appealing, tangy taste. As they chewed, she chanted the song she had learned from Mahina. *Aloha mai no, aloha aku . . . o ka huhu ka mea e ola 'ole ai . . . E h'oi, e Pele, i ke kuahiwi, ua na ko lili . . . ko inaina. . . ."*

She brought holy water out of her black bag and sprinkled it on the sacred *ti*-leaves, then she shook the leaves in the four cardinal direc-tions, in the corners and dark places of the room, toward the windows and the fireplace, and lastly she shook the wet leaves over Jamie.

Finally, she said, "We may begin. Whatever is unhappy in your hearts, reveal it now. Expose your pain so that it may fly away."

When neither spoke, both men stubbornly refusing to appear weak, she said, "Jamie's trouble began when you two had a fight, is that true?"

Peter crossed his arms and sat stiffly in the straight-backed chair. "I don't have anything to say," he said. "Let Robert tell you about it."

"It was a silly argument," Robert said. "A misunderstanding."

"A 'misunderstanding?' I assume you mean, on my part. You

were in the right, of course. The fight was all my fault." Peter turned to Theresa. "I accused my brother of something and he told me I was mistaken."

"What was the accusation?" she asked, glancing at Jamie, who was watching from his chaise.

"Peter, I told you at the time—" Robert began.

"You killed the only thing I really loved! And you've known all these years that it was all your fault."

Robert took a step toward Peter, hands out in a placating manner. "You have to listen to me—"

Peter shot to his feet and shouted, "You let her go! You didn't even try to stop her! You just stood by while Leilani went down to the beach to drown in the surf with the quarantined patients!" His face grew red with rage. "Why didn't you stop her? My God!"

"Peter," Robert said, "I did try to stop her. And I tried to tell you this, eight years ago, when you wouldn't listen." He turned to Theresa, speaking quickly. "Leilani insisted on going to the quarantine pavilion on the beach, to help take care of the victims of the chicken pox epidemic. A week after we buried her, Peter accused me of *letting* her go to her death."

As the truth dawned on Theresa—that Peter had been in love with Robert's wife—Peter growled, "Why don't you tell the good Sister why you were married to Leilani in the first place? Tell her how you have hated me all these years because I wouldn't stay in Honolulu and run the company after Father died. I wanted to follow my dream of owning a cattle ranch. I wasn't like you and Father. I didn't give a damn about the sea! But I went to Waialua, and you were forced to put away your ship's logs and seaman's spyglass and run the shipping company from an office at the docks. So you seduced Leilani. You purposely stole her from me. That was how you punished me."

But Robert shook his head. "That just is not so."

"Then what? Have you another explanation for why she married you instead of me?" Peter waited. "See? There you have it! When I asked you this before, you had no answer and you still have no answer!"

"Let's stop this. It isn't going to work. Peter, I'm sorry I sent for you."

But Theresa sensed that Robert was holding something back,

something that perhaps he had carried for a long time. "Captain Farrow," she said softly. "Tell Peter what is in your heart."

"There's nothing," he said flatly. "Only that I did try to keep Leilani from going to the quarantine pavilion on the beach. She said her people needed her. That's all there is. Peter and I had a fight about it. We struggled at the top of the stairs and he fell. I'm sorry you broke your leg, Peter. I truly am."

But his brother said, "A half-confession is no confession. Admit that you stole Leilani from me because I made you give up the sea. You resented me for moving to Waialua. You seduced her into marrying you. There will be no peace in this family until you admit the truth!"

Peter reached for his hat and cane.

"Wait," Jamie said in a threadbare voice. "Uncle Peter, don't go ..."

Peter stopped and looked down at his nephew, pain in his eyes. "I'm sorry, Jamie boy, but your father isn't holding up his end of the *ho'oponopono*."

Theresa looked at Robert and saw that he was in torment. He was holding a secret close to his heart. Why didn't he confess it? He had so willingly agreed to the ritual, but now he was holding back.

"Robert," she said, putting a hand on his arm. "Whatever it is, please, for Jamie's sake, talk about it."

Robert's eyes were filled with agony as he looked from her to Jamie and then to Peter. She saw that he struggled—was it a moral dilemma? A secret shame? Finally, Robert relaxed his shoulders in a sigh. "Peter," he said, "the truth of it is, Leilani was never in love with you."

Peter stared at him. "That's a lie," he growled. "Confound you, Robert, that is a devilish lie!"

"No, Peter. She told me herself. Leilani didn't love you, she never intended to marry you. I never told you this because I didn't want to hurt you."

"I refuse to believe it! You stole her from me because you wanted revenge for my making you stay in Honolulu when you wanted to go to sea."

"It's true, Peter, that I hated you for that. I loved the sea and when Father died, you announced that you were not going to step into his place and run the company. You wanted a cattle ranch. So you ran off to Waialua and bought your damn cows while I had to close my logbook and resign myself to life in a shipping office! But Leilani didn't love you. When you found us together in the garden . . . Peter, she came to me. She told me she loved me. I told her she must go back to you. She said she didn't love you. She didn't want to marry you."

"I don't believe you! You're lying!" Peter rushed at his brother with fists up. He got one hit in, across Robert's jaw, but when he moved to strike again, Jamie wailed, "No, Uncle Peter! Stop!"

Peter stared at his nephew, then looked at his fists, as if wondering whose they were. Finally he slumped into the chair and cradled his head in his hands. "All these years . . . you let me hate you rather than hurt my feelings with the truth. You let me think you stole her from me, when she didn't want me in the first place."

"I knew it would devastate you, Peter. It was better you hated me than you hated Leilani."

Peter lifted bereft eyes. "I could never have hated her."

"You think that now, but how can we know? If she had rejected you to your face, how do we know you would not have come to hate her over time? It was better that your bitterness was aimed at me."

The wind picked up outside, sending kukui branches to scratch against windows, like ghosts trying to get in. Drafts found their way into the drawing room, causing candles and lamps to flicker. Shadows shifted and crept around. Theresa felt a sense of waiting.

Something had not yet been said.

"Peter," Robert said at last, as if the whispering wind and stealthy shadows were urging him to make one last confession. "About Father's death—"

"I know what you have thought all these years," Peter said, rising to his feet again, to look around the room, as if for an escape, or an explanation for why he was there. "You never said it, Robert, but I could see it in your eyes. My God, don't you think I would have stopped it if I could? But I got there too late!"

"Peter," Robert said again, reaching out to touch his brother's arm. "I never thought you could have stopped it. I never thought that. And I am truly sorry that you were there alone, that you witnessed such a horrific scene."

Robert turned to Theresa and said, "The night our father died, when he went out onto the cliffs to save Mother . . . Peter saw Father lose his footing and plunge into the sea. His body was never recovered—" Robert's voice broke and Peter took up the narrative.

"I saw Father fall," he said to Theresa, "but that wasn't all. It has been our secret all these years. Our mother pushed MacKenzie Farrow into the sea."

"Lord have mercy," she whispered, crossing herself.

"I never blamed you, Peter. I never once thought you could have stopped it. Mother was out of her mind. She didn't know what she was doing." Robert turned to Theresa. "We told the authorities that he slipped and fell, that it was an accident. You understand that we couldn't tell anyone that Mother killed our father."

She nodded, and felt great sadness for the two brothers who had kept such a secret, and who had been haunted by such a memory all these years.

Jamie suddenly cried out from his chaise, "I'm sorry, Uncle Peter, that Reese died and I lived!"

They turned to look at him. His face was distorted, and he was sobbing. "What?" Peter said.

"I'm sorry I lived! I wish it was me in Reese's grave!"

"Oh God!" Peter rushed to him, gathered Jamie into his arms and held him tight. "I didn't mean it, dear boy. It was my grief talking! Oh God, I could not have borne it if you had died as well!"·

Uncle and nephew clung to each other and cried together while Theresa stood with Robert, thinking of the things he had said, the two truths that had come out. She thought of families and secrets and wondered for the first time if her own family kept secrets locked away in a forgotten cupboard. Mother, in their Oregon cabin, weeping bitterly and cursing Father's name as he stayed away at the gold fields. Father, inventing a lie about a man named Barney Northcote getting his legs crushed and then receiving wonderful care from Catholic nurses—just so he could save his pride and let his daughter go into a Sisterhood.

But perhaps some lies are good, like Robert not hurting Peter with the truth about how Leilani felt about him. Sometimes, Theresa thought, secrets and lies keep a family together.

Peter finally laid Jamie back on the pillow and Theresa could see that the boy had fallen asleep. He rose and turned to Robert. The life, and the fight, seemed to have gone out of him. Theresa could not predict what their relationship would be like after this night, if the *ho'oponopono* had worked or not, if Peter and Robert could ever be friends, if they could ever speak words of forgiveness to each other. Perhaps that would come later, with the healing of time.

"About the decommissioned warship," Peter said. "Go to Boston, Robert. I'll run the company while you're gone. I'll make sure everything keeps going smoothly. Go and bring back the fastest and safest passenger ship that has ever sailed the seas."

Not exactly a reconciliation, but a start.

While Peter sat in the study, keeping an eye on Jamie, Robert and Theresa went out onto the lanai for air.

"I think everything is going to be all right," he said as they stood among the fragrant blossoms. "I think that, in time, Peter and I can be brothers again. And I hope that what we did tonight helped Jamie. I thank you for that, Anna."

He stood close to her, the man of her heart, and whom she would love for the rest of her days. And to whom she must now say good-bye.

"I'm leaving for America right away," he said. "But there is solace in one thought: although the voyage there will take weeks, the voyage back will be only days."

"Robert, I'm leaving, too."

"What? Where? Why?"

When she told him, he shouted, "I won't let you go! I'll go directly to the bishop."

"It is not up to the bishop! I must do as Mother Agnes says. Robert, please. I beg of you, let me go, forget about me."

He took her by the shoulders and said, "Take off these ridiculous robes, Anna. Be a woman. Be as God made you. Let me show you the world. Let me take you to the fjords of Norway, the green islands in the Mediterranean. Let me show you the East where people pray to giant Buddhas and I will put cherry blossoms in your hair."

"Robert!" she cried. "I cannot!"

"Come away with me, Anna! Sail the seas with me. Let me show you the world! Oh, the places we could go, the grand adventures we could have, and I would love you every single second of every single hour of every single mile we sailed."

"Please," she sobbed.

His grip tightened. "From the time I could first walk, my mother reminded me constantly that New England is my home. But you reminded me that *Hawai'i* is my home—and what a beautiful, magical home it is. You once told me that Hawai'i is a symphony. I saw the magic in the Birthing Stones because of you. I have seen Hawai'i through your eyes and it is a beautiful place that I took for granted! Damn it, Anna, I'm in love with you."

"Robert, I took sacred vows. I owe a debt to the Sisterhood. Please," she whispered, tears streaming down her face. "Be strong for me because I cannot be strong for myself."

Their eyes stayed locked for another long moment as the warm trade winds stirred her veils and she saw moonlight in Robert's dark eyes. His body shook as he wrestled with passion and conscience.

Finally, he loosened his grip and he stepped away, his hands falling to his sides. "Though it pains me, I will respect your honor and your vows. But I will not stop loving you, and I will fight again for you."

The secrets had become too much of a burden. They were weighing her down as surely as the nun's habit was. She had carnal desires for a man. She had allowed lepers to go into hiding and told no one. She had conducted a heathen ritual that had been banned by law. And she had confessed none of these things to her priest or her Superior. So perhaps it was best that she be sent back to California to start anew with a clean slate.

Theresa told herself this as she packed her few possessions while trying to find joy in her heart at leaving Hawai'i—after all, she would see her mother and father again, her little sister, and possibly Eli. But she was also leaving Robert, and the pain of it far outweighed her joy.

She knew that her life would never be the same. She would always love Robert Farrow. Her heart would always be here with the palm trees and rainbows and Mahina's people. Perhaps she had, after all, become, as Robert had said, *kama'aina*, a child of the land.

Mother Agnes came in as Theresa was finishing up. She was going to accompany her to the docks. "Sister Theresa, a week ago you went to Farrow House to leave a tonic for the boy, Jamie. What else did you do?"

Theresa had anticipated this. "We prayed." It was close enough to the truth. "I encouraged Captain Farrow and his brother to make amends. I explained how confession is good for the soul, and that forgiveness is sometimes the best medicine."

"I see."

"Why do you ask, Reverend Mother?"

"It has come to my attention that the boy is recovering in a fashion that people are calling miraculous. It seems, Sister, that the cornerstones of the Catholic faith—confession and repentance—have saved the boy where other means did not. I would gather from this that perhaps there is hope for bringing that family into the Church yet, and through them, the boy's Hawai'ian grandmother and the recalcitrant natives at Wailaka. Father Halloran agrees. Therefore, we have decided that you are doing admirable work here, Sister Theresa. You are an asset to our Order. Unpack your things. You are remaining in Hawai'i."

CHAPTER TWENTY-THREE

It was a big day for the citizens of Honolulu.

The first all-passenger steamship was arriving after departing San Francisco a mere ten days prior. The vessel was the SS *Leilani,* flagship of the Farrow Line, and everybody turned out to see her glide majestically into port.

Weeks before, Robert had sent home the prototype for an advertisement that was going to appear in newspapers and magazines and would be posted on walls and lampposts, announcing the maiden voyage of the SS *Leilani:* "Find Yourself In Paradise In Mere DAYS! Travel the sea in luxury and comfort on the only All-Passenger steamship dedicated to YOUR safety and pleasure. Amenities include a card salon, where men can retire for a game of poker or cribbage with cigars and whiskey. A separate salon for the ladies, where they can drink tea, read books, and write letters. Enjoy fine dining while listening to entertainment provided by a pianist and a chanteuse of popular songs. Separate cabins for ladies are available."

The maiden voyage from San Francisco had sold out within days.

Robert had won the Pacific Mail contract for the lucrative West Coast–Hawai'i run. Today's historic arrival of the SS *Leilani* marked a new era in faster travel and speedy communications. Every man and woman in the crowd on the docks eagerly anticipated the letters from home that would be filled with recent news, rather than news that was weeks out of date. The newspapers would not even make it into town, they would be snapped up quickly by those hungry for the latest word from the United States.

Excitement ran high. Inside the reef, the magnificent ironclad *California* and another American war vessel were moored in line with a British clipper. Two coasting schooners were just leaving the harbor, and the inter-island steamer *Puahe'a,* natives crowding on deck, was just coming in. In between, countless canoes paddled by natives were going this way and that. All eyes were turned to the harbor entrance, to the ocean beyond the reef, anxious to glimpse the *Leilani.* Every available place along the wharves and roads was crowded with citizens eager to witness the dawning of a new age.

Jamie's former governess, Miss Carter, was among the throng. She had come to Honolulu to visit her mother, Mrs. Carter, who was still Robert's housekeeper. Sister Theresa had not seen Jamie's former governess since she'd left for Kona four years prior. She smiled at Theresa and seemed happy. She was no longer Miss Carter, but Mrs. Freedman, having married the owner of a prosperous coffee farm.

Mr. Gahrman the druggist was on hand for the big occasion. He did not smile at Theresa. He had not been cordial to her since she'd given Mr. Klausner the idea of selling patent medicines in his shop. Mr. Klausner was doing a booming business while Mr. Gahrman was only getting by.

Of course, the Klausners were there, greeting Sister Theresa with enthusiasm. Little Theresa was the light of their lives. She was a healthy, lively five-year-old who called her "Auntie Sister."

Miss Alexandra Huntington, daughter of the judge, held onto the arm of a gentleman whom Theresa knew to be a wealthy mill owner from New England, visiting Hawai'i for business prospects. Alexandra glanced at Theresa but gave no sign of recognition.

Dr. and Mrs. Yates were in the crowd with their two children.

King Lot Kamehameha and Queen Emma sat regally under a fluttering canopy while the Royal Band played loud music. Theresa sat in a place of honor with Peter and Jamie Farrow. Sixteen years old and robust, Jamie had taken up sports such as sailing, canoeing, and riding the surf on a long board. As a result, his coloring was more Hawai'ian now, and Theresa saw how the girls looked at him.

He was ambitious now, too. When he had gained physical strength after the *ho'oponopono,* his mind had also gained new strength and now he suddenly had so much that he wanted to do. Foremost among his ambitions was going to law school and entering Hawai'ian politics, like his father. Jamie felt strongly that, by being both Hawai'ian and white, he would have the proper balance and perspective needed to properly guide Hawai'i's future.

Unfortunately, Emily Farrow's health made her unable to attend the arrival of the *Leilani.* She was at home, under Mrs. Carter's care.

Mahina, though invited, had not come. Nor had Chief Kekoa or any of the people from Wailaka. Theresa suspected they did not want to bring themselves to Dr. Edgeware's attention. All of Honolulu was aware of the health minister's intensified crusade to remove all lepers from O'ahu and send them to an off-island colony.

Finally: "There she is!" someone exclaimed, and the royal band struck up the tune of the United States national anthem, *America* (which, interestingly, had the same melody as both the Hawai'ian national anthem and the British "God Save the Queen"). The crowd erupted in cheers to see the mighty ship enter the harbor under her own steam. Outriggers raced out to meet her. Flowers and leis were tossed on the water as if to perfume her path. They saw passengers at the rails, waving and calling to those onshore. What an uplifting sight, and what a difference from the weary and seasick handful of nuns who had arrived by slow clipper with Father Halloran six years ago.

Leilani was a sleek three-master with a prominent bowsprit, but her sails were furled as she came in under her own steam, a long plume of black smoke streaming from the funnel in the center of the ship, a great sign of progress and the modern age. Theresa anxiously searched for Robert, whom she had not seen in months, but she could not see him as he was piloting the ship.

When the lines were secured and the gangplank raised, she saw him appear from the wheelhouse, looking smart in his marine costume of brass-buttoned naval jacket and white trousers, a white captain's hat on his head. He stood at the head of the gangplank, shaking the passengers' hands as they disembarked, to be greeted on the dock by young women draping leis over the heads of the new arrivals.

When a gentleman behind Theresa said to his companion, "Annexation to the U.S. can't be far off now," she scanned the vessels in the harbor and realized that while she saw only three British flags flying over other ships, and two French and one German, she counted forty American flags. The *Leilani* was the forty-first.

It startled her, and she wondered if Robert was aware that he had just been instrumental in bringing Hawai'i a step closer to the very action he opposed.

C ome with us, Sister," Jamie said. "You must!"

Theresa had to look up to meet his eye, he had grown so tall. "But it's a private family outing," she said, although she was pleased they were inviting her. In the years since Emily Farrow had come back to live with them, the Farrows had taken up the habit of going down to the beach for occasional excursions. Robert had said his mother loved walking along the shore. It seemed to clear her mind and restore her spirits.

"The woman who save my son's life is family," Robert said now.

Peter added with a smile, "After all, we *do* call you Sister." In the year since the brothers' *ho'oponopono* and reconciliation, Theresa had seen more of Peter in Honolulu, especially after Robert had left for the States to purchase the steamship.

They had just come back from a party at 'Iolani Palace, celebrating the arrival of the SS *Leilani*. All of Honolulu society had turned out—even Father Halloran had attended. Among the first passengers on the new steamship was a newspaper man from Sacramento. He was familiar with San Francisco, and Theresa was able to spend a few pleasant moments talking with him. He was in Hawai'i for six months, he said, to write a series of articles for his newspaper. Theresa was familiar with his work. His name was Samuel Clemens, although he wrote under the name of Mark Twain. She was pleased to tell him how much she enjoyed his story about the jumping frog. Although the day was warm, Theresa placed a woolen shawl around Mother Farrow's shoulders. She was enjoying one of her "strong" spells, in that she was able to leave the house, and able to walk with Robert's assistance. Emily seemed to grow more frail each day, yet her spirit and faith remained strong. She attended church on Sundays, and joined prayer groups with friends on occasional evenings.

The beach wasn't far, but they went by carriage.

When they arrived at Waikiki, with Robert and Peter helping their mother down to the ground, Jamie said, "I'm going to hunt for shells. I'm thinking of starting a collection."

"We'll help you," his father said.

"Oh, I'd rather I was the one to find them."

Theresa and Robert shared a knowing smile. Of late, Jamie had been making frequent mention of a girl at his school, named Claire. By the frequency with which he brought up her name, and the way he said, "Claire says this, or Claire says that," Robert and Theresa suspected the boy was smitten and that the hoped-for seashell was intended more as a gift for Claire than for a collection.

"You know, Robert," Emily said as they helped her down to the sand, "your father once flew an enormous Chinese kite for me on this beach. It was before your time, of course."

"That was in Hilo, Mother."

"So it was, but still . . ." Theresa knew why these excursions were such good tonic for Emily's body and soul—they reminded her of better times.

"When I was a girl in New Haven, we loved going to the shore and searching for treasure. We would find bits of glass and wood and shell. Jamie, see if you can find something from home along here. Something that traveled the thousands of miles from New England to the Sandwich Islands."

Home, Theresa thought as she walked at Emily's side. How strange that a woman can live in one place for forty-six years and still call another place home.

As for herself, Theresa was in high spirits. She had received a letter from her mother, informing her that Eli had returned to San Francisco and was joining their father in the family business. Another letter had arrived on the *Leilani* from Mother Matilda in San Francisco. She had written that, as tragic as the War Between the States was, something good had come of it: "Nursing Sisters in Britain and Europe heard the call and came to our shores to take care of our wounded soldiers, both Union and Confederate. I am told that religious Sisters now number in the thousands in America, with more girls joining every day. We are no longer curiosities in the streets, people no longer stare at us, and I have faith that our numbers will continue to grow and that we will continue to serve the Lord in the highest capacity."

She wondered if she could send Eva Yates' nursing textbooks to Mother Matilda, and what her reaction would be. Mother Agnes's reaction had been a negative one.

"But there is some wonderful advice and information in them, Reverend Mother," Theresa had said.

Agnes had pursed her dry lips. "The Sisters of Good Hope have been offering excellent nursing care since the Middle Ages. Our practices are based upon centuries of learning and making improvements upon the teachings of those who went before us. We do not need the experimental writings of newcomers and outsiders. Return the books, Sister."

But it had gnawed at her. Florence Nightingale spoke of the environment. She spoke of health reform. Sister Theresa thought of the Sisters' practice of closing windows in a sickroom with curtains drawn against sunlight and fresh air. She was beginning to suspect that what might work in cold, damp Europe would not work here in the breezy, sunny tropics. And Florence Nightingale promoted fresh air and sunlight.

She also recommended that the knowledge and skills of nursing care should be made available to the public, not just to nurses and doctors, so that people could help one another if professional care weren't available. Perhaps Mother Matilda in San Francisco would see the wisdom of pursuing these ideals.

It was a warm and cloud-free day, and the fivesome enjoyed a view of Diamond Head as they combed the beach. The gentle tradewind rustled palm fronds overhead, and they seemed to whisper, "Enjoy the day . . ."

Theresa and the Farrows were not the only white people on the beach. She noticed that many others had "discovered" this secluded spot not far from the mossy boulder called Pu'uwai, the heart of O'ahu. Several American ladies were enjoying the water, wearing bathing dresses that, thanks to Amelia Bloomer and her innovations in women's clothing, covered every inch of skin. With wide-brimmed bonnets and Turkish pantaloons under jacketed dresses made of heavy flannel, they were assured that not a speck of their white skin would be touched by the sun. Where the water was very shallow, the ladies undressed in little cabanas on wheels. Curtains surrounding the "beach side" of the cabanas allowed the soaking wet women to come out of the waves without being seen.

It wouldn't be long, Theresa thought with a trace of sadness, before Waikiki became a white man's beach and perhaps Pu'uwai would be dug up and removed to make room for a tourist hotel.

She looked out over the water, to see natives cavorting in the surf. She envied the Hawai'ians' freedom to swim clothing-free in the sea, instead of just enjoying modest dips as the white women were doing. Hawai'ians went into the water every day and spent hours in it—even Mahina's people at Wailaka, three miles from the ocean. They plunged into inland lagoons created by waterfalls and creeks. In public places they wore loincloths, even the women. But the ladies were admonished by the authorities to cover their breasts, and so they sought hidden coves where they could swim as the gods had done—in the nude.

Theresa had experienced it only once, and wished she could again strip off her habit and swim in the ocean. And suddenly she was in the grip of an impulse. She thought: Why not? It was all so very tempting. She could not resist! She removed her shoes and stockings, lifted her hems and waded into the water. As the water washed over her feet up to her ankles, she closed her eyes. The surf and wet sand were deliciously reminiscent of the creek back home

When she saw the Farrows staring at her in shock, she wondered if she had gone too far. And then Robert bent and pulled off his shoes and socks, hiked up his trousers, and joined her in the water. "It's been years since I've done this!" he said with a laugh. "By God, it feels good!"

As she walked at his side beneath the tropical sunshine, Theresa heard his words, spoken a year ago, echo in her mind: "Come away with me, Anna! Sail the seas with me. Let me show you the world! Oh, the places we could go, the grand adventures we could have, and I would love you every single second of every single hour of every single mile we sailed."

How she had wanted to cry, Yes I will go with you!

But she had vows and obligations and debts to honor. She wasn't her own person. She doubted she ever would be. But she would continue to love him, as he had promised to love her, and it was a silent, secret passion they both knew was doomed.

And so Theresa told herself she must be content with moments such as this, to be at Robert's side, if only to walk in the warm surf and look for seashells. *I will savor every moment for as long as they are given to me and I will ask for nothing more. . . .*

The five strolled along, scattering beach birds from their path. They picked through seaweed and driftwood. They were hailed cheerily by inhabitants of the huts who were working on canoes and surfboards. They saw youths climbing the slender, curving palm trees to knock coconuts to the ground. Peter's progress was a little difficult, as his cane slipped into the sand, but he managed to bend once in a while, pick something up, examine it, toss it back down.

After a time, Emily grew tired and so they turned back, with Jamie still in need of a gift for Claire. They climbed back into the carriage—Robert and Theresa wearing shoes and stockings again—and struck off for home, but when they neared the docks, they saw a great commotion going on along the wharves.

"What is it?" Emily said.

Robert brought the carriage to a halt and shaded his eyes against the sun. To Theresa's eyes, the scene was of wooden buildings, tall ships with masts and rigging, and a milling mob of what appeared to be angry people.

"Wait here," Robert said and he jumped down from the carriage.

Theresa watched as he pushed his way through a confusion of horses, wagons, people shaking fists. He was stopped by soldiers who barred his way with guns. Wooden barricades had been erected to keep the mob from swarming down to the dock. Beyond, Theresa saw a huddled mass of people—men, women, and children—holding bundles of possessions and looking frightened. They were surrounded by soldiers.

When she saw Dr. Edgeware appear from a small office in one of the buildings, she stepped down from the carriage and made her way toward Robert. Knocked about and jostled by the mob, she reached him and had to seize his arm to keep from getting swept away. "What is it?" she said. "What is going on?"

Dr. Edgeware did not acknowledge her as he said to Robert, "These people are lepers. They are being sent to an isolated colony on Molokai."

Now she saw more closely the wretched state of the pitiful cargo of over a hundred people, holding onto one another. They were a mixture of Chinese and Hawai'ian. There were no white people among them. And now she distinguished the emotions of the crowd—some were shouting their support of the new isolation laws, and were demanding that the authorities get the diseased people off the island as quickly as possible. Others were protesting this brutal treatment of people who needed a proper hospital. Threaded throughout the shouts and yells were mournful cries and calls of *"Auwe!"* as Hawai'ians begged Edgeware to let them take their loved ones home.

Theresa and Robert watched helplessly as soldiers marched the line of shuffling lepers onto a waiting ship. Everyone knew where they were going to be dropped: on a narrow strip of land surrounded on three sides by unfriendly surf and a two-thousand-foot wall of sheer rock at their backs. They would have no doctors, no nurses, no priests. Their isolation would be total.

When they returned to the carriage, Robert said grimly, "I'm sorry, Anna, I did not know. I've only been back a few days and haven't had a chance to get caught up on government business. King Kamehameha passed the isolation law while I was away. I have fought it for two years, and would have fought it this time, too. But I sailed to America and Edgeware saw his chance. Anna, Edgeware said he isn't going to give up his hunt for lepers until he has scoured every inch of this island."

Before he helped her back up into the carriage, their eyes met in silent communication: both were thinking of the secret leper camp north of Wailaka.

They rode in silence, their hearts heavy with sadness for the lepers they had seen the day before.

The wagon was loaded with supplies: blankets, clothing, food. Especially needed were the shoes and gloves, which they were going to have to convince the villagers to start wearing. Theresa had also brought special ointments, which she feared would do little good, yet she had to try something.

What had once been the secret hiding place of a solitary boy was now a secret leper camp of thirty individuals.

Robert and Theresa rode past the village, where they saw torchlight and heard voices and drums, but no laughter. Here, Robert paused to look back down the road, to make sure they hadn't been followed. Dr. Edgeware had intensified, with his soldiers, his ruthless hunt for lepers. But Robert saw no one. They continued on.

They rode past the path that led to the secret fertility grove. They kept going on a rutted track that made their wagon rock and creak and stall in places. When they could advance no further, Robert cupped his mouth and called out. They waited, and presently they came—like ghosts from out of the forest, weak, shuffling creatures who walked as if ashamed of their very existence. Mahina was among them, of greater stature than her companions because she was not sick. At her side, a weakened Liho limped. He had lost the toes on his right foot.

The boy who had ridden the ocean waves like a young god, who had been cured through *ho'oponopono,* was dying, and this time there was no cure.

Theresa gave Mahina the ointments, saying, "Make sure you check for cuts and burns every day. They cannot feel such injuries anymore. Apply this ointment to prevent infection. And try to get them to wear shoes and gloves, for it is the fingers and toes that are affected first."

Theresa retrieved the oil lantern from the wagon and lifted it up to Mahina's face. Her skin was clear and without blemish. Theresa touched Mahina's nose. "Can you feel this?"

"Yes."

Theresa examined her fingers and pinched them. She still had sensation. As yet, Mahina did not have leprosy. But there was a great melancholy about her. The joviality Theresa had known in her for six years was gone. Mahina said, "The night Pele took my mother was the night the curse began. We have no hope, Keleka. The gods have left us. For a thousand years, and another thousand years, the healing stone from Kahiki kept my people well. We were without sickness. And then Pele took the healing stone and now we will all die. Tomorrow, there will be no more kanaka."

"Mahina, why did your mother sacrifice herself to the mountain?" Theresa needed to know, she needed to understand what was eating away at the souls of the people, causing them to die in alarming numbers.

"Mahina not know, Mahina never know. The night my mother walk into Pele's fire, she say she sacrifice to lift curse. But it never work. Curse still upon us. Before she walk into Pele fire, my mother say, the day come when babies torn from mother's arms. Husbands and wives torn apart. Brother taken from sister, and daughter taken from father. They go across the water and we never see them again! Auwe! That is the end of Hawai'i nui. That is when Pele destroy all the people. Now Mahina know. The leper colony. This my mother's prophecy." She bowed her head and shook it from side to side. "My mother, great kahuna *lapa 'au*, High Chiefess, descendant of the great Umi. She see future. She see end of kanaka."

Mahina turned away while the others accepted the supplies and blessed Robert and Theresa before they disappeared back into the night.

CHAPTER TWENTY-FOUR

Robert sent a message to the convent. Emily Farrow had taken a sudden turn. Mother Agnes gave Sister Theresa permission to go.

Mahina opened the front door of Farrow House, and explained that Jamie was at the ranch in Waialua, and that there was no time to send for him and Peter.

While they waited for Dr. Yates and Robert to come downstairs, Mahina asked Theresa about Western doctors. How are they chosen? How do they learn medicine?

Theresa said, "Men who wish to become doctors, in America and Europe, go to school. They take classes, read books, train in hospitals. Afterward, they might apprentice with an established physician to gain more experience, or open up their own practice."

"How long they in school?"

"Six months, a year. It depends on the school."

"And how old when they start?"

"About age twenty or so."

She frowned heavily over this, working her lips in and out of her teeth. "And wahine?" she asked. "Same for *wahine*?"

"Women can't become doctors."

"Why not?"

"I don't know. They just aren't allowed."

Mahina thought some more, then said, "In Hawai'i, healers are men and women. But they not choose. It is *kahuna kilo 'ouli*—character reader, like Uncle Kekoa—who choose. He come to family hut and sit with children. He drink *'awa* and chant while holding sacred *ti*-leaves. He ask each child many questions—what month and day and hour he was born, what omens at the moment of his birth, what dreams he had, what were his good luck signs. All through night. When everyone too tired, the *kahuna kilo 'ouli* finally point with the sacred *ti*-leaf and say, 'This boy will build canoes. This boy will be bonesetter. This girl will be kahuna lapa 'au. This was Pua, my mother. He said she would be a High Chiefess and learn the ancient art of healing."

They both looked up at the ceiling when they heard muffled voices. Theresa wondered how serious it was.

"Pua seven years old," Mahina said, "leave her family to go live with supreme *kahuna lapa 'au* in Puna. There she learn all the kapu—the rules of what to say, what not to say, what to eat, what not to eat, what special prayers to say, which gods to please. Pua must remember everything her teacher tell her. She learn all the magic and healing of the islands, all the secrets of bad magic and evil spirits and how to chase them away. She study all the parts of the body and how to cure their sicknesses. She learn plants and animals and all the treasures of the sea. She live with her teacher many years, and when gods say Pua is ready, a great ceremony is held and my family sees Pua again for first time. The ritual goes on for days, and the kapu must still be observed. If Pua eat the wrong food, if she step on wrong mat, she is outcast and no one look at her again. In this ritual, she is taken into heiau and allowed to look upon sacred stone of Lono. No one but healing kahunas may look upon Lono's Penis. Anyone look, he die.

"But my mother now kahuna lapa 'au. She allowed to touch the sacred Lono stone, and place a lei on him and pray to him."

She smiled. "That is how kanaka doctors are made."

Theresa rose and paced. Dr. Yates was a pleasant young man, but was he competent? She had spoken of medical school just now, but in truth any man could call himself a doctor and carry a black bag. There were no official rules, no governing body to regulate a profession that held life and death in its hands. Theresa wondered why that was.

More Western medical men had come to Hawai'i and yet the

native population continued to shrink. The secret leper colony above Wialaka had received nine more victims. For all their science and knowledge, Western doctors were helpless against so much disease. Mahina had told her that in the days before the arrival of the white man, there was little illness in these islands. Theresa wondered if that was true. Or if such health could be attributed more to their beliefs than their way of life. Mahina spoke of the sacred stone her mother had hidden somewhere near Kilauea Volcano, thirty-six years ago. Although Theresa believed a stone was simply a stone, what mattered was what the Hawai'ians believed of it. If you think a stone can keep you healthy, then perhaps it can. Certainly Mahina's son, Polunu, had thought that death-words could make him die.

Robert and the physician finally came into the parlor. Dr. Yates said, "I have given her arsenic. Her color and stamina will improve over the next few hours, but it is a temporary measure only. Nothing further can be done, I'm afraid."

They went upstairs where Robert's mother lay among white sheets. Dressed in a white nightgown with a white cap on her head, the pale woman could hardly be distinguished against the linens.

She asked Mahina to come forward. "I need you to forgive me."

"For what?" Mahina said gently, with a smile. "You no hurt Mahina."

But Emily Farrow seemed agitated. Theresa wondered if it was the medicine. "Before I stand in judgment before the Almighty," Emily said in a raspy voice, "I must make reparations here on earth. I know you believe in forgiveness, Mahina. *Ho'oponopono.* That is what I need before I meet my Maker. I cannot stand before the Almighty in a state of sin."

Theresa was puzzled. Emily Farrow was a pious, God-fearing woman whom she doubted had committed a sin in her life. But she seemed to need to get something off her chest.

Emily drew in a labored breath. Her face was the color of chalk. "We came to these islands with the best intentions, and our accomplishments cannot be denied. In less than forty years we taught an entire race to read and to write. We gave them an alphabet and grammar. We created schools. We taught them to sew, to plant, to be self-sufficient. We found these islanders a nation of half-naked savages, living in the surf and in the jungle, eating raw fish, fighting among themselves, slaves to feudal chiefs, and living in sin and carnality."

Emily paused, her chest lying dormant for a moment, then she opened her mouth and struggled to draw in a deep breath.

"Now they are decently clothed, they recognize the law and sanctity of marriage, they know arithmetic and something of accounting. They go to school and church. The more elevated of them hold seats on the judicial bench and in the legislature, and fill posts in the local magistracies."

Another pause for breath.

"All my life," she continued, "from earliest girlhood, I wanted only to serve God. And when I heard about savages who had never heard of Jesus or the Gospel, I was consumed with a burning desire to deliver these precious things to them! But unmarried women were not allowed in the Mission, nor were unmarried men. I married a distant cousin, Isaac. But I never loved him. And then I met MacKenzie Farrow and my heart surrendered."

She plucked at the bedclothes with frail hands. "You have to understand . . . the loneliness of those years! I was the only white woman for miles, surrounded by strange, savage women whose ways I could not comprehend. I could not eat, from the loneliness. My throat closed up with loneliness, my stomach turned to stone with it."

"Mother," Robert said, sitting on the edge of the bed. "Don't tire yourself. You need rest."

"No, son, I must speak." Her filmy eyes did not meet her son's, but wandered above his head, as if she were telling her story to the ceiling.

"Isaac was gone for days, sometimes weeks, while I endured empty hours and an empty bed. I filled my time with busywork—teaching them sewing and English and writing and reading. I would gather the women every day, such as those I could find or who were inclined to join me, and I would sit them down and read from the Bible and tell them about Jesus and God. And I would look past those brown faces, past the huts where dogs and children ran wild, I would look at the path that emerged from the trees that would bring my husband home. The yearning was unbearable . . . not for Isaac, no, never for him. But for Captain MacKenzie Farrow. I would go for walks in the afternoon to stand on the cliff and watch for ships, praying that the sails on the horizon were his. . . ."

She closed her eyes, and her lungs seemed to search for breath.

A smile lifted her lips as she said, "I had never known such happiness was possible. I had never known such *love* was possible. MacKenzie was my breath and soul. I was incomplete without him. And so when the Board said that if I married a sea captain I would be dismissed from the Mission, I chose MacKenzie! I gave up my first love to be with my second love. I turned my back on God for carnal reasons. That is why He punished me. That is the reason for the events that took place in the summer of 1830, what other reason could there be?"

"Mother, please—"

"They're here, Robert," she said with urgency. "They've come for me. Don't let them take me! I am so afraid!"

"Mother, there's no one here but Sister Theresa and Mahina."

"The ghosts . . . Sorrowful phantoms who cannot rest. They demand that I tell the truth. I never told anyone. I never told MacKenzie. But I have to tell it now. That night, in the summer of 1830, when it was so hot and humid, and the volcano was spewing lava and noxious fumes, and the earth trembled and shook. That night, I burned with fever. My chest was severely congested. I could not breathe. I was in the throes of influenza. And then I heard thunder. It hurt my head. I needed to find the thunder, to silence it somehow."

The three listened in silence to a startling narrative, Robert's face going white, Theresa's throat tightening in sadness and sympathy, Mahina trembling beneath her flowing muumuu. Breezes came through the French doors while Emily spoke, and the three pictured the spectacle of that hot night thirty-six years ago. . . .

Emily's skin on fire, her nightgown drenched. She had chills and sweats and aching muscles. Although she was greatly weakened from days of coughing, she needed to find the thunder. She looked in on Robert and Peter, and saw that they slept like angels. She stumbled out into the night. The other mission houses were dark and silent, as her neighbors slept through the noise. She staggered toward the native village and found it deserted. She had never seen it thus before and wondered where the people were. She managed to make her way down a dirt path between taro patches, until she came to the edge of dense forest. She pushed in, tearing vines and green growth from her way until she came to a clearing, and there were all the villagers.

Beneath the full moon and flickering torchlight, they were engaged in their lewd dance called hula. *Emily knew some of the women. They came to her church. Isaac* had baptized them. They called themselves Christians but they were naked. To the beat of island drums, they made lascivious moves. Emily was sickened by the swaying, naked breasts with large, prominent nipples. The men with their sweating, muscled bodies, their genitals barely covered, slapping their chests and thighs, stomping their feet as they barked loud, manly grunts. Animals, Emily thought in horror. They are no better than beasts.

But she could not move. She felt strange, hot emotions flood her body. Fresh aches that had nothing to do with illness gripped her. They felt primeval. She felt as Eve must have felt before being cast out of the Garden. Emily felt desire. She felt sexual yearning. She felt lust. She wanted to tear off her nightdress and join them in the dance.

Filled with self-disgust and revulsion, Emily bolted into the circle of light and screamed at them to stop the depravity. She ran from drummer to drummer, hitting them, kicking their drums until they toppled, until the dancers stopped and the night fell silent.

Then she saw what was on the altar and she could not believe her eyes. She had seen it before, when she had looked into the heiau. The stone, which they called Lono's Stone, was an abomination. She had thought it destroyed, as other idols had been destroyed, but there it was, on an altar, draped with flowers. She shouted at the natives. She told them that they had turned their backs on Jesus. But Pua smiled and said, "No, this is not about Jesus. We make new babies."

A more depraved and degenerate sight Emily had never seen. Naked women dancing in a most disgraceful way around a stone carved like a man's member. It crazed her. She became a lunatic. She lost all reason and sanity. What sort of wicked land was this that women danced naked to obscene stones?

Emily picked up a spear and ran to the obscenity on the altar, intent upon smashing it to bits. She swung, but in her weakened state did not strike hard. The obscenity toppled and fell off the altar, landing on the grass. She shouted at the natives that they were going to burn in the eternal fires of hell for what they had done.

Emily, in her nightgown, spun in a circle to look each of the offenders in the eye, men and women with whom she had taken meals, who sat in her meetinghouse on the Sabbath. "I wanted to befriend you! I wanted this to be an adventure. I wanted to be brave. But you made me feel weak and cowardly. You reminded me that I don't belong here. That I am a New England woman born and bred. I hate you for that. You stole my dream and threw my flaws back in my face."

She pointed at each as she cried out, "You are not Christians anymore! Jesus hates you! He does not want your souls. He gives them back because you are not worthy of God's love."

As the natives stared at her in stunned silence, Emily Farrow screamed, "Jesus Christ has put a curse upon you—all of you!"

Warriors rushed at her. Emily swung the spear in a circle until she was so dizzy she nearly fell to the grass. And then there was a shrill cry and everyone stopped. Silence filled the glade. Emily saw Pua standing there with her arms raised, her skin glowing in the light of flames. She called out words that Emily could not understand, and in an instant everyone fled. Before Emily's unbelieving eyes, they vanished into the forest, leaving her alone with spears and drums and a satanic altar with the obscenity lying on the grass. . . .

"Friends found me the next morning," Emily said to her audience of three, "wandering at the edge of the forest. I was told that I burned with fever for three days, delirious, crying out in a jumbled speech that no one could understand. After I recovered from the influenza and was prepared to put the nightmare of the hula ritual from my mind, the local natives began falling ill. One by one, those who had been in the clearing when I said that Jesus didn't want their souls, became stricken with an illness that no one could diagnose. We sent for a doctor from Honolulu who did his best to help them, and the missionary wives—as well as those from Kona—worked night and day to nurse the natives back to health."

She paused as tears rolled from her eyes. "But they died. . . . Each and every one who was in that clearing that night perished and nothing could be done for them. Over a hundred men and women, moaning on their mats while their families prayed and wailed and wept. After they were all buried, Chiefess Pua came to my house and told me that it was my curse that had killed her people. They could not be cured because they knew they were condemned to death by Jesus. She turned her back on me and that was the last I saw of her."

Emily fell silent but the others didn't move, didn't speak.

"Robert," she said, squeezing her son's hand. "I knew about the power of the spoken word and the people's susceptibility to things that were said to them. I was irresponsible in my speech. I should not have said what I did. But the resentment had been simmering for ten years. I blamed them for making me aware of my failings, when I should have blamed myself."

"Mother—"

"I blamed them, Robert, and resented them for exposing my weakness. It wasn't their fault. For ten years I kept my resentment buried, but when I burned with fever, I lost control. In that moment, I hated them for not having fulfilled my naïve dream. I knew the power of the spoken word. It was as if I had I taken a pistol to that clearing and fired. I killed those people."

Emily turned to Mahina and said, "Forgive me, I am the reason your mother sacrificed herself to Pele. I am the one who sent her into the fiery lava."

Mahina cried out, beating her breast and shouting, "Auwe!"

Theresa watched helplessly as the Hawai'ian woman slapped herself and pulled at her hair and cried out. What Mahina had learned just now was a secret beyond comprehension. She had not been there that summer night thirty-six years ago when Emily, burning with fever and loneliness, had gone out among the natives and did what she did. Mahina had not known what drove her mother to walk into Pele's fire. But now she knew and it was worse than anything she could have imagined.

"That was when the ghosts started haunting me," Emily said as she struggled for breath. "Their torture was endless. They tried to kill me. One strong spirit chased me out to the cliffs one night where he tried to fling me to the rocks below, but I struck him and the ghost fell into the sea."

Theresa gave Robert a look. He met her eyes and she saw surprise there. What he had believed for so long to be an act of murder turned out to be not so after all. The two brothers had lived in the terrible belief that Emily had purposely pushed MacKenzie Farrow to his watery death. But now . . . she hadn't known it was her husband whom she had pushed.

Emily spoke with diminishing strength. "Do you think I can be forgiven for such a monstrous crime?"

"In the asking is forgiveness," Sister Theresa said.

Emily looked at Mahina, whose face was twisted with sorrow. "My dear, I am so sorry for what I did. I was unprepared for that life. I was not strong. I need your forgiveness before I go to God."

Robert and Theresa watched the gigantic Hawai'ian woman with long white hair contrasting her copper skin. They thought of the lepers she was caring for in a secret camp, sacrificing her life to make theirs more comfortable. They thought of all her losses—mother, husband, sons, and daughter—and they marveled that her heart had remained so big and loving.

Robert choked back a sob. He knew that Mahina had been there the night he was born and Pua had laid him, minutes old, on Lono's altar for a blessing.

When Mahina did not respond, Emily said, "Please know that I came to these islands in love. I came for aloha but followed a crooked path. Forgiveness will set me on the right path again."

Mahina came slowly to the bed and looked down. They were close in age, but the small white woman seemed so much older. "You kill my mother," Mahina said in a low tone. "You kill my people. You take healing stone from us."

There was nothing so blood-chilling as the sound of Hawai'ians wailing in grief. Mahina lifted her arms heavenward and released such a howling cry that Theresa feared she might wake up the whole district.

Emily began to cry. Deep, racking sobs that Theresa would have thought her frail body incapable of. Robert looked at his mother with a woebegone expression.

Mahina fled, taking her shrieking wails with her. They heard her heavy body thunder down the stairs and out into the night.

Theresa stayed with Robert as he held his mother in his arms. Presently, she grew quiet. She closed her eyes. Her breathing grew irregular. She struggled for breath. Theresa saw, beneath the closed lids, her eyes move rapidly back and forth. She was not at peace. Was she seeing her invisible demons?

Robert started to cry, his tears falling on her white nightcap. When Emily grew still, Theresa could detect no heartbeat. "I'm sorry," she whispered.

When Robert lifted anguished eyes to her, her heart went out to him. He rose from the bed and wordlessly took Theresa into his arms. He held her tight, his face buried in her black veil. She felt his body shake with dry sobs. She cried with him. Emily Farrow was taken by the Lord at the age of sixty-six. And with her passed an era the likes of which this world would never see again.

But something good had come out of this night as well. Drawing

back, Theresa took Robert's anguished face in her hands and said,
"Your mother was not insane. Her spells of mental instability came
from that night. They were nightmares driven by feelings of guilt.
Remember that, Robert. Keep that in your heart. Your mother had
burned with fever. She was delirious. She didn't know what she was
doing. And out of that, she imagined ghosts haunting her. But that
was all it was, Robert. Imagination compounded by insomnia. She
wasn't insane."

He nodded mutely. He knew what she was saying, and he thanked
her for it. Through the darkness of his grief and sorrow, Robert saw
the light of hope. If his mother wasn't insane after all, then Jamie was
free.

CHAPTER TWENTY-FIVE

An agitated crowd had gathered in front of the courthouse, the word "Kilauea" on everyone's lips.

Sister Theresa couldn't climb the steps to the entrance, the throng was so dense. Not a man stood without a newspaper, each reading aloud from the many reports pouring out of the beleaguered island of Hawai'i where, six days prior, Pele had awakened from a long sleep to remind the islanders that she was as mighty as ever. The eruptions were accompanied by earthquakes, a destructive tidal wave, and a strange rising and falling of the sea. Everyone was saying it was an omen portending disaster, a sign spelling the end for the dynasty of the great Kamehameha. The crowd was worried. Many had friends and relatives on Hawai'i Island. "I heard that up to a thousand shocks were counted in one night!"

"Where is the new lava coming from?"

"Fissures are opening up everywhere!"

"They're saying that the heaviest damage is in Kau. An avalanche fell on a village and thirty-one souls and 500 head of cattle were buried instantly."

"A new vent's been reported near the 1830 lava flow."

"Theresa!"

She turned to see Robert pushing his way through the crowd. "Sorry

I'm late. I keep getting waylaid by people wanting to know what the government is going to do about the earthquakes." He shook his head. "As if we had control over that! Come on. I'll take you to the rear entrance. Only members of the legislature can go through the front entry."

After months of crusading for the cause of lepers, writing letters to the newspapers, writing to the king and his ministers, pleading with the bishop, talking to anyone who would listen—after doing what she could within her limited power to create a leper colony here on the island of O'ahu and bring them back from Molokai—Theresa had finally appealed to Robert, who said he would lay her case before the members of the legislature and propose new laws governing this disease that was finding more victims every day.

The legislature met daily from eleven in the morning until four in the afternoon. The sessions were held in the Supreme Court room, as stately a chamber as any found in America or Europe, with flags, royal portraits, tall windows admitting sunlight onto a wood-paneled room with a judge's bench, a speaker's pulpit, rows of seats and desks for the members, and a wooden railing separating the lawmakers from the visitors' gallery, where Theresa was to stand.

There was no demarcation between the Nobles or the Representatives, but all sat as a body, between forty or fifty men (the natives outnumbering the whites). The king's ministers—Englishmen, Americans, and one Frenchman—sat in thronelike chairs at the far left wall of the assembly. She saw Robert sit at his desk, with his back to her. She found a spot among the visitors, who were all men, kanaka and haole, and all talking and smoking.

Presently the chaplain opened the session with the Lord's Prayer, first in English, then in Hawai'ian. Roll call was taken and, understandably, the Representatives from Kau, Puna, and Hilo districts were absent. Only the man from Kona represented the Big Island. Following this, as Robert had warned her, was an hour of men taking turns to rise from their desks to propose a new act, to rebut a point of law, to table an ongoing debate, to call for a vote, to question a member's meaning, to propose a bill, to challenge a recent ruling, to complain about insufficient pay, to discuss a measure—all in such a hodgepodge fashion that Theresa wondered how the clerks and reporters could keep up with it all.

It was a noisy, almost chaotic affair, with members arguing amongst themselves, or snoozing with their heads on their desks, all smoking (pipes, cigars, cigarettes), spitting tobacco, munching on snacks of cheese and crackers, and peeling oranges while ignoring the various speakers. A representative from Maui was "recognized" and given the floor. He was a native in Western attire, requesting a clerk for the sheriff of the island, with a salary of one thousand dollars. A discussion followed, the request was granted, and the gavel went down.

Theresa's heart raced as she waited for Robert to choose his opportunity. All her hopes and plans rested on what he said here today.

Although in the year and a half since Emily had died, Theresa had had little occasion to visit Farrow House (Jamie had grown into a big strapping 18-year-old almost as tall as his father, and so she no longer had patients there), she had not lost touch with Robert. Because Mother Agnes allowed her to continue to visit Mahina's people at Wailaka village, Theresa often encountered Jamie there, visiting his Hawai'ian relatives. And she met secretly with Robert at the village, from where they took the wagon to the hidden leper colony to dispense supplies and to treat the patients as best as she could in her limited capacity.

Robert and Theresa had not spoken of their love since the night they had cured Jamie with the *ho'oponopono* ritual. But when he looked at her, she saw the desire in his eyes, she sensed his longing, his wish to overstep bounds and forget vows and honor. But, out of respect, he held back, as she held back.

And she yearned for him now, as she stood in the visitors' gallery.

As she was wondering when Robert was going to speak, suddenly there he was, rising to his feet and asking to be heard. Younger and taller than those around him, better dressed and with a more dignified bearing—to Theresa's mind, anyway.

The Speaker of the House recognized the "Representative from Honolulu, Third District," and gave him the floor.

Theresa would never cease to be amazed, and moved, by Robert's impressive skill for oratory. While most members had murmured and coughed and snored and chomped into apples during other members' speeches, as soon as Robert rose to his feet, the chamber fell silent. Everyone wanted to hear what Captain Farrow had to say.

But when he began by addressing the issue of a leper colony, an undercurrent of grumbling and displeasure rippled through the chamber.

"Yes, in the beginning," Robert said in a commanding voice, "the Royal Board of Health provided the quarantined people with food and other supplies, but it did not have the resources to offer proper health care for them. Everyone in these islands knows that the leper colony has become so abandoned and wretched, and with such appalling living conditions, that the lepers cry, *'Aole kanawai m keia wahi*—In this place there is no God.'"

Dr. Edgeware, Minister of Health, rose, cleared his throat, and said, "Everyone knows that we are taking all necessary steps to ensure the safety of the lepers." Tall, thin, and bony, Theresa thought that everything about him seemed narrow, including his politics.

"Everyone knows exactly the opposite," Robert shot back.

"Captain Farrow, you bring up an issue that has been debated endlessly, examined and studied, voted on, and is now law. Please do not waste our time with an old problem that has already been solved."

"I would say the problem is far from solved, Sir. The inhumane treatment of the victims of leprosy is appalling and a disgrace to this kingdom! We don't even allow visitors to sail anywhere near the island of Molokai, for fear they will discover Hawai'i's dirty secret."

"You are out of place, Captain Farrow!"

"And you shame the title of Minister of Health!"

The Speaker banged his gavel and a thunder of shouts and insults suddenly filled the chamber. When the Speaker got everything under control, Edgeware said, "My Lords and colleagues, let us put it to a vote right here and now—"

Theresa could not keep silent any longer. She stepped to the wooden railing and said, "My Lords, please hear our plea. We speak for those who have no voice."

Edgeware leveled a cold gaze at her. "Then why don't you go and help them, you care so much?"

It was a topic that had already been discussed at length in the convent house. While the Bishop of Honolulu believed that the lepers needed a Catholic priest, he realized that the assignment could become a death sentence. Hence he had announced that he would not assign anyone to the task. Instead, he would call for volunteers. So far, no one had. And Mother Agnes said the Sisters were not to get involved.

Theresa said, "Establishing a leper colony here on Oʻahu would alleviate the terrible isolation and suffering of the poor lepers."

"I believe there already is a leper colony here on Oʻahu, is there not?" he said pointedly.

The chamber fell so silent, as everyone awaited her reply, that she could hear a fly buzzing high on one of the windows.

"Come come, woman. We know there is a secret camp where lepers are being harbored. I instruct you right now to give us the location of that camp."

As a religious Sister, she was unused to speaking in public. But, thinking of the poor sufferers in the hidden camp north of Wailaka, she found the courage to say, "Why has everyone turned a blind eye to the terrible conditions on Molokai? The area is void of all amenities. There are no buildings or shelters. No fresh drinking water. The people live in caves and in the most rudimentary shacks built of sticks and dried leaves. When they arrive by ship, they are told to jump overboard and swim for their lives. Some drown, some are eaten by sharks. The crew throws their supplies into the water, relying on currents to carry them ashore. Women on their own are grabbed by men on shore and dragged off to be assaulted."

"Rumors and lies," Edgeware said in a flip manner. "I order you again, young lady, to tell us the whereabouts of the renegade lepers."

"What she says is true," Robert interjected. "My own ships' officers have observed these loathsome actions on the transport ships. You cannot turn a blind eye to it, sir. And let me ask you a question, *Mr. Minister of Public Health*," Robert added in a louder, more commanding voice. "When was the last time you personally conducted an inspection of the colony on Molokai? Or have you *ever* visited there?"

An eruption of "Hear hear!" filled the chamber so that it was some minutes before order was restored.

Theresa gripped the railing. "Dr. Edgeware, *please*. The dwindling of the Hawaiʻian race is alarming. At last count, there are only 49,000 native Hawaiʻians; and if the decrease is not arrested, in a quarter of a century there will not be a Hawaiʻian left!"

"And I suppose you have a miracle cure for this problem?"

"Yes. Lift bans on native practices, such as hula and chants to the old gods."

An uproar erupted in the gallery and the Speaker had to bang his gavel several times before the din quieted.

Edgeware chuckled and said, "You can't be serious. Surely even a Catholic wouldn't condone the reprisal of such satanic practices."

"Western medicine is not saving the Hawai'ians," she said, and received a smattering of applause and cheers from the gallery. "Their only recourse is to their own traditional methods."

Edgeware waved a dismissive hand. "Hawai'i wishes to move forward and enter the modern age and be recognized among all the world's powers as an equal. You would have us turn back the clock. Now stop wasting the precious time of this august assemblage and tell us the location of the secret leper camp."

"Sir, how can you, a physician, criminalize illness? You have made a crime of this disease, punishable by exile to a prison that is a living death."

"Young lady, I will have you arrested and put in prison if you do not disclose the hidden leper camp!"

They were interrupted in that moment by a court clerk who went up to Dr. Edgeware and murmured something to him. "Your Honor," Edgeware said, addressing the Speaker in the pulpit. "May we break for a five-minute recess?"

"This is most irregular, sir."

"It is a matter of the utmost urgency."

A few members called for the argument to go on, while others agreed that a recess would be fine. Theresa went outside for some badly needed air, where she found an agitated Mother Agnes informing her that she had brought instructions from Father Halloran and the bishop that Theresa was to reveal the location of the hidden camp.

How they had received word so quickly of the debate in the legislature, Theresa did not know, but she told Mother Agnes that she could not tell them where the camp was. She would go to prison first.

Mother Agnes appealed to Captain Farrow, who had joined her outside. But he said, "I stand with Sister Theresa."

Mother Agnes tried to think of something to say. But it seemed Robert Farrow had all the power. Three years ago, when she had told

Theresa she was to return to San Francisco, Jamie Farrow had experienced a miraculous cure to his mysterious malaise. The next day, Mother Agnes had received a surprise visit from Father Halloran to inform her that Robert Farrow had gone to him in agitation about a rumor that Sister Theresa was to be sent back to the mainland. "He offered to donate a great deal of money to the Church," Father Halloran had said to Mother Agnes, "and the promise to support Catholic interests in the legislature in exchange for my intervention in the deportation of Theresa."

Although Mother Agnes had really wanted to send Theresa home, Father Halloran had said that part of the money was to go to the convent, and Mother Agnes was tired of struggling to make ends meet. One stipulation was that Theresa herself would never know any of this.

They were called back inside and Theresa was prepared to continue to press for a leper colony on Oʻahu when Dr. Edgeware surprised her. With a smug smile, he said, "You are no longer needed for questioning, young woman. We have found the secret leper camp above Wailaka. They've all been rounded up and are being taken to the docks as we speak."

Robert and Theresa literally ran, surprising pedestrians and carriage drivers as they flew down King Street to the docks. They saw soldiers forming a cordon around a group of frightened natives. They were all from the Wailaka camp. Theresa saw poor Liho among them, Tutu Nalani, and all the rest. She did not see Chief Kekoa.

But Mahina was among them. Theresa dashed forward, breaking through the soldiers, and went straight into Mahina's arms.

When soldiers tried to grab her, Robert ordered them to step down. Recognizing Captain Farrow, and his authority as a member of the legislature, they backed off.

Theresa frantically looked around. A large crowd had gathered on the dock. Many were natives from Wailaka village who were wailing and weeping. And more were arriving, as word spread that Mahina—daughter of High Chiefess Pua and one of the last of the aliʻi—had been rounded up with lepers. "Who's in charge here?" Theresa shouted. "This woman is not sick."

"No no, Kika," Mahina said. "I go. Be with family."

"But Mahina, you aren't sick. You don't have leprosy."

Mahina couldn't put into words the feeling of responsibility and duty that compelled her to go. Because she was influential with the kanaka, even the Christianized ones, and because she had told them not to work for haole on their big plantations where they would be exploited, the growers had had to import labor from elsewhere. Because of this, the importation of Chinese to the islands had commenced in 1852—and with them had come leprosy. Mahina believed it was her fault that the leprous plague had broken out among her population.

"Mahina go take care of them," she said. "Who take care of Liho?"

The poor boy had worsened since the first signs had appeared. He had lost fingers and toes, the tip of his nose was gone, and his face was in the early stages of deformity.

Theresa searched the faces of these people whom she had grown to love, and she thanked God Jamie had not been visiting his Hawai'ian family when the roundup had taken place, but was safely in school at O'ahu College in Punahou.

"No cry, Kika Keleka. This meant to be. Hawai'i Nui coming to end."

Theresa could not help the tears. Her heart was being torn by the pitiful sight of how they huddled together, frightened, knowing they were being sent to a living grave. "What do you mean?"

"Big Island shaking now. Big Island falling into sea. Pele angry. Pele destroy all islands. Chiefess Pua say this many years ago. She see it. When we go to Molokai, Pele wake up and destroy Hawai'i."

"Mahina, you can't give up!"

"Poor Kika Keleka," Mahina said, stroking Theresa's face. "So sad. You good heart. You good aloha. Don't cry for Mahina."

Theresa turned to Robert. "If these people believe their blood will die out, then they will succumb and allow it to happen! Just as Polunu did. Just as the natives did after your mother said Jesus cursed them. We have to stop them from fulfilling Pua's prophecy. How can we convince them that this isn't the end of their people?"

"I haven't a clue. Other than a mass *ho'oponopono* ritual—"

"The healing stone!" Theresa cried. "If it is restored to the people, they will believe they can be saved!" She turned to Mahina. "We need to find the healing stone and bring it back. Where is it?"

"No no, Kika! Kapu! Gods punish you!"

"It won't make much difference if Hawai'i is going to be destroyed anyway. Think! Where did your mother hide it?"

Mahina frowned. "Too long ago. Mahina too frightened. Pele very angry."

"Would Uncle Kekoa know?"

She thought for a moment, then she nodded. "Uncle Kekoa know where to find Pele's Womb. You find stone. You take to Wailaka. Keep village healthy. Lono Stone keep Chinese sickness from Kekoa's people."

Dr. Edgeware arrived with a military escort. "Why aren't these people in the quarantine camp?" Theresa cried. "Surely you aren't sending them to Molokai *today*?"

"They have been quarantined long enough," he said dryly.

"For God's sake, man!" Robert shouted. "You're treating these people like animals."

"For *God's* sake?" Edgeware said coldly. "I'm thinking of the sake of the citizens of Honolulu. The sooner we ship these people off the island the safer it is for everyone."

Edgeware waved to the captain of the steamer, and the soldiers began herding Mahina and her people to the gangplank. The moaning and wailing grew louder, and a few tried to resist. But the soldiers overpowered the victims and pushed them onto the boat.

"Robert, can't you do something?"

He shook his head grimly. "In this case, Edgeware has full authority. Theresa, he's right. For now, we have to think of the healthy population. I won't let the matter of an O'ahu colony drop. I'll convince them, I promise. We'll find land, isolated enough so that we can contain the spread of the disease, but with access to family and friends. We'll fight it, Theresa, I promise."

Tears streamed down her face as she watched Mahina, with her long flowing white hair, her statuesque form draped in a red muumuu, walk onto the boat with pride and dignity. Theresa whispered, "Aloha," and silently promised her that she would bring her and her people back to O'ahu.

Dr. Edgeware turned to the lieutenant of the cohort. "Arrest that woman," he said, pointing to Theresa. "She is charged with harboring lepers."

A soldier grabbed her arm but Robert stepped in, seizing the man by his other arm, swinging him around. "Let go of her!" Robert shouted, and when the soldier refused, Robert curled his hand into a fist and slammed it against the man's jaw, sending him reeling backward. Turning to Theresa, he said, "We have to get out of here."

"Robert, take me to Wailaka."

Edgeware stepped in their way and Robert, with a curled fist, growled, "Move aside or I'll give you the same."

Dr. Edgeware smiled and stood aside. "There will be an arrest warrant for the Catholic woman within the hour."

They ran to the row of carriages for hire and jumped into the first one.

The village was deserted.
"They're all down at the harbor by now," Robert said. "They'll camp out on the beach and wail all through the night."

"I didn't see Chief Kekoa among them."

They went from hut to hut. Theresa looked into the women's quarters while Robert checked on the men's. They had even taken their pet dogs. All that moved in Wailaka village were a few chickens.

"Kekoa's hut is empty. I mean, everything is gone. His ceremonial robes, helmet, *kahili*—all personal items."

"He wouldn't have gone to the docks with all that."

"No, he wouldn't." Robert looked around at the silent huts, the smoldering fires. The settlement had a feeling of having been abandoned and Theresa wondered if the people would come back. There had been leprosy here, and the old ways. Perhaps, with Mahina gone, the remaining natives would join the rest of the kanakas in embracing Western culture.

"There might still be a few around," Robert said. "Maybe they went into hiding when the soldiers came. We have to find them."

It was not easy, in the darkening jungle now that the sun was setting, to conduct the search, and after an hour they gave up. They had moved northward, into the foothills that began the gradual climb up to the Pali. "Wait," Theresa said, stopping when they reached a small clearing that she recognized as the place where the fertility hula had been performed. She recognized the flat stone with the petro-glyphs depicting human sex acts. "What's that sound?"

Robert paused to listen. He turned slowly. "I hear it. But . . ."

"Is it a bird?"

He stopped and looked off into the distance, over the treetops to a rocky outcropping several hundred feet above them. "There!" he shouted.

Theresa looked up and saw, silhouetted against the pale dusk, the figure of a man. He stood with his arms outstretched, and he was chant-ing—loud and in a high pitch, and in such a mournful way that she thought it was one of the most beautiful sounds she had ever heard.

"It's Kekoa," Robert said.

Now she saw the cape of yellow feathers, the high, curved helmet. He had anchored the sacred *kahili* into the ground. His voice carried on the wind, it echoed off the steep cliffs and swept through koa and ohia trees. It startled birds, causing them to fly up out of the forest and wing across the darkening sky.

It was a long, lonely chant of old. Theresa imagined the thousands of people who would have stood in this forested valley to listen to their great chief, to receive his blessings and the blessings of the gods. But the only people to witness it now were two haole.

Finally, his voice died, he lowered his arms, and he stood very still.

"My God," Robert murmured. "Kekoa is standing on the very spot where he fought side by side with Kamehameha the Great during the battle for O'ahu."

"Shall we go up to meet him?" Theresa said quietly.

But before Robert could reply, Kekoa leaned forward and flung himself off the precipice. They watched in horror as his body bounced on boulders below, and then off another edge, tumbling, twisting, like a broken doll. They saw his head fly off and then his body plunged into a gorge that was a thousand feet deep.

Theresa screamed and covered her face. Robert pulled her into his arms.

"It's wrong!" she cried. "It's all wrong!" She pulled away from him, ripping the rosary from her belt and flinging it to the ground. "This is all meaningless!" She yanked at her veils, tearing them. She pulled at her sleeves, she wanted to strip herself of all the meaningless trappings of a world that had betrayed her.

"It's all wrong! Everything is backward and upside down! Why are we here? My God, what have we done? What have I done?"

Robert took her by the shoulders and said, "You have done wonderful things here, Theresa. You have saved lives. You have given people hope. You gave me back my son. And you made me realize that my mother wasn't insane after all."

His grip tightened. "Theresa, listen to me!"

But she wouldn't listen. She struggled against him. "Theresa!" he said, seizing her wrists. "Look." He was pointing to the night sky.

She looked up and saw, across the face of the gibbous moon, a rainbow of wondrous colors. She blinked. She wiped the tears from her eyes. And as she stared at the miraculous sight, she thought: Mahina is gone. And now Kekoa. The last of their line are *Alaheo pau'ole*—Gone forever.

And she knew beyond a doubt that it was Chief Kekoa's spirit they were looking at in the rainbow, and that he was sending her a sign.

She took her eyes away from the rainbow and filled her vision with an even more miraculous sight—the handsome face of Robert Farrow. After tonight, she would never see him again.

And so she wanted to say good-bye without him knowing it, for if he did, he would do his best to prevent her from leaving.

She suddenly understood something, on this night of revelations: before she could know who she was or what she was meant to do, she must start over. She must be reborn. Not as a nun or a nurse, but as a *woman. . . .*

She lifted her chin and he lowered his head until their lips met.

Her veils and skirts came away with ease, and then the starched linens and the wimple. She felt vulnerable yet on fire, as they stood in Eden among ancient ferns and flowers.

"How is it . . . how is it?" Robert asked as he took her face in his hands. "How is it that you walk into the huts of lepers and bathe their sores . . . how do you straighten broken bones and clean up sickness, and see a side of life no one is meant to see except those it's happening to . . . how do you witness the tragedies and inequities and unfairness in life and yet remain untouched, still hopeful, childlike?"

Her tears tumbled over his fingers. And then tears streamed down his own face until they held each other and silently cursed the destinies that had been assigned to them at the hour of their births. Because she could not go away with the man she would love always and with every breath she drew for the rest of her life.

He lowered her to the grass and they lay entwined in a jungle glade beneath the light of a rainbow-moon.

The night air was heavy with dampness and fertile scents. Giant hibiscus—scarlet and bright yellow—nodded on thick stems, dewy leaves swaying in the tropical breeze.

Robert could hardly bring himself to touch her, now that the cumbersome habit was off and he saw her as she really was, a little doll with ivory skin. "My God," he whispered, "you are so small, so pale." She still wore the linen coif that encased her head. He pulled it off to expose surprising red-gold hair, thick and wavy and shoulder-length.

Theresa closed her eyes and sighed beneath the tender fluttering of his hands on her body. *Just this once, my love,* she thought, *and then I will be gone from your life forever. . . .*

She had never known such desire, such sweet aching. The world and all its people no longer existed. The pain she had felt over witnessing Chief Kekoa's death became consumed in a raw passion that was new and exciting. She touched his chest. She squeezed the muscles in his arms.

Robert bent his head and kissed her neck. She moaned. When his hand cupped her breast she gasped. She arched her back and opened herself to him.

"My God," he groaned, "I love you so much. I have wanted you since the day I first saw you."

And I, you. . . .

The night was filled with nocturnal birdsong. Nearby, a stream trickled over stones. The symphony that was Hawai'i. Theresa drove her fingers through Robert's hair and brought his face to hers. When his lips touched her mouth, she thought the fires of Pele had invaded her blood. She had never known such heat, such wanting. She perspired in the cool air. She heard groans of desire escape from her throat. No sexual fantasy had come close to this reality.

His tongue startled her. She was learning as they went along, and Robert was a patient teacher. With each new, sudden gesture and sensation, she hesitated, then mimicked. When his hand reached down for her moist place, she parted her thighs.

It is so right, she thought. How can this be a sin? How can it be forbidden? It is what the gods created us for.

And when he entered her it wasn't startling at all but the most natural and delicious feeling in the world. He held himself up on elbows, as if afraid she might break, but Theresa pulled him to her, to feel his damp chest against her bare breasts. His breath was hot on her neck. She wanted to cry out with joy.

As he filled her with his hardness, she began to feel a new sensation that made her lift her legs and wrap them around him. A hiss of pleasure escaped her throat. Oh my dearest love, her mind cried. My dearest Robert . . .

A wave of pure ecstasy lifted her up, like a warm wave cresting at a beach, and it carried her high on a ride so sweet that she thought she would die from the joy of it.

They lay entwined, exhausted, damp with perspiration, the night air on their bare skin. Theresa marveled at this man who held her in his arms, his power and strength, but his tenderness also. His eyes were closed, his breathing deep and slow. She wondered if he was asleep. He was so handsome in the moonlight. She gently ran her fingers through his hair, and kissed him lightly on the lips. This is what it is like to be married, she thought. Having the luxury of enjoying each other in private and peaceful quiet. "I love you," she whispered and closed her eyes to savor her last moments with him.

A cloud sailed across the moon. Mist rolled in. Chill crisped the air. Robert woke from his brief slumber to look at the pale beauty in his arms. She seemed so vulnerable and fragile, innocent and helpless, and yet only hours ago she had stood up to one of the most powerful men in the kingdom. She had pushed through a line of armed soldiers and had shouted in protest. Her fragility was deceptive. This woman was stronger than most men he knew.

"Wherever I go, my love," he murmured against her cheek, "I see your face in the moon, I hear your laughter in creeks and streams, I see your eyes in rainbows. You are my compass and anchor, the wind that fills my sails. Your depths and mysteries are as the ocean's, you are the golden lighthouse in a storm. You breathed life into me when I thought I was dead. You gave me purpose and strength and hope. How can I live without you?"

She stirred and opened her eyes. "Hold me," she said, and he pulled her tightly to him. She clung to him as if she were drowning. And then she said, "Robert, I am going to search for the healing stone. I will go to Hawai'i Island and find it and bring it back."

He raised up on an elbow and looked down at her with stormy eyes. "Kilauea is wreaking havoc on the island. It is dangerous. Jamie and I will search for the stone for you."

She offered him a sad smile. "You and Jamie can go with me."

"We'll take the afternoon steamer."

"Yes." *But I will be on the earlier one, that departs at eight o'clock in the morning. . . .*

As she looked up at the moon following its ancient, eternal path across the sky, she thought that when the heavy veils came off, and the confining starched linens were flung away, when there were no more bells or hours or rules, all that remained was truth. In the clarity of that moment, as she lay naked beneath the Hawai'ian stars, as surely as Eve had in the Garden of Eden, Theresa knew what she had been called to do.

To bring *ho'oponopono* to Mahina's people. To make things right. To go to Hilo alone, to find the healing stone and take it to the lepers on Molokai.

It was past midnight when Theresa let herself in through the garden door. Mother Agnes was waiting for her.

"You made a spectacle of yourself today, and of our Order," Agnes said. "I have tolerated your impossible behavior for eight years but I will no longer. This time, I assure you, I will not change my mind. I do not care how much money Captain Farrow gives to the church, Sister Theresa, your actions are drawing scandalous attention to the Sisters of Good Hope. You leave for San Francisco on the first ship that sails."

"No, Reverend Mother," Theresa said calmly. "I am going to the island of Hawai'i."

"I forbid you to leave this house."

"Mother Agnes, thirty-eight years ago Emily Farrow was burning with the fever of influenza, and in her delusional mind she cursed a group of Hawai'ians who had converted to Christianity. She told them that Jesus hated them. In the days that followed, they all died. To mollify Pele, a high chiefess walked into lava and set herself on fire."

"Merciful heaven," Mother Agnes whispered, crossing herself.

"And now I need to bring the healing stone back to Mahina's people, and restore their hope and faith in their future."

"It will be suicide," Mother Agnes said bitterly. "All day, we have heard news of the terrible quakes and lava flows on Hawai'i Island. I cannot let you go into such danger."

"I will go," Theresa said softly. "I must. Reverend Mother, you know that I have questioned our effectiveness as nursing Sisters. Perhaps we should allow the natives their ancient rituals, for those were what kept them healthy before the white men came. Have we the right to tell the natives how to conduct their lives? If prayer can be a healing tool for Christians, then can't the same be said of Hawai'ians' prayer in the form of the *ho'oponopono* ritual?"

"It isn't prayer that heals, it is God. And God has nothing to do with heathen ritual. Whoever prays without directing that prayer to God is praying to *nothing*."

"How do you know, Reverend Mother?"

Their eyes met in the silence of the convent, of Honolulu, while the stars over Hawai'i embraced them.

"In eight years," Mother Agnes finally said, "you have broken the law, thumbed your nose at authority, kept secrets, failed to report incidents of leprosy, went your own way when you thought it best— you even wrestled with desires of the flesh and I daresay you might have even given in. You are as headstrong as you were the day you donned the postulant's veil. You are intractable and, quite frankly, a handful."

When Theresa started to defend herself, Agnes held up a hand. "I envy you. I have since the day you came to our convent in San Francisco and asked to be admitted into the Order. I envied you because you knew what you wanted out of life. To be a nurse. And in order to do that, you were willing to give up everything. I have known it all along,

Sister Theresa, the sacrifices you made. I envy you your courage to follow your convictions no matter what. You see, I don't have an imagination like you, I don't have drive or vision. I need rules, I need hours and bells. I need to be told what to wear and when to pray. I don't know what it's like to be a free spirit . . . and then to give up that freedom to follow a destiny."

She said, "Let us kneel and pray together."

"There isn't time, Reverend Mother."

"Daughter, I fear I have let you down. I knew you were struggling with your vows and your conscience. I should have been more of a help. I should have guided you more. Please forgive me."

"There was nothing you could do. Since the day my father delivered me to the convent in San Francisco, eleven years ago, I have been an outsider. In a way, I have dishonored you and my Sisters because I have been living a lie. I owe the Sisterhood a great debt. You took me in, you clothed me, put a roof over my head and food on my table. You educated me beyond anything I could have hoped for outside the Order. And so I will honor you by going to Molokai to take care of the lepers, in the name of the Sisters of Good Hope."

"What are you saying?"

"Reverend Mother, I joined the Order for reasons other than a desire to serve God. I have struggled with this for eight years. I can no longer wear the symbols of your sacred calling. It would be hypocritical, and disrespectful of this Order. Mother Agnes, I honor you and my Sisters. I will not sully your trust with secrets and lies."

"Think what you are doing!" Agnes cried when Theresa began to remove her ring. "To break your solemn vows—"

"Forgive me, Reverend Mother, while the Sisters of Good Hope do remarkable things, there is so much more that can be done. Florence Nightingale's book opened my eyes. You say we do not need the experimental writings of newcomers and outsiders. But I believe we must listen to them. I know deep in my soul that I can offer so much more. But here, I am under constraint. I cannot turn my back on those who are in need."

As Mother Agnes looked on in sorrow, Theresa methodically removed the wedding ring, the rosary, the veils. When she was done, and standing only in her white shift, her red-gold hair standing out in tangles, she said, "I am no longer Theresa. I am not worthy to carry the name. I am Anna again."

There was a duffel bag full of clothes in the parlor, donated by parishioners to be distributed to the poor. Mother Agnes watched as Anna went through them, finding a day dress that fit her. She stood silently, hands clasped within her wide sleeves, as Anna slipped the dress over her head and did up the buttons that closed the snug bodice from her waist to her neck.

The top buttons were missing and so the collar fell open to expose her throat. Tears streamed down Mother Agnes's face. She could not say why she wept—or if they were tears of sadness or joy. The transformation from Theresa to Anna overwhelmed her.

"My dear, be careful," she said. "Soldiers came to the convent this evening with a warrant for your arrest. They are searching for you."

"Thank you, Reverend Mother. I will be careful. I am going to write a few letters before I leave for the steamer. There is a book among my things, *Walden*. Could I ask you please to see that it is returned to Farrow House?"

"I will see to it," Agnes said in a tremulous voice. "And I will pray for your safe return."

For the first time in years, Mother Agnes embraced her and Anna felt the gentle touch of Agnes's kiss on her cheek.

As she watched the Mother Superior wearily climb the stairs to her bedroom above, Anna could not help but ponder the chain of events set off by Emily that summer night, thirty-eight years ago. If she had not burned with fever. If she had stayed in her house. If she had not happened upon the secret hula ritual and the sacred stone. . . .

Many Hawai'ians might not have died because of her ill-chosen curse. She would not have been plagued by visions of the dead. She would not have pushed MacKenzie to his death. Robert would not have had to give up the sea and perhaps he and Peter could have been friends all these years.

But then, Jamie would never have been born. Anna would never have met Robert.

The workings of fate and destiny would never cease to amaze her. Our actions have more consequences and far-reaching effects than we know, she thought as she sat at the parlor's writing desk. And who is to say these effects will stop after I find the Lono stone? Perhaps the events of 1830 will continue to reverberate down through the years and touch the lives of people not yet born. . . .

The harbor was bustling with morning commerce as passengers arrived at the docks to depart for various destinations, or people came to greet an arriving ship, stevedores loaded and unloaded cargo, captains barked orders—a hub of maritime industry.

Anna knew which dock the inter-island steamer departed from. She had taken care as she had made her way through the early morning streets, to make sure that no soldiers spotted her. Now she paused at the dock, seeing redcoats here and there, with their muskets. But they would be looking for a nun in black and white. She knew they wouldn't recognize her.

When she found the dock, she saw Robert standing beside the gangway, smiling at her. He was casually dressed in a loose flannel jacket and trousers, with a canvas rucksack slung over one shoulder. His smile faded as he looked her up and down and the significance of the pale blue gown, with the tight bodice and full skirt, the collar exposing a pale throat, dawned on him.

"Did I cause this?"

"No, Robert. I have emerged from a dream. A very long dream. I have made my peace with God. My own *ho'oponopono*."

"I had a feeling you were going to try to do this on your own. I'm coming with you, Anna, so don't protest. I think we'll find the cave near the 1830 lava flow."

"Robert," she said, as he started to go up the gangway, "Mother Agnes said you gave money to the church to keep me in Hawai'i. Is that true?"

"She wasn't supposed to tell you. But, yes, it's true. I was going to move heaven and earth to keep you here. And now I suggest we hurry. I explored a lot of Hawai'i Island in my youth. I know the boundaries of the 1830 lava flow. But with all the seismic activity that's been reported, and fresh lava flows, the cave might not even still be there. It could have collapsed or gotten covered in lava."

"Let's pray it's still there!"

They ran up the gangway, hand in hand, but when they reached the top, they heard an authoritative voice shout, "Stop right there!"

They turned to see Simon Edgeware striding through the crowd on the dock, with soldiers in redcoats. "You!" he cried, pointing at Anna. "I thought you might try to run away. But you should know by now that I have eyes everywhere. Come down, young woman, you are under arrest."

But Anna remained where she was, standing on the deck at Robert's side, looking down at the Minister of Public Health with a resolute expression on her face.

He stared up at her, frowning over the change in her appearance, trying to figure out what had happened, what was happening.

The deck of the steamer was crowded with natives traveling to the other islands. They sat among their possessions, along with pigs and dogs and crates of chickens. A man in a uniform pushed through and said, "What's going on here? We have to cast off. We have a schedule to keep."

"You may cast off," Robert said.

"Now see here!" Edgeware shouted, turning red in the face. "I have a warrant for that woman's arrest."

But Anna remained defiant, standing above him like an avenging angel, her red-gold hair flying in the breeze to create a blazing halo around her head.

Edgeware shifted on his feet. He looked right and left, and then back at Anna. The tight-fitting bodice outlined the curve of her breast, the narrowness of her waist, with the skirt flaring at her hips. She was no longer a meek, shapeless, and subservient nun, but a *woman.*

He was speechless.

Dockworkers pulled the gangplank away while sailors cast off the last line and signaled to the skipper of the steamer to get underway. The engines chugged to life, smoke billowed from the stack, and the mighty paddle wheel started turning.

Robert and Anna left Edgeware standing wordlessly on the dock, growing smaller as the harbor receded from view.

CHAPTER TWENTY-SIX

"Mamy God," Robert said as he stood in the bow of the SS *Bird of Paradise* with other passengers. Maui had dropped far behind them, and the Big Island now drew near. All were silent as they saw enormous clouds of steam rising from the surf where lava was pouring off the cliffs to boil the ocean below. Smoke and volcanic gases filled the sky. Up and down the coast, fires raged as villages burned.

As they chugged into Hilo Bay on choppy water, they saw a crowd on the dock, men and women and children, laden with bundles and boxes, carrying pigs and dogs and chickens, clamoring to get off the island.

The steamer pulled up to the dock and stevedores ran up to catch the lines. Anna saw a portly man in shirtsleeves standing on a box shouting something at the panicked mob. Able-bodied seamen with clubs kept the crowd back.

"That's Clarkson," Robert said. "He's the dock agent. His grand-father was the dock agent when my mother first arrived here."

"Ahoy!" Clarkson called up to the wheelhouse of the *Bird of Paradise*. "How many can you take on?"

The First Mate surveyed his crowded deck and shouted back, "Just six and no animals!"

As the gangway swung into place, the crowd on the dock surged forward and Clarkson raised a pistol in the air, firing straight up, a crack so loud it stopped the mob in their tracks. "Only those who can pay!" he shouted. "And we only take coin!"

"Bastard," Robert growled as he and Anna disembarked. "Profiting from people's fear. What those poor devils don't know is they will have to pay again once they get on board."

People wailed and begged to be let through. Mothers held babies high in the air, hoping for priority. An old man hobbled on crutches, pleading with Clarkson to let him on the ship. But only those who could produce coins and drop them into his fat hands were allowed to pass.

As soon as the fortunate six were on board—two men and four women, all kanaka, clutching their few possessions—and the crowd strained at the dockworkers, threatening to overrun the vessel, the gangway was pulled back and the steamer's great air horn sounded. The paddle wheel began to turn and the steamer pulled away. The skipper had told Robert in advance that it would be a quick port of call, just as it had been up at Kona, because of people desperate to get off the island. The *Bird of Paradise* would make landfall at the much less populated southern tip of the island, to take on fresh water and wood for the engines.

"It's been eighteen years since I was last here," Robert said as he and Anna pushed through the crowd to get to the dock agent, who was counting his money. "That's when my father died and I moved the company headquarters to Honolulu. A lot has changed. Clarkson will know where we can get horses."

The dock agent's eyes widened. "Why, bless me, it's Captain Farrow! Been a long time, sir!"

"We need horses and quickly."

He scratched his scruffy jaw. "Your best bet would be Jorgensen. He's just up the road, if his stable is still standing. A lot of horses got spooked when the tremors began. Ran off. Owners can't find them. Where do you plan on going?" he asked, eyeing Anna in frank curiosity.

"South of here, in the Kahauale'a forest."

Clarkson released a long whistle. "That's a mighty dangerous area. Too close to the caldera. You looking to rescue someone?"

"Something like that."

"I don't recommend it. Lot of hot activity around there. New vents popping up all over the place, like sinkholes. Liable to swallow you up."

They found a town in chaos, where people milled about in terror, searching for lost loved ones, asking after escaped animals. Many of the wooden houses in the town had collapsed into rubble. People wrapped in blankets and looking frightened squatted in front of flattened homes. A makeshift camp had been erected in the center of town, opposite the small town hall and government offices, where missionaries were offering cots and distributing food and clothing to people who had no where to go.

Jorgensen's Livery was still standing, although the proprietor, an immigrant in his late sixties, was so rattled that it took some minutes before Robert could make their needs known.

"A horse?" he said, his eyes blinking owlishly. "I only got one left. The rest, they ran off after the first earthquake. Thank God my wife is visiting her sister on O'ahu. They say the island is going to sink into the sea!"

"A horse, please, we are in a hurry."

"Yes, of course."

As Jorgensen set about to tacking up the mare, searching through equipment that had fallen from the walls and rafters—the stable looked as if a tornado had raced through—he found a bridle and handed it to Robert.

"It started in the middle of the night," Jorgensen said, picking through a tangled mess of straps and reins and leads, "lava suddenly burst out from the ground in Kahuku and flowed rapidly down to the sea. They say that a fissure a mile long opened up, disgorging lava, spouting jets high into the air, burning the forest and spreading out a mile wide."

He found the leather breastplate and handed it to Anna, who helped Robert with the horse. "The way I heard," the old man said, "the flow separated out into lateral streams on the grassy plain while the main flow poured into the sea, causing the waves to boil with great violence. A ranch with thirty head of cattle was overrun and destroyed, but the family managed to escape in just their nightshirts. Then the earthquakes started—"

The ground gave a sudden jolt. "Not again!" Jorgensen cried.

"We need to hurry," Robert said, and helped the old man to strap the saddle on.

Once the horse was ready to go, Robert hung his canvas rucksack on the pommel, then he mounted and leaned down to pull Anna up behind him. She held on tight as they galloped away from the town.

They raced past small wooden houses and grass huts, following a narrow path between cultivated fields. Then the dwellings were gone while the countryside grew denser and greener, and Hilo fell far behind. To their right, beyond the rain forest, great plumes of smoke and gas rose up to the sky, while to their left, up ahead, they saw massive steam clouds erupt from the boiling surf where the lava poured into the sea.

Robert brought the horse to a halt and said, "Pele's Womb is somewhere in there."

He pointed at the edge of a forest so dense that it looked to Anna like a solid green wall. "The way Mahina described it, the cave is at the edge of the 1830 lava flow. We just have to find the field and search in the neighborhood." He shook his head and added, "But there are a lot of old lava fields in there."

The ground gave another strong jolt and Anna saw a flock of red and blue birds, perhaps a hundred of them, suddenly fly up from the forest and head out to sea.

"Hang on!" Robert shouted and they plunged into the trees.

Anna pressed her face against his back as they raced through branches and sharp leaves and hanging vines. Through the trees she saw bare patches of ground—ancient glassy lava, splintered into pieces with green ama'u ferns struggling up through the cracks. They galloped through clearings where the horse's hooves made a sharp clattering sound on stretches of old lava where seedlings flourished and the brittle surface of the hardened lava was crumbling, turning into soil. They came to another open space where Anna saw more green growth, shoots and creepers that were the beginning of a young forest now covering what was once a bleak field of lava. Looking at the waist-high ferns and 'ohelo bushes putting forth berries that were sacred to Pele, she thought: The lava, once destructive, has now produced a new forest.

The earth suddenly rose and sank beneath them like the sea in a storm. Rocks tumbled around them, boulders split apart. "Look!" Anna cried. Wild boar had burst from the trees, squealing in terror. Robert struggled to control the mare as the large beasts with fearsome tusks ran past them.

They proceeded forward again, more slowly, as Robert tried to find space between densely packed flowering ohia trees, the prickly red lehua blossoms brushing Anna's arms.

When the ground shook again, the horse reared, nearly throwing them. "We have to let her go!" Robert shouted over the noise of the rumbling earthquake.

He helped Anna to the ground, untied the rucksack, pointed the animal in the direction of Hilo, and watched it gallop away. "She'll find her way home," he said.

As they continued on foot, upward on the gently rising slope, over mossy ground, the earth swayed to and fro with everything crashing about them, the trees thrashing as if torn by a strong rushing wind. They heard an explosion and saw, through the trees, a fountain of lava burst from the ground less than a hundred yards away, spewing rocks high into the air. Robert quickly pulled Anna to the safe cover of a thick banyan tree and waited for the end of the raining debris. From there, they could see the ocean. They stared in horror as the tide suddenly withdrew from the shore, rushing back to the ocean to leave bare, wet sand. A moment later a gigantic wave rose up a mile out to sea, to rush back to land and crash over the cliffs and run inland, a swift, deadly tidal flood sweeping away everything in its path.

Robert and Anna ran. Through moist ferns and vines and creepers, thick damp branches and dewy leaves. A forest of green and mist. The ground moved beneath their feet. Rumbling, shaking.

Anna fell.

Robert pulled her up and held her arm as they ran.

The mossy soil under their feet trembled and shook. Nearby, something roared. The acrid smell of sulfur filled their nostrils. The shaking grew stronger. They could barely stay upright, as if forces were determined to knock them to their knees.

Then they saw, just yards away, the molten river emerging through a fissure with a tremendous force and volume. Before their terrified eyes, four huge lava fountains boiled up with fury, throwing rocks high into the air. They were knocked off their feet. The heat was so intense that green plants around them rapidly grew brown and withered. Behind them, far below, they heard screams, and the violent hissing of a boiling sea. While great dollops of lava, having been spewed into the air, came down around them, they pressed on.

"I don't think we're going to make it!" Robert shouted, and at that moment the ground swayed and a giant lehua tree snapped at its base and came crashing down inches in front of them. "There's no way around this!"

Anna looked up at the sky, at the rolling black clouds of volcanic gas, she gagged at the stench of sulfur, felt the heat of Pele's wrath on her skin. And she remembered something . . .

"We have to find a way through," Robert shouted as he dug into his rucksack and brought out a hunting knife. As he began to hack at thick branches, Anna looked at the moss beneath her feet, saw how ferns trembled, how leaves shook.

She thought: This is Pele's home—an island old beyond counting. It knows nothing of new ways. It demands to be honored in the old way.

But what was it . . . ? She tried to remember. Something she had learned from Mahina.

Yes! That was it!

Anna held out her arms and let her head fall back, as if she were about to execute a swan dive. As she kept her face to the sky, with her eyes closed, she began to chant in a high voice: *"Aloha mai no, aloha aku . . . o ka huhu ka mea e ola 'ole ai . . . E h'oi, e Pele, i ke kuahiwi, ua na ko lili . . . ko inaina . . ."*

Robert turned and looked at her. He recognized the chant and the stance from a ritual Mahina had performed many times.

Anna sang louder, over the roar of the earth. *"Aloha mai no, aloha aku . . ."*

She slowly lowered her arms, the words tumbling from her mouth. Now she made gestures as she sang, punctuating phrases with sudden, precise, and fluid jabs and stabs with her hands.

Anna crouched suddenly, her eyes still closed, and waved her hands over the rocky ground. *"E h'oi, e Pele! i ke kuahiwi, ua na ko lili . . . ko inaina!"*

Robert watched in awe. He had seen skilled dancers, had heard professional chanters all his life. Anna was doing a damn good job of imitating them. Had Mahina been secretly teaching her? Her chant was perfect, with glottal stops and elongated vowels in all the right places, her hands doing their own dance as her fingers fluttered over the lava, tapping the hard rock.

And then her voice died and as she slowly rose and opened her eyes, she and Robert looked around and realized that the shaking had stopped.

"Hurry," he said, reaching for her hand. "We can climb through these broken branches."

They fought their way through sharp branches and cutting leaves and when they emerged, Robert pointed up ahead. "Look!"

Anna stared in wonder. One would never have guessed that in the heart of this vast, dense rain forest there lay a barren black lava field miles wide. She had never seen such a bleak landscape. Not a tree or shrub, not even a blade of grass broke the endless sea of hardened lava. She could only imagine what it had been like, a rolling red river, giving off unimaginable heat.

"This is the 1830 flow," Robert said. "I'm sure of it."

Where Pua had walked into Pele's fiery blood and sacrificed herself in a column of flame.

"The cave will be somewhere along the perimeter. This way."

They stayed in the trees, keeping the vast lava field to their left. The air grew thick with smoke as the wind shifted and stirred the gases and fumes from several vents. Anna wondered if there was one nearby, if she and Robert were going to pass through the next wall of trees and find a red, burning river on the other side. As Robert hacked a path with his knife, holding back branches for Anna to pass, she glanced frequently at the old lava field and saw, here and there, patches of grass and vegetation where, in 1830, the lava had separated and traveled in a circle to embrace untouched forest.

Might that happen to Robert and her? *Will we find lava running in front of us, but when we turn, will we find it has circled around us, trapping us?*

They came to a small clearing where moss carpeted the ground and emerald ferns grew like plants from a fantasy. On the other side, a curious grassy hillock squatted among the trees. "That could be an old lava tube," Robert said.

Anna scanned the unusual rock formation, rising from a flat

forest floor, with no other hills nearby. It was covered in ferns and sweet, flowering bushes, and vines and creepers, which Robert hacked away at until he exposed a gaping black maw.

"Is this the right one?" Anna asked.

"It fits Mahina's description. A cave large enough for people to enter without having to stoop over. I hope it's stable."

"The tremors have stopped."

He listened, then smiled. "Whatever it was you did, Pele seems appeased. For now. We'd better hurry before she wakes up." Robert removed his canvas rucksack and brought out a lantern. He lit the flame and stepped cautiously into the cave.

It took a moment for their eyes to adjust. The cave was dark and dank, but there was enough room for them to walk side by side, and the ceiling was high.

"According to Mahina's description," Anna said, "Lono's Stone is tall, carved from soft lava, and polished to a shine. It is very explicit in shape and meaning."

Robert swept the lantern light over rocky walls and found the sacred artefact perched on a natural shelf. "It's still here," he said.

"Mahina said there was something else in this cave. Something kapu that she wasn't supposed to look at."

Robert moved the light over the walls, ceiling, and floor. "I don't see anything."

"Wait," Anna said. "What was that? Bring the light back. . . .There!"

"Where? I don't see anything."

They ventured deeper into the cave until they reached a crevice in the wall. "Here it is," Anna whispered. "What Mahina saw when she came into the cave. The highest kapu."

Robert moved the light inside, the flame quivering over the bones and objects that had been buried with them. The remnants of a cloak made of yellow feathers. A high, arched helmet. Spears. The wooden idol of a god.

The skull. The long bones.

"Good Lord," Robert whispered, "is that—?"

"Chief Kekoa was one of the young men who sailed away with Kamehameha's body, to bury him in secret so that no one would find him and steal his mana."

"*Ka iwi kapu*—the sacred bones," Robert murmured, stunned to realize that they were standing in the presence of Hawai'i's most supreme symbol: the legendary hero himself, King Kamehameha the Great.

And then Pele woke up.

A powerful tremor jolted the region, and debris rained down in the cave. Robert and Anna started to run, dirt and grit pouring down on them, when the ceiling suddenly gave way and came down in a thunder of rocks and boulders. When the shaking stopped and the air cleared, they saw that their way was blocked completely so that not even a sliver of daylight showed through.

"Anna, you're bleeding," Robert said, lifting the lantern to examine her forehead.

"It's all right," she said, "just a small cut. It looks worse than it is." Ripping the lace cuffs from the ends of her sleeves, she wadded them into a ball and pressed it to her forehead. "Robert, how are we going to get out? We can't move these rocks!"

He ran the lantern over the chunks of ancient lava that had created a new wall, pressing here and there, pushing at stones, searching for a weak spot. Then he stepped back and surveyed the whole of it. "I see only one way out," he said, pointing to the largest of the boulders. "If we can somehow roll that away, we'll have a hole we can crawl through." He rubbed his face, which was covered in soot and grit and perspiration. "The thing is, it won't budge."

He thought for a moment, then said, "Archimedes."

"I beg your pardon?"

"An ancient Greek who said, 'Give me a lever and a place to stand, and I shall move the Earth.'" Robert looked around the cave, sweeping the lantern light over the walls. "A lever amplifies an input force to provide a greater output force, so all we need is—"

"What are you doing?"

He had slipped inside the crevice, and Anna heard him moving things around. When he emerged, he was holding a long, thick rod. "The old king's spear. In amazingly good condition. If what the Hawai'ians believe is true, that a person's mana is in their possessions, then we should have Kamehameha's power working for us. Now we need a fulcrum, which should be fairly easy to find."

The ground trembled, as if Kamehameha were protesting the

prosaic use of his royal possessions. Or perhaps, Anna thought, he was voicing his approval that his mighty spear would be put to such valiant use. Lono's Stone lay on the other side of the rubble. If she and Robert couldn't get out, then they wouldn't be able to return it to Kamehameha's people.

Setting the lantern down, Robert rolled a stone into place, positioned the spear, moved the stone back, repositioned the spear. He did this several times until he announced that this would be their best shot. Wedging the tip of the spear under the lava boulder, he pushed down on the other end.

Nothing happened.

He pushed down again, straining until his neck veins bulged. Still no success.

Anna ran to help him, standing in front of him so that, on his count, she pushed down with all her might. Fearing the spear would break, she increased the pressure while Robert, behind her, pressed down until he groaned.

And suddenly the boulder moved, shifted, and then with one last push, they rolled it all the way out, exposing a large enough opening for them to crawl through.

But when they were on the other side, they couldn't find Lono's Stone. It had been buried by the collapsing ceiling.

The ground started to shake again, in a sickening, rolling motion that felt like the sea. Robert and Anna stayed where they were, despite more dust and grit spilling down from above as they frantically dug into the rocks and boulders.

"Here it is!" Robert cried. "And it's undamaged!"

Anna pulled the last of the rocks away while Robert gently pulled the lava phallus from underneath.

The earthquake increased in magnitude. "Run!" Robert shouted as he held tightly to the Lono stone. The ground shook so violently he was nearly knocked off his feet, but he dashed through the entrance right behind Anna, and at that moment the entire cave came crashing down.

With a roar and an explosion of rocks and dust, the ancient lava cave collapsed entirely, sealing it off forever.

Anna waited on the upper verandah. She stood next to Robert's brass telescope, but she wasn't looking out to sea. She was watching the road that came from 'Iolani Palace, where Robert had spent the past four days conferring behind closed doors with the king and the few ali'i left in the islands.

After leaving Hilo and buying passage on a crowded steamer where they kept to themselves, protecting their priceless treasure, Robert and Anna had said little. They were exhausted, and the experience of the volcano had left them numb.

Upon returning to Honolulu, Robert had insisted she stay at his house—where else could she go?—but she had seen little of him since.

Now she watched for him, anxious and wondering about the future.

And there he was, coming down the road. But his face was shaded by the wide brim of his hat, she could not guess his emotions. He had met in private with Hawai'i's royalty and nobles to determine the fate of Lono's Stone. Robert wanted it to go to the lepers on Molokai, but others wanted to put it on display at the palace.

She hurried downstairs, holding up the skirts of her long gown—borrowed from Mrs. Carter until Anna could decide what she was going to do next—and met Robert as he came through the front door.

"Well?" she said.

He faced her with a serious expression, but then he removed his hat and broke into a grin. "They have agreed to let us take the stone to Molokai!"

"Oh Robert, that's wonderful news!"

"Yes, it is," he said quietly, holding her with his eyes. Anna felt a jolt go through her, felt her heart race with rising excitement to be so close to Robert Farrow. They had yet to speak of their night together at the foot of the Pali, the night Chief Kekoa fell to his death. She had thought that would be her only time in Robert's embrace, that she would never see him again. But here they were. . . .

"Anna," he said, reaching for her hand. "Come with me. There is something I want to say."

He led her through his study and out through the French doors onto the lanai, where flowers bloomed in dazzling colors and filled the air with tropical fragrance.

He turned and, facing her, said, "My dearest Anna, mere words cannot express the profound feelings that fill my heart. To say that I love you seems paltry. There isn't a big enough word that can describe how I feel about you."

"But there is a word," she said. "Aloha," and she said it the way Mahina and Kekoa had, with a heavy breath and drawing out the middle vowel, so that the word was love itself.

"Aloha," he whispered, and then Robert startled her by dropping down to one knee, to take her hand between his and to say with ardor, "Anna Barnett, you are the one true love of my life, and I know that I would perish should I not be able to walk this earth with you at my side. Please marry me. Be Mrs. Anna Farrow and share my life with me. I promise to make you as happy as is in my power to grant."

She smiled. "Yes, dearest Robert, I will marry you."

He returned to his feet and brought her into his arms for a deep kiss, after which he drew back, his smile wide, his eyes glistening, to declare, "I am the happiest man on earth! Oh Anna, the things we will do, the places we will see! A whole, beautiful world awaits us."

She trembled with excitement, imagining the possibilities. Then she said, "But first we go to Molokai. . . ."

A crowd saw them off at Honolulu, all agreeing that Lono's healing stone should be taken to the lepers.

But Robert and Anna had decided to tell no one about the other find in the cave. The burial place of Hawai'i's hero must forever remain a secret, to preserve Kamehameha's very potent mana.

And now Robert and Anna and Jamie were approaching the eastern side of the Kalaupapa Peninsula on the north coast of the island of Molokai, gliding into a bay where no other ships rode at anchor, where there was no dock, no customs shed, not even a rowboat. The deserted, desolate crescent of beach and small valley were embraced all around by sheer cliffs and forbidding, mist-shrouded peaks.

The three stood on the bow of the ship, watching people on shore emerge from crude huts and shelters, crowding onto the rocky beach to wait for crates of supplies to wash ashore.

When they dropped anchor, Robert and his son and Anna climbed into the longboat, where supplies had already been stowed, and sailors took their places at the oars. The boat was lowered and the visitors to the isolated leper colony were rowed ashore.

The sailors pulled the boat onto the beach and began unloading the supplies while a silent crowd watched. They were in various stages of the disease—some horribly disfigured, others looking quite healthy. Many wore rags tied around their fingers and toes, some had even hidden their faces. There were old men and little girls. A few of the women held infants.

"What a terrible place," Anna said with tears in her eyes as a lonely wind whistled down from the sheer cliffs.

The quiet and watchful crowd on the beach parted and a robust figure emerged, her bright blue muumuu billowing out around her, her white hair lifting like ghostly tatters. "Aloha!" she cried, raising her arms.

Mahina embraced her son-in-law and grandson, weeping with joy at the sight of them. But when she turned to Anna, her eyes grew big and her mouth dropped open. "Keleka!" she cried.

"Not Theresa anymore. I am Anna now."

Mahina grinned. "Anna! Sound Hawai'ian. You have hair. You very pretty."

They didn't tell Mahina that Kekoa was dead. She had enough sorrow on her plate.

Robert scanned the crowd, saw how they eyed the wooden crates that were being stacked on the beach. He looked at Mahina. "How is it going, Mother?"

She smiled. "Before, things very bad. They throw us overboard. They throw supplies into water. Before I come Molokai, big fights over food. When boxes float ashore, only big and strong men eat. Everyone else hungry. But they listen to me because I am ali'i. There is peace here now."

"Mother," Robert said, "I am going to send supplies to build proper houses. Food and medicine and clothing will come regularly. When new people arrive, they will not be thrown overboard and forced to swim. They will be brought onshore in boats."

Then he said, "I have a gift for you," and he handed her the canvas bag he had carried from the ship.

When Mahina opened it, her eyes stretched wide. Then she looked at Robert with such naked joy and gratitude that he felt his chest tighten with emotion. "You find it," she whispered. "You go Pele's cave and find Lono Stone. Now my people can be healed."

Robert turned to the sailors, who had retreated to the safety of the longboat from where they nervously eyed the lepers. "Hey, you lot! Get these crates open."

But they didn't move. Mahina laid a hand on his arm and said, "They no come near the sick. You go, son. You and Anna and Pinau. No come close to us. Mahina open boxes and share out food and clothes."

Robert looked at the blank faces, some horribly scarred, others with barely a blemish, beautiful women and handsome youths, but cripples as well and the elderly with hands twisted into claws.

"Mother," Robert said. "Why don't you come back with us?"

She shook her head. "Many years ago, when Mika Kalono and Mika Emily come to Hilo, my mother Pua say she want to be friends with haole. She learn read and write. She listen to stories of Jesus. She tell Mika Kalono she pray Jesus. But he say, only Jesus. Only haole god. My mother say, we have Pele and Lono, we have Kane and Laka. We have goddess of birth and god of war, we have goddess of milk and god of thunder, we have goddess of moon and god of wind. We have lizard goddess and shark god. We have the 'aumakua, our ancestors' spirits. Where they go, we not pray to them, we not give them gifts and sacrifices and sing sacred chants? So we keep. But we pray Jesus, too."

She shook her head in sadness. "Mika Kalono say only Jesus, only haole god. So Mahina stay with her people and remind them of the old ways, and now with Lono's power, they will be healed. I will create a sacred heiau and my people will begin to heal."

She paused, stared for a moment at the polished lava stone in her hands, then she looked at Robert and said, "I remember Mika Emily the day she come Hilo, many years ago. She very pretty. My mother Pua stroke her and kiss her and want to be her friend. My mother Pua bring you into the world, my son, and place you on Lono's altar for his blessing. I am sorry about Mika Emily. I am sorry she make my people die." Her great bosom heaved with emotion. And then she said, "I forgive her."

As she embraced them, Mahina said, "Mahalo for the gift of Lono. Now the sacrifice of my mother will not go forgotten. I will tell the people what she did, and the great Pua will join the many legends of these islands. And now that we have the healing stone, Hawai'i Nui will not come to an end. The kanaka will live for many generations."

Mahina embraced Jamie, calling him her little Pinau. Then she turned to Anna. "You go now. You go home. Back to Honolulu and help my people. And haoles, too."

As the ship weighed anchor and the engine began to chug and the paddle wheel turned, Jamie said, "Do you really think the Lono stone will heal them?"

"If it doesn't give them a cure," Anna said. "It will at least give them hope."

The three stood in the bow of the ship, facing the open sea, the sun and wind on their faces. The future, as always, was unknown. But they knew that they were going to take a great part in shaping it: Robert Farrow, son of a courageous missionary and sea captain of conviction and vision; Jamie, with the blood of ancient Hawai'ian kings and warriors mixed with that of hardy New England seafarers; and Anna, herself the child of brave pioneers who had traversed a continent fraught with danger to settle the American West.

Jamie looked ahead with excitement to a future in law and Hawai'ian politics, with himself as a bridge between kanaka and haole.

As Robert fixed his eyes on the horizon, he thought of the innovations he was going to bring to the islands—the telegraph, steam technology, faster and safer ships, tourist hotels. But modern progress wasn't all he was interested in, not anymore. His focus had broadened now, thanks to Anna. He was going to legislate better reforms to protect native rights. He planned a campaign to lift the ban on hula and other rituals. He had also started his campaign to get Edgeware ousted from office for gross negligence and lack of regard for natives' welfare.

But most of all, Robert Farrow looked forward to a bright and exciting future with his bride, Anna Barnett, a young woman who had brought magic and love back into his life, and reminded him of who he really was.

Anna, too, had plans. She was free now to continue and expand her nursing practice. She was also going to open a nursing school for Hawai'ian girls. But she was not just going to teach what she had learned with the Sisters of Good Hope. Anna planned to draw upon

Florence Nightingale's progressive programs. And more: Mahina had given Anna the names of healing *kahunas* on O'ahu and the Big Island. She planned to visit with them, gain their confidence, and continue to expand her knowledge of the secrets of kanaka medicine. Her school would combine both systems.

Anna turned and looked back at the emerald green island where mists created rainbows and sunlight sparkled like gold on the water, and she marveled at Mahina's ability to forgive Emily Farrow.

Slipping her hand into Robert's, Anna shivered with anticipation. She could not wait for the future to begin.

AUTHOR'S NOTE

After 1868, three more monarchs sat on the Hawai'ian throne until, in 1893, the wealthy and powerful businessmen who controlled the legislature staged a bloodless coup. Queen Liliuokalani, the kingdom's last monarch, acquiesced under political pressure. The Provisional Government proclaimed themselves the Republic of Hawai'i and by 1898 they received status as a U.S. Territory. In 1959, Hawai'i joined the Union as the fiftieth state.

Today, the Hawaiian Sovereignty Movement, viewing the annexation of the islands as illegal, is pressing for self-determination and self-governance for Hawai'i as an independent nation.

The leper colony on Molokai no longer exists except as a point of historical interest and a place of religious pilgrimage.

In 1873, Belgian priest Father Damien was the first to volunteer to work with the lepers. He built a church there, ministering to the victims' spiritual needs, but he also built houses, treated the sick, made coffins, and dug graves until his own death from leprosy in 1889 at the age of forty-nine. Shortly before his death, Father Damien was joined by Mother Marian Cope and two other Sisters of St. Francis, where they took up his work with the lepers.

Both Damien and Cope have since been canonized, therefore distinguishing Molokai in the Roman Catholic religion. The island is visited by Catholics from around the world as a place of veneration.

In 1873, Norwegian physician Gerhard Hansen identified the bacterium that causes leprosy, now known as Hansen's Disease. No one knows why some people become infected while others don't (nor is it known how the infection is transmitted), but modern medications have brought the disease under control.

Kilauea Volcano has been erupting since prehistory, and many of the flows have been identified and dated. The 1868 event was triggered by an earthquake with an estimated magnitude of 7.1, causing massive landslides and tsunamis that claimed lives and property.

The most recent eruption started in 1983 and continues to produce lava to this day.

The native population has continued to shrink. It has been estimated that during the reign of King Kamehameha the Great, there were between 500,000 and one million natives. But in the late 1800s and early 1900s, more foreign workers arrived: Japanese, Filipino, Portuguese. Through intermarriage with this new population, and continued decimation through disease, the number of pure Hawai'ians has diminished. It is estimated that, today, there are less than 8,000 pure kanaka left.

The location of Kamehameha's burial place remains a mystery.